EURO TRIPPED

SALLY BRYAN

First Printing, 2018

ISBN-13: 978-1985580008

ISBN-10: 1985580004

CONTENTS

For my readers and fellow travellers.
I hope you forgive my long absence. May this story stir fond
memories of special places past.

PROLOGUE

"I'm glad you could make it. I know how busy you are but this couldn't wait any longer." He shook Gable's hand, patting him on the shoulder also, about the most physical contact the two had exchanged since that first nervous handshake the day they met, which hardly served to diminish Gable's trepidation, mixed with more than a little curiosity. "The drive was ok?"

No threats as yet and Mr Argyle's tone suggested that perhaps none would be forthcoming. Gable exhaled a long relieving sigh. "I enjoyed the trip, thanks."

"Relax. Perhaps you thought I might demand you stop seeing my daughter?" He smiled, still standing uncomfortably close.

Gable tried to smile in return but he'd been so anxious about being asked, nay, commanded to make the trip north with only a few days' notice he was sure it came out more as a squint. "Yes, well, no. I mean, not really. There's no reason why you would have." At least Gable didn't think so but who could say? Right now, everything was so perfect that something was bound to go wrong somewhere and this was the most likely place for it. And after five years the request had been quite unusual.

He prodded Gable in the rib. "Believe me, I'm not about to demand you stop seeing my daughter."

Gable emitted a high-pitched laugh, "well, that is good news," and, not being able to wait any longer, was about to enquire upon the nature of this summons when Mr Argyle placed his arm around

Gable's shoulder and, skirting the edge of the pond, guided him across the lawn in the direction of the summerhouse. Nope, more painful small talk would be in order before getting to the matter of business, whatever that might be, and Gable didn't wish to come across to the father of his beloved as being too socially inept because he wasn't, apart from, that is, whenever he was in the company of Mr Argyle. "It's a, um, beautiful garden you have, Mr Argyle, and the birds certainly seem to think so."

"Too many gulls, blackbirds and crows. They scare the real birds off. This way, Son, and you'd best get used to calling me Angus." Somewhat mystifying, oh, how the questions were piling up. He pushed open the door to the summerhouse, a strange name, given it was barely south of Inverness. "Take a seat and relax, and I do mean *relax*. You drink whisky? You'd better not." He said, with what looked like a smirk, so it was probably a joke. Regardless, he bounded towards a minibar in the corner as the planks beneath his feet shuddered, shaking the entire structure. Thank God Freya didn't possess her father's grace and elegance, or for that matter his warmth or looks, or anything much else. Come to think of it, were they even biologically related?

The upholstery within the summerhouse clashed and stood out like blood on a bandage, a true man cave, and the stuffed stag head above the wood burner was in particularly bad taste, making Gable grimace before he softened his gaze in sympathy for the poor dead animal.

"I see you're admiring Old Wilcox there." Mr Argyle strode back, bringing with him a decanter and two small glasses. He waited for the planks to settle before continuing. "Shot him myself with the Prince of Wales near Balmoral." He rolled the r of the Queen's Scottish home to an insane degree. It was a blessing Gable could even understand the man, just so long as his full and undivided concentration was given, because asking Mr Argyle to repeat himself was to risk death itself, a risk that was mitigated, mercifully, due to having spent rather a lot of time with his daughter, who happened to share the same almost unintelligible Scotts drawl. Except with her, it tended to be somewhat more appealing, even sexual, not quite the same with her father though, who now filled the glasses with the dark nectar. "This one's from a small distillery on the Outer Hebrides. They make a nice whisky near a town called Portree, which is the *Inner* Hebrides if you know your geography. They boast it's the most north-westerly Scotch in the world but this, what I'm holding here, is evidence to the contrary. It's mild and smoky, a strange contradiction, and they make only a few barrels every year. Son, you're about to try something truly special."

"Good. I mean, yes, I'd be happy to try some. And I'm privileged." Gable had to lean uncomfortably forward to take the dram and he clinked glasses with Mr Argyle before sending the dark fluid home. It burned in the most appallingly wonderful way, as contradictory as the mild smokiness of it, and he suppressed the urge to clench a fist to his chest and cough. Must keep the side up for the English and besides, if a man's dating the daughter of old Scottish nobility, he'd better learn to take his whisky because you can bloody well bet, there's more on the way.

Gable was suddenly aware he was being studied, like something of great value could be learned from how a man drank his whisky. Mr Argyle's glass was still full, was being slowly turned by his long aged fingers and Gable experienced a sudden rush of panic - Was he not supposed to have knocked it back so readily? The silence persisted to the extent of discomfort. Finally, Gable drew breath and heaved. "And that was *mild*, you say?"

Mr Argyle grinned. "Not partaken much in Scottish culture have you?"

Unless your daughter counts, Gable almost said but thought better of it at the last moment. Instead, he shook his head and said, "no, well, not as much as I'd like." Would that count against him?

Gable thought about the long drive back down to Edinburgh and how relieving and pleasant it would be after this business was out the way. He'd take his time and enjoy it, knowing that what he'd been dreading the last few days was finally done with. He'd take the scenic route through the Cairngorms and maybe go on the lookout for golden eagles. And all the while, the love of his life would be awaiting his return in Edinburgh.

Being sworn to secrecy by her father, Gable had told her that he was going home to visit his parents in Yorkshire. It was about the only lie he'd told her in five years and although, he assumed, it was for the greater good, he still felt bad about it. Freya would forgive him like he'd forgive her anything because they were in love and that was all that mattered.

"You're a good laddy." Mr Argyle finally concluded and occupied the seat beside him, stretched out his legs and crossed one foot over the other. "She's at least made a better choice than her sister and for that alone, I'll drink." And with that apparent compliment, he sent the liquid back, which touched him about as much as expected.

Freya's sister had involved herself with a soldier whose regiment was based somewhere in England. Mr Argyle had taken issue, possibly due to the man's low rank, low birth, low income or low IQ, it was all speculation. It hadn't mattered in the end because he'd been posted, she'd followed and they'd married in Gibraltar and as a consequence, Lizzie had been disinherited.

There was also Lachlan, the eldest sibling, and a wheelchair-bound paraplegic with severe learning difficulties and although he was loved and would be well taken care of, was unlikely to ever breed and therefore alternative considerations had to be made.

These minor details left Freya the sole hope and heir to the Argyle estate, which likely explained why Gable had been scrutinised the way he had; family, background, career, hobbies (there was no time for any), drug use history (there was none), friends (he had some) and now this new one, how he handled his Scotch, everything but having a pair of Marigolds applied in ano est.

No, Gable was about as safe a prospect for a son-in-law as any overprotective father, with a fortune to think about, could hope for, which was how he'd consoled himself about this visit - But all that was way off into the future.

Not that the money wouldn't be welcome. Aye, that was no word of a fib and anyone who said otherwise was a bloody liar. Though Gable hadn't known about any of it when he fell in love with Freya, pretty much the moment he first met her, and she'd kept the specifics secret until almost two years into the relationship. That was when Gable had first come to Inverness for a nervy Christmas and been read the riot act in a basement filled with muskets and cavalry blades from the Napoleonic era. A memory of sorts. And not unreasonably, he'd expected something similar this day, hence his nerves. Instead, he was getting whisky, and not the mass-produced crap that barely deserved the right to be called Scotch, but apparently the good stuff, from a secretive distillery that was the most north-westerly in the world. It was probably the soldier who could be thanked for that, for lowering Mr Argyle's expectations because Gable was about to become a mere doctor, and that, it seemed, was acceptable.

Gable had tried extra hard not to alter his behaviour after being told about the Argyle wealth, insisting on going dutch as always and no vacations until after graduating from Edinburgh, as per the original plan. Indeed, he'd been scrutinising Freya for any signs of change in her, of superiority perhaps? But no, she continued being her usual single-minded, determined, almost serious to the point of being a robot self - She'd make a fine emergency doctor, for sure.

But no. If anything the money was a hindrance because Gable now felt the overwhelming pressure to prove himself on his own terms, to make his own pile and accept no charity. That was the only way he could maintain his independence as a man and not be constantly reminded of who it was who held the bloody purse strings, even if Freya never made mention of it, Gable would still know it. Not that any of that mattered right now though because talk of marriage had not once been raised by either of them. And why would it? The timing was far from right. Not that Freya wouldn't say *yes* because Gable believed that she most definitely would - All hypothetical though, of course.

After five years of Medicine at the University of Edinburgh and prior to two years foundation training, followed by another six of specialism, now was the only convenient time to take a break because if it didn't happen this summer, it never would and Gable had once been told there was more to life than study.

"Mr Arg...um, Angus, why did you invite me here?" He finally found the resolve to ask, surprising himself. He'd be pouring himself a fresh dram next.

At that, Mr Argyle leaned forwards and refilled both glasses. "Gable, you've been dating Freya for what, five years? Well, that's quite long enough, my lad, and now it's about time you stopped pissing about and married her."

Gable had been in the process of reaching forward to take the whisky but suddenly found his arm unable to progress to full extension. But he had to hand it to the father of his beloved, he didn't 'piss about' much himself. In fact, Gable wasn't completely certain he'd heard correctly and had to risk triggering his ire by asking the oaf to repeat himself.

"You heard damn well what I said." The skin at the bridge of his nose reddened a few shades. "Don't think I'm not aware of what you and my daughter get up to in your wee student house. What are you? Did you think this would be allowed to continue indefinitely? You're clearly quite fond of the girl, don't think I haven't noticed and I've seen the way she looks at you, the way she speaks about you. Well

Laddy, when are you intending to stop wasting hers as well as my time and do the decent bloody thing?"

Gable saw that his arm had somehow found its way back to his side and had to remind himself of what the year was (2017 at last check), all whilst Mr Argyle, as well as Wilcox, stared back most offputtingly. For some reason, Gable recalled that Christmas interrogation and how he'd had the fear of God instilled in him as an unknowing Freya played charades with her brother on the floor above. It had taken him three days to recover his sexual drive. "Mr, um, Angus, you do know we begin our residencies in October?"

"Excuses! Of course, I bloody well know." He leaned forward, causing an obscene creak of wicker, and came to within a nose of Gable's face. "And after your two years, you'll make the excuse you're about to begin *six* bloody years of specialism, for treating junkies overdosing on skag and drunkards who get a glass bottle to the face on a Friday night. And after those six years, you'll make the excuse you're both only just starting as fully qualified hospital doctors and that now ain't the right time to finally start acting like a man. By that time the stress of work will cause you to drift apart, that is if you even get to see much of each other, and then what if all that causes you to break up? You'll be a thirty-one-year-old doctor in the prime of your life, pick of the women, but Freya? She'll be a single, thirty-one-year-old woman with the best of her childbearing years behind her and all because *you* didn't have the balls to do the decent thing when you were twenty-three."

Feeling more emboldened, Gable plunged forward for the dram, downed it in one then refilled the glass. "So, Angus, this is all really about grandchildren?"

With an elaborate sweeping use of his hand, he waved about the vicinity, the summerhouse, the mansion, the moors and everything else. "Of course it bloody well is. Listen, she may believe she wants to become some doctor in a hospital but she'll soon change her mind about that when she hits forty and has only money and apathy to show for it. You should see my sister and how miserable she is. Put it off, put it off and put it off and now she's past it, no man wants her, not even with all her money and she'll die alone and miserable. Aye, I can tell what you're thinking, that it ain't any of my business but you'll understand someday when you have your own bairns."

Gable wasn't quite sure how to respond to all that and worried he wasn't doing a good enough job fighting his corner. Clearly, the subject had been on the mind of the father of his beloved for some time and had come into this bout well prepared, meanwhile, Gable's primary preoccupation had been on bird spotting in the Cairngorms, putting him at somewhat of a disadvantage. He was tempted to advise the old man to seek reconciliation with Lizzie because, for all anyone knew, she may well already have dropped a grandchild or two, which would solve this whole dilemma. Though after only two drams, he was nowhere near inebriated enough for that. "And, um, what ... what if I say no?" Which, he felt, was perfectly within his rights.

Mr Argyle bared teeth. "We both know how fond she is of you but she ain't her daft sister. She ain't quite so enamoured as to give up her inheritance, like her daft sister."

Again, Gable was unsure how to respond. Was it the truth? He couldn't be sure. He hoped not but what did hope have to do with anything? Freya's inheritance, and it would be substantial, represented status and security and no woman would readily give that up. Except, of course, her daft sister, who Gable had never met and had no intention of ever so doing, and her father had already proven a man willing to do the unthinkable. But where Lizzie had been a young lovestruck girl, swept up in what must have seemed to Mr Argyle a bad idea, Freya was more logical and not prone to such short-term idiotic thinking. Freya always had the bigger picture in mind, she was training to be a doctor, after all, and it was quite possible that it might only take a few words from her father to persuade her that a hospital, in fact, employed many other doctors. And some of those doctors would be taller, more rugged without Gable's receding jaw and possibly even more charismatic.

To put it simply - Why risk it? Especially considering he was in love with Freya.

But marriage? Gable had always considered himself in favour of it, his parents still being together presented him with a good model to follow. But to marry Freya now?

The truth was, he couldn't imagine life with any other woman. Freya was levelheaded and rational, which he'd noted was a rare thing amongst even the women who were studying medicine. That she was beyond intelligent could not be disputed and she challenged Gable in every way. For all her foibles, seriousness and dedication, she knew how to laugh, which was an important attribute. Best of all, even after five years, she still made Gable catch his breath and go fuzzy in the head. It was the way her lab coat rested over her arse and how that thick Scottish red mane flowed over it to contrast with the white. Her perfect proportions, elegant, feminine features and accent that always made Gable think she'd been a wild girl found roaming the Highlands with a pack of wolves - She wasn't though, she'd assured him of that.

Marriage to Freya? Aye, that would very well make Gable happy. The obvious problem being that the present was far from the right time and besides, what kind of man would succumb to such suggestions under pressure, from a father-in-law, no less. He may be happy Gable had 'manned up' but on some level, he'd always know that in doing so, he was less of a man simply for going along with it. Though in all honesty, such concerns weren't even tertiary right now.

Gable downed another dram. "Angus, it's not just the workload and that we have residencies approaching. The type of wedding I'd love to give my future wife would cost more money than I have right now and over the last five years, I've accrued rather a lot of..."

"Debt!" He cut Gable off by showing a large palm. "Money, ain't an issue, so let's not hear that idiot excuse again. I have it and you know it. And besides, it's custom for the father of the bride to pay and so be it."

Gable found his voice rising in pitch. "That's very kind of you, Mr Argyle, but wherever we end up at residency, we'd be sharing accommodation with other young professionals, out of necessity, which is hardly how Freya and I would envision beginning our married life." Gable thought he detected the flicker of a smile on Mr Argyle, perhaps even admiration like there was a mutual, unspoken understanding that Gable was coming around to the idea and was even now indirectly hustling for as much as he could get. It was how his tone had sounded even to himself, unintentional as it was.

Mr Argyle refilled the glass. "If you marry Freya, I'll agree to buy you a house near whichever hospital you end up. No need to squat it out with other young'uns and certainly no living in some hospital provided basement." He prodded the dram toward Gable who took it and began sipping, provoking a look of derision from the opposition.

"A house?" Gable blew out air and pushed up his glasses. He was training to be a doctor, not a negotiator and took his time choosing the next words. "A place in the suburbs is always preferential to a city centre flat."

Mr Argyle leaned back and interlaced his fingers. "I'll not have my daughter living in some English dung heap, so don't you worry."

"And a car?"

"I'll get you a Land Rover, perfect for a large family but I want the proposal *this* summer and a quick wedding before you begin residency."

"I'll propose this summer but we'll have the wedding *after* our two-year residency but before we begin specialism."

"Very well but you'll have to forego the vehicle and settle for a smaller place in the city."

"How about we just wait *one* year?"

"Then you'll have the house in the suburbs but no vehicle."

"We have the wedding *this* year and you pay off our student debts."

"Done! But I want you to start working out. It's bad enough my first grandson will be short-sighted with your ridiculous hairline, I don't want him also having your man tits."

Gable straightened but didn't challenge him on it. He knew that last point would be the hardest to get Freya to agree to, she just wasn't prone to whimsy short-term thinking like most women. Her agreeing to marry Gable was one thing but getting her to go along with a snap wedding before this coming October was another thing entirely and would require much thought about how to guide, twist and steer her into accepting, even if it was for her own good. But there'd be time to think about all that and Gable hoped he'd come up with something sufficiently persuasive.

"And I want my first grandchild *before* you begin specialism, which gives you two years to get it done, otherwise my daughter will end up going through with it and knowing that girl it'll be six years heads down, no break and we may as well just go home and not bother with this whole thing. Once you've had two then she can go back to work if she chooses."

Gable closed his eyes and squeezed at the flesh above his nose. He'd hoped kids wouldn't come into it. Getting married was one thing, as it was only really an official seal on what he already had and, practically speaking, it wouldn't really change all that much. Aye, the joke would have been on Mr Argyle for sure because marriage certainly wouldn't have prevented Freya from continuing with her dreams but children would and Gable now felt foolish for underestimating her father. For the first time, Gable felt dirty about negotiating Freya's future without her input or consent and hoped the feeling would pass after a few days.

"One child and then she can return to work and we can think about the second *after* she completes her specialist training," Gable implored.

For a while, Mr Argyle rubbed at the bristles on his chin. "No." He finally declared. "I want two *before* she returns."

Gable had to look on the bright side because at least the man wasn't insisting on any son being named Angus, which was a stupid name if ever he'd heard one. "Very well. But I want ten thousand pounds transferred to my bank account by Monday morning." Ah, the whisky was finally beginning to work its sweet magic.

The skin wrinkled on the old man's forehead. "Ten thousand pounds? What on earth for?"

Gable tried to stand, in what he'd hoped to be a physical stamp of the upcoming point but only ended up slumping back into the wicker. "Because we're off on a Euro trip." Where apparently he would propose to the love of his life.

And then Gable realised his mistake.

Because he was too intoxicated to drive home.

Which meant spending the night at the in-laws.

Chapter One

DINAN

"*I*t's not too late to turn back." Gabe had said as the line of cars crept forward at the port.

"I bet you've been waiting to say that since Edinburgh." It was the closest I'd ever been to a ferry and couldn't believe the sheer scale of the ugly thing, a marvel of engineering, a monster that seemed to enlarge as we approached. How such a craft stayed afloat was beyond me. "And, while technically it's not too late to turn back, it would have made more sense before driving all the way down here."

The drive from Scotland's capital to Poole in Dorset had taken eight hours, almost the entire length of the island of Britain, which I was about to leave for the first time in over five years. Why would I want to turn back?

And then we'd rolled into the ferry and parked as though it was any ordinary, if slightly claustrophobic, carpark.

My eyes fixed on Gabe as we exited the camper and it was that moment I'd always remember.

He'd lovingly caressed his hand over the large round VW badge like he always did the curvature of my hips, the same pervy expression on his face as he watched for my reaction.

"You imbecile," I tutted.

But it was exhilarating and I could feel something coursing through my veins. We were going on our Epic Euro Trip, me and my incredible boyfriend and it was the feeling of freedom because for the first time ever, we had no commitments, no cares and Europe was ours. We'd intentionally made no schedule so we could go wherever we chose and do whatever we desired, no constraints, and now I pulled him away from the van, grazing his hand with my thumb and dragged him towards the steps where the other passengers were filing.

"And the camper, tell me again how?" I'd been astonished when, the night before, he'd rocked up in it, stopping outside our student house, honking the horn, revving the engine and generally causing a scene amongst our jealous peers.

He pulled the same knowing grin of the night before. "Oh, you know, the trip of a lifetime, why not go all out and do it properly?"

I didn't necessarily disagree. It's just that money was already a big enough concern for us. After years of comparatively frugal student living, we'd managed to save a reasonable wedge for the trip but still, we'd budgeted everything, had a strict daily spending limit and, apart from our final night on the continent, when we intended to splash on a four-star hotel somewhere, we'd be staying in hostels. I never nagged him and didn't wish to put a downer on this wonderful feeling before we even stepped foot on the ferry so I decided to let the subject go but now Gabe sensed my trepidation and gave my hand an encouraging squeeze.

"It's ok, trust me, the van'll actually save us money. It's called a *camper* van for a reason."

That was a fair point and it was reassuring to know that if some far off town only possessed the one dingy hostel and it was full of snorers, or worse, then all we needed to do was step outside and sleep in the vehicle.

It was one of those bright orange Volkswagen camper vans, of the type you often saw in old movies where runaway teens drove off into the sunset with a bunch of rowdy friends and doubtless a copious supply of soft drugs. The stories it could probably tell, it had the full authentic look to it, like it better not require a part or two over the next few months and a tonne of rust around the skirts. I'd soon become accustomed to the unpleasant fust smell but more importantly, it was in good working order. I just worried about our finances, conscious as I was to the level of debt being massed by students of medicine.

He saw my concern, "if we're doing this..."

"...We're doing it right." I'd finished for him then smiled because the steps had given way to the ferry atrium and the feeling of exhilaration intensified.

Now, after seven and a half hours and a quick change on the Isle of Guernsey, we rumbled off the ferry and into the beautiful port town of St Malo, Brittany, in the middle of the afternoon.

I buckled in. "I should probably have asked but you've driven on the right before, yeah?"

His neck was probing forward, eyes squinting in that cute way he always did whenever he was giving something his full concentration. "Huh? Oh, no, I was sort of with you every single day for the last five years."

I flicked him on the arm and told him to find somewhere to park because, as it turned out, this town was incredible.

St Malo was indeed beautiful, possessing star-shaped medieval defensive walls with cannons, a long pier and beaches. The July tourist flocks were dense and enforced a crawling pace on us as we explored the streets but that was no matter because I was in France and away from Edinburgh, responsibility. What stood out were the crêperies, evidently a Bretagne speciality and it seemed like every other storefront, as well as many of the street stalls, were making great exhibits of men pouring batter over hot grills, using giant ladles to spread out the mixture before flipping it over and adding all kinds of goodies, sweet and savoury before folding over the edges to trap the filling inside. Gabe bought a banana filled crêpe and I had Nutella and as the sun burned down, we enjoyed the treats sitting on a wall overlooking the English Channel from where we'd sailed.

The two ports were only a hundred and eighty miles apart though the difference in mindset was huge. English port towns tended to be disgusting industrialised crap holes, like no consideration was required for the beauty of such places since they were merely transit points where people said hello and goodbye to the country. The French obviously had different ideas, like they were the first place a visitor would see, so best make a bloody good first impression.

I rested my head on Gabe's shoulder and watched the gulls dipping into the waves to pluck out fish. We were finally here, alone and together. We'd previously managed the occasional day trip and even a weekend away once but the workload was such that it could never be a regular occurrence. It wasn't only that time was an issue but also money, as with most students, which was why after two years I'd been happy to take him to visit the family home in Inverness.

Despite Gabe having a "wonderful time" with Dad, there were always reasons we could never spend subsequent Christmases at the family estate. Gabe was either too ill to travel or one of his grandparents was poorly.

"This could be my final Christmas with Grandma Camilla," he'd said, "but you go ahead and we'll see each other at the start of term." Which was why it was so awesome to finally have him to myself, all without study groups and insane deadlines and stress and anxiety. I'd enjoy this trip.

"Your dad," Gabe churned banana in his mouth whilst staring down into a tourist pamphlet, "you ever recall him hurting anyone?"

I shot him a glare as my body went rigid. "What? Of course not. Why?"

He flipped the page and squinted at something about a local arts and craft shop, hardly his thing. "Huh? Oh, nothing."

"Ok." I turned back to the sea, crammed my mouth with Nutella and considered how that had hardly been the first odd question about my dad, pulled from nowhere, he'd asked since leaving Scotland.

Gabe had first suggested an *Epic Euro Trip* three years before, though it was only the last few months we'd determined to actually go through with it. The stress and workload had beaten us both and he was right about now being the only convenient time there'd ever be because after this summer, if we thought the workload had been tough before, well then, that was nothing but a dress rehearsal compared to what was coming. I hoped that after recharging over this summer, we'd be ready for it.

Of course, it never helps having your face stuck in a book when all your so-called friends are repeatedly posting images of their world travels. Never having been out of education, it was the one thing I'd missed and didn't everybody like to rub it in. Gabe had one friend who'd been nearly everywhere, experienced everything, photographed it, lived it and had not been home in over two years. It was certainly one way of living though not quite for me, but it was hard to tell how much Gabe had been influenced over the months as the photos and stories gradually chipped away at his soul.

"Where to then, my love?" I asked Gabe, who'd spent the last few minutes researching the local towns.

"I'm thinking Dinan looks interesting." He showed me a screenshot of a medieval cobbled street with timber-framed houses meandering up a hill, plants pots on every windowsill, not an imperfection in sight. "It looks like a scene from a calendar."

I nodded enthusiastically, humming my affirmation and within a few minutes we were back in the camper, making the twenty-mile drive south. I used the time to research the area. "Brittany is one of the six Celtic nations, along with Scotland, Ireland, the Isle of Man, Wales and Cornwall."

He shook his head and grinned. "Even now, you can't help yourself."

"Oh, shut up. I suppose you were hoping to breeze through Europe without learning a single thing, Doctor? Well, that's not how *this* MD operates."

"Sorry, Doctor," he smirked, "ok, ok, so tell me this ... does that make the Bretagne British or the British Bretagne?" He squinted, "hang on, isn't that the same word?"

That quandary went unanswered as we pulled into the auberge di jeunesse, or youth hostel - How much better it sounded in French. It was an old watermill set within woodland about a one-mile walk from the old town. The whole area was beautiful woodland and although we could have spent the night in the camper, I really wanted to stay in the incredible building.

We checked in and then made the pleasant walk down the hill, reaching Dinan after ten minutes. It was our introduction to fairytale France.

Dinan was built at the bottom of a valley on the River Rance, with the forest so close you could smell the leaves and hear the birds in the trees. The stone buildings were in that impeccable old French style as though every inch and detail was designed and planned with absolute love and care. Small boats were moored from the ancient stone bridge until the river bend took them out of sight. In the distance, a viaduct loomed over all like a lord.

"Welcome to France." I gasped whilst surveying the line of restaurants along the riverbank. It was a hard choice but we decided on a bistro.

Gabe pulled out my seat and the waiter presented us with menus. My French was non-existent but the numbers beside each item were easy to understand. "These prices, Gabe?"

His hand reached across the table to clasp my arm. "Aye but it's our first night here so I think it's all right to make an exception."

I hummed, knowing I'd inevitably order simple fish rather than the fillet steak.

He was studying my expression. "I must say, I've always admired that about you."

"Admired?"

"Yeah, well, you know, you're frugal when you needn't be."

I shrugged. "I do need be, I'm a student and a Scottish one at that. You ever hear the story of how copper wire was invented ... two Scotsmen arguing over a penny?"

He tutted, "you know full well what I mean, Miss Argyle."

And indeed I did. But just because my family came from wealth didn't mean I should do what other people might and ask for endless handouts, only to waste it. Thinking about it, I'd most likely inherited my dad's frugality. No, first I'd earn my own money and then if I wanted to blow the lot on sparkly trinkets then at least I'd only be harming myself.

I kicked him beneath the table. "Anyway, Mr Scrimp, what happened to you?" I'd always known Gabe as a spendthrift. Not once in five years had he even bought me flowers and our anniversary usually meant a meal and bottle of wine in our student accommodation, not that I didn't adore that kind of thing but right now I was a tiny bit concerned about the state of our budget and the fact we'd probably have to strangle our spending over the next few days just to make up for tonight.

He folded his arms. "Nothing, nothing, I just wanted this to be the best trip ever, that's all, and there's no harm in having an expensive, *real* French meal on our first night here, is there?"

I held up my hands, "hey, it's ok, I was hardly being serious."

The waiter returned and we both ordered moules-frites, or mussels and fries which, we were told, was a popular Bretagne dish. Gabe added a bottle of Muscadet, a white wine made in the Loire Valley.

"Gabe, you shouldn't have, fifty Euros, for one bottle?"

"Exactly. And you're about to taste the best wine of your life." He stretched out his legs beneath the table. "Relax, we're having fun."

That, at least, was true and we held hands as a small boat passed on the river and a pair of birds landed near our table and began singing their song as if they'd come to serenade us. His thumb gently grazed my skin as the last of the evening sun provided a pleasant warmth. An elderly couple smiled as they walked past, like it was genuinely pleasant for them to see an attractive young couple so much in love. Perhaps we reminded them of how they used to be and I wondered if Gabe and I would still be together when we reached their age.

I turned back to him and couldn't help but smile, remembering our encounter on the very first day of university. I'd been so nervous that day and found him lost, blundering around the biomedical sciences block. Together, we'd found where we were going and have been getting lost together ever since.

There was, however, one thing that worried me because it seemed that whenever my friends and their boyfriends went on holiday, they always broke up soon after returning home. It was like taking a holiday was a test of what a partnership was made of. If a holiday was all it took to break them up then obviously it was for the best because how would they survive a marriage, or kids? Surviving had been easy for us because thus far the biggest obstacle we'd faced was not annoying each other during joint study sessions. Now, we were undergoing our first major test and I wondered if our friends were speculating on whether we'd still exist come the end of it and if so, well, I'd be happy to show them how strong we were.

The mussels arrived still sizzling in the pan and were presented to us in the same, quite a touch I was unused to and the garlic, chilli and white wine sauce was like nothing I'd ever experienced. Once I forgot the wine's price tag, it wasn't hard to enjoy that too.

"Better than our usual four quid bottle from Tesco." Gabe remarked as he poured my second glass.

"Agreed." And we sat back and spoke about where the trip might likely take us. "Paris is a must, obviously, and Lisbon, and Spain has some incredible cities."

"If we make it as far as Southern Spain, perhaps we could drop by and visit Lizzie?"

I tensed and glanced over at the viaduct, the river, the other couples eating. "Yes, yes, we could. But time's an issue. Spain's a big place and if we'd like to see Italy then driving all the way down there and back will kill several weeks. Besides, Gibraltar's technically Britain, not Spain, so why bother leaving home at all?"

He reached over and grabbed my hand. "Hey, it's all right, it was only a suggestion, we can skip Gibraltar or even Spain altogether. In fact, I don't know why I even brought it up." Indeed, it was one of the few times he'd even mentioned my sister, though it was obvious the reason being we were now on the continent.

I squeezed his hand and slowly sipped some wine. Lizzie, my elder sister who I'd not seen since her elopement, was understandably a sensitive topic. She'd met her now husband whilst visiting friends in the south of England, which was all I knew and I'd certainly never met the man and neither would my dad tell me why, in his opinion, he was unsuitable for her. What I did know is that it caused one heck of a shit storm in my family, which had far-reaching consequences for her and although I was kind of fortunate to have been away studying at boarding school at the time, it also meant I was never able to say goodbye, or learn the truth. That had been eight years ago and although I'd wanted to contact her, I could never get any assistance from Dad and, of course, the longer these things are left the harder they become.

"Are you ok?" He asked after several minutes of silence.

I nodded. "I am." And it was only right that Gabe might be curious about the sister of the woman he'd been dating for five years and I wondered how the two of them would get along. "And I'm so happy it's just the two of us."

My melancholy was interrupted by Gabe's phone beeping and he let go of my hand to read his message.

"Gabe?"

He was grimacing into the screen and then his head sagged to the table.

"Gabe?"

"I'M SO, SO SORRY."

He clasped his head and sat on the edge of the bed, one of six singles in the room. By the window a girl rustled through her bag, politely ignoring us. If she understood English she was doing an excellent job of concealing the fact.

"This is why I don't use social media." I was clutching his phone, scowling at his latest well thought through Facebook declaration. "I mean, who cares that we're in France, really?" I wasn't overly angry, more annoyed and disappointed but as on the rare occasion Gabe managed to get me this fumed, my dialect became more broad Highland, meaning he couldn't always understand me, however, my stomping about the room could be understood in any language. The girl coughed, removed a book from her bag and rushed out the door.

"I know but come on, everybody does it and how was I to know he was here?"

My foot tapped an involuntary rhythm against the floorboards. "Who is *Danny Belcher* anyway?" I almost spat the name. "And why can't you just tell him to fuck off?"

He appeared small on the bed where he perched. "Because he's my best friend who I've not seen since the day he left to travel over two years ago. If Kirsty was heading to Bordeaux, you'd insist we followed her too."

That was probably true. "Don't you dare bring Kirsty into this!"

"It's true then."

I clenched my fist and stomped over to the window from where I could view a group of travellers loitering by the stream, cooking on a barbecue and drinking beers. "No," I finally thought up a better response that might get the result I wanted, "I'm here with you so I'd tell Kirsty that if she wanted to see me then we'd best meet *here* or somewhere in between. I certainly wouldn't drive three-quarters of the way down the length of the country, go *completely* out of my way for her, skip Paris and who knows what else in between. Bordeaux's almost bloody Spain. Are you listening?"

He threw up his hands. "Of course, I'm bloody listening."

"You're just not taking notice."

"I am taking notice, I'm just not about to miss this opportunity, that's all."

I crashed onto one of the spare beds, the one furthest away from Gabe.

"So you're not sleeping with..."

My expression cut him off. "So much for our bloody Epic Euro Trip. Now we're sharing with some smelly traveller." I was probably being unfair but screw it, I'd suffered an injustice.

He dropped his bag to the floor and tried to sound reassuring. "It'll be one day, Doctor, that's all we agreed and then we'll find a lay-by, or maybe some travelling circus to ditch him."

I peeped up from the pillow. "You promise?"

"I promise."

Chapter Two

BORDEAUX

$\mathcal{I}$t's true what they say about sleeping on your problems.
Waking up to the French sun shining in through the blinds followed by a continental breakfast and good coffee tends to improve the mood.

There were about forty of us in the canteen, munching on pastries, fruit and what looked like slices of cold, hardened toast pulled from individual packets, quite bizarre.

I kissed Gabe on the cheek and he patted my leg beneath the table. "Sorry I blew up last night."

He turned inwards and slid a small dish of jam in my direction. "No need to apologise, it was totally my fault. I should have thought. Social media and all that..." he sipped from his mug of black coffee, "and I should have told him his request was out of the question, or to wait until we made it down there in our own time. I was just so excited to hear he was in France. Last I heard, he was still in Asia and then to find out he was back in Europe, I kind of just, I don't know, got a little nostalgic."

I sniggered. "Oh great, when you put it like that, now I feel like the unreasonable one."

He waved it away. "It is what it is but I think you'll like him."

"Well durr, he *is* your best friend."

"And once we've met, had a meal, a few beers and reminisced, we'll go wherever you want." He left his words with an upward inflection, as if to enquire where that place might be.

"Paris, no Barcelona, Madrid, oh, I don't know. It's too damned hard." I slapped him on the arm because he was laughing at my indecisiveness but knowing we'd soon be back on the road, and free, had brought that indescribable feeling of exhilaration back. "So, how long's the drive?"

He sucked in air. "Uuuum, well..."

———

"ARE you going to be silent all day?" He asked for the third time.

I grunted and turned to look out the window, to the rolling green fields of Pays de la Loire, its vineyards, castles, the entire Loire Valley and the great city of Nantes, all of which we'd miss. "This Dan Belcher guy better be worth it." I sulked under my breath, he didn't hear and asked me to repeat myself. "Never mind."

He rubbed me on the knee. "Is poor little Doctor Frey-Frey hungry? Is that why you're being so grumpy?"

I slapped him on the leg and he laughed, which hardly helped my mood. "I'll eat when we see this Dan guy you love so much. After all, it'll be free food with his ability to turn water into wine."

"What are you talking about?" He asked through hysterics. "I thought you'd decided you were ok with it all now."

I folded my arms and angled even further away. "Anyway, how do you even know this guy and why's he been on the run so long?"

He exhaled in an exaggerated way. "Oh dear, doesn't travelling bring out a different Frey-Frey. That didn't take long, did it? I hope you'll give him a fair chance."

"What? Even after he butchered our plans?"

"And what plans are they exactly?" He cast me a sideward glance. "We don't have any, which is the beauty of this whole trip. Tomorrow we might meet a hobo with tales of an Eldorado one hundred to one twenty miles due south by southeast and be so enthralled that we drop everything in search of this mystical new land. And then what of our plans?"

He always had a way of making me smile, even when I was trying to be angry with him, an often impossible task. "Yeah, and you'd better stay off the drugs, Doctor." I playfully hit him but it turned into more of a caress of his knee.

"Promise me you'll give Dan a fair chance." He urged.

I sighed. "Of course, I will. You've known me sulk but you've never known me not be fair."

"Good, and since you're so interested, we grew up together. I've known Dan since we were five and went to the same school. We were both central midfielders on the local team, we had our first beer together, I even had a crush on his sister at one point though the less said about that the better." He smiled and shook his head from some memory best left unsaid.

I'd since turned back to face him because he was speaking with such warmth and feeling it was hard not to be caught up in it. "You're close," I said as a matter of fact. Of course, I knew all Gabe's friends in Edinburgh, and he mine because most of them were mutual. But I'd never met any of his friends from home.

His chin wrinkled. "Like I said, he's the best friend I ever had and I've not seen him in far too long."

"Because he's been travelling whilst you've been studying to become a bloody doctor." Which meant I'd bagged the good one.

He was quick to intervene in defence of his friend. "He's not a bum. He just never had my brains. I guess we took two very different paths after school with my going to Edinburgh and his taking a job as a welder in the next town." He shrugged, "I don't know, how much can you change in two years?" then shook his head, "I suppose he got fed up of welding and took off. Can't say I blame him really."

"And he's been travelling alone ever since?"

"Alone?" He barked and overtook another vehicle. "Not according to his Instagram. No, it looks to me like he's been picking up and letting go of, shall we say, *characters*, every day for the last two bloody years." He laughed and I thought best not to pursue down that road. "There was that one time we both spent a night in a cell."

My mouth fell open. "What? You? MD Gabe?" I mean, what? Really? "No, no, no, you can't go silent on me now. You have to tell me what happened?"

And then he pulled his annoying smirk, the one he always did when he knew I was exploding inside, and kept quiet, suddenly giving full concentration to the road and all I could do in response was grunt and turn away.

MY CARDIGAN WAS DISCARDED IMMEDIATELY upon arrival and I shut my eyes, held out my arms and faced up into the sky. "How nice does that feel on the skin."

Bordeaux was a big city with lots of traffic and we were in the centre of it. Thus far we'd not seen anything to write home about, driving straight to the hostel and dumping the camper as close as we could whilst ensuring to close all the curtains. Earlier, Gabe had intentionally driven through a soggy field and now both flanks were caked in mud.

"Nobody'll bother breaking in now." He said, thrusting out his chest and that was probably an accurate statement because it truly resembled nothing that any person with anything of value would possess, which was also true of us.

Our shoulders burdened with backpacks, we entered the hostel and checked in, also grabbing a handful of tourist pamphlets on the way. Shockingly, our room possessed no fewer than twelve beds and although it was only six in the evening, there were already three people asleep and not one stirred when Gabe accidentally slammed the door.

I don't know what I was expecting but as I quickly learned, not all hostels were created equal. It was accommodation for fifteen Euros a night but after the pleasant stay of the previous evening, this was a crash back down to reality. In comparison to the Bretagne countryside, money obviously didn't go quite so far in the city of Bordeaux. It wasn't the cramped conditions necessarily, or the dusty floor or the broken lockers. It wasn't even the many large backpacks and people's belongings strewn all about the place that made my toes curl and soured the excessive saliva building in my mouth. What did it was that after such a long drive, all I desired was a mere ten minutes alone time, Gabe excepted, to sit, gather my wits and revitalise my soul. The last thing I'd wanted was to arrive and feel so inhibited, like I couldn't change clothes because one of these people might happen to be watching the redheaded Scots girl.

I opened a window overlooking the main road and one of the sleepers, a heavily bearded man in his fifties turned over, scratched down below and muttered something foreign. My instinct was to find a bed as far from the door as possible so that if any of these people turned out to be an escaped convict, I'd be the last target. It was all paranoia, of course, but survival instincts are deeply ingrained and hard to shut down and it wasn't like I could even share a bunk with Gabe, inconveniently narrow as they were. I was being stuck up, which wasn't like me at all, despite my upbringing and hoped I'd soon become desensitised and get used to it, or otherwise just stop caring. After all, squatting is a big part of travelling and there was no way we'd be able to escape it, at least not on our budget.

The door flung open and, expecting Gabe's friend, we both twisted around but after a second, Gabe lowered his head and continued making his bed from the supplied sheets.

The newcomer, a man in his mid-twenties with closely cropped brown hair and the lazy demeanour of someone who'd long been on the road held my eye contact as he squeezed his way bedwards. "Evening, speak English?"

I nodded, "I'm Scottish, so only just."

He flashed teeth, "and me Irish, which makes us fellow Celts." He held out his hand and I had to reach over my bed to shake it as we exchanged names. His gaze passed over my neck, shoulders, breasts, abdomen, hips, thighs and back to my face, all very quickly. "How long you been out from the ginger factory?"

I snorted and neglected the sheets for the moment. "Only since yesterday." I glanced over at Gabe and found him slowly spreading his sheets, making as little noise as possible with an ear turned towards us.

The Irishman scooped up the mess on his bed, only to throw the lot against the wall at his feet. "Don't mind me, Freya. You had chance to see Bordeaux yet?"

"It's hard to make the place much worse so go right ahead and no, not yet."

"Ah," he collapsed on his bed and propped his hands behind his head, "tis a beautiful place. I recommend the river walk but Bordeaux's all about the wine, we're surrounded by the best vineyards in Europe, did you know that?" He continued to talk about the city and wine, a friendly guy with a certain charm, which kind of made him attractive.

It was all fun and we were on this trip to make friends but I kept wondering when Gabe would bound to my side and drape his arm about my shoulders in some non-verbal declaration I was his woman but after four or five minutes he still hadn't come forth, or even said a word, and now he was perching awkwardly with one leg on the bed, pulling items from his bag before stuffing them back in again.

It wasn't completely strange for me to receive admiring glances from men so I knew there were some out there who found me attractive and I'd often be approached on the rare occasion I ever hit the Edinburgh bars with university friends but for the most part, everyone on my course knew I was with Gabe, so it wasn't something I regularly had to deal with. But here and now, I looked and felt dishevelled from the journey and couldn't imagine how any man could find me appealing.

"You won't have seen any of the bars they got here then? There're some great old worldy ones serving wine from St Emilion and I promise, you won't have tasted anything like it. I'll take you there when you're ready," he said almost as an afterthought, "there's this one place that serves a very particular red Pessac Leognan Graves, its earthy and tastes of blackcurrant and cedar, goes well with the lamb you can order on these little crackers." How the Irish could charm and if it hadn't yet clicked with Gabe I was being seduced, it certainly had with me but what could I do? You can't begin every conversation by declaring up front that you have a boyfriend because by doing so is to make the presumption they're even interested and how would that look if the guy was just being friendly? No, the responsibility had been Gabe's from the outset, to at least do something, to make some kind of a gesture, verbal or none, to show we at least knew each other.

"It does sound wonderful." I glanced again at Gabe who was pretending to find interest in a brochure about some local wax museum and when I looked back, the Irishman's eyes snapped back from my breasts to my face.

"Well, I can show you this great place, Le Wine Bar on Rue des Bahutiers, and we'll see the river on the way and discuss where we're both heading next, as well as other things." All in all, it wasn't a bad attempt at seduction, except for one thing.

Which now rushed forwards, startling his rival and wagging an anxious finger. "Ah, you know, sorry there, but she's my girlfriend … just letting you know that," he trailed off and scratched his head.

"What?" The man looked from him to me and back again with an expression of something between puzzlement and anger. "You should have just said. What you been doing sat there like a pudding all this time while some guy's hitting on your bird?" He shrugged and stood, making a point of the three or so inches in height he had on Gabe and although his back was now to me, I was able to make out the contemptuous grunt. Gabe looked down and stepped away as the

Irishman turned back to me. "If you fancy that drink with an actual man, I'll be around."

The words punched through my head as he strutted to the door before turning back for one last remark directed at my man, "you look like you'd probably enjoy being cucked," followed by a mocking snigger and then he was gone, leaving Gabe forlorn and head hanging in the small space between the beds.

One of the sleepers snorted then Gabe stamped over to me, thrashing his arms about. "Why didn't you bloody tell him you had a boyfriend?"

My mouth plunged open. "I thought he was just being friendly, how was I to know where he'd always intended on leading it?" I shoved him on the shoulder, "and all along you did nothing. All you needed to do was ask 'are you hungry, Frey?' or chuck me the suntan lotion and he'd have been clued in."

He twisted away and rubbed the back of his neck, plonking himself down on his mattress. "You're right, I'm fucking socially inept."

I didn't disagree though neither did I say he was looking just a little bit emasculated too, a man needed his pride and besides, it was over and done with so I returned to the task of making the bed.

Afterwards, we headed down to the communal area to see what the hostel offered. The facilities were numerous, including a large dining area with flat screen TVs, sofas, books and magazines, an internet cafe, washing and drying machines and a kitchen for those who'd brought their own food.

"We'll have to find a supermarket and buy something to eat." I cautiously peeked into the kitchen and grimaced, not enjoying the prospect of having to use it. I was used to my own student kitchen, of course, and having to share it with five others, Gabe included, and it had been the source of a hundred arguments about hygiene. It was occasionally possible, after telling people for the tenth time to properly clean their plates and utensils, to find something adequate to eat from but that was only because they'd become so worn down by my nagging. Here, however, the punters were only breezing through and what did they care about scouring the plates of all remains? Do a half-arsed job, stick it back on the pile and disappear, next city, next country. And even now, two long-haired men in their early twenties, shirts unbuttoned, chest hair protruding from within, were bounding out holding plates, sucking up spaghetti as they came.

"Doctor?" Gabe waved a hand in front of my face.

I was half tempted to call Dad and ask for money, something I'd not once done since leaving home, living frugally as I did off my student loan. There'd be hotels in Bordeaux and they'd be clean and I'd have privacy and wouldn't have to deal with unkempt strangers, from God only knew where, sharing bedrooms and kitchens, oh, and the bathroom, which I hadn't yet had the privilege of witnessing. But calling Dad went against my ethics, tempting as it was, and that I still needed to eat on a budget didn't make the thing any easier. "I'm gonna really struggle on this trip."

"What?"

I breathed and shook off my negativity. "When's your friend arriving?"

A horn blared and we both turned toward the large window that overlooked the road because a small, green, battered, rusty hatchback was pulling into the loading bay.

And a man exited.

"GAY BOY!" He bounded in our direction, smile stretched to its painful limit as I took an instinctive step back.

"Dan, you crazy bastard," Gabe strode to meet him halfway, "what's with the hair?"

The newcomer's eyes roamed over me then settled back on Gabe as they both opened out their arms and embraced. Now, Dan was holding my gaze over Gabe's shoulder and gave a little wink as everyone else in the room turned to watch the commotion. They stepped back and my eyebrows quirked as they commenced some strange handshaking, rhyming routine that even included a chest bump halfway through.

"Ok, this is interesting," I mumbled under my breath.

Gabe punched him on the arm then turned to me. "Frey, I want you to meet the best friend I ever had, Dan." As though the introduction was necessary.

He took two large steps in my direction, face reddened from the exertion of the last minute and a half. "I knew it, I know his type. Always the redheads."

I made up the remaining distance between us and held out my hand. "Well, I hope there've not been too many other redheads."

His hand was sticky and he squinted, like he was replaying my response over in his head and taking his time to decipher it. "Yee're Scooooteeesh?"

"I found her in the Highlands, running wild with the wolves." Gabe put in, helpfully.

Dan raised an eyebrow. "You mean, it's possible to domesticate a Scot?"

"Just so long as you catch them early."

"Otherwise, admit defeat and cut them loose."

"That's about right."

"Don't mind me," I said, still standing there but finding it all very cute. I could take a joke at my expense, no probs.

The lady from the front desk approached us but directed her question at Dan. "Excuse me, is that your vehicle outside, parked in the loading bay?"

I swivelled to look out the window. If it could even be called a vehicle then technically it wasn't in the loading bay but more one-third loading bay, one-third disabled spot, one-third pavement.

"Huh?" Dan looked from the window and back to her, scratching his head. "No, that's not mine."

She placed her hands on hips and if she was about to challenge him, she evidently decided it wasn't worth the hassle and returned to her post.

Gabe bit his lip, "but that *is* your car, ain't it?"

"Nope, that's my hunk of junk. Can you believe it actually got us here? I bought it for less than four hundred Danish Krone, which is Denmark," he said this last bit to me, "and you can actually see the road moving through the passenger side footwell."

Gabe blinked, "I'm sorry, you said *us*?"

Dan didn't hear and continued, "and you think I'm paying city centre parking charges? No chance. And I ain't parking that tin can three miles out and walking either. Now there's a nice little life hack … buy a shed on wheels and they don't bother ticketing you. The car's just not worth the price of the bureaucracy, you see." He patted Gabe on the shoulder, "*bureaucracy* … now, doesn't that sound French to you?"

Gabe smirked at me. "If only we'd thought of that, right Doc?"

"It's very clever, I must admit." And I was sure he'd still look clever after it got towed, if at all he cared, which I doubted. Meanwhile, I was still watching the vehicle because...

"So how long have you been here?" Dan asked me, stealing my attention.

My eyes twitched up to his head, distracted because he had one of those man buns, tightly tied upon his crown, a style I'd already seen a few times amongst Frenchmen. "We arrived in France only yesterday."

"No, I meant, how long have you been in Bordeaux?" He clarified with a good-natured smile. He was an attractive man, or rather, would have been if it weren't for the hair and the major stubble growth, like he was caught between deciding whether to grow a beard or not. I loved stubble on a guy and even a nice beard but his between look made me wonder if he was just unkempt, life on the road perhaps. He was a touch taller than Gabe, which made him more or less average height but far slimmer and his cargo shorts hung off his legs like a scarecrow's rags. Malnutrition from travelling or simply a case of bad style? Either way, Gabe didn't seem too concerned over his friend's almost emaciated appearance.

I squinted, "how long have we been in Bordeaux?" I thought that would have been obvious from the conversations he'd had with Gabe and was about to give a more satisfactory answer when I was distracted by movement in my periphery.

Dan cast a sideward glance at Gabe, as though silently enquiring upon my intelligence and spoke slower. "Um, yes, when did you arrive here?"

"Um," I was staring at the vehicle now, "is there someone in your car?"

"Yeah," he shrugged, "so they won't tow it."

Ah, clever boy, so he *had* thought of that.

"Really?" Gabe interjected, "who?" One of his travelling 'characters' no doubt.

"It's a woman," I confirmed and winked cheekily at Dan, "definitely a woman, you Casanova." If I narrowed my eyes, I could just make out the girl's long blonde hair and even a few coloured braids weaved in. She occupied the passenger seat and was thus closest to us, staring blankly forward.

"A woman?" Gabe asked, excited. "Not that I'm surprised, judging by your Instagram."

Dan made a clicking sound with his mouth. "Aye, well, we met in Copenhagen and she followed me all the way here," he moved closer to Gabe so he could whisper the next bit into his ear, "and I've not had chance to seal the deal yet," I still heard, "and she's kind of blowing on the wind, a bit ditzy but a good laugh and company for those long drives," he leaned into Gabe again and I got the impression he didn't care whether I heard or not, "or, I expect, she will be."

I cringed inwardly. Yeah, I most definitely bagged the better of the two here and hoped Gabe never spoke in such a way about me when I wasn't around.

I nudged Dan on the arm. "Aren't you going to bring her in? I mean, you are staying here, aren't you?" More importantly, with the arrival of Gabe's friend, and making a judgement after having met him, a female companion for the night might probably be an alleviating thing.

He leaned back and shook his head. "I'm not sure that's a good idea, she..."

I flapped a hand, "oh, don't be silly, I'll help her with your bags, you two can catch up." I was already on my way and wasn't stopping, even as he made a halfhearted protest. But really, leaving a young woman in the car just to avoid getting a ticket? What a jerk.

I exited the hostel and the vehicle was only a few steps away. My eyes briefly surveyed the mangled bumper and half missing number plate before shifting upwards to fix on her. *Oh, hello, a photogenic one, if a little miserable*, was all I had time to think as we made eye contact but her gaze didn't follow me around as I approached her at the opened window.

I stooped to look in, briefly clocking tanned legs as I propped my forearm on the doorframe. "Hi there, I'm Dan's friend and I just thought I'd help you with the..."

Her head turned swiftly, red, flared and screaming, "fuck off!"

I leapt backwards, almost falling over a man walking his dog and scurried back further as I openly gaped at the bitch who was now winding up the window. I turned back to the hostel, aghast, from where Gabe and Dan were both looking out through the communal room window, Gabe fidgeting with a sleeve as Dan was using his hands to silently wave *no* - A bit late.

Thank fuck it was only for one night because the sooner the pair of these gatecrashers were gone, the better.

"...AND how about all the times I stopped Jimmy Smith from beating the crap out of you?"

"It became almost a full-time job after I took his place on the team." Gabe's glazed over eyes stared into air.

"He didn't like your face much either." Dan laughed and slapped his back, almost spilling all three of our beers over the table. He glanced my way, stealing a quick peek at my cleavage in the flowery summer dress I'd worn and I felt a small prickle. "Losing your place to a four-eyes is the ultimate humiliation, might as well lose it to a girl, but Gay Boy was almost a clear foot shorter than the rest of us, to add insult to that already large injury, and built like an anorexic ballerina. No, no, no, that couldn't be allowed to fly. But he could run faster than any of us, even if he couldn't kick a ball straight, or very far, and that surprised a lot of people."

Gabe absorbed it all, clearly enjoying the banter, compliments and memories, and liking it even more that I was around to hear it. And I must admit, it made for interesting listening, to learn things about my love's childhood from the eyes of someone who arguably knew him better than I did, certainly, he'd known him long before I ever did and I always enjoyed such stories, even if it meant being left out of the entire conversation which, on this occasion, I didn't mind.

We'd come to one of the main squares in the centre of the city, where restaurants encircled a huge fountain at the focal point and pigeons caused chaos hopping around our feet in search of scraps. I loved animals but pigeons were so often a nuisance, especially when you were eating. The soft sounds of an acoustic guitarist floated across the square, to be almost completely drowned out by several hundred conversations, which created an all over pleasant hum that enveloped us. There was no comparative place in all of Scotland where so many people could gather outside in the evening to eat and be entertained whilst not feeling cold and after the day I'd had, I wanted nothing more than to sit back and relax, listen to the sounds of the world passing, to eat and drink knowing my momentous responsibilities were postponed, if only for a few months. Despite the temporary interruption, I'd do my best to enjoy it all.

"You remember when I set you up for that goal in the cup semi-final?" Gabe asked his friend.

"Aye, and we'd have won the final if I hadn't been suspended."

"For punching an opponent, if I recall."

Dan flapped a dismissive hand but smirked, all proud. "For

pushing *you* off the ball. The blind ref missed it ... didn't miss me flooring him though, funny that." Their accents were identical, with every word pronounced and inflected in the same way, which I thought sweet and evidence to their proximity growing up.

I was happy to let them reminisce as I sat back and ordered more beers for the table, pushing aside the empty plates when they arrived. It seemed to me, as they discussed classroom mischief, playground incidents and even more football team near glory that theirs was a relationship dominated by Dan, who was clearly the alpha to Gabe's beta, except now they'd grown up and gone their separate ways. Gabe was the one who'd grabbed his own life by the balls, so to speak, and taken the route he wanted whilst Dan, from what I could tell, was a bit of a drifter, working as a welder before leaving home with almost no money to his name, to travel the world doing the odd job whenever a couch or floor was available. He told me he could also play the guitar and had survived the first year busking in every far-flung corner of the planet.

"And where's your guitar now?" I imagined sing-songs around a campfire as Gabe and I drank with strangers from a dozen different countries. It would probably make tolerating him easier.

"G string snapped." Was all the reply he gave, leaving me wondering why he didn't just get a new one, enabling him to continue busking and thus earning to fund his travels.

The conversation returned to football and I blanked out, recalling in my own head taking Gabe aside to complain about my earlier treatment. "Did you hear how that bitch spoke to me?" I'd asked after stamping back inside the hostel.

"No," he shrugged, "the glass is pretty thick but I saw you trip over that dog."

"I did not trip over that bloody dog." I stamped my foot, hurt it on the tile and cursed my ridiculously thin flip flops, as well as almost the entirety of the trip up to this point. "If you think I'm spending even one night near that ... *girl*, or whatever it is then you're mistaken. So let's buy some food, cook it, eat it, maybe see something of this city and go to bed."

He knew my moods and how to treat me when I was being like this, which was why he'd rubbed my arm and spoke soothingly. "It sounds wonderful, Frey, but you did promise me one night with Dan, one decent meal out somewhere and just look at him," he nodded toward the huge plate glass window that revealed Dan stooping down, head poking through the car window as he seemed to be placating the bitch squatting inside, "you see?" He rubbed his face, "I've never seen him so thin and I'm worried. He's been travelling so long on too small a budget." Perhaps he could teach Gabe a thing or two. "The man needs a good meal and I'm paying and I'm gonna make sure he sits there and eats the lot. But please come…" he said hurriedly, "it'd mean the world to me if you could get to know my best mate."

I'd bit my bottom lip and drawn it out for effect, knowing full well I wasn't about to wander the streets of Bordeaux all alone, but he didn't need to know that. "Ok but only on the proviso that you buy him a razor blade and that whoever it is in that vehicle does *not* come," I spoke with conviction on that last point and Gabe knew better than to challenge me on it.

"Buy him a razor blade?" He looked horrified.

"Not for suicide." I'd slapped him on the arm. "What do you think I am?"

And thus, in arriving at our present location, we'd at least walked along the riverbank and seen much of the sites and beautiful grand architecture of Bordeaux.

As it transpired, there was nothing wrong with Dan's appetite. For sure, he'd devoured a starter, main course and the largest crème brûlée I'd ever seen. Gabe had matched him, whilst I'd foregone the starter and opted for a basic pasta dish with no dessert, although I, along with the boys, had commenced drinking in earnest.

"Who was that bitch, anyway?" I all but shouted, startling the two of them, who'd been discussing something or other. I'd spent the last few minutes sitting with one leg crossed over the other, my foot air tapping so much it was beginning to fatigue.

Dan caught my eye from across the empty beer glasses. "Her name's Anna and I'm sorry about all that."

"Anna?" I grunted the name and hoped she'd been towed away with the vehicle.

His eyes again roamed over my breasts and I made a mental note to wear a jacket if ever again I was in his company. "Don't mind her too much, she's been in a sulk most of the day because we drove straight through the Alps, no stops. You know, for a *traveller*," and he made air quotes with his fingers, "she sure gets cranky when she, um, travels." He laughed and rolled his eyes. "Some women, though…" he left the rest unsaid and turned back to Gabe, though not before ogling me once more.

"So, is she merely tagging along for a cheap ride or are you actually travelling *companions*, for lack of a better expression?" Gabe asked a little too enthusiastically whilst leaning away from me and I felt like kicking him.

I'd seen the woman, briefly, at least from the neck up, and the less Gabe was around that one the better. I'd been given an explanation as to why she reacted to me the way she did, as unsatisfactory as it was and other than that, no more details were necessary. In fact, the sooner I could forget about the pair of these interlopers the better and then Gabe and I could commence doing what *we* wanted.

Dan flapped a limp hand. "She's been tagging along since Denmark. People come and go, you know? They pay for the petrol, I drive. Apart from the cramped conditions and stench coming from the back, it works well. I nearly bagged her in Paris, city of romance and all that but the hostel was crammed like a Hong Kong high-rise so I could never get the privacy to proposition her and my car's way too small and uncomfortable for any hanky-panky, not that she wouldn't be worth the attempt, as well as any knock on cramps and bruises." He sipped his beer and leaned back. "Just biding my time."

For a brief moment, I almost felt sorry for this girl, Anna, then remembered the reception she'd given me and decided she and Dan were probably a logical match.

"Anyway, enough about her. Barcelona is where it's at." Dan declared, slamming down his empty glass to emphasise the point.

I wouldn't dispute that.

"I wouldn't dispute that," Gabe said, eerily mirroring my thoughts and I pulled him back into me, "and I'm sure we'll get there eventually."

"Eventually?" He gaped in an exaggerated way, "you're four hundred miles from the greatest city outside of Vegas and you're telling me *eventually*? We're talking the three Bs; beer, beaches and the best women in Europe. I can see we need to work on you, my friend."

I sat forward, awaiting Gabe's response and he shot me a quick look before returning to the oaf. "It's just that the next stop's Freya's choice but I'm sure we can meet you there."

Oh, I wasn't so sure about that. I leaned forward, rubbed my chin and made a small sigh for Dan's benefit. "Barcelona sounds really great, Dan The Man, but tomorrow morning, we're heading to Carcassonne." I grabbed ahold of Gabe's hand beneath the table and pulled it into my lap.

Dan squinted, "where?" His cluelessness was hardly a surprise.

"It's in France, Dan, not much of a party place, more cultural and historical than anything else." Which meant it probably wasn't for him.

"Oh, ok." He frowned as my heart filled with blossom. "Well then, I'll make sure I'm up early to wave the two of you off."

Gabe's chin wrinkled and I felt a pang of guilt, which, I was sure, would pass. "But the night's not over yet. It's what, ten o'clock? We'll hit a few bars, drink some more dreadful French beer and reminisce."

Dan nodded, even as his bottom lip protruded most beautifully. "Aye, we can do that." And then bizarrely, he pulled out from his back pocket a small sachet of vinegar and I studied the strange man, aghast, as he proceeded to make a small tear before sucking out the contents.

I was frozen to my seat and unable to react but luckily Gabe asked the question that was still trying to form in my befuddling head.

"Still get vinegar cravings?"

"Huh? Oh, I sort of moved on to Lea & Perrins Worcestershire Sauce now. It's slightly less acidic ... probably not as many long-term consequences either but it's hard to come by in most countries. Still, chilli sauce works well enough if you're in a bind and there's always trusty vinegar no matter where you are."

I hastily called for the bill, assuming Dan would offer to pay his third but he didn't and I winced at the total as Gabe produced our joint travelling account card and settled up.

Thankfully, it was only one night.

———

IT WAS a pleasant enough return walk along the riverbank with a gentle late evening breeze that felt so good on the skin. Dan had managed well, going a full twenty minutes without saying anything that made me want to shove him into the Garonne River and then we arrived back at the hostel.

"It's too bad we ain't travelling further together. It would've been awesome to get to know you better." He kicked at a can on the pavement, not knowing it was full and splashed beer over his cargo shorts.

I leapt back but such a trifle thing could hardly diminish my glee. "Aye, as you say in Yorkshire, it's too bad but I'm sure we'll meet again." I held out my hand but he moved in for the hug, which I had no choice other than to reciprocate as my breasts crushed uncomfortably against his chest.

And four and five and six...

"Well, safe travels," I pushed him off and turned to Gabe, "have fun. I don't mind driving tomorrow."

His face brightened at the invitation to drink as much as he wanted and we kissed before the two of them strolled off.

I stepped toward the hostel and caught sight of Dan's car, still parked in the loading bay except now the girl was no longer inside and a ticket was taped to the windscreen.

"Tut tut and good luck finding him, you may as well just write that off now." I giggled to myself and held onto the bannister before using the keycard to enter the hostel.

It was about an hour before midnight, hardly late, but around my usual bedtime. It was probably inevitable I'd end up going to sleep later and later as the trip progressed though right now, I was still on Scottish student doctor time, and contrary to popular belief, it meant that by now I was dead.

The communal room was still alive with the expected late night activities of travellers who'd long forgotten what it was like to have responsibility, how much I envied them. The screen blared a football game, a small crowd converged around an air hockey table, a solitary figure on the sofa was reading a celebrity gossip magazine with a glass of wine, a long-haired man left the kitchen with a plate of food and the warden yawned from behind the front desk.

I grabbed a glass in the kitchen, pre-washed the thing and filled it with enough water to last the night before heading upstairs and entering the dorm room, noting the door's stickiness and a black patch at hand level from a million people like Dan. Of the twelve dorm room beds, only three were presently occupied, which meant I could anticipate being roused multiple times throughout the night as each fellow guest staggered their grand entrance. I collected my kitbag and traipsed to the bathroom.

"Oh, Christ." It was as expected with filth and bugs and long strands of hair stuck to the walls and mirror and an extra special clump in the plug. Someone had made a big effort in trying to make the place look hip and trendy by diagonally overlapping posters of local shows and pinning beer coasters sporadically to the wall when I'd simply settle for a damp cloth and some bleach. The stalls were cleaner than expected and I used one to change into my night clothes before plodding to the sink and delving bagwards for my toothbrush.

Brush, brush, brush this way, keeps our teeth clean all day. Under, over, round the sides, makes our teeth nice and white.

I spat out the foam, rinsed with water and then the door creaked open.

"Oh, hey, there you are, I've been searching the whole hostel for you."

I could see who it was in the mirror and, not wanting any drama when I was this beat and desiring only my bed, decided against turning to greet her, which was rude, I know, but then what did she expect? "You've been searching for me? Why?" I asked in a tired, barely interested tone.

She stepped closer, "I just felt so terrible for the way I spoke to you earlier..."

I stuffed my toothbrush back into the kitbag "...where is it..." and rooted within for my contact lens case.

"...And I just wanted to say, I'm sorry."

My eyes flicked up to the mirror, briefly catching a tower of blonde piled atop her head with a single red dyed braid left loose to fall over her cheek where it came to rest on a slender shoulder. I continued rustling within, feeling tweezers, nail file and other crap. "You know, it's fine, I'm over it. There's no need to apolog ... ah, got it." I opened the case and squirted in a quantity of liquid before moving closer to the mirror and delving into my eye socket.

"Ah, phew," her silhouette's hand moved to brush her forehead in a cartoonish way, "and I've been feeling so bad all this time. I'm not usually like that, just so you know."

"Um hmm, so why did you do it?" My eyeball throbbed as I clamped the lid open with thumb and finger, slid the lens to the side, pinched and pulled it home.

She laughed and leaned too close, making me shimmy to the side. "Oh, it was the guy I'm travelling with." She giggled and covered her eyes, "I shouldn't speak badly of a guy who's not here to defend himself but believe me, it was the journey from hell." She spoke with what sounded like an Australian accent and her tonality was friendly and inviting, quite the opposite to the vibe I'd have expected, or the vibe I was giving now.

But what woman doesn't love her gossip? And since whatever I learned might relate to Gabe, I finally turned to face her and in response, she made a small tilt of the head and displayed her teeth.

"I know Dan," I began, "he's best friends with my boyfriend and I'm not sure there's anything you could say that would surprise me."

She was wearing a light blue sleeveless pyjama top with the logo *L♥ve Sleep*. Her arms were slender and toned with hints of feminine muscle, a girl who hadn't been on the road long, or if she had then unlike Dan, she hadn't been neglecting her health. Her pink shorts cut off a little too high for my conservative style, but whatever she thought would gain her the most attention from the boys, I guess, it was surely working on Dan and doubtless her orange thighs were working on him too. My overriding thought was that this was precisely the type of bird best kept as far away from Gabe as possible, not that I believed for one minute my man would stray.

She nodded in acknowledgement. "I really shouldn't, but gosh, he drives so fast, my nerves were shattered by the end of it. France has very long, straight roads, you could literally fall asleep and not veer off course but I don't enjoy going over a hundred miles per hour on them, oh and the hairpin bends ... I thought he was about to drive us off a mountain and when you ask him to slow down, he gets so bad-tempered. And you wouldn't believe the sites and views we missed. He wouldn't even stop for a photo. It makes me wonder why he even bothers travelling. Meh, he just wanted to see his friend, I guess." She spoke with incredibly animated expressions, her eyebrows, in particular, appeared to dance around her face as her small nose waggled and her blue eyes never left my own. Indeed, it was hard to believe this was the same girl from before.

I'd spent the majority of the last few minutes facing away whilst she'd been giving me her whole attention and such was her warmth that I almost felt bad, almost. "Sometimes it's good to breathe," I nodded, "see? But yes, he did mention something about missing the Alps. It's a bummer."

She wasn't discouraged by my indifference. "Well, I've got the rest of my life to see them, so no harm done. I'm sure I'll be back someday. I recommend Bruges if you've not seen it. They say Belgium's boring but I didn't find that, unless you think wonderful buildings and great chocolate's boring." There was a brief pause for air. "So tell me, what's been your favourite place so far?"

I turned back to the mirror, exhaled and went for the other lens, feeling my eyeball quivering in its socket as I plunged my finger into it. "You know, I really haven't seen all that much..." I shook my head and sighed, why not just humour the moron, she'd be gone tomorrow, "the port of Poole in Dorset was great. I especially enjoyed the long lines waiting to embark the ferry."

She slapped me playfully on the shoulder. "Oh, don't let the French hear you say that."

My jaw clenched, another inch to the side and she'd have had my eye. "I'll remember that."

"Anyway, my name's Arwen." And as she brought her hand up, all I could do was snort.

"Arwen?" It was hard to hide the derision in my tone but again, she showed no sign of taking offence.

She nodded and again displayed that annoying set of perfect teeth. "That's correct."

"As in Lord of the Rings, Arwen?" And not, as Dan had said, Anna - Oh, Dan.

"Partly and partly because of my Welsh ancestry, but in my parents' defence, I was born way before the films were made so at least I was named so because they'd read the books." She grinned and I couldn't tell if she was sadistically enjoying my almost mocking tones.

"Well, that makes it much better." I was a bad, bad person. And then I noticed her hand still lingering near my belly and so I troubled myself to take it and as I felt her warm smooth skin, all I could think was whether she'd touched one of the doors in this place. "I'm Freya."

"Freya?" One side of her mouth turned up as the corresponding eyebrow drooped. "Dan said you were called Frances."

I laughed and it probably even sounded genuine. "Trust me, that one's a lost cause and if you're sticking with him then my advice is to..." I stopped myself, remembering he was Gabe's best friend and what business was it of mine anyway. The girl had travelled this far with him so either she was only using him for a cheap ride or was the stupid sort of girl who went for the boorish, overconfident, all talk type of man and judging from her almost stereotypical blonde bimbo appearance, apparent ditsy demeanour and probable bipolarism, I wouldn't put it past her. "Freya, my name's Freya."

"Well, Freya, I brought this as a peace offering." She produced a bottle of red wine from behind her back, which to my astonishment, she'd managed to conceal this whole time whilst I'd been preoccupied with ignoring her.

My hand found its way to my chest as I waved the other dismissively. "Oh, that's kind but unnecessary, it's already forgotten, really." And now *I* felt bad for snorting at her name, for being impudent and for being told to 'fuck off' in the first place.

She bobbed it in front of my solar plexus as the skin around her nose turned red. "No, I insist, I'd like you to have it."

Wow, so she really did feel bad about telling me to fuck off.

"Well, if you insist then I'll take it."

She handed it over and again wiped her brow in that cartoonish way. "I never go to sleep on an argument or unresolved bad feelings, I'd be having nightmares otherwise."

"Well, you can now consider all bad feelings resolved." I nodded and then we both stood in awkward silence until I felt compelled to say something else and so I turned the bottle to read the label. "Château Haut-Brion."

She bounced on her toes. "It's a Cabernet Sauvignon and Merlot blend. The guy in the shop said all Bordeaux wines are like that."

"Um, ok, I gotcha." More silence. "And I'll enjoy this, so thanks."

She got the message and backed up. "Then I'll say goodnight and best of luck with the rest of your trip. Maybe we'll bump into each other again at some point down the road."

"It's always possible," I smiled and nodded again to finalise this exchange, "goodnight, Arwen." I turned back to the sink, heard her feet patter toward the door and felt the draught as it opened and closed after her.

I poised the bottle over the plughole and moved to unscrew the cap. "Damn, a cork?" She must really have been sorry. "Oh well, maybe I'll enjoy this at some point down the road."

Chapter Three

CARCASSONNE

*I*f I was grumpy then there was a bloody good reason for it.

It happened just after three in the morning when the door opened, flooding the room with light before crashing back into its frame, rousing every man and woman within the twelve man dorm, ear plugs be damned. And in case that hadn't done the job, Dan had then stumbled into the metallic lockers, knocking off a glass vase and smashing it on the floor. As it transpired, there were plenty of French people in the room and all were keen to teach us some of their more colourful words, not that those additions to my limited French vocab soothed my mood now as I sat back on the couch, sunglasses donned whilst waiting for Gabe to shower and collect his bags so we could finally get out of Dodge.

It was already midday, long after when we should have been on the road and I wasn't convinced as to Gabe's suitability to drive. Carcassonne was two hundred miles away; not excessive, but long enough we'd see little of the place if we didn't get moving. The sun burned down in a way that would imperil my Scottish skin and there were yet many more southern roads to travel.

Gabe, looking washed but still groggy, lumbered into the communal room, to where I had a plate of pastries and mug of lukewarm coffee waiting. "Doctor, we need to talk." His voice was hoarse enough to match his pained expression.

Already anticipating what this might be, I could feel the blood pressure rising within me but I held my tongue in case I was wrong. I mean, he wouldn't, surely. "Yes?"

"It's Dan." He confirmed my nightmares whilst collapsing into the seat beside me and clutching the coffee to his face.

"Yes?" I asked through clenched teeth.

He sensed it at once, replaced the mug and went for my hand, clasping it between his and looking into my eyes and because he could barely open them, the result was a strange imploring expression mixed with pained squint from the sun coming in through the large window. "Frey, it's only until Barcelona."

I threw down his hand. "*Our* Epic Euro Trip, right? That's what this was supposed to be."

"Frey, I promise it's only till Barcelona." He tried to speak soothingly but couldn't even manage that with his voice in this state. "I think he wants to stay there forever, all the women and parties, he's somehow talked himself into believing it's a utopia and I'll spend the entire journey reinforcing that image in his sweet little head." He groaned and rubbed his temple following the long verbal exertion.

"You're not helping, Gabe." And nor was he. It felt like a large chunk of life force had been yanked out from me. I knew travelling was meant to be about discovery and exploration, which included meeting and spending time with new, worldly, intelligent and interesting people but having met Dan, I was dubious any of those labels could be applied to him. And why couldn't Gabe and I just have a week, one measly week alone to have some peace, quiet and culture before we were descended upon? Had we not spent the last five years working hard enough to deserve that? I exhaled deeply and then my hand made a sudden forlorn lunge for my bag that was on the table. "You two concocted this last night, didn't you? Whilst you were getting pissed off your trolleys." I threw the bag back, having made my point. "And were you not even going to consult me about this? You know, travelling with another person, all the way to Barcelona, however long that will take. That's quite a change from what we had in mind, don't you think?"

"I know, I know." He tactfully agreed and rubbed my arm. "If it makes you feel better, he'll be asleep most of the journey." Which, I reasoned, would at least be true, given Arwen had confirmed his philistine nature. And then I froze as my mind threw back Gabe's last words.

"What do you mean, he'll be asleep most of the journey?"

IT WAS TRUE.

Dan's stupid little car had been towed away, or stolen, or hidden by Dan during the dark hours and I now glared at the oil stain on the pavement where the vehicle had been only the night before.

"So you see? There's no choice, he has to travel with us." Gabe leaned in and raised his eyebrows in an imploring gaze. "Please?"

When I'd first heard of this master plan to venture as far as Barcelona with Dan, I'd innocently assumed we'd be travelling in separate vehicles, which at least meant respite during those long, uncomfortable, sweaty hours on the road and, if he turned out to be as intolerable as expected at the rest stops and services, I could make my excuses and avoid him at the hostels. But now?

"This is a very, very poor excuse, Gabe." Especially given the man had bought the thing for practically nothing and could quite easily do so again, not to mention public transport which, I was told, existed even in France. But as so often with Gabe, I felt my resolve weakening. Worse, it felt like I was the one being unreasonable. Dan was my boyfriend's best friend, after all, and they'd not seen much of each other in recent years. The last thing I ever wanted was to be one of those women who came between her man and his friends. I knew one or two such women studying medicine and pitied them. What were they afraid of? That his friends might lead their man astray? Which meant really that it all came down to trust and I most certainly did trust Gabe and knew without doubt that he would never cheat or even be tempted. Not only was I being irrational but I also realised I was only feeling this way because our special trip was taking a detour, both geographically and, with the addition of male competition, emotionally, which meant that for the first time, I had to learn to share. Besides, might it be possible Dan could grow on me if I just gave him a chance?

Gabe sensed my resolve weakening and moved in for the hug and then he kissed me and everything was all right with the world. "I love you, Doc."

"I love you too." I clasped him tight as I felt his arms around my back. "But we're going to Carcassonne today and any deviation from that and we're breaking up."

He plucked my bra strap and the elastic snapped against my back and I tried to hit him on the shoulder but couldn't because he was holding me too close, so I melted into his embrace instead and then our lips met and his hand clutched one of my buns that I knew tipped him over the edge with lust as my breasts pressed against his chest and the air between us became intense and all I could think was that we'd not had the privacy to be intimate in too long and when would we have it again and his tongue entered my mouth as I felt him hardening against me and I was about to grab his hand so that I could rush him inside, to find any room that may or may not be free and to hell with anyone who might happen to walk in and then...

"Don't mind me, you two horny little love birds," came Dan's deep Yorkshire rumble from somewhere too close.

We instinctively broke apart like we were two teenagers caught doing something wrong, even though we had no right to feel that way.

He bounded from the hostel in our direction, dragging a large backpack along the ground. "Is that the camper?" He looked across the street to where Gabe had parked it earlier as his stupid face came alive. "Oh, mate, looks like you've got me the entire summer."

I wasn't sure if that was a remark intended to compliment Gabe or annoy me, indeed, all that was missing was a slap on my back. So far, I'd not given Dan any reason to know how much of an annoyance I was finding him and hoped the peace could be maintained, for Gabe's sake, at least until we parted ways. Things would have been better had we met in Edinburgh, knowing I could escape Dan The Gatecrasher at any moment but for now, I could only reconcile myself in the knowledge it was temporary, probably only two more stops, and then Gabe and I would have the rest of the summer to ourselves.

"Trust me, you're gonna fall in love with it," Gabe told Dan as he slid open the side door and they commenced an animated discussion about the camper, how old it was, how fast it could go, had we had sex in it yet and was Dan allowed to drive it.

All this whilst I took it upon myself to load all our belongings without their help and then I stood, hands on hips, as I wondered why the heck we were still standing around.

"Did you have to drive it through a sewer though? It's filthy." Dan used his finger to scrawl 'Also Available in Orange' on the side panel. "I'll drive when you get tired then you and Freya can go in the back and do your thing."

"Mate, I'm not letting you drive this. Don't think I can't remember how much of a liability you are behind the wheel of any..."

Their words petered out as the rumble of wheels increased in volume and their gazes shifted in unison toward the hostel from where Arwen was casually approaching with a trolley bag. She wore flip flops and a frilly red short jumpsuit that cut off closer to the arse than knees, though the top was elegantly tapered into a V, covering her cleavage, not that the girl's assets weren't straining against the material from within. No, she looked good and she bloody well knew it, but at least was decent enough not to outshine me too much to the best of my capabilities in front of my own boyfriend. I mean, what girl likes being upstaged at her own supposed party.

Because apparently, Arwen was joining us, which considering everything up to this point, should not have surprised me one bit.

And then my cynical side kicked in as I surveyed the girl, her looks, physiology and sweet-natured demeanour. She'd travelled with Dan all the way from Denmark. Yet Dan was skint whilst she was buying expensive bottles of wine, unnecessary as it was, for people she didn't know. Sure, Dan was probably a spendthrift and maybe Arwen had rich parents but somehow, I still doubted she was paying her way, as Dan had suggested, and was likewise teasing the idiot with promises. Let's face it, too many men were blind to a pretty face and made easy prey for the type of woman who was all too happy to take advantage. Well, she could try that with me and see how far it got her, I'd be watching closely.

I turned back to Gabe, who along with Dan had not only gone silent but had a deranged glazed look in the eye. "So you can see straight now, can you?" I could have throttled him and then I realised that this was the first time Gabe had seen her in full, up close and I got the distinct impression he wouldn't be all that against her joining us.

I snatched the keys from his limp grasp, "I'm bloody driving," and stomped toward the driver's side door.

I OPENED the window as far as it would go, breathed and worked my head around its axis. Two hours driving that had brought us from the region of Aquitaine to Occitanie, where the terrain became noticeably more mountainous, had gifted me with a stiff neck, doubtless from a poor night on a bad bed, possibly exacerbated from stress and kicked off from spending too long in the same position.

Beside me, Gabe was reclined back with his feet on the dashboard from where he occasionally muttered nonsensical claptrap and I wondered with a smile about what he was dreaming.

For the first hour, Dan had been rattling around in the back with the pots and pans as he explored the camper's furthest recesses, lighting the stove and playing with the TV, radio, coffee machine, drinking shots from the minibar, pulling out the chemical toilet and its septic tank and generally driving me crazy.

To her credit, Arwen spent the time lounging back on the seating bench, keeping quiet whilst reading a book, occasionally sitting up to gaze outside the window whenever we passed something of interest and altogether somehow managing not to get piqued by the Gatecrasher's proximity. I don't know how she managed it, as even now he was sifting through Gabe's collection of board games he'd brought for a rainy day, finding everything yet nothing of interest like a teenager with ADHD. Either she'd somehow tranced out or she possessed the patience of a saint which, considering our first encounter, I thought unlikely.

I adjusted the rearview mirror and peered into it, trying to see what it was she was reading, except I couldn't tell because it was in French. I made a small appreciative hum and muttered, "not such a bimbo, after all."

Gabe stirred, mumbled something incomprehensible and again, I worked my neck with a hand pressed down on my shoulder. "Ugh, I've done something to it."

The motorway bypassed the city of Toulouse and in so doing the signs were indicating I had to pay the second toll charge of the journey. So far I'd had to stump up fifteen Euros of my own money, whilst Gabe slept and the freeloaders pretended not to notice.

That was one difference between the UK and much of Europe. We so often complained about having to pay the most expensive fuel costs in the world but at least we didn't have to pay tolls. Here, fuel was much cheaper but having to make regular stops to feed money into a machine was irritating and, I was sure, more than made up for what they didn't collect in fuel taxes. However, where our roads were continually congested, here you could drive for miles and miles and not see another vehicle in either direction. It was a trade-off, I supposed, though on balance I'd go with the French.

Stopping at the barrier, I sighed loud enough for Dan and Arwen to hear, made a deliberate jingling noise with the change in the door's side pocket before getting out to pay the toll. That was another thing about driving a British vehicle on the continent and I assumed it was something we'd have to get used to, leaving the vehicle to walk around the other side in order to pay. Of course, I could simply have slapped Gabe awake so he could feed the machine through the window at his side but I wanted to make a point and see how the gruesome twosome in the back reacted. After I'd paid, that was another ten Euros from our diminishing fund gone and I hoped I wouldn't have to make that phone call to Dad.

I resumed my seat and Dan, for the first time, was sitting quietly, conspicuously looking out the window as though the other lanes of traffic were a fascination to him - Noted. I shifted my focus to Arwen who, to my surprise, was looking straight back and caught my eye in the mirror. I hastily looked away, as was the learned British custom of avoiding eye contact and silently cursed myself. Was she about to offer me money?

I clenched my hands around the wheel and restarted the engine, drove through the opened barrier and clamped a hand on my shoulder in an attempt to stretch out my neck muscles.

Gabe awoke half an hour later. "I feel better after that."

I reached over the dashboard to tickle his feet, causing him to instantly pull back in giggles.

The upcoming road sign stated we were approaching the Millau Viaduct and intrigued, Gabe looked it up on Google.

"Oh, wow," he rubbed his hands together and announced, "we're about to cross the tallest bridge in the world."

There was a rush of feet from the back and a blonde head poked through the gap between our seats. "Really? Any chance we can stop for a photo?"

I gasped and leaned away then was about to demand she resume her seat or risk being dropped off at the side of the road when Gabe spoke up from his phone.

"No, according to TripAdvisor the only place to stop is below, which means going to the local town of Millau and we've already passed the junction." He stuck out his bottom lip. "Sorry."

I was briefly distracted by the rearview mirror, presently trained on Dan, who was busy leering at Arwen's behind as she leaned forward, a long pink braid with its accompanying wooden bead coming to rest an inch from my knee with its faint accompaniment of peach. Gabe inhaled, pushed his glasses up and seemed to pause before returning to his phone.

My face flared in Arwen's direction. "If you sit down, I'll drive slow so you can get your photo as we cross." I sounded curt as intended, prompting a wavering smile from Gabe.

She didn't argue and a minute later we arrived at the Millau Viaduct that crossed the Gorge Valley, a structure taller than the Eiffel Tower that presented the most impressive views of fields and trees and mountains and towns that looked like specs and rivers and of birds that were actually flying below us. There was the patter of feet and expressions of awe with Dan and Arwen moving from one side of the camper to the other as Gabe filmed the crossing on his phone and I simply sat back and enjoyed the intoxicating air that flooded in through the opened window so that it almost felt like I was floating and finally I was here, in beautiful France and for a moment, everything was bliss.

If only it could last because my neck was giving me such discomfort, I had no option other than to stop at the next services.

"I'll drive the rest of the way," Gabe said, taking the keys from my palm.

I didn't argue and the rest would be most welcome, "thank you."

The intruders were waiting up ahead and Gabe caught up with them to buy some food whilst I went to the chemist to get some ibuprofen. As the boys continued, I was surprised to find Arwen waiting for me. It was nice to finally stretch my legs and I caught her up after a few seconds. It was only now I could see, and almost appreciate, what Dan had been so fascinated by.

It was the ass and how it filled out her red shorts the way all women wanted and most men craved, glutes that could only be built over time, as a result of heavy barbell squats, going deep, three times a week, every week. I knew that arse, the booty of fitness women whose programmes I'd purchased with the promise that I too could have buttocks shaped like that, just so long as I was willing to suffer and sweat and spend the week hobbling around on sore legs. Was it worth the sacrifice? In a word, probably, to have a rear like that, we women were willing to put ourselves through that kind of torture, to attract and keep our men.

My own buns were passable, I knew this from how Gabe reacted to them and the other attention I received but due to my ridiculous workload, it was more like deep squats only once a week for me and I'd be lying if I said I didn't feel a pang of jealousy and probably some insecurity. I didn't want her around Gabe and I certainly didn't want him looking, to compare me to her.

"Isn't it a beautiful day." She was wearing a stylish pair of sunglasses, whilst I'd left mine in the camper and because the sun was positioned behind her it caused me to shut one eye and squint with the other.

I continued and she walked alongside me. "That it is, that it is."

"You have a problem with your neck?"

I turned inwards and raised a curious eyebrow. "I think I slept very badly and I'm off to buy some painkillers. Aren't you hungry?"

She shrugged, "I'll eat when we get to Carcassonne. You know, it doesn't help being so stressed," which was probably her polite way of saying uptight, "you do seem very tense."

I stopped and stood arms akimbo. "Oh really, and you can tell that I'm stressed and tense, can you?"

She nodded and her feet scuffed against the ground as she took a small step closer. "It's all in your shoulders and the way they're being pulled. I don't know, you spend long hours at a desk? At a computer? That'll do it long term, and stress too, a bad night will kick it off."

I stood almost stupefied, unsure what to make of this. I *did* spend long hours at a desk studying and had suffered the occasional past complaint but nothing a quick dose of chemicals couldn't mitigate. And of course I was stressed, both chronically and, thanks to Dan and this bloody woman, acutely. I was under no doubt all would be well just as soon as they were gone from my life for good.

She continued, "and I don't want to tell you to relax," she said with a sympathetic hand searching forwards as my arms avoided it by moving from my hips to fold over my chest, "because I don't know enough to judge but stress will mess you up in all kinds of other ways."

I gave her my hardest glare and considered that she too might suffer from stress if she knew what actual work was. "Why don't you just come out and call me an uptight bitch?"

The girl didn't even flinch, "because I don't think that but we could all benefit by chilling every now and then, especially when we're on holiday."

I didn't disagree with her on any of that but wasn't about to be given medical advice from a bimbo and so I rolled my eyes and continued toward the chemist. "Yeah, well, you know, Arwen, I'm training to be a doctor, so you can keep your advice for Dan because I don't need it." That was something I hadn't wanted to divulge about myself because people always reacted in the same way, with reverence and admiration, which I usually found awkward dealing with and it wasn't like I was trying to impress the girl. So why had I told her when I could simply have ignored her?

But in response to my disclosure, she displayed only a subtle smile and other than that, simply continued walking alongside. "Well then, you know best. Ah..." she thrust a hand into her bag and pulled out a ten Euro note, "here's for the tolls. It's more than my quarter but I don't have anything smaller. Let me know what I owe you for the petrol or diesel or whatever and I'll make up the difference."

I stopped mid-stride and felt my facial muscles softening. Now, that was a pleasant surprise and I wasn't quite sure what to make of it, other than that I needed it. Had I misjudged her? At least on that score? I took the money. "Um, thanks, Arwen, it's appreciated."

"No, no, I feel so grateful to have met all you guys and I'm just happy to contribute." She smiled and as we entered the shop, we diverged onto separate aisles.

When I came out, the others were all waiting by the camper and I watched as Dan handed a sandwich and banana to Arwen. When I neared, her face perked up and she dashed to close the remaining distance.

"Frey, I was thinking..." *Frey?* "...you wanna know what the best thing for a sore neck and shoulder muscles is?" She spoke in a low voice, all conspiratorial like, despite the fact her dash had drawn the attention of the other two who were even now scrutinising her behind.

"I'm all ears, Ar." I caught Gabe's eye and he quickly spun back to the camper, rubbing the back of his neck.

She leaned even closer, "a massage cures all ails, including your stress and tension. I don't mind doing it. I'm not very good but I took a course back home so I can at least promise not to make it any worse."

"I am not stressed!" I growled, provoking a smirk from Dan.

She held up her hands and stepped away. "Ok, I was just offering. Did you find your pills?"

"I got my bloody pills."

"Uh huh, so what's your plan once they wear off? Will you be taking them indefinitely?"

For a moment, I actually looked at her inquisitively, genuinely curious if she was truly concerned for my wellbeing, albeit in a pushy way, or was actually trying to provoke me and was in the process of formulating a response when again, I caught Gabe ogling her. "I'm not stressed!" I snarled as I marched over to Gabe and plucked the keys back from his grasp.

———

Is it true that bad vibes make bad things happen?

If it was then I could blame my stress.

Twenty minutes was all it took.

And what made it worse was that we were less than thirty kilometres from Carcassonne, from relaxation, good food and a lie down in an air-conditioned room.

"Why didn't you take a piss when we were at the services?" Dan demanded of Gabe, as though he had a right to tell my boyfriend when he can and can't relieve himself.

Gabe flecked back his hair and blew out air.

"Is that all you have to say?" Dan demanded again. "We're fucked and all because you couldn't wait a few more minutes. How old are you, man?"

Gabe continued staring into the soil before shuffling to the front of the vehicle and leaning against the bonnet.

I stomped up to the moron. "You have no right to complain. You're lucky to even be here."

He turned on me, a few strands from his man bun falling loose and limp over his face. "Lucky? Will I be lucky to die of thirst? Oh, and nice driving Sabine Schmitz."

"Ugh." I clenched my fist and stomped into the cornfield for respite, lest I do something I'd regret. And who the fuck was Sabine Schmitz?

It was true that Gabe had needed to pee and, being on a minor road as we neared the destination, I'd stupidly gone off the beaten track and in the process, popped a tyre. It was just one of those things, they happen, and then we get heated and say things we don't mean and so I was right to withdraw from the argument. I also had no desire to be close enough to provoke another infuriating lecture from Arwen, this one about how we were only in this situation because my karma was bad and that somehow I'd intentionally driven into a big hole as a cry for help. I plucked at a corn reed and tore it into strips, closed my eyes, breathed and thought about the future, all the great places I was still to see, hopefully.

When I returned they were still bickering, although slightly more civilly as they scowled into their phones.

"Hey Gabe, do we have international breakdown assistance?" I asked and he nodded.

"We do but they can't make it out until tonight. It's a rural area."

I sighed but tried to remain positive. "And how far to the nearest town?"

"Like he just said, it's a rural area." Dan shook his head and made a mocking laugh. "If you're volunteering to walk all the way to Carca...wherever, then go ahead, I'm sure you'll be missed."

My jaw dropped and I looked to Gabe, expecting him to reprimand the jerk and for a second it looked like he would.

"Carcassonne is the nearest town, Frey." He said instead, astonishing me.

"Are you kidding me?" I stared wide-eyed at my man, who apparently was too weak to rebuke his friend for speaking to his girlfriend in such a disrespectful way. "Gabe?" I implored but he just looked down at the dirt.

I was seething and the mid-afternoon heat burning down hardly helped. I pulled out my phone, "right, I'm calling a bloody taxi and we can go quarters on the fare."

It was bait and Dan immediately turned away in embarrassment.

"Ah hah." I pointed and felt a surge of glee, "what's the matter, Dan? Can't pay your share?"

He whipped back on me, "I can pay, Freya, just not right now, that's all."

"Yes that's right, you need a stupid guitar string to pay your way but can't be bothered walking into a shop to get one." I stomped closer, tilting my head up to meet his eyes and feeling the ache in my shoulders. "What are they, like two Euros? Not once have you even offered to pay your share for anything." There was a slamming sound from somewhere close. "Well, it stops here. From now on you pay your way or we're off on our own, right Gabe?"

Gabe threw up his hands as Dan grabbed and squeezed at the man bun atop his stupid head, dislodging yet more strands. "Well sorry, Princess, we can't all have parents who own half of Scotland and maybe you should show a little more charity to those less fortunate."

My mouth plunged open again as I cast an accusing eye on Gabe. "What crap have you been feeding him?" I turned back to Dan, giving him my best scowl whilst having to yell above a new rhythmical squeaking sound that was coming from somewhere nearby. "And so what if my dad has money, it's not like I go begging for handouts every day, is it? There is such a thing as trying to make it on your own, you know, but you wouldn't know anything about that, would you?"

"And what's his name?" Dan ignored my point and smirked, "Angus? Angus? If that ain't the stupidest thing I ever heard..."

My dad's name had nothing to do with anything and I was about to berate Gabe for talking about my family like that when everyone's attention was seized.

Because the camper was vibrating. No, not vibrating, it was springing and rising up from the ground.

Gabe stepped forward, "shush."

"What the heck?" I murmured and we all ran around to the back of the camper. I gasped, "Arwen!"

She was there, thumping down with her foot, flip flops and all, onto the jack, working away as her thigh muscles strained from the effort. The boot was open and a panel from below had been removed, I guessed, to access the jack. She made an exaggerated expression of exertion, sticking out her tongue and panting. "For your information, we're quite close to the town of Bram ... a strange name, I know ... and it even possesses a garage, but French prices? I don't think so."

The camper was rising, it was actually rising, to the extent I could now slide my hand underneath the flat.

"I'd like to jack her up," Dan muttered in monotone.

She strutted over to the tyre and in one motion tore off the hubcap before crouching, grabbing the wrench and unscrewing the nuts, one by one, and tossing them to Gabe. "Don't lose those."

I snorted into my hand as his eyebrows dipped and I knew he was feeling more than just a little emasculated but, like a good boy, he put them in his pocket for safe keeping.

"Oh, and your international assistance?" She eased the wheel off, which wasn't light, and carried it to the boot, returning with the spare. "You'd might like to consider changing companies," she slid the wheel into position and gave it a spin on its axis, "or possibly even a refund. You got nuts?"

Dan slapped Gabe hard on the back and doubled over laughing whilst I was compelled to watch, absolutely impressed and feeling more than a little bad for poor Gabe.

He shambled forward, red-faced and coughing into a closed fist. "Um, yes, here they are."

She replaced the nuts, tightened them with the wrench, clipped on the hubcap and made everything right again in the boot, setting the flat tyre, wrench and jack back into place before closing the hatch and beaming at the three of us, oil and dirt covering her hands, forearms and jumpsuit.

"Ready? Carcassonne awaits."

"GABE? WE'RE NEARLY THERE."

His head turned from the window and he gave me a small smile in response, which was the most I'd got from him since rejoining the road.

Arwen laughed from the back and I checked the mirror to see Dan sitting beside her on the bench, their shoulders and knees touching. He made a sweeping movement with his arm, followed by an engine sound from his mouth and she laughed again. He leaned further into her and they bumped knees and then there was a terrible grating noise as I drove over the rumble strip.

"Freya!" Gabe perked to life and corrected my steering. "I think we've already used our spare wheel."

The vibration shook us all and it felt like my brain had been rattled in my skull. "Sorry, guys." I waved to them in the back and made a double take as I stared ahead.

The approach to Carcassonne was on flat ground, which meant we could see it from miles out, a double ring of fortifications beside a river, atop a steep hill and countless towers that sprouted up from within. I ached to be there because from out here it appeared as some other world from a different age, a place I was never meant to see, preserved through time by a thoughtful, cultural people. Britain possessed no place like it and if it did, I wondered if my people would protect it the way the French had, or would they simply modernise it, demolish the ancient walls to build roads, replace the cobbles with ugly asphalt, sink telegraph poles into the turf and worst of all, a McDonalds and Starbucks on every corner, the cancer that made every town and city the same. Not so here and my arms tingled as we drove past the sign 'Welcome to Carcassonne.'

Carcassonne, like other similar towns, was actually two places; the old and the new, the latter built up due to the tourism brought by the former. Mercifully, they were separated by a respectful distance, by fortifications and a river and never before was I so happy to have to park in the new and make the long walk to the old, which included the steep hill and an ancient drawbridge spanning the river.

After the eventful journey, we made the walk in fine spirits, Gabe and I lugging huge backpacks as Dan dragged his unceremoniously over road and turf. The excitement shone from Arwen who seemed to bounce, even up the steep hill, as she wheeled her exceptionally large case as though it weighed nothing, her filthy oil stained clothes not harming her mood.

The posters on TripAdvisor had repeatedly told of Carcassonne's legendary resident and as we entered the hostel, we met him in person.

He was standing behind the desk as we joined the back of the short queue and watched, intrigued. The man, French, slight of build and bespectacled was the type you'd normally walk past without a second thought. The guest at the front of the queue was Japanese and what made the hostel warden particular was that he was speaking to him in Japanese. Money was exchanged, a room key was handed over and the tourist went on his way. The next man was Chinese, who began speaking in English, and when the warden commenced speaking in the traveller's native tongue, he physically jerked back, scratched his head, took a second to adjust to the shock and continued. I watched, fascinated and carefully scrutinised the warden's face for his own reaction and although he'd make a great poker player, I decided there was the slightest hint of enjoyment displayed in the eyes and cheeks, to surprise people.

Languages have always fascinated me, I love listening to people speaking them, they're like riddles that have to be decoded step by step and if I hadn't been in intense training to become a doctor, I'd have been a linguist instead. Unfortunately, the joy of being in a foreign country and speaking to the locals in their own vernacular was one more thing I'd almost certainly never get to experience and I hated that none of my high school French had stayed in my head.

When the transaction was completed, Dan stepped up.

"Language?" The warden asked in English.

"I can, yes." He dragged his filthy bag up to the desk and traipsed leaves all over the clean floor. "Whatever costs the least."

"Ah, well let's see. You have the option of a bench on the walls, the gutter in the alleyway, the moat," he winked at me and I giggled, "or you can pay fifteen Euros for a reasonably comfortable dorm room bed."

He slapped down his money. "Aye, it'll have to do then."

"And would you like breakfast?"

Dan glanced over at Gabe, who nodded, "that'll be a yes," and consequently had to pay an extra five Euros. Dan took his key and shambled up the stairs as his bag clattered against every step.

Arwen stepped up and began speaking in French. The man's face lifted, although whether it was from talking to an English speaking girl in his native tongue, or from being face to face with a girl like her, it was hard to say. And she was good too, I could tell despite not understanding any of it. She was certainly fluent and spoke with swagger and at one point the warden laughed, which made me feel like I was being left out. Arwen handed over forty Euros and received a key with a different coloured tag.

"I'll catch you guys whenever." She addressed us both with a wavering smile.

I stepped abruptly forward. "Wait, aren't you sharing our dorm room?"

She jangled her room key and broke eye contact. "Sorry, I kind of need my own space."

That was a bummer. Come to think of it, she'd been the only one of the four of us who hadn't shared our dorm back in Bordeaux.

I frowned, "oh, ok then." She was about to turn away but I reached out and tapped her shoulder, "but you can come for dinner tonight, right?"

Gabe rubbed his chin, "um, Doc, you do remember we're on a budget, yeah?"

I could have kicked him. "Shush." Who was he to talk?

Her chin tilted up and she smiled cautiously, her feet already pointing towards the stairs. "Um, only if you're really sure?"

"Of course I'm bloody sure." I insisted with a nod.

She mirrored my nod and grinned. "Oh, well, then that's a yes, I'd love to meet you all for dinner."

"That's great." And it was. Still, a bummer about the dorm though.

When Gabe and I arrived in our six-man room, the contents of Dan's bag were already strewn across his bed.

"Oh, Jesus." Gabe protested, making a dash for the window and prising it open. "He must be in the shower."

I recoiled, yet couldn't look away. "He's a pretty laid back guy, huh? When he ain't causing stupid arguments."

His clothes were all spread out, mixed with tokens and keepsakes from all over the world; South America, North America, Russia, the Japanese text on the empty KitKat wrapper especially stood out. He'd even visited countries I'd never considered viable destinations; Tajikistan, for example. Mixed in with all this was a fine layer of sand, no doubt unwittingly collected from a hundred beaches, which he'd managed to scatter across the bed and floor. Though why he'd exhibited his underwear for the benefit of everyone else, I couldn't fathom, and yet it was hardly surprising he had.

"Next stop, Barcelona," Gabe said in a low voice as he closed the distance between us, maintaining firm eye contact all the way.

I instinctively reached out and pulled him into me. "And it can't come soon enough." I looked away, regretting the words as soon as I spoke, a revelation that piqued me.

His hands slipped down my body as he gripped and experienced my curves before pressing his lips into mine. Our breathing increased in volume as our tongues clashed and he pulled me hard into his crotch and rubbed, his other hand sliding up to clutch my breast, which felt full in his grasp. We hummed in unison, his tongue explored my mouth as I felt him growing further down. He groaned, I groaned a different pitch, his tongue delved deeper, mine remained steady, his eyes were closed, mine opened.

He pulled away, fire in his eyes, "I'm locking the door. Fuck anyone else." He took a stride but I pulled him back.

"Gabe, we can't do that. What if someone has a key?"

His nostrils flared in the direction of the door. "Then I'll use the bed to block the entrance, the wardrobe, Dan's crap to add extra weight." He growled and bounded over to the large bunk bed against the adjacent wall, giving it a tug, it barely moving, heaving again with an added grunt, his shirt coming untucked from the back of his cargo shorts.

I sighed, "Gabe, Gabe, we can't, we really can't. I'm sorry.

Someone might come in or knock and complain and I don't want to get kicked out of this lovely hostel."

He gestured out the window. "Kicked out? Good! We have a camper."

"And what about Dan if he's in the shower? He'll be waiting in the corridor wearing only a towel."

"Good, he'll understand, in fact, he'd probably encourage it."

I spoke in a soothing tone. "I'm sorry, Gabe, we'll get our own room in Barcelona. Either that or we *will* spend a night or two in the camper, I promise." I took some ibuprofen with a gulp of water and gave him another apologetic glance. "Are you heading out to explore this wonderful place?"

His shoulders slumped and he sighed deeply, surveying the three inches of movement that were the fruits of his exertion. "You bloody well go ahead."

I swallowed, "ok."

THE MINUTE you step out the hostel, you're transported to another world, a place of cobblers, blacksmiths, all kinds of tiny specialist shops, of narrow streets with stone arches converging into small squares, cobbled ground, of timber framed buildings where the upper floors overhang the lower, of every window with a wooden shutter, their ledges filled with flowers, of streets so clean you could almost eat from them, except I wouldn't recommend that last one, a labyrinth where you actually wanted to lose yourself and in the air, always, a sense you were treading in history and not once would you see a motor vehicle.

All this before you even make it to the walls.

There were two, an inner and outer and I strolled on the grass between them, craning my neck to view the tops, the spires and towers. The outer wall descended into the moat, was a solid bastion with steep steps at strategic points giving access to the summit whilst the inner wall possessed numerous archways leading into the town.

I pulled out my phone and took photo after photo, knowing the images would never do the place justice.

Ahead, Arwen was crouching in an archway, facing up and pointing what appeared to be an expensive camera, an actual real one, at something of fascination. She'd changed into a loose flowery dress, the most modest thing I'd yet seen her wear and I had to squint, slowing my approach to check that it was really her. But there was no confusing her long blonde hair and those three coloured braids with any other girl and even from this distance, her athletic figure was just as conspicuous.

And knowing it was her, I halted, paused and turned around to go back. She hadn't seen me, no harm done, I could have a pleasant evening in Carcassonne without the drama. I stepped once, twice and then for whatever reason stopped, scuffing my flip flop on the grass.

"Bugger it." Maybe it wouldn't be totally unpleasant to exchange a few words with the girl.

"Hi," she said, standing and brushing a long twist of blonde from her eyes, "isn't this the most magical place?" On one wrist she wore a band of wooden beads whilst on the other was a stylish looking red leather bracelet that I assumed to be the source of the pleasant scent around her, of what reminded me of Aloe Vera. She also wore another on her left ankle, a blue one, which I guessed meant they were probably to repel mosquitoes. The total cost of her accessories was probably somewhere in the region of zero, whilst still looking totally cool.

I nodded, "you seemed enchanted by something there. Care to share?"

She backed up to the wall and invited me forwards to peek through the archway, the other end revealing a stone wall and not a lot else. She anticipated my confusion. "It's the intricate patterns in the stones, the way they all fit together so snugly, each piece is a different size and shape. I just find it fascinating and beautiful. To me, this is art." Even though she spoke in a low voice, it came out amplified with the faintest echo.

I turned back and our shoulders brushed, "sorry, yes, it's beautiful," I stepped away, back onto the grass, "the small details, things you don't normally consider, or appreciate."

"The beauty is always in the small details and I find you have to take a closer look to appreciate them fully." She spoke with complete seriousness and it was bad of me to think such profundity sounded weird coming from her.

And why was that? Was it because she was blonde with a small, innocent face? Was it because she was around my age and it isn't considered cool to speak in such ways? Or was it because our first encounter had been such a horrific car crash? I had to be honest with myself because up to this point, I'd been wrong about Arwen at every single juncture.

She gestured to the path and we set off at a sauntering pace. The outer wall blocked the sun, which cast much of the walkway in shadow where ahead, it curved out of sight and I assumed it would be possible to circle the entire town if we wanted. I fidgeted with my blouse cuff that cut off at the elbow and then nodded to a middle-aged Chinese couple, who ignored me.

"So, how're your shoulders?" She asked, louder than before as her body angled slightly into me.

I made a small, embarrassing bark, "you don't give up, do you?" I shook it away. "Anyway, how come *you* know how to change a flat?" It sounded patronising, even to myself. "Oh, I didn't mean...ugh..."

She laughed and shook her head. "All I did was change a flat tyre. It's not like I cured cancer, fed the world or disabled all nuclear weapons, you know."

I could feel my muscles relaxing and assumed it had something to do with her not feeling anywhere near as tense as I did, "yeah but still..." and I had reason to be agitated. I'd been mean to Arwen and she'd returned only warmth when she had every right to give back what she got, told us to fuck off, find new friends and alternative means of travel.

"I'm sure your boyfriend had it taken care of, I just didn't give him much of a chance to prove it, did I." She sounded almost apologetic.

I gave her a knowing look and smirked, wondering if she was taking the piss but I couldn't tell. "You're too kind. No, give him a few years and he'll save your life if you happen to overdose on opioids or get ploughed down by a bus but as for anything practical..." I left the rest unsaid, knowing that poor Gabe, for all his capabilities, would struggle to change a light bulb - Not that it was his fault and not that I was much better. When you spend your life studying human anatomy, other things tend to get neglected, which kind of explained why the simple act of witnessing a young girl saving our arses was so impressive to me.

"You love him very much, don't you." She said as a matter of fact. "How long have you been together?"

"Five years," I stated. "Five years. He's a great guy. One of the best. Ah," I pointed to some steps that appeared in the outer wall, "let's go to the top."

She glanced across at me then led the way up, grabbing ahold of the rail and stepping carefully because the ascent was steep and we were both wearing flip flops. Her dress cut off at the knees, revealing calves that popped in a way that mine didn't.

The reward atop was a spectacular view over the earthworks, moat, river, new city and surrounding countryside and in acknowledgement I gasped something incomprehensible before enjoying the next few minutes in respectful silence, leaning against the parapet and gazing out in awe, occasionally turning around for a view over the old town.

It was a mystery how such places could be built during times of supposed lesser enlightenment, before the advent of modern machinery and medicine and it was hard not to make comparisons with modern structures, towns and developments. Were we even capable of creating such beauty anymore? The future was coming but were we really going forwards?

I pulled out my phone, "how about you," and checked the home screen for alerts, "is there anything going on between you and Dan?" I glared into the screen, nothing new since last check.

"Dan?" One side of her mouth quickly raised. "He's a fun guy, I like him, but only as a mate. Oh, God," she giggled harder now, after having apparently given the scenario some thought, "no, no, no, that wouldn't work. We're travelling buddies and that's all it'll ever be."

My feet shuffled, scratching the stone. "To be honest, I couldn't picture the two of you together." It would have been too much of a mismatch, for sure. "So, no boyfriend on the road? Or back home?" I checked my home screen again, still no alerts.

"Nuh-uh," she shook her head, "free as a bird, which is how I'm able to travel for as long as I like and not answer to anyone."

I brushed the hair away from my face. "I expect it'd be a problem, you know, being away from home so long, with your relationship, if you were in one, which you aren't, not that I even know how long you've been away. How long have you been away ... travelling?"

She smiled and briefly broke eye contact as her eyes snapped upwards. "About six months, not as long as Dan. He's been everywhere and knows a thing or two about travelling on a zero budget. I know it might not seem like it sometimes but he can improvise when he wants, you'd be surprised. I just think that now he doesn't need to use his head so much because he has you and Gabe to do all that for him, he's happy to sit back and let someone else drive and plan and think for a change ... pay, even?" She shook her head and grinned. "I've seen him arrive at a hostel and within minutes there's a group of nine or ten of us all heading to the pub. People like that are very rare. Yep, he's the guy you see when all you want is a bit of fun. Oh, hey..." and she made a swift half spin, grabbing my wrist, "the things I said about him last night, the mean things, I shouldn't have said them, not really, I mean, I was still quite angry with him so they don't count."

"Hah, that was you being mean?"

It was a true friendship then. She wasn't using him, as I'd previously and judgementally thought. And I could tell from the light in her eyes, the warmth in her voice and the animation of her face that she genuinely liked the guy and enjoyed his company. Of course, Dan obviously wanted more, he was a bloke, after all, and Arwen looked like the heroine from an anime series. But that didn't mean it would happen and he'd be far from the first guy to have been placed firmly in the friend zone.

Not for the first time, I felt ashamed about my rush to judge Arwen.

But I'd learned my lesson.

"I'm glad you're here with us," I said without thinking, feeling immediately silly but she showed no sign of being startled or unsettled.

"I'm glad to be with you." She said in the kind of laid back Oz way I was beginning to find refreshing and likeable.

And although, I realised, I knew next to nothing about her, it'd be fun having Arwen knocking about, if only until Barcelona. A feminine counterbalance to the overwhelming levels of testosterone in that camper would not be unwelcome.

The sun now resembled a glowing slither that further sank and diminished beyond the horizon.

"Selfie?" I asked with raised eyebrows and without hesitation, we positioned our backs to the parapet and as I brought up my phone, I felt her hand slip across my lower back. I did the same.

I tapped the screen, an instant was all it took but it would be there forever.

DAN STOOD and used the back of his seat for balance as he stretched out his quads. "Ok, ok, I'll take a hit for the team." He retook his seat, flexed his fingers then held a napkin, using it to hold the shell, *escargot*, and breathing deeply, "can you believe it even comes with its own fork?"

Arwen slapped the table. "You can do it."

Gabe patted him on the arm. "I have faith in you."

"Ok, I just need a sec…" he made panting sounds and plunged the fork in, twisting and extracting the snail. "Fuck, fuck!"

"Now, dip it in here." Arwen pushed the garlic butter sauce closer.

He submerged the delicacy then brought it towards his grimacing face, "ok, team, here goes," and closed his mouth around the snail.

"No, no, you have to chew it." I declared, my belly hurting from so much laughter.

"I *am* chewing. Oh, Christ, I'm really eating a snail."

Gabe was filming the whole event on his phone. "Down the hatch, buddy."

His Adam's apple bounced, he winced and the wine was quick to follow. "Actually, that wasn't too bad."

"Then you'll want another, right?" Arwen teased, gesturing to the remaining snails.

"Balls to that and I don't know why you're laughing, Frey-Frey, you're up next." He shoved them closer to me and sat back, arms folded in satisfaction.

In these types of situations, I find the ripping of the band-aid approach to be best and so I plucked up a snail, removed it from the shell, dipped in it the sauce and sent it home all within a matter of seconds.

Oh, bloody hell, but I was actually eating a snail, chewing the thing, and then everybody was slapping the table in raucous laughter and nearby diners were staring and all I could think was how much it reminded me of the moules-frites from our first night in France, which wasn't bad at all. "Wine." I croaked, grasping for my glass and pouring a large quantity down my gullet. "Ugh, I'm so happy that's over and you're up next Arwen," I pointed an index finger and made a clicking sound.

Dan looked at me then back to her with a questioning expression before silently mouthing, "Arwen?"

I burst out in laughter but the mood was so great this night that I just couldn't embarrass the guy by announcing he'd had her name wrong for so many weeks and thankfully, Gabe hadn't connected the dots and then I watched enthralled as she picked up the snail, removed it from the shell before sending it between her wide, thin lips and holding a hand over her mouth to conceal the discomfort she must surely be undergoing.

"I think she's more used to barbecued shrimp." Dan declared and when she swallowed, he pulled her in with an arm and kissed her on the cheek.

Gabe raised his glass. "To the girl who saved our arses, without whom we'd still be walking here."

Arwen flexed an impressive bicep, "just let me know when you need your oil changing."

"Awe, poor Gabe." I gave him a sympathetic hug as his cheeks reddened.

We were in a small, very beautiful square lit by gas lampposts and candles, surrounded by flowers flowing from hanging baskets, where the tables from the surrounding restaurants merged into the next and I wondered for how many hundreds of years people had sat and eaten and laughed and cried in this exact same spot. Certainly, there was an ethereal, almost unworldly feel about the entire town, the old part at least, which had only been exacerbated by the onset of night. It was just something you felt down your spine, that same Christmas morning tingle you remember from being a kid, or the first day of summer, or the last day of school, a feeling you experience only a few times in your life and it made you feel alive. The doctor in me logically attributed it to the dopamine being produced from a combination of Carcassonne's magic, alcohol, good food and present company. I doubted I was the only one who was feeling it, which only added to the mystique because it appeared to be something we were sharing as a group, at least tonight, where everybody got along and everything just seemed to click. Even Dan was acting pleasant and had not, thus far, caused offence.

The waiter arrived with the sea urchins, *oursins*, which resembled small spiked balls cut through the middle to reveal the orange goo within, a supposed delicacy here in the south.

"We're gonna need more wine," Arwen announced before speaking to the waiter in French, impressing everyone.

"Oui, madame."

"And don't have a heart attack, Gabe, it's on me."

He winked, "we need wine so I won't say no."

There were eight halves, two each, and it was Gabe's turn to go first.

He removed his glasses and squeezed at the flesh above his nose. "And I have to do this twice?" Come to think of it, he looked a tad paler than normal.

Dan slapped him on the back. "It can't be worse than all that haggis your missus force feeds you."

"Hey, Gabe loves my haggis."

"And can you believe they even have a special spoon just for these little things?" He picked it up and dipped it into the yolky substance with bits of red and black floating in it, scooped it out and closed his eyes as it went down, swallowing in one.

Arwen was leaning forward, her little face alive. "Doesn't that just glide right down there?"

Gabe opened his eyes and breathed, "actually, it's kind of creamy, not unlike oysters, not too bad. I've certainly had worse in a Scottish greasy spoon."

And then came the pigeon, frogs legs and finally, just in case we hadn't already been sufficiently open-minded, or drunk, enough this evening, the tête de veau, which for the lesser informed, was boiled cow brain. This final bright idea had been one of Dan's, which by the rules of the game meant we all had to choke it down before he did. It looked exactly as expected, with a leaf or two of lettuce for garnish. Dan blanched as he took his knife and began slicing the monstrosity into four equal pieces.

"Having second thoughts?" I asked, genuinely hopeful so we could forget this whole silly idea.

He looked up from the plate with a disapproving glare. "I've eaten worse than this. You'll understand if you ever see Beijing. What was it Prince Philip said, 'if it has four legs and is not a chair, has wings and is not an aeroplane, or swims and is not a submarine, the Chinese will eat it.'"

I shook my head, having thought too soon about him not causing offence - Oh, Dan.

"Bon appétit, Freya, oh look, they left the skin on." He sat back and clasped his hands behind his stupid head.

Gabe assisted by transferring one of the portions to my plate and leaning in close to my ear. "It's supposed to be very good for people with arthritis."

"But I don't bloody have arthritis." I was almost trembling at the sight of it and pulled my wine closer.

He soothingly rubbed my forearm. "And after eating this, you never will."

I nipped the skin on the back of his hand. "And I don't know why you're being so smug because you're next."

That shut him up and he leaned sombrely back.

A hand began rubbing my other arm and I looked across the table to find Arwen reaching between the empty glasses to offer comfort. "You can do it, just one mouthful and then you can relax and watch the rest of us attempting to choke it down." And there was something so very reassuring to her tone, her eyes.

"Well, when you put it like that." After all, I was here to try new things, even if cow brain hadn't been high on my list.

I grimaced before the pink, rubbery goo and skewered it with my fork, brought it to my nose and inhaled, "smells like French mustard," which, I guessed was the sauce they'd used to kill whatever vile taste it had.

Gabe's hand was back on my knee and Arwen was leaning forward, elbows on the table.

"Ok, here goes." And there was an inhalation from somewhere as it touched my tongue and I closed my mouth to commence mastication in earnest. "It's chewier than I'd hoped, kind of rubbery, can taste the mustard, faint hint of caper," it finally broke up and I swallowed, resisting the urge to purge, to give Dan the satisfaction and I smiled, carefully replaced my fork, dabbed the side of my mouth with a napkin and invited the rest to give it a try.

Arwen applauded and then added to the wine already in my glass. "You deserve that."

And never was I so relieved to have wine.

It wasn't that it was bad because it was no different to eating a large piece of particularly gristly pork belly. It was more the psychological aspect, the knowledge I was eating brains and then not going straight for my wine afterwards, to wash away the unpleasantness because to do so would be to give the boys satisfaction and to show weakness in front of Arwen, which for whatever reason I did not want to do. No, this one was a victory for the girls.

Arwen soon followed with the band-aid approach, swallowing so fast I doubt it even touched her mouth. The boys, however, were somewhat less dignified, drawing it out, trying to distract, to get more drunk, huffing and puffing, offering money and favours so they wouldn't have to go through with it until finally surrendering and submitting to a forfeit at some time of our choosing.

"No more food tonight," Dan proclaimed to everybody's relief, "only drink." And he regaled us with tales about the food he'd eaten on his travels; chicken feet and one-hundred-year-old egg in China, eyeballs in Japan, fried spider in Cambodia and tequila worms in Mexico, although judging from his performance tonight, it was hard not to be sceptical.

On her travels, Arwen had also been adventurous, having tried snake in America, grasshoppers in Thailand and even kangaroo in her own country, though only because she'd been told it was beef. Meanwhile, the height of my exotic food experience stretched only as far as the occasional kebab and eating the fish we'd caught ourselves in the Highlands.

Then Dan tried to one-up her by speaking of the rivers he'd rafted down, the tribes he'd spent time with, the mountains, planes and valleys he'd camped on and the crowds he'd entertained with his music as he'd travelled the world.

Not subdued, Arwen entertained us with anecdotes of the exotic wild animals she'd photographed, the castles she'd been in, mountains she'd climbed and more than one story of being propositioned by rock stars and hip-hop artists who, she assured us, she'd turned down.

I listened in awed silence, enthralled by it all and barely daring to breathe in case I should happen to miss an important or even minor detail. Yet conversely, I felt so empty.

As I sat and listened, all I could think was that there was indeed so much more to life beyond the student halls I'd spent so long shut away inside and as Arwen and I made brief eye contact from across the candlelight, I couldn't help but feel regretful about the lost opportunities, which I'd never see again.

Why was I only feeling this way now? Was it hearing of Dan and Arwen's adventures? Or was it the food? That I'd finally done something crazy myself and opened the floodgates? I had to admit, it was funny it took a cow's brain to make me see it.

I was nearly twenty-four years of age, was only now going on my first independent holiday, had no real hobbies to speak of and had known only one lover. I'd never had a part-time job and thus never earned my own money. I'd never run a marathon or competed in a sport. I'd missed celebrating my twenty-first birthday because a group presentation had been scheduled for the next morning. The drunkest I'd ever been was arguably this moment and I'd never used drugs of any sort, although that was unlikely to ever change. I was educated and, I'd thought, extremely happy but now I couldn't be sure I'd even lived a life at all.

Worse, I knew that as soon as this summer was over, I'd return to Britain, back to a life of routine, of doing the same things, of having to shut myself away in a hospital for half the day and a study the rest, of not having time for anything else and I'd always know that this magical euphoria I was presently experiencing may never again return.

Don't get me wrong, I wanted nothing more than to be a doctor, there were very important reasons why I'd chosen this particular career path and knew I'd make a bloody good one but there are points where everyone gets hit by melancholy and the lamentations of what could have been.

Should I have waited a year before going to medical school? I didn't think so because at the age of eighteen, I had no interest or urge to travel and the thought of doing so would have struck me down with fear. But I was certainly travelling now and sometimes things happen in life at the right moment for reasons. And although I couldn't take back the time spent locked away, nor more of the same that was yet to come, what I could do was ensure I made the absolute most of *this* summer by making a vow to myself this very moment. That vow was that I would seize every opportunity to live this summer, this one magical summer, to the utmost of its extremes. I would say yes to every opportunity that presented itself but more than that, I would create my own opportunities. I would laugh and cry and for the first time, I would live.

I gulped from my glass, suspecting the wine was probably responsible for my strange mood, for my vacant eyes and Gabe brought me further back to clarity with his deep voice up close.

"Hey, Doctor, are you all right?"

I smiled from the mouth, as warmly as I could. "Yeah, I think so." I reached out and he took my hand, kissing my knuckles as I glanced across the table.

Dan was leaning into Arwen, speaking so low I couldn't make it out and it became clear the table had split into two groups, one couple and what, to me, was increasingly beginning to look like another couple, despite what Arwen might have said.

"We can't leave this place tomorrow," Gabe gestured out with his hands, "it's too soon and it's a good base for other nearby places."

I nodded in affirmation, "what are they talking about?"

He hesitated, looked across and frowned, "oh, dunno, um, maybe what they're gonna do after we've ditched them. Europe is our oyster, Frey, and we can go wherever we want."

"Wherever we want," I said, sounding hopelessly monotoned.

"Hey, guys," it was Arwen, who was raising her glass, as Dan to her side likewise mirrored her.

Gabe and I obediently did the same and waited for the Australian to make her toast.

"I just wanted to say that I'm so happy to have met you all so, let's make a toast to us, to friendship, to Mother Europa and to whatever's around the corner."

I couldn't agree more and then we all clinked glasses.

And drank.

———

THE LANGUAGE GUY watched bemused from behind the front desk as Gabe and I shambled into the hostel a little after midnight, using each other for support, Gabe chanting the first verse to Auld Lang Syne.

"Shush, Gabe, I want to ask the genius a question."

A bushy eyebrow perked from behind the desk and we shared a moment of telepathy, *another rowdy lot from north of the English Channel*.

"Sorry for my Scottishness, can you understand me? Of course, you can, you understand everybody, even those people from the Amazon jungle." I leaned against the desk and began shuffling through a stack of pamphlets about nearby attractions or something. "You obviously spent most of your life studying stuff and languages, so I just wanted to ask ... No, Gabe, stop that, not on my neck ... I just wanted to ask if you'd have rather done other stuff instead? ... Gabe!" I giggled and shoved him half-heartedly away, forgot my question and reached out again for his support, heading in the direction of the steps and calling over my shoulder, "there's a pretty girl behind us and she's with some guy who's not got a chance, so could you do him a favour and say he should just forget about her."

Gabe's tongue found its way into my ear and I shivered. "What are you talking about? Dan'll soon be having his way with her."

I slapped him playfully on the side of the head. "No, he bloody well won't."

"*Should old acquaintance be forgot, and never brought to mind? Should old acquaintance be forgot, and old lang syne?*"

"Shush," I urged him, watching every step on the creaky stairs, "Gabe? Do you have any regrets? Anything you might have done differently?"

"Nope," he kissed me on the cheek, "everything's perfect."

Chapter Four

CATALONIA

We spent a total of three nights in Carcassonne, using it as a base to see other nearby places, like the town of Avignon to the east, which during the fourteenth century had been home to the papacy, with its twelfth century bridge to nowhere, the Pont Saint-Bénézet that traversed halfway across the Rhône river before stopping, the other half having been destroyed by floods four hundred years earlier. We enjoyed a beautiful river walk on a hot sunny day with ice creams before driving the short distance to see the one place I'd have picked out of a million, somewhere that was bound to show up on any travellers list of places to see, the Pont du Gard, a largely intact Roman aqueduct that dominated the Gardon River with its imposing size, beauty and countless arches.

Standing on the south bank, Gabe and Dan were arguing over whether the structure had been altered to accommodate the tourists that were even now walking across from one side of the aqueduct to the other.

Dan thrashed his arm in the direction of the structure. "They're not gonna alter a two-thousand-year-old Roman pile just so you can waddle your fat arse over it."

Gabe jabbed his finger with equal intensity. "Are you blind? Just take a look underneath the thing? The stone at this side's a different bloody colour, size and texture. And why do you think that is? Because it's been cut from the quarry nearly two thousand years later, using different tools and techniques. It's not been in the bloody sun as long."

"The sun makes stone lighter, does it? Then why is the older stone darker?"

"So you're admitting it's older stone now?"

Dan momentarily found himself unable to reply, which was rare for him.

Gabe, sensing victory, delivered the death blow. "And you think they won't alter a two-thousand-year-old aqueduct for reasons of posterity but they're perfectly happy to allow thousands of tourists to trample all over it?"

Arwen and I had been listening close by and we looked at each other, rolled our eyes in unison and waded into the river. We were both in summer dresses and flip flops and, not knowing we'd be doing this, neither of us had thought to bring a change of clothes. Not that it mattered because the sun was imposing its power on us today and the water was a beautiful cooling contrast against the skin.

"What do you do back home, for a living, I mean?" My hand was making small, incomplete movements in the direction of Arwen's arm, in anticipation of needing her for stability as the water gradually began to cover our lower legs.

Her hand was doing the same and at one point, her fingers briefly wrapped around my arm. "I dance."

"Ahhh," I nodded, as though it explained a lot, "very cool. What kind of dance?"

Her face brightened as the water made slushing sounds with our every step. "I spent most of my life training in ballet, tap and jazz. They were my passions but after I hit eighteen, I kind of needed to go where the money was so I learned salsa and hip-hop too."

I glanced across as my lips made an appreciative pucker. "Do you teach?"

"Um hmm, there's just not enough music videos to go around so I kind of have to spend most of my time teaching but that's ok, cos I love it, it pays well and feels like I'm giving something back."

"You've been in music videos?" I asked in a tone that failed to hide how impressed I was.

Her hand jutted out again for my arm and I helped steady her by reaching around and placing a hand on her shoulder. "Thanks, Honey, yeah. Have you heard of Tiny Biggz?"

My eyes widened. "He's a huge hip-hop star! You've been in one of *his* videos?"

She nodded as the bridge of her nose turned red. "Oh, he's a rotter ... offered me money to sleep with him so I told him to go eat shrimp."

I snorted and gave her another appreciative glance. Most women would probably have done whatever a world-famous multimillionaire demanded of them but not Arwen, no. "Wow." I finally said.

"I've actually been in several of his videos and was on his world tour last year. I lived and travelled for free for six months, performing in shows every night and living in hotels but I didn't actually get to see anything, not one thing, which was such a disappointment, so I saved a huge stack of cash and came back to Europe to do the whole thing again, only this time properly." She giggled, "if you think Dan's an ignoramus, you've not seen anything until you've met a guy who's obsessed only with diamonds, gold, fast cars and flashing money around to impress people." She rolled her eyes and I wondered of what memory she was thinking. "No, Dan's an angel compared to some guys, oh, and Gabe too, of course."

I agreed, "of course."

From atop the aqueduct, at least two male tourists were taking photos of us and we stopped as the river came up to our knees, we both almost slipping on the goo coated rocks of the river bed. I fell into her and she steadied us both by threading an arm around my hips, where it remained.

"I have to agree with Gabe," her voice was calm, easy and natural, like holding onto me was nothing, "you can see where the stone changes ... not clearly perhaps, but if you look hard, you can sort of tell."

"Oh, don't let him hear you say that or else he'll be gloating the rest of the day." I felt her fingers pulse around my flesh and the cold water sent a shiver up my body. "The fact we're even discussing this shows how great a job they did. They've fooled thousands of people into thinking that walkway is ancient."

I silently mused how Gabe would complain that had the aqueduct been built in England, they'd have long since pillaged the stone to make sheds, demolished it altogether as a health and safety risk, or else kept the structure but built the walkway from ugly breeze blocks or solid steel and I had to agree with him. There were reasons Britain possessed no comparable aqueducts, despite the Romans having occupied most of the island for nearly five hundred years. One only needed to look at Hadrian's Wall, or what was left of it, to understand the problem.

Two men in a kayak glided past, their oar blades coming to rest on the water's surface as they leaned back to relax, enjoying the break and majestical view for a few moments.

She hummed and brushed a long pink braid away from her eyes. "Still, I'm not sure I'm totally in favour of altering such an old structure just for tourists."

I sighed in agreement. "Yes but it's probably preferential to having them trample over the real thing."

Together, our heads turned to the bank from where the boys were still bickering. We giggled and, feeling her hand slip from my side, we started for the bank. Two steps, three, four and I spun around, throwing up water to soak Arwen's grey summer dress.

She stopped and gaped, unable to believe what I'd just done. There's nothing that reveals damp patches in clothing quite like the colour grey and, approving of my handiwork, all I could do was laugh.

"Oh, you drongo." She finally managed to squeak after adjusting to the additional cold and wetness.

"I'm a what?" I was briefly crippled with laughter until she sent a stream of cold water my way, soaking the front of my flowery summer dress. The chill was brief because it was soon overwhelmed by the delivery of more and so I sent a cascade back until we were both thrashing and kicking water and only coming to a stop when neither of us had anything left to soak.

"I can't believe you." She grinned as water trickled from the tip of her chin, from the point of her nose and the lobes of her ears but I didn't care because never before had I stood in such a beautiful river with a friend and endeavoured to soak her as my belly hurt from laughing so hard.

The material clung so tightly to her curves that for a moment I thought it'd shrunk as her hips and buttocks and breasts stretched every inch of that dress to its very limits. Breathing heavier, she appeared to be surveying her own handiwork, her eyes casually passing over my thighs and abdomen as I felt my breathing tighten from the added water weight and constriction of my dress until a damp clump of red fell over my eyes and I swept it aside with the backs of my fingers.

More men were leering from atop the aqueduct and then the boys wolf whistled and almost as one, we jerked around to face them and waded back to the bank.

Dan nodded his approval and stroked his chin as his eyes completely ate up every inch of Arwen, the constriction from her dress enforcing small steps upon her. "You guys look awesome." He turned to continue glaring at her arse as she trudged past.

"Not sure about your forward planning though, or lack thereof," Gabe said lightheartedly, concealing what I knew to be a subtle reprimand as he doubtless hoped I wasn't aware he was tracking Arwen's damp buttocks from behind his sunglasses. "And I hope you're dry by the time we get back to the camper." He said in a lower voice, reserved only for me.

I flicked water over his sunglasses. "Oh, you're such a drongo."

"Am not." He returned to the back of my head.

Before leaving Carcassonne, I dashed into the new town to buy something for Dan and upon returning to the hostel, made a second embarrassed apology to the language guy. Finally, we made our way on foot, out through the walls, across the drawbridge and down the slope to the camper from where I sat in the passenger seat next to Gabe.

"Barcelona." He declared profoundly.

And my chest was hit by a sudden thud.

IT WOULD HAVE BEEN a journey of a mere three hours had we taken the fastest, most direct route to Barcelona through the Eastern Pyrenees. But Arwen, having been denied the French Alps, had expressed her regret at the thought of also missing what she'd been told were some of the most picturesque mountains in Europe.

"Right!" I'd said, needing no more convincing before pestering Gabe to take the scenic route.

The consequent drive through the central Pyrenees was indeed nothing short of spectacular and I took more photos during this stretch than everywhere else combined so far. It was the snowcapped mountains that ranged into infinity, the lakes and their tiny islands, the rivers and streams as pure now than at any other time past, the beautiful roads that meandered in countless loops sending us up and up to bring those perfect views of the sun reflecting on the water below, the hamlets, the birds, everything surrounded by thick forest and the knowledge that nothing had changed from time immemorial. Arwen's camera clicked constantly and I do believe there was the occasional gasp even from Dan.

And then we arrived at the Andorran border.

As we queued, Gabe opened Wikipedia to learn more about this strange microstate. "Andorra is the sixteenth smallest country in the world and its capital city is the highest in Europe. Hear this ... the people of Andorra have the highest life expectancy in the entire the world."

There was an "ooh" from the back, followed by Arwen saying, "must be all this mountain air."

"Doesn't mean they're happy," came Dan's voice, "just look at this miserable lot."

He meant the extremely bored and almost redundant border guards who, because of the Schengen agreement, simply waved us through despite being in a UK registered vehicle.

From there it was a short drive to the capital, Andorra la Vella, and despite the one road leading directly there, Gabe still insisted on using Google Maps, perhaps because he assumed that with it being the capital city, he'd somehow get lost. As it transpired, Andorra la Vella had a population of only twenty thousand people, which made it equivalent to a small English town.

We stopped for a late lunch before splitting up to take a look around and from then it required only one minute to realise the purpose of this entire country. It was, after all, a tiny nation sandwiched between two great powers and there had to be a reason as to why it had been allowed to exist. That reason - Tax-free goods.

Doubtless, Andorra had been the place that for centuries the French and Spanish had travelled for cheap tobacco, fine clothes, jewellery, alcohol and God only knew what else. Its principal street possessed shop after shop selling these items as well as prescription, electronic and other such modern goods at exceptionally tempting prices.

Dan disappeared, despite his supposed financial circumstance and after Gabe and I had purchased several bottles of red wine, Cognac and Cointreau, as well as some spicy Spanish sausages, cheeses and rustic bread, we found him with Arwen, leaning against the wall of yet another shop selling spirits.

She was standing upright, hands on hips and neither were speaking when we crashed.

"All ready to go?" Gabe lifted his two plastic carrier bags filled with the good stuff.

"Yes." Dan snarled before pushing between the two of us and bounding in the direction of the camper.

Arwen sighed, "sorry about that."

I looked from Dan's brown man bun bouncing up and down to Arwen's three coloured braids. "What was that all about?"

"Perhaps best not repeated in polite conversation." She had no bags so I assumed whatever it was had stolen her shopping time, not that I had her down as the consumerist sort, even at discount.

Before reaching the Spanish border, we took advantage of the cheap fuel prices, filling the tank to the top whilst undergoing the usual routine of Dan's silence and Arwen's insistence on paying more than her fair share. I waved her away on this occasion and gave Dan a cold stare.

At the border, we had to stop for an inspection and we waited outside the camper whilst a gloved woman examined the contents of our shopping. Satisfied we weren't taking the piss too much, we were sent on our way.

Spain.

But because we were still in the central Pyrenees, it still very much resembled France, at least from the inside of our camper.

Gabe's phone chimed, he read the message, scrunched up his face and smashed his hands against the wheel. "Fuck! Fuck! Fuck!"

There was a dash of feet from the back and then two heads were poking between the seats.

"What on earth?"

He handed me the phone and I read the news that apparently, because he'd been using his data constantly whilst in a 'rest of the world zone 3 area,' he'd accrued over four hundred pounds in charges.

"Gabe?"

His hands were clenched around the wheel as the sweat began to shimmer on his forehead. "Fucking maps." He swept a hand through his hair, dislodging the neat parting and propped up his glasses.

Arwen made a tactful retreat back to her seat but Dan made his presence known by bursting into laughter.

"Wait, wait, wait, you mean, you passed through a zone 3 country without switching off roaming?" His head thrust further through the gap as he slapped Gabe hard on the shoulder, barking out loud.

A vein in Gabe's neck bulged, something I'd never seen before. "I needed to use the maps."

"Watch where you're going," he said sternly before returning to a mocking tone, "there was one road; from France to a capital city, to Spain. How hard could it be?"

Gabe flushed and not from the Spanish heat. "Did you or did you not see the European flag at the border crossing?"

"Andorra is not in the European Union, you idiot."

I turned on Dan. "Return to the back at once. Gabe, pull over and let me drive."

He did, we switched sides and I waited thirty minutes for him to calm down before reaching over to rub his knee.

"It's just one of those things, Gabe, it could have happened to any of us."

He turned away and growled. "But it happened to me and now you all think I'm stupid."

"Well, we'll see how stupid people think you are when you're saving lives, right?" Although he had a point. If it were to happen to any of us, it was always going to be him, or me a close second. A result of spending a life in education, of not getting out and experiencing that life but I was determined to use this summer to put that right.

"Are we really in Spain?" Arwen asked in a rhetorical tone.

I knew what she meant. One could be forgiven for thinking we were in fact in some other country, that country being Catalonia because thus far, the only Spanish flag we'd seen had been at the border crossing. Ok, perhaps the Spanish weren't big with the flag waving, we British were similar but what soon suppressed that thought were the hundreds, thousands of red and yellow horizontally striped Catalonia flags that adorned every lamppost, every tree, every road sign, every parked vehicle. It became even more apparent as we drove through the first town, a place that went by the name of La Seu D'urgell, and it was here we were provided with answers.

'Catalonia Is Not Spain' and 'Independence For Catalonia,' the signs declared in English, which was the remarkable thing. 'Freedom' and 'We Are Ready' were other popular slogans.

Arwen was busy with her camera, "I wouldn't want to be the one guy flashing the Spanish flag around here."

I smiled at that comment, which I found to be funny.

"A bit overkill, don't you think?" Gabe remarked, finally coming around, to my delight. "We get the message, you don't like Spain."

"Best not stop, they might not like outsiders either." Dan chirped in.

"Well, Barcelona is Catalan. You know, that place you want to go so badly?" I said, watching him in the rearview mirror. "What will you do when you get there? Hide?"

He shuffled and had nothing to say but it served as another reminder to me that it would be our last stop together as a group and loathe as I was to admit it, I'd taken at least a small shine to the oaf, as well as to...

"Are you scared to visit Scotland?" The girl asked him in a testing tone. "There are people there who also want independence and they wave lots of flags too."

For some reason, the mention of my home country, coming from her, whilst being so far from home warmed my heart and I peeked again into the mirror to see she was already smiling back at me.

"I've been to Scotland loads of times." Dan returned.

"Yet you think some big, bad Catalan's going to hurt you? Oh, bless." She spoke with such playful mockery that I snorted and had to reach for a tissue. Other than a grunt, no response from Dan was forthcoming.

We emerged from the town and I checked Google Maps, Spain being a roam free destination, and found we were a little over two hours from Barcelona. My lips turned down and I called into the back. "Hey, Dan, what will you do when we arrive?"

There was a pause and when I checked, he had his nose in a magazine, despite the scenery. "Huh? Oh, we're off to a beach party."

His response was a little ambiguous and I glanced across at Gabe. "Are you going to this?"

He was filming a large lake in a valley and answered without moving. "He means he and Arwen are going to a beach party."

"Oh," I squirmed, "I see. Gabe, my Ibuprofen's in your side pocket, could you pass it over please with my water?"

He did and I took a few pills before rolling my shoulders and flexing my neck.

I remained silent as we descended for several miles, the air gradually heating to what we'd come to expect, before entering the Parc Natural del Cadi-Moixero.

We were parting ways tonight then.

I wound the window down and checked the map again. "How about dinner tomorrow night?" I called over my shoulder.

Arwen perked and swiped the hair away from her tiny nose. She seemed about to answer but Dan spoke first.

"Dinner? You're being serious?" He spoke in a sceptical tone with eyes narrowed and it stung more than a bit.

I was quick to answer on the defensive. "Of course, why wouldn't I mean it?"

He didn't answer and I exhaled, turned my attention back to the scenery and decided the national park we were driving through was probably on the southern edge of the Pyrenees as we were indeed in lowlands now, a valley green as anything in the English Lake District.

Catalonia.

It was a different kind of beauty. Of green meadows, picture perfect ancient villages of uniform grey stone, of more than one waterfall tumbling from the always present distant mountain ranges, of timber bridges spanning streams and of wild deer keeping a safe distance.

Catalonia was even more beautiful than the Scottish Highlands and, feeling so agitated about Barcelona's proximity, of what that city would mean, I hated not being able to enjoy the moment.

Just ahead, a small dirt road veered further down into the valley, isolated and perfect.

It was a split second decision.

And I surprised even myself by taking it.

"Um, this isn't the way to Barcelona." Gabe bounced and swayed in his seat, giving his voice an odd vibrating rhythm as I drove over bump and mud and dirt.

Ahead it was only green and what I optimistically hoped to be a crystal clear stream that meandered through the short grass. We passed a barn on the right and there was another not far in front, which is where I assumed the track finished.

"I just fancied taking a look. It's really beautiful, don't you think?"

Dan, slow to react, wobbled up front and held onto the countertop as he came. "Freya?" He said cautiously, his eyes scanning to his bro as in, *why are you with this mad woman?*

Arwen remained seated from where she bobbed up and down with a questioning frown.

I rounded the grey stone barn and saw I was right about the track, that it ended, and so turned left onto the pastureland and, remembering we were without a spare tyre, reduced speed and aimed for the stream.

"She's not gonna drive us into that, is she?" Dan asked Gabe, not joking.

"I don't know, Frey?"

"Oh, settle down. Where's your sense of adventure?" I shook my head and tutted. "You're making more out of this than necessary."

Slowly approaching the stream, I angled the camper around, stopped and applied the handbrake. It was approaching seven in the evening, hardly late, especially by Spanish standards but still, it was the perfect time.

"I've never wild camped in a valley surrounded by mountains beside a stream before," I turned off the engine and pocketed the key, registering Dan's funny look, "don't you look at me like that. You've done it, you said so, and now I want to do it. Problem?" Anyway, it wasn't his decision.

For a while, he remained expressionless, save for the gnawing at the side of his lip and then, almost like the idea was slowly growing on him, his face began to illuminate until finally he glanced slyly at Arwen and clapped his hands together. "Actually, that's fine with me." He stepped away, turned and ogled Arwen's legs, who was leaning with her forearms on the back of my headrest.

"I'm up for it." She enthused, to my relief. "Barca tomorrow, no probs."

I turned to Gabe, who was tugging on an earlobe, and I knew he'd be uneasy with the idea. Camping? He'd indeed packed a tent and inflatable double mattress along with foot pump but that had been more in the expectation we'd be camping, just the two of us, on an actual campsite with facilities, legally. Wild camping probably wasn't his thing but we were here to experience life, he'd said so himself.

"Gabe? We have food, drink, a stove and the most incredible location we could ever hope for."

He surveyed the scene outside, the stream that trickled so close then turned to Dan and Arwen who were watching him in expectation. He sighed and pushed up his glasses. "Sure, why not."

There was no sign of civilisation anywhere, not a single town, village or house. The barns we'd passed were ruined and probably hundreds of years old. There were, however, some cows plodding on the flatland and even a few deer where the slope merged with forest but they were too far away to be of any concern or distraction to us. No, we could have been the last people on earth as far as civilisation knew.

We exited and breathed the air and I watched Arwen as she held out her arms, closed her eyes and spun around, her grey summer dress flaring outwards from the warm breeze.

She caught me staring and skipped in my direction. "This was a wonderful idea, Frey, kind of the reason to travel in the first place, right?" There was a genuine sparkle in her blue eyes. "People come to Europe and only go to Paris, London or *Barcelona*. They forget about all this." Again, she spread her arms and whirled around as my hand gravitated to my lips.

I stepped forward and when she stopped, my hand reached out halfway towards her. "I'm so glad you're happy with it."

"Of course. I used to wild camp back in Oz and loved it. People have always done it and never needed to ask permission from anyone. Doesn't it just annoy you that they make laws stopping you from doing it?"

Oh gosh, was she serious? It was something that had been at the back of my mind but screw them, nobody could see us and the fact they might have made some prohibitive law stating we couldn't sleep out in the open, in nature, just as our ancestors had done for millennia, well it just made me want to do it all the more, just to show them.

"Yes, it annoys me very much, Arwen, so screw them." And then I felt a renewal of electricity surging through my veins.

"Yes, screw them. It's natural for us and for them too." She nodded in the direction of the cows and stuck her tongue out at them and I found myself still watching her as the camper door slammed shut and two large blurry shapes passed in my periphery.

The boys were wandering off for a stroll downstream, evidently in clandestine discussion about something and so Arwen and I returned to the camper to sort through the food supply. There was not enough for a banquet but easily plenty to provide adequate satiation. Besides, we had wine.

Over the next hour, the boys returned, Arwen dawdled off with a backpack for a hike and I headed the other way, into the trees for a call of nature.

When I returned, Dan was occupying himself in a manner more enthusiastic than at any other time I'd witnessed - Erecting the tent. It was one of those two-man things that required only a minimum of sense to put up, with no features, bells or whistles. The inflatable mattress and foot pump lay in a heap nearby.

"You're good at that," I observed, handing him a peg, "is Gabe in the camper?"

He nodded, "and all along you thought it was a faulty septic tank."

I hit him with the peg but couldn't help laughing.

The side hatch was open and when I stepped inside, Gabe was busy opening a bottle of red.

"A perfect idea." I stood behind and wrapped my arms around his belly, giving it a little jiggle and upsetting his steady arm that was attempting to pour the wine.

He waited for me to cease. "This whole thing was, sorry if I didn't seem so enthusiastic before but yes, we should be doing more things like this. It is what I'd wanted for this trip." When he'd poured four glasses, he handed me one.

I took a sip and enjoyed the delicious nectar as it made my mouth dance. "Maybe I should have discussed the idea, rather than..." I let it slide as he waved it away.

He clinked his glass against mine and his pupils shrank as he stared through the opened hatch into the distance. I turned around to see that Arwen was pottering through the field several minutes away, making her way back.

"But we do need to discuss the sleeping arrangement." He said with a flat tone.

"Ah." My glass paused halfway to my mouth. The subject of who was sleeping where had probably been lurking in my head somewhere, though I'd given it little conscious consideration and I remained silent for Gabe's suggestion.

He too was pausing in anticipation that perhaps I'd put forth the obvious and when I didn't he finally said the words himself. "I'm sure you're aware that Dan fancies the arse off of Arwen, yeah?"

I straightened, sipped wine, tasted nothing. "Well sure, but that doesn't mean that..."

"Look, we can't all sleep in the camper. We have a pullout double bed, which will be comfortable but any more than two and somebody'll have a severely cricked neck come the morning." He spoke fast and looked at me with an impatient expression because Arwen was even now sauntering her sweet little way into our proximity.

"I see. The camper *will* take four. You slept for hours in the passenger seat the other day and there's a bench just here." I pointed futilely to the narrow bench that was barely wide enough to fit an average sized bum.

"No, no, the bench gets covered when you pull out the bed and you can't expect anyone to spend a full night on the front seats." He was tapping his foot and making a circular motion with his hand like he was telling me to be quick and see sense. "Of course, it *could* feasibly sleep four but it won't be comfortable and besides, that's not the point and you know it." He shook his head. "Please, don't play dumb because I know you're not. You know what I'm getting at."

I took a sharp inhalation that he didn't hear. "Gabe, they're not dating. They're not a couple..."

He made a clicking sound with his mouth. "Well, it's gonna happen eventually ... maybe this'll help things along."

I laughed at that because it was just so ridiculous. "You can't force these things. If it happens, it happens but you can't expect that poor girl to share a tent with a guy she may have no romantic interest in." I was momentarily distracted by a loud rhythmical squeaking from not far away and I glanced over my shoulder to find Dan stomping up and down on the foot pump, mattress pulsing from his efforts as long clumps of hair dislodged from his man bun.

Gabe shook his head and spoke with a straight face. "Like I said, this might help them along. You want them to be happy don't you?" He grabbed the other two glasses from the countertop. "Besides, we need our privacy because we're having sex tonight." And at that he strode past, leaving me speechless. "Arwen, have some wine."

"Ugh!" I tugged at the frilly material at my collar then, taking my wine, decided to occupy myself with the food, frying some Spanish sausage goodness in the pan.

Within minutes the smoke was attracting the attention of the others and when they were ready, I brought the sausages out on a plate with some cheese and rustic bread.

"That's one devil of a combo," Dan remarked and I had to agree. Spicy Spanish sausage and red wine.

The sun was beginning to sink over the western horizon and

although it wouldn't be cold tonight, the boys had collected sticks for a fire.

I went to the nearby stream for a moment of serenity and to enjoy the gentle trickling, a sound older than Spain, the butterflies of white and black, red and purple and a magnificent green and red combination. I swatted at a mosquito then another and cursed the blighters, for it was yet another thing I'd not considered but screw them. Beyond, on the horizon, the Pyrenees with its natural border made me feel small and insignificant, reminding me that my time was finite and when it was gone it was gone, I'd never have it back. "I'm not a mountain." I sniggered, knowing I probably sounded profound in the moment but would be embarrassed if only I could hear myself later as clearly, the first sign of the red taking effect was manifesting, which meant I was liable to say even more foolish things as the evening progressed.

"I'd say you're more a medium sized hill."

I whipped around, tasting wine in my sinus, to find Arwen treading over in that slow, carefree way of hers. "You shouldn't do that. What is that?"

She was grinning and approached with what I now saw to be one of those leather mosquito bands. She had one on her wrist and another on her ankle and I'd always liked the way they looked on her, totally complementing her almost hippie look.

"I saw you swatting like a madwoman and I have like a whole bagful of these, so..." without even asking permission, she took my hand and I felt her fingers grazing my flesh as she wound the strap gently around my wrist, the sweet scent of Aloe Vera from the band, hers and mine, filling the small space between us as the gentle rhythm of her breathing seemed to match the flow of the stream. My limp fingers were pressed against her abdomen, lithe and taut beneath her dress as her biceps held the weight of my arm. Her eyes were fixed on my wrist as she gave her full attention to the small task, tying the ends together and then, after what seemed like only a few seconds but was probably a lot longer, she gently returned my arm to its side.

She looked up and caught my eye as she brushed away the red braid that had fallen over her face.

"Thank you," I said, holding her eye contact before finally, looking down and stepping away. "Damned mosquitoes are everywhere. You enjoying the wine?"

It was a worthless, damned obvious and nothing of a question but she didn't treat it that way. "It's delicious and I'll be having lots more of it."

"We should get some now." I raised my almost empty glass and looked beyond her to where the boys were sitting on two deck chairs, leaning back, hands clasped behind their heads. "I also have another idea."

We returned to the camper and as Arwen refilled our glasses, I delved into the glove box before finding Dan's guitar partly hidden beneath a pile of dirty t-shirts.

Dan's eyes narrowed as we approached. "You can see it has no G-string?"

I handed him the instrument then pulled out from my pocket the nylon coil in transparent plastic bag. "You're a jerk but I still love you."

His eyes widened and then he leaned forward to pluck the bag from my hands. "Freya, I'm gonna snog you later. Where did you get this?"

I held up my hands. "Just a little shop in Carcassonne." I wouldn't say that I hoped he'd be able to start busking again so that he could earn and feed himself. "All I ask is that you'll play us a few songs?"

"Of course." He beamed and began securing the string in earnest.

Gabe slapped his knees. "I suppose I'll get this fire started then."

It took around twenty minutes, which included finding anything flammable from the camper we could use to ignite the twigs and sticks. Gabe had even arranged a small circle of stones around the periphery as a precaution against it getting out of control and once the fire was going, the whole setting was beginning to resemble something from my ideal, imaginary camping adventure. Even the sky was darkening now whilst Dan tuned the guitar and Arwen brought out the frying pan filled with the next dose of pork.

Within minutes we all had wine, the meat was sizzling on the flame, the smoke doing what it should as twilight enveloped Catalonia and finally, Dan began to play.

I hadn't been sure what to expect but my first thought was that yes, he was a competent musician as he played what I recognised to be an Ed Sheeran song, in his own style, with his own twists.

I unscrewed another bottle of red and filled everyone's glasses, handing Arwen hers.

"You seem surprised." She said with a smirk, though her words carried a slight rebuking tone. "He's managed to travel the world off the back of his musical ability."

I smiled reluctantly, "I've been unfair to him." I held my eyes closed as I considered the bitch I'd been to these people. It wasn't me. At least, it wasn't the me I wanted to be. "And I was unfair to you too and for that I'm sorry."

We were slouching on the grass as Gabe perched forward on his deckchair, tending the frying pan out of earshot.

She waved it away. "I deserved it. The first time we met, I screeched at you." She turned to face me fully, propping up her head with a hand as I unconsciously did the same. "And for *that*, I'm sorry."

The effects of the wine made my head swirl in a delightful way though despite the alcohol, or perhaps because of it, I momentarily couldn't think of anything to say and there was a silence, not totally unawkward, as we shared eye contact from across the small space between us. Finally, I demonstrated my social ineptitude.

"I've not been bitten." I held up my wrist, just in case she wasn't aware of what I was referring and cringed inwardly.

She grinned, showed no reaction to my discomfort and held the back of her wrist toward me. "Bump."

I smiled and lightly touched my wrist to hers.

This girl was seriously cool. "Ah." She held up a finger and jumped up and there was a mis-chord played as three sets of eyes watched her skip through the camper's open door. Ten seconds later she returned, holding another mosquito band. "For your ankle."

I almost knocked my glass over as she skipped back and plonked herself on the grass to my fore, facing away so I couldn't see as I felt her fingers glance over my ankle and the leather lightly caressed my skin. She leaned against the outside of my thigh and hummed to the new song being played. Her hair was bunched over to one side, coming to fall between my legs and giving me a first glimpse of the back of her neck and the yin and yang symbol tattooed there in black ink, very cool, in case I hadn't already taken her for the spiritual type. My eyes slowly traced a path down, from where her shoulders projected over her narrow waist, her back tapering into a v until it met her midriff, impossibly tight, from where her hips broadened to mirror the width of her shoulders.

"Almost didn't want to disturb you there." It was Gabe, who loomed above us with a plate. "They're cooked."

Arwen patted my leg as if to say she was done and stood,

revealing the blue band on my ankle to match the brown one on my wrist.

And then we enjoyed an exceptionally relaxing late evening eating, drinking more wine and generally unwinding, talking and even singing along with Dan who eventually began playing songs we knew the words to, the old classics like American Pie, Wonderwall and House of the Rising Sun, proving he also had an awesome singing voice.

At one point Arwen began to dance and I wondered if it was the wine or simply the fact we had music. We all watched mesmerised as her body moved in perfect symmetry with the song like she'd rehearsed the routine over and over, yet for all I knew she was probably inventing it all on the spot. She moved with her eyes closed, like the only things that existed were the music and her body's own movements in her own world. Her body flexed and twisted and rolled and turned with a grace and poise I'd never seen so close, a fluidity that merged one move with the next as though they were one, her arms lightly glistening from the exertion, the fire crackling and illuminating her curves and when the song ended she finished as though it was anticipated and we all clapped, the master had shown us her thing.

She blushed, waved it away and crouched to retrieve her wine. "Whew, that's my exercise for the night."

I was already walking over, my wrist extended for the bump, which she returned because apparently, that was our thing now.

The temperature had dipped due to the breeze, we were in an open valley, after all, and Gabe went scavenging for more sticks whilst Arwen strolled off into the trees. It provided a natural break in the evening and, surveying the wreckage of the food, four beer and two empty wine bottles, I teetered into the camper to retrieve a third along with whatever food remained.

Dan clobbered his shoulder into the doorsill as he staggered inside after me and I laughed, almost rubbed him on the offended arm but thought better of it at the last moment.

"I'm glad you were able to stumble your way in because I just wanted to say that even though you're the most obnoxious person I've ever met, I'm still bloody glad to have met you."

He leaned against the threshold, propping his arm on the panel above his head, effectively the thin end of a sheet of metal that was propping him up, for now at least. "I'll remind you of this moment when you're sober."

"Just you do, Dan Belcher, and I'll say the same thing, that it's a tragedy you're not staying with us ... and Arwen, Arwen too."

He beamed and shook his head. "Believe me, I really would but I think Gabe has, um, plans, he..." and at that, he abruptly stopped, like he was having to force himself.

"Well, I want those plans to include the both of you." I sulked, knowing how silly I sounded for changing my mind.

"Be careful what you wish for." He squinted and readjusted his arm as I wondered what he meant by that. "There's no guarantee the girl'll stick around forever and then it'll be just me ... a Frey sandwich and I've no real desire to get that close to Gay Boy."

I assumed I understood the innuendo he was getting at but my mind jumped back to his other words. "What do you mean, there's no guarantee she'll stick around forever?" As I awaited his answer, I was mostly unaware of just how hard I was twisting the bottle in my grasp.

He belched and thumped his chest. "She's a bit of a free spirit, in case you hadn't noticed and precisely the kind of bird who'd get along in *any* group." And any group would be happy to take her. He sighed and for the first time I saw in his face what appeared to be a vulnerability, of doubt and I knew at once what it was. Everything he'd been through with her up to this point, the way he always looked at her, how he reacted back in Andorra la Vella - Dan was besotted with Arwen.

And now that I realised it, I could see it so clearly. How the mere mention of her name had made the skin bunch around his eyes, giving him a pained stare as we faced each other in the dim light of the camper and even now, the hand hovering over his head was clenching and unclenching in a subconscious display of anguish. It was a side to Dan he'd managed to keep concealed beneath his often disagreeable front but now that alcohol had been added to the mix, and was doing what it does, his true feelings, or some other part of himself, were being revealed.

His mouth moved to speak but there was only a croak and he inhaled a deep breath before trying again. "I'm just terr..." he hesitated and changed tack, puffing out his chest just enough for me to notice, "I recognise the possibility that she might find another group in Barcelona, or some man, or something, and that'll be fucking it."

"Dan?" I stepped forward but felt useless.

He flapped a pathetic hand and I felt for him. "Nothing seems to be fucking working. It's like she has literally no interest in me." If it had been any other moment, I'd have probably laughed at that, but now? "What is it about me, Frey?"

I blew out air and tasted the faintest sour whiff of what had to have come from his armpit, a smell, I remembered from the time Gabe had helped me with a bunch of boxes from Ikea. "I..."

"I mean, I'm fun to be around. I know I'm not completely ugly, I've had girlfriends before but..." he shook his head in exasperation, "...useless. I've lost my powers, Frey, what is it?"

How could I tell a guy I'd grown to like and could easily grow to like a lot more the kind of truth that would devastate him, that from how I saw it at least, there was an awful lot wrong with him. I could only say it from my own point of view, that he'd probably need to spend years working on himself. Put simply, some guys you could never be attracted to and I hated that I felt so bad about that. But it was Arwen's opinion that mattered and I knew she felt more or less the same as I did, she'd already told me so, that Dan was a friend and would never be anything more.

My hand was touching my chest, "I wish I could help you, Dan, I really do."

"You can," he said deliberately.

I wasn't sure where this could possibly lead but I had to hear him out. "Yes?"

He looked me straight on. "I'm hoping to be alone with her tonight, either in the tent or camper, I'm not too bothered which, so it would be pretty cool if you could assist in any way you're able." Oh, not this again.

"Assist? How am I supposed to assist in making Arwen have feelings for you?"

He continued with conviction, despite the words tumbling out with barely any coherence. "I don't know, I don't know. Perhaps you could make it known, in case she asks, or kicks up a fuss ... maybe you can tell her up front, I don't know ... that it's been ages since you and Gay Boy have given each other a good panelling, which is probably the truth anyway, and you were both hoping to be alone tonight in the camper, or tent, to thump each others' brains out.

You got anything better? You're a girl. And we have more wine, so..."

Most of that waffle had to have been at least in half-jest although I managed to establish, I think, that I was supposed to help him get laid and after that, because he was presumably so good in bed, Arwen would magically fall in love with him - An infallible plan.

I recalled their clandestine walk along the stream. "You and Gabe have been discussing this, haven't you."

"Look, all I'm saying is that it makes sense, because you and Gay Boy are a couple and he's been complaining about the dry spell you're going through, blaming it all on crowded hostels and your mood swings, so now's your chance. Take the camper tonight, which leaves me and Arwen to sleep in the tent," he registered the wine in my hand then his gaze followed to the other bottle still on the counter behind me, "sounds kind of logical, yes?"

In fact, the only thing missing was Dan saying she'd be 'well up for it.'

But I was beginning to panic on Arwen's behalf because something was likely to come to a head tonight. There would be a bust-up, bad things would be said, friends would be lost.

I put the wine down and folded my arms. "Listen, I'm telling you this as a friend and as my boyfriend's best friend. You cannot expect Arwen to sleep with you just because, to your mind, it sounds logical. I've got news for you, women aren't always logical, at least not like you're thinking. She has to *feel* something first or at least I'd hope. If you were already a couple then obviously, that would be great, but you're not, you just said yourself that nothing's working, so take that to mean she's not interested in you that way. She's your *mate*, Dan, which means you cannot expect the girl to share a bloody tent with you, not to mention the one sleeping bag when there are other options. Please, will you see sense." Oh, Christ, I sounded so harsh and doubted I'd have said any of it had I not been on the way to being drunk but damn, it needed to be said.

But my words had barely touched him. On the contrary, they seemed to have given him a renewed sense of purpose. "Well, we'll see, won't we." And at that, he reached around my back, grabbing the wine and strode outside, to where Gabe and Arwen were busy tending the fire.

"The idiot." I rubbed my temples and pondered the options. Assuming Arwen had no desire to share a tent with Dan only left the one alternative, that she shared the tent, or camper, with me. The boys could share a bed and not think anything of it, no problems or issues and likewise with Arwen and I.

But it was all a big fuss over nothing. The way the night was going, we'd still be drinking and talking and singing until daylight, from when the soberest amongst us, myself most likely, would begin the drive to Barca whilst the rest snored in their seats.

I waited a few minutes for myself, and Dan, to simmer down before stepping cautiously in the direction of the fire. There was a pleasant breeze and although the temperature had dropped noticeably further, it was still the perfect climate for spending a summer night in the elements.

Dan was standing with the others, already laughing about something and showing a remarkable ability to flip from one mood to another, though it was a relief in a way because it meant I wouldn't have to deal further with this manufactured problem and could return to enjoying the magic.

"Here you go, Doctor." Gabe handed me a glass and, sensing my agitation, came in for a hug. "I just wanted to say how fucking stunning you look in this dress."

It was the same flowery thing I'd worn at the Pont du Gard and yes, I knew how good I looked in it. "Hmmm." I hummed and leaned into him, feeling my worries melt away.

He nuzzled my neck and inhaled and then I felt his lips on the tender spot beneath my ear. "You turn me on so much," he whispered with the sweet scent of red wine on his breath, grabbing an arse cheek with his free hand, "I'm gonna go fix up the bed so I can take you without delay," he groaned, stealing away, just as Arwen slipped into my line of sight.

I turned away from them both and feeling a throbbing sensation building in my neck and shoulders, began to rub. It provided minimal relief though I knew even that wouldn't last and I was about to take another couple of pills, not a great idea with the alcohol, when I felt a pair of small hands clasp my trapezius muscles.

My first reaction might ordinarily have been shock but the wine had taken the edge off my reflexes and instead I almost crumpled from the instant release of tension as my head slowly tipped sidewards.

"Shhh, relax," Arwen whispered from behind while just a little further away, some wordless folk song began playing. She pressed her thumbs upwards and this time my legs almost buckled as I let out an audible sigh and it was like half the tension in my body evaporated with it. "Perhaps you'd better sit for this."

There was no way I could possibly disobey and her hands remained clutched on that sensitive area between my neck and shoulders as we both took to the floor. I was able to manoeuvre into a cross-legged position as her knees came to rest either side of me and then my body disintegrated in her hands as she did whatever it was she was doing.

I closed my eyes and allowed the world to dissolve as I put all my being into feeling and enjoying her fingers and palms that were working some kind of spell, kneading and squeezing away all the pain and soreness and tension that'd built up, not just over the last few days but possibly over five years, five years of study and stress and family shit. How could Arwen's small, feminine hands possess such vicelike strength as they ironed out the knots and tightness and I continued to sag and wilt and wane, feeling more and more relaxed with every cinching of her hands. There was a strange tingling in my feet, which I put down to sitting crossed-legged on a hard surface but then it spread slowly upwards through my legs. I ignored it, concentrating instead on the wonders happening on my back, as I hitched lightly forwards, my shoulders pinching towards my ears. I groaned and shifted as the tingle intensified until finally there was the strangest feeling brewing from somewhere deep within my belly. I recognised this sensation. A sensation I'd only ever experienced alone in my room with the light out after spending fifteen minutes inside my head, mentally visualising my presence on a desert island before being taken by Ewan McGregor as the sun burned down and the waves lapped about our feet. Whatever it was fluttered in my belly, swelled, pulsed, rocked and unfurled as I realised my fingers were digging into the earth. Suddenly, I was conflicted, caught between riding out these fucking tremors that were even now on the cusp of enveloping me in uncontrollable convulsions as I let go and surrendered entirely and remaining still, shutting the fuck up, squeezing hard and suppressing it, to demand she stop at once because, fuck, girl, you were about to make me come.

Was it even possible to climax from a fucking massage?

Because she was about to make it happen for me. Inappropriate much?

And then, just as I was on the edge of ecstasy and was about to summon all the willpower I had, to control myself, to bring myself back from the edge, I felt her warm breath in my ear.

"I think that might be better now." There was more than a hint of mischief in her tone but surely I'd imagined *that*, because that couldn't have been deliberate, could it? No fucking way! Not possible!

And then she pushed herself up from the ground and I felt her move around before stepping in front and sashaying towards the fire and Dan and Gabe, who were apparently still here, and the music that, as far as I could tell, was still playing.

I was plastered to the grass, almost afraid to move lest the slick substance between my legs give me away and confirm my fears.

And so I waited, drank wine, pretended to hear the music.

"WHAT ARE you doing over here all on your own?" Three songs later, Gabe pulled me up by the hands and ushered me into the gap on the grass beside Arwen.

She was half turned the other way, focusing entirely on Dan as he made music, singing Cast No Shadow by Oasis, her head nodding along to the chords.

"Imbibed too much, huh, Doctor?" He raised his voice above the sound, almost losing balance as he plonked himself down by my side and bopped me with his shoulder. "Well, you ain't the only one." His glasses were off slightly to the side and I straightened them for him, smiling then gazed up at the sky.

It was one of those cloudless nights where every single star in existence could be seen, the kind of night that due to the clouds you rarely saw in Scotland but was probably commonplace here. The North Star was the one that shined brightest, I knew that as a child but as for finding any of the constellations, I was clueless.

"You looking for Libra?" Gabe croaked into my ear, referring to my star sign and pointing up. "There it is."

I followed the point of his finger but was totally stumped as to which were my stars and even if I was looking straight at them, they were lost in an infinity. But one thing I could tell from looking up was that my shoulders knew they'd been through a treatment with some kind of flat iron. They still pained me but it was a different kind of pain, not the stress and irritating ache of before but instead, they felt like my thighs and buttocks had the first time I ever picked up a barbell for a heavy squat session at the gym. Either that or a large animal had walked all over me.

The fire crackled from nearby and I checked my phone to find it was after one in the morning. Slowly, I was adjusting to the late nights of the continent and before spending even a single night in Barcelona, I'd already be in sync with the locals. It'd be midday siestas from now on.

Arwen gently rolled her shoulders to the music, taking the occasional feminine sip from her glass and I watched her intently for the entire duration of Let It Be, almost in expectation she might cast a mischievous glance at me from the corner of her eye with a sly smile in accompaniment, knowing full well she'd very nearly caused a major accident in my underwear. But she didn't. Which then made me wonder if that was also deliberate, like she was playing the innocent. Or perhaps she had no idea she'd almost brought me off? Even now her small nose and lips, her flawless skin illuminated by the flame and general outward appearing naivety, gave her the look of innocence. Although, as I was beginning to learn, this naivety was probably a front, something she used not to get what she wanted, as I'd originally thought, but simply to amuse herself. No, I was becoming certain that Arwen was more streetwise and worldly than any other girl I knew.

Dan finished with a flurry then slapped the back of the guitar and propped it up against the side of his deckchair. "Done with that shit, my voice is going. Freya, I trust that's two Euros repaid for the string." He used his teeth to remove the cap from a beer bottle, passed it to Gabe then repeated the process for himself before taking a large pull. "Anyone got any ghost stories?"

"Oh, no, Dan." I moaned, gesturing into the pitch black that shrouded us. "Are you insane?"

"Best not answer that, mate," Gabe slurred, "and she hates ghost stories."

"No, no, you have to hear the one about the licked hand. Now..." his face was full of mischief as he was about to launch into the story.

It needed to be stopped. "Dan!"

"Ok, how about The Missing Boyfriend?"

"You leave Gabe out of this." I tugged up a fistful of grass and futilely threw it at him. "We will at some point have to retire to the trees for a call of nature, you know."

"And besides," Arwen added, "you just said your voice was going."

The boys both laughed at that and Dan pulled his seat closer and leaned toward her. "Fine, we could play Truth or Dare instead." He glanced at each one of us, fixing his stare on me. "No objections, Freya? You surprise me."

"Truth or Dare's a stupid, child's game but at least it won't prevent me from sleeping tonight." I crossed my legs and deigned to play, shuffling a little closer to Arwen, who turned inwards as Gabe moved closer to Dan.

It was all so sweet. We could have been thirteen-year-olds again, having our first ever camping experience with friends in the parents' garden. If only my fellow junior doctors could see me now.

"I'll go first," Gabe picked up an empty beer bottle and gave it a spin. It stopped on the girl. "Ok, ok, Arwen, um, let me think, um, now, let me see, what is your best talent?"

Dan slapped his forehead. "What a missed opportunity to get her to take off her clothes." It was hard to tell whether or not his rebuke was in jest and Gabe looked momentarily to the ground and swept back his hair.

"Thank you, Gabe," Arwen shook her head at Dan, "at least there's one gentleman present. My best talent would be dancing."

"Yes but we already know that. We've seen you. So strip, woman." Dan raised his bottle in a gesture of cheers that nobody returned.

Arwen stood and for a second I thought she was about to remove her dress but instead she pressed both hands into the ground then kicked her legs up one after the other, landing in a perfect handstand.

My lips parted and the boys both came out with a "whoa." The girl was far from sober yet here she was demonstrating her ability, once again, to kick all our arses.

Her toes were pointed, as they were supposed to be, which made her calves pop spectacularly and she'd even managed to snag her dress between her knees to prevent it from falling over herself, revealing all. "I'm not sure how long I can hold it after all the wine, the floor's spinning even now but on a normal day I can go on and on. I used to watch Neighbours in this pose whilst Mum cooked dinner, so I guess you can call it a talent of sorts. How long's that now? Will it do you, Dan, or do I need to stay here all night?"

"That'll do Arwen," I clapped and stuck my tongue out at Dan, "you showed him."

She came down, flicked the braids out from her eyes, "my turn," and spun the bottle, it coming to point at Dan. She cracked her fingers.

"Ooh, gross." I leaned away from her.

She leaned back into me and grinned. "Dan, Dan, Dan, what's your wildest fantasy?"

He laughed and spoke without hesitation. "Soooo easy. I'd banish Gabe to the camper, grab a beer, take you and Freya into that tent, zip up the flap, watch as you both slowly undress and then you'd start kissing and rubbing each other. Then you'd have full-on sex, or whatever the girl on girl equivalent is, as I sit close by. After an hour or two, when I can no longer take it, I'd then take turns on the pair of you as..."

"Ok, we get the idea." I finally made him stop.

The three of us shook our heads in unison, having listened to that with a mixture of amusement, at least at first, before it turned to eye rolls, disbelief and then finally, almost disgust. His graphic description had brought up an image, it was just a shame he was in it, though it should hardly have been surprising that a drunken game of Truth or Dare, and one involving Dan, should have degenerated so quickly.

"You had to ask." Gabe and I both said to Arwen.

"And you're not even ashamed one bit, are you?" I said to Dan more as a statement and reaching for the bottle.

"Hey, it's my turn and no, of course, I'm not. Now, hand it over." He took the bottle and gave it a spin and it whirled for longer than the other two rounds combined, slanting a few inches over the grass before coming to a stop - Pointing at me. My body tensed and he tried to crack his fingers as Arwen had before but nothing happened and we all laughed. "Ok, ok, Freya, Frey, Frey-Frey. What's the worst thing you've ever done to someone?"

"Is that it?" Arwen asked, looking blankly at me. "This is the best you pervert could come up with?"

He tipped his bottle to me. "Thought I'd go easy on the girl, she's my buddy's girlfriend, after all."

It was an unexpectedly tame question but I couldn't think of a single thing and I wasn't sure if it was due to being put on the spot or because I'd lived such a sheltered, boring existence. "Nothing. I haven't ever done anything bad to anyone." Oh shit, I'd cut in line once in the dinner queue back at primary school but they'd never accept that and such an answer would rightly invite ridicule.

"Nothing," I repeated, shrugging and fearing the wrath of what was to come. "Oh shit, I'm sorry, there's nothing." I buried my head in my hands.

"Because you're so perfect, aren't you," Dan remarked, bringing his hand up to stroke his chin. "There's only one option, as per the rules of the game. You'll have to take a dare instead."

I breathed, "then give me what you've got," I said, in a rare moment of alcohol-fuelled valour. What was the worst that could happen? I'd make an arse out of myself attempting to emulate Arwen's handstand, inevitably falling on my back. Maybe I'd have to down a beer or something typically mature or at the very worst, the absolute very worst, I'd have to walk alone into the trees and stay there for a count of sixty.

Dan was still rubbing his chin. And what's more, there was an evil, sly expression on his stupid face. "One second," he raised a finger and swaggered over to Gabe, "I'd like to discuss this with my business associate."

They huddled together as I heard the whispering and Arwen and I just shrugged at each other. Gabe caught my eye and bit his bottom lip, displaying the same concerned expression I'd seen a few times before. He shook his head but Dan placed his arm around his shoulders, turned him away and the whispering continued. "It'll be fine." I thought I heard. "She'll be good."

Finally, Gabe nodded, Dan clapped and returned to the fire, both retaking their seating positions.

"Right." Dan again tried cracking his knuckles and this time I cringed as there were at least three pops. "You ready to hear it?"

I sighed, "oh, I'm all ears."

That grin, "I want you and Arwen to kiss for one whole minute," and with that, he stamped his foot to add emphasis.

I rolled my eyes and slapped the turf. "Oh, how predictable, you moron. I don't know why I agreed to this stupid game and Gabe? I'm surprised at you the most, yes, hang your head. Try again, Dan." I folded my arms then unfolded them to take a sip of wine before refolding them across my chest.

Dan rushed to bring his hands up. "No, no, it's Truth or *Dare* and you failed the truth part so now you *have* to do this. There's literally no other way. You and Arwen *will* snog the face off each other, as sure as this night will turn to day, it's happening."

I appealed to my so-called man for backup. "Gabe?"

He exhaled and showed his palms, looking a strange contradiction between defeat and exhilaration. "You probably should just do it."

"Ugh. Men!" And I'd never thought my boyfriend was one of *those* types. Or maybe he'd just become even more subservient to his sidekick than I'd originally thought.

Of course, I was fully aware that all throughout this exchange, I'd not once looked at the girl. Indeed, I'd tried extra hard not to look at her. But now she was being conspicuous by her silence and so I had to swivel slightly to appeal to her for help.

But Arwen was just leaning back on her hands, taking it all in her Oz stride, a slight amused expression on her angelic face whilst the rest of us bickered. "It's just a kiss," she actually said, straight-faced and all, "and it'll clearly make this pervert's whole life complete." How could she joke about this?

I whipped around on Gabe. "And you, Dan's wing boy, you really want to see your girlfriend kissing another person?"

Dan quickly interjected, "*girl*, kissing another *girl*," and he was absolutely shining.

"Gabe?"

His eyes flicked from Dan to me. "It's ok, Freya."

"See." Dan urged, bringing out his phone.

"And you're most certainly *not* filming it, you super perv," I said a little too reactively and regretted it because at that Dan almost jumped up and squealed.

"So you've agreed!" He clapped his hands and beamed at Arwen and even she seemed to take it as my agreeing.

She was turned into me now and shuffled a few inches closer, her eyes locked on mine as she tucked a few loose strands of blonde behind her ear.

I had absolutely no idea what had happened but suddenly all eyes were on me, including Arwen's, especially Arwen's.

"It's just a kiss and it'll shut him up," she said, her voice so soft and dainty compared to his.

"But..." I began and stopped, not able to think of anything else that hadn't already been said. Of course, I could just flat out refuse. I was in a relationship and had always been completely monogamous, save for the occasional glance at one or two hot lecturers. But like Arwen said, "it is just a kiss."

Dan sizzled at my verbal acceptance, Gabe leaned further forward and Arwen simply remained where she was, her weight placed over one arm and waiting for me to complete the small remaining distance between us.

Yes, she was cute *for a girl*. I'd noticed that the very first time I ever saw her, right before she exploded on me. But I'd noticed it the same way I'd notice a cute dog; good for getting attention and lots of fun but you wouldn't want to take a bath with it.

I swallowed and used my hands to assist in shuffling closer, trying to avoid eye contact. "I suppose..." I made a small coughing sound and touched my neck, "I reckon best no tongues."

"No tongues." She agreed in a sweet voice.

There was a small, high-pitched mewing sound, only just audible that had to have come from Dan, though it could just have easily been Gabe, I couldn't tell either way because I was still looking down, from where the tips of her red and blue braids with their small wooden beads were resting on the grass. They'd all gone quiet, not wanting to breathe lest it proved sufficient to change my mind - And I still couldn't believe I was even considering this.

I glanced up then back down again, briefly glimpsing Arwen, looking all neutral like she was in the line at the post office. Maybe this was no big deal.

I reminded myself of the vow I'd committed to in Carcassonne, to make this trip one of living to the utmost of my means, so I could return to the UK and a lifetime of work, toil and drudgery knowing I'd at least had that one summer where I'd gone out of my way to have as many wild experiences as I could. I'd always have this summer. I hadn't known at the time that making such a vow would include kissing Arwen, another girl. It was a far shout from eating cow brain.

That's right, just think of cow brain.

Not that kissing Arwen could possibly arouse me but then she already most certainly had aroused me with her massage.

Ok, just stop stalling and get it over with.

I shuffled the rest of the way, stopping when my knee bumped hers. "Sorry."

"That's ok." And how could she be so composed at a time like this?

I was shaking, I was actually shaking, despite being well beyond the tipsy point and I took the weight off my arm lest my elbow buckle, which shifted my position and forced me to meet Arwen's eyes.

Oh God, but she was close, inches away, the nearby flames reflecting in her eyes, the sweet scent of Aloe Vera mixed with peach and grass strong in her proximity.

I'd seen lesbian kisses on those silly TV shows and the girls involved always seemed to be overly enjoying it, grabbing the other's face and running their hands over each others' body. Instinctively, my hand probed forward, just to have something to touch, to anchor around, for balance as much as anything else but I lost my nerve on the way and my hand sort of just flopped, grazing her thigh before finding its way back into my lap where it awkwardly remained.

I could feel the boys' eyes burning into me, into us, but the only sounds were Arwen's breathing and the occasional crackle of the fire.

I tilted my head to the right and she followed my lead, after all, this was *my* dare and it would be by far the wildest thing I'd done in my entire life, or was likely to ever do.

I leaned slowly forwards, briefly catching her gaze before my eyes dropped to her lips, wide, narrow, red.

And then our lips touched.

It was just a tap at first because I pulled back, I wasn't sure why, perhaps I was expecting something unpleasant, like how you check a panhandle to see if it's hot before wrapping your hand fully around the steel but after a second I tilted forwards again and our lips connected fully.

Both our mouths were closed, almost like how you'd kiss your aunt, no tongues remember, and it was exceptionally light but that was because neither of us were in a position to pull the other closer but then she adjusted herself, forcing me to do the same and I felt her hand slowly glide up my back to nestle in my hair. The pressure increased but only a little and now it almost felt like the sort of platonic kiss you'd give a male friend, still closed mouthed and I don't know why I did it, I could have copped out and denied the boys their little moment and rode out the minute with a minimal level of enthusiasm but instead I opened my mouth, just a little and the response from her was a little extra added pressure. Perhaps I didn't want her to feel insulted by my lack of passion, or to think I was a cold fish because I wasn't and I opened my mouth further, fully aware my hands were resting uselessly in my lap. For a second, I opened my eyes and found hers closed and the sides of her mouth turned up. Her mouth closed around my top lip and I felt her ever so gently pinch, suck and pull. She moved closer again but did it by arching her lower back, which pushed her chest, neck and head forwards and she opened her mouth a little more and it became clear she was now the one leading me, perhaps even enjoying it?

But I had to admit, it wasn't altogether unpleasant. Strange, yes, and certainly a heck of a lot more gentle than Gabe, with no scratches from his five o'clock shadow and dryer too, with no spittle running down the side of my face, which was a common occurrence with him.

Almost together, we inhaled deeply through our noses and her hand clutched tighter around a large clump of my hair. I found myself increasing the tempo and heard a hum from her. Her tongue flicked across my teeth and then I was surprised as I felt the backs of her fingers lightly graze my jawline.

My hands were still on my lap and although both were trembling, one had been unconsciously stroking the inside of my thigh but for how long? Her knee was pressing against mine but other than that it was only our lips and her hands making contact but then we both inhaled again and I couldn't stop my hand from stroking her knee and then it was floating up to glance lightly off her ribcage and settling on the back of her neck. It meant a more comfortable position for us both and she rewarded me with a barely noticeable tremble before increasing her speed and applying even more pressure to my lips.

In contrast to before, we were now kissing fully open-mouthed and our heads had started moving in slow, tiny circles from her to me as we transferred the pressure from her lips to mine and back again, finding a rhythm. I hummed from somewhere deep within my chest and then it was more out of curiosity than anything else, or perhaps I was caught up in the moment, or maybe I was enjoying it a little more than I wanted to admit, but I probed forwards with my tongue. It didn't have to search far because I discovered hers already lingering in my mouth's entrance and, remembering the rule I'd made, sharply retracted it. But why? They'd already touched and it wasn't like there could be any more or less of Arwen's saliva in my mouth and so my tongue reached forwards again and this time they connected properly before commencing an enjoyable rhythm of tangling with the other.

Our breathing increased in tempo as I pulled her harder into me and then there was a clink of glass and a cheer and suddenly, almost devastatingly, Dan was howling with approval.

"Fuuuuuuccckkk! Yeah!" The noise was awful.

Arwen and I pulled away as I felt my heart thumping so hard through my chest I thought it was trying to get out. Somewhere to my side, there was the slap of skin on skin, a high five perhaps, as the howling continued but in truth, I barely noticed any of it. My sight had partially blurred, probably due to a crazy concoction of alcohol and something else?

But I was aware of Arwen because I just couldn't bring myself to look away, her heaving chest, the flames in my periphery as her eyes burned into my own. I could hear her breathing, panting almost, and watch as she rubbed her lips together and brought a hand up to touch her mouth.

And what could she see? That I was still taking deep breaths? That I couldn't take my eyes from hers? That I was shaking? That I was terrified?

"Oh, fuck yeah!" Dan howled again. "Didn't I tell you, Gay Boy?"

"Aye. Yeah, that was interesting, I'll say that." Gabe sounded quite shaken.

I felt Dan's hand on my shoulder, wrenching me from the moment I was still sharing with Arwen. "I know we only agreed one minute but you looked so into it, I just couldn't bring myself to interrupt."

My chin tilted upwards, to where the oaf was looming over me, beer bottle in hand. "How long?"

He snickered and bounced several times on his toes. "Three minutes twenty-five seconds."

"And you'd probably have carried on longer if we hadn't interrupted," Gabe slurred, matter of fact.

"Oh yeah." Dan seemed to dance around to Arwen's side, sitting and placing his forearms on her shoulder. "Don't mind us, ladies but I must confess, I feel it almost prudent to retire to the trees for a few solitary moments of privacy." He blew out air and Arwen turned away from him.

I rolled my eyes and wanted to suggest he did just that but was too shaken in the moment to say much at all. Come morning and sobriety, I'd have some introspection to do, all right. That's if I wake and even believe what had happened tonight, which couldn't be guaranteed.

Dan stretched his arms over his head and yawned. "Tomorrow, the beach."

For a noticeable while, there was silence as Dan looked to his amigo with raised eyebrows.

My eyes tracked from the oaf to Gabe, who stood, hands in pockets with an almost half asleep, dopey expression.

Dan coughed, "I said, *tomorrow, the beach*."

Gabe perked and shook away the brain freeze. "Ah," then rushed over to me, draping his arm over my shoulders, "I think it's late enough and we've a long drive ahead tomorrow, so let's call it a night, I think."

Dan nodded and I turned to Gabe with narrowed eyes as he pulled me in the direction of the camper.

And then my legs were moving as I heard from behind in a masculine voice, "goodnight, you two lovebirds," as I imagined him winking.

Gabe opened the camper door and before steering me inside, I managed to glance over my shoulder, to see Dan sitting beside Arwen at the fire, the tent and its opened flaps waiting just behind.

The door was closed behind us and Gabe flicked on the lamp, turning to face me. "Well, it's been quite a night, hasn't it." He croaked, loosening the top button of his shirt and glaring at me with fire in his eyes. "Not sure I'm into it as much as he is but it was something worth seeing once, right?"

"Right." I'd turned away to squint through the window, trying to see what was happening out there but the angle was no good and my line of sight cut off too early. Damned parking.

Gabe approached from behind, his shirt half undone and closed the curtains. "You know what he's like. Can't be having those two peeping in."

I stepped away and caught his eye. "That was code, wasn't it?"

"Huh?" Another button undone.

I folded my arms across my chest. "When he said, 'tomorrow, the beach.' That was your code to drag me off to bed so he could be alone with Arwen."

He exhaled and nodded, kicked off a flip flop. "So? Where's the crime?"

"What are you, his procurer?"

He ignored me and strutted closer to slip the dress strap from my shoulder. "Shush, now, it's been so long. Let's get you out of these clothes." His lips were on my neck and I pulled away, tugging the strap back into place.

"Anyway, I'm on my period. I'm sorry, I should have told you but it's not happening tonight." I spoke as sternly as I could, holding his eyes all serious.

His eyes darted up and I knew what he was thinking. "Bit early, ain't it? Hmm, you might be right." He came forth again whilst trying to remove his arm from a sleeve and only succeeding in getting it stuck. "Look, just this once, I don't care. I want you now."

I maintained the same position and tapped my foot on the floor. "Gabe, I already told you, it's not happening tonight."

There was a crack of wood, which made me jump, and then Gabe let out a cry as he crumpled to the bed holding his foot. "Fuck sake."

After a second, I figured out that in his frustrated anger, he'd kicked the storage unit with nothing covering his foot. The door was now hanging from its lower hinge, exposing the wine and beer within.

I turned away and covered my face. "Gabe? Don't … please … I …" I began to sob, heard a commotion outside, quietened to listen then restarted when he spoke.

"Shit, Freya, I'm so sorry," the bed springs squeaked from his weight, "I didn't mean to upset you … fucking hell, my bloody foot."

I sniffed, hunched my posture and shuffled to face him. "Let's just sleep, shall we."

I jabbed the camper door open with my foot, being careful not to spill any of the tea I brought out in two mugs, the steam visible in the crisp July Catalonian morning air.

Dan was asleep on the grass in a space between our camper and the fire, a towel half screwed up and covering one leg, his brown leather man bag acting as a pillow, beside which was splatted a large cowpat.

I studied him as he lay there. It was the first time I'd seen him with his hair unbound and now it was spread out across the grass in a fan of long brown. His top lip was turned up and a crust of yellow had formed on the lower part of his cheek. He grunted, scratched his head and I nudged him with my foot.

"Morning, Dan The Man, you get any action last night?" I smirked, proud of that one. "Or did you retire to the trees?"

His reaction was a slow stirring and I waited for him to open his eyes. "My balls are so blue right now."

I strangled the urge to scold him with hot tea and instead crouched to leave the mug beside his head, sidestepping and turning toward the tent.

"Freya..." he croaked and when I turned back he was sitting up trying to work some feeling into his neck, "you don't um ... you don't remember anything embarrassing from last night, do you?"

"Embarrassing? What in particular are you referring to?" I knew exactly what he meant but couldn't resist playing.

He regarded me with uncertainty and I could tell his brain was far too smushed right now to be doing any kind of thinking on this level. "You know?" And he nodded as though it was obvious.

I hummed for his benefit. "Do you mean getting kicked out of bed or showing your true feelings?"

He shifted away. "Never mind." Because that answered his question. "Well, at least Gay Boy got some action last night."

"Of course, Dan." I humoured him and continued toward the tent, unzipping the flap and poking my head inside. "Good morning, Arwen."

She was awake because she scrunched her eyes tightly closed. "Daylight ... it hurts." There was a sweet smell within the small confines of the tent. She was still inside the sleeping bag and her curled up shape looked so snug through the material.

"I have tea."

"Tea?" There was a rustling sound and a squeaking of the rubber mattress as she sat up and took the mug. "Thanks, one sugar?"

I nodded, "a lucky guess."

"You British and your tea." She sipped at the fluid and made a small appreciative hum. "What a night that was; singing, dancing, eating, drinking." She drew the last one out and if I'd been slightly trepidatious about speaking to her this morning, perhaps with good reason considering it was only last night we'd had our tongues down each others' throats, she didn't seem bothered about it at all as she sat there, slightly slumped and fanning out her hair as the braids made small whipping sounds through the air. Indeed, I'd wanted to get this out of the way immediately, to avoid the inevitable awkwardness that would only exacerbate the more it was stretched out. I needn't have worried. "We got any more of those sausages?"

I shook my head. "Sorry. We have some cheese and rustic bread though."

"Meh, I'll hang on till we pass somewhere."

"We're thinking of leaving in about an hour. It's not too far to Barcelona from here, a couple of hours at the most." I inhaled the sweet air, stronger now after that hair performance.

"An hour? That's plenty of time. I just need to wash."

"Wash?"

"I DIDN'T THINK people actually did that." Gabe and I were leaning against the side of the camper, staring in the direction of the stream. "I thought it was just a movie thing."

"And only those movies set in ancient times."

"Or post-apocalyptic times after the world's been reclaimed by nature." He sipped his tea and pushed up his glasses.

Arwen was facing away, in her bikini, standing a few minutes downstream, *in* the actual bloody stream and I could just make out the toothbrush protruding from her mouth. She bobbed upwards prior to plunging herself beneath the water and remained submerged for a count of ten before thrusting up and flicking her blonde mane backwards as the water jettisoned in all directions. The toothbrush was still there and she devoted the next minute to that task, before taking a second dunk below.

"She is the type, don't you think? One of those *of nature* girls." I don't know why I asked for Gabe's opinion on *that* but he didn't answer anyway.

"All I can say is, it's a good thing Dan ain't back yet to see it cos I don't think he'd be able to control himself." He sniffed and glanced over at the trees. "How long's he been?"

It was a question I had no intention of even considering and instead watched as Arwen stepped out from the water and tilted sidewards to squeeze long trickles of water from her hair. How cold must that have been? Granted, it wasn't Scotland but it was a comparatively dull morning by Spanish standards. The goosebumps she must have right now. She wrapped a towel around her hips and threw a second over her shoulders before beginning the short stroll back to her tent and disappearing inside. The fascinating woman.

There was a throb down below and I knew what it was, I was a healthy young woman, after all. The girl had left me in quite an agitated state after that massage, not to mention the kiss, which now left me with two options; either ignore it or follow Dan into the trees.

———

WE STOPPED for a quick breakfast at the first town we drove through, mostly pastries and yoghurt with lots of strong coffee and soon afterwards Gabe had the camper on a fast road to Barcelona.

I leaned against the passenger side door and faced inwards, not just because I wanted to appear more sociable to the two in the back but I needed to conceal the screen of my mobile phone as I conducted research. Having a medical degree, I knew the answer already but felt the deep desire to learn about the experiences of other women.

I typed into Google, 'is it possible to orgasm during massage,' and scrolled through the results. The overwhelming response was a definite - Yes! And reading through the posts from some of these women, it soon became clear that they, like me, had experienced their first orgasm through massage. Well, it would have been my first non-self inflicted climax had the Australian not left me high and dry and just a little bit frustrated.

I clicked on a female problems page, swallowed and braced for the read.

'Dear Aunt Agnes, I have a real problem and don't know what to do. Almost every time I go for a massage, I experience an orgasm. It seems to happen when he's working on my lower back and is unpredictable, occurring when I least expect it and am not even aroused. It doesn't matter if my masseuse is a man or a woman either, it still happens. Sometimes I have up to four or five mini tremors per session, others it's one or two big ones and I have to try extra hard not to scream out at the top of my voice. The funny thing is that no matter how hard my partner tries, he's unable to make me come, no matter with oral or penetration, in fact not once in my life have I ever climaxed from penetrative sex and some of my most dedicated partners have given up trying. I find myself returning for massages, sometimes up to four times a week, and it's draining my entertainment budget. Worst of all, I feel like I'm cheating on my partner, going to a masseuse and paying for sexual release, almost like I was visiting a brothel and paying for sex. I feel like I need to give it up but don't think I can. Am I alone in this? Help!'

I shut down the screen, opened the window and considered how that unfortunate woman could have been me in so many ways.

Poor Gabe. I remembered the time he'd surprised me with candles and soft music, wine and a bunch of pillows on the floor.

"Strip and lie faced down." He'd ordered, squirting lotion on his hands and I'd obeyed.

"Awe, such a wonderful idea, is it my birthday?" It had been a long day at the library and a massage, however that might go, sounded most welcome.

"Does a chap need a reason to pamper his bird?"

I suppressed a yelp and shivered as he squirted cold lotion over my back and then had the wind thrust out of me when he sat on my arse. "Um, Gabe? You're hurting me."

He readjusted himself and set to work and it felt like being tickled by a feather duster, his hands slipping and sliding across my back, shoulders and neck. Downstairs, our housemates were blaring out Metallica, which overwhelmed Tchaikovsky trilling softly from the speakers in our room and there were bits of cork floating in the wine.

No, I'd not felt much during that massage, certainly not an orgasm and neither had Gabe tipped me over the edge any other way in five full years of dating. I was just one of those women, one of the unlucky ones but he was a good man, intelligent with a bright future and I loved him. And at least he'd tried.

But last night, when she'd touched me...

I mean, it wasn't right.

In five years, not once had Gabe made me come and here was this *girl* succeeding on her first attempt. By massaging my bloody shoulders!

What the fuck?

I peeped over at Arwen, looking so sweet and innocent reclining back on the bench, one hand propping up her head, the other holding a book. What was she reading? I squinted but couldn't read the cover because it was in Spanish.

"What the fuck?" I yelled out.

They all shot glares at me. "What?" Dan called. "You woke me."

"Sorry, false alarm." I waved to Arwen, who'd sat up with a perturbed expression. "Good book?"

"It's fine." She remained rigid, posture stiff. "Are you sure you're ok?"

"Yep, I'm ok." I turned back to lean against the door and after a minute realised I should have blamed it on a rabbit running across the road but by then it was too late.

We were on a three-lane motorway now, traffic was building and the Pyrenees had long vanished. We'd soon be in Barcelona and it was looking to be another scorching hot Spanish day. The clouds were thinning out by the minute and the roads were producing that wavy haze that comes from the heat.

Dan clapped his hands together. "What must I do to get one of your famed massages?"

Arwen slammed her book closed. "You'd like one?"

He pressed his shoulder down and worked his head around its axis. "After that night on the grass..." he said in a playful accusatory tone.

She grinned and stood. "Serves you and your pervy hands right, doesn't it? Go on ... remove your vest and take to the floor."

He whipped his vest off and flexed his pectorals, making them dance individually.

She cupped them in her hands and gave each a playful squeeze. "Ooh, but you know, there's really nothing sexual about a massage, Dan."

He grunted, made a dopey expression and positioned himself prone. Meanwhile, I flexed my neck and shoulders, which still felt like they'd been steamrollered but the awful tension of the previous days was a fraction of its former self.

Arwen began rustling through her trolley bag and brought out a small bottle of lotion, dripped a small quantity over his back and knelt by his side.

But Dan was good, keeping his eyes closed with a neutral expression, making only the occasional audible whimper as she pressed over a tender spot and unlike some people I wouldn't mention, he certainly wasn't getting off on it, which perhaps came as a shock.

She was good too and I could be forgiven for assuming no bad altercation had taken place between those two last night. She was beginning to seem more and more like a compassionate girl who hadn't so far let Dan's unrequited love damage their friendship. Why he couldn't just accept things, I don't know. To watch them now, Dan could have a friend for life in Arwen, just so long as he didn't screw it up. And as for the massage, she knew what she was doing, as if I didn't already know, was attentive, thorough and possessed obscene strength in those tiny hands.

I tasted blood. "Shit." I murmured, dabbing a finger to my lip. Yep blood. Great.

I needed a distraction, so went back to Google and typed in, 'kissed girl and enjoyed,' nope delete that, try again, 'kissed girl and didn't dislike it, am I a lesbian.'

Ugh, that search turned up nothing but guff, try again. 'Have crush,' nope delete, try again, 'have small crush on hot girl, am I a lesbian."

Ok, I found an article that looked promising.

'If you think you might be a lesbian, there's no need to freak out. Just buy a plaid shirt and get yourself to the nearest gay bar.' Ugh. 'These days, it's no big deal if a girl is into other girls. If you're into girls, that's all it means, you're into girls. You might still be into men too, which is cool, or you might not. Who you're into at any specific moment may even flip between the two. There's no need to change your life plans or prepare for any massive coming out ceremony. When it comes to your sexuality, you need to do whatever makes you happy. And neither is there any need to define yourself, however, if you'd like to stick a label on your forehead then the following questions will help determine if your crushing on girls is a passing phase or you need to start streaming Orange Is The New Black and get down to the local cat rescue shelter.'

I coughed, wound the window down further, glanced over at Arwen, still massaging Dan on the floor and ensured my back was fully against the door, bringing my phone closer.

1. You follow lots of hot women on Instagram.
Answer: No I do not. I don't have time for social media.

2. You get excited when you meet a lesbian.
Answer: There was one on my course, that I know about, and no, Julia does not excite me.

3. You flirt with girls too.
Answer: Not once have I ever flirted with a girl.

4. You're obsessed with your idol.
Answer: My idols are Edward Jenner, Louis Pasteur and Joseph Lister.

5. You're crushing on your BFF.
Answer: At this point, I would hardly describe her as my BFF.

6. Your favourite TV shows have strong female leads.
Answer: I have no time for TV shows.

7. Women get you all tingly.
Answer: It's too early to say, it happened only once.

8. You're craving the experience of ravishing a woman.
Answer: No comment.

9. There's something that's just not right when you're with a man.
Answer: No, Gabe and I are strong! We've never been stronger and will always be strong.

10. You fit the stereotype.
Answer: I do not and never have.

11. You kissed a girl and you liked it.
Answer: Now, that I will admit to.

12. You're resisting the lady loving.
Answer: That's ridiculous, I'm open-minded but right now, I'm only at the stage of research.

Such garbage, I rejected the article in its totality and shut down my phone.

It was just a kiss, as well as a massage, a surprisingly pleasant kiss and yes, Arwen's absolutely gorgeous and mystifying but I'd get over it.

I knew I would.

WE ARRIVED AT LUNCHTIME, which meant we had the full day to explore Spain's second municipality. Or we would have but arriving in any big city takes time with the heavy traffic but I was able to appreciate Barcelona's famed grid system, even if we saw nothing of any real tourist interest. Finding a safe spot to abandon the camper took longer than hoped and from there it was a fifteen-minute walk to the hostel.

The Rock Palace hostel was huge with a giant front desk staffed by seven guys and girls with dreadlocks, nose rings, bandanas, their badly pressed clothes indicating they'd been a long time on the road. Large groups of travellers were in and out through the doors constantly, a man in his early twenties who'd forgone wearing clothing on his upper half kicked a vending machine, the corridors were filled with stragglers leaning against walls and talking in languages I couldn't identify, a trail of water led from the bathroom, down the hall and into one of the dorms as an elderly Spanish lady mopped the floor two doors from our room. The place was as clean as could be expected under the circumstances, even if I couldn't help thinking the poor woman was fighting a never-ending losing battle.

With the hostel being so busy, there were no options for Arwen to reserve her own solo room and after quietly voicing her objections to me, that she wouldn't be able to dance or meditate, which was a new one, we entered our four-man dorm on the fifth floor.

"Standard." Dan threw his bag across the entire length of the room for it to crash against the far wall and flop to his bed. "And claimed." He stretched out his arms after the exertion of dragging it so far, slipped his hand into his back pocket and pulled out what I thought to be a condom but then I saw what it was and winced even harder when he punctured the vinegar packet with his teeth and commenced sucking out the contents.

Arwen and I both went to the window, the view merely encompassing the street below, just as a young tourist emerged from the hostel, hand over eyes and scanning both directions, trying to decide where to go. A horn blared from somewhere close.

"Not a great intro to the city, is it? I'm going back downstairs to get a map." She exited just as Dan followed after her with a towel slung over a shoulder, leaving just Gabe and myself in the room.

He plonked his bag on the bed next to mine then came over for the embrace. "Last stop for the gatecrashers, this is where we part ways, just the two of us from now on."

"Um hmm," I rested my head against his shoulder.

"You are ok with that? It's what you wanted."

My hands connected around his back and I nodded into the crook of his neck. "It'll be a pity, right after I was getting a little attached but probably best in the long run."

He brought himself to arms' length. "In the long run?"

"Because now we can go where we want and not have to think about them, duuur." I held onto him and inhaled the natural scent his neck was giving off. "Anyway, I've taken to him, a little bit at least, he's not as bad as I'd originally thought. There's a decent guy in there somewhere."

He laughed and leaned back. "He's changed a bit over the years but not much, he's still the same guy who protected me from the bullies. And Arwen, she's been a pleasure to have around too." He waited for my response but I remained silent. "Don't you think?"

"Oh, yeah," I pulled away and pottered towards my bed, "she's cool I suppose."

"Whew, I'm glad I don't have to worry about you going all lesbian on me. What was that girl's name who everyone thought was into other girls, the one on our course?" He went to his own bed and began rustling through his bag.

"Her name was Julia and she *was* into women."

"Julia! That's the one. Did she graduate? Anyway, It's just that..." he sat and brought his kitbag into his lap, "it's just that last night..."

I twisted around to face him. "Last night? What are you talking about?" I had a funny feeling where this was going.

He regarded me from the next bed as his mouth opened and closed like a fish against a fish bowl. "I don't know, I'm being silly, I guess, I've just never seen you kiss anyone else before."

"Well, obviously." My hands gravitated to my hips. "And? I was just going along with your silly game, remember?"

"Yes, I know that," he rushed to say, "but still, it lasted for an awful long time."

"And you can blame yourselves for that." My foot tapped the floor. "Really, Gabe, two doctors coming to Spain to play Truth or Dare, it's pathetic."

"Yes!" He stood and closed half the gap in one large step. "You're right." He slowly exhaled and his face lifted. "Not into girls then."

"Nope, I'm not into girls. For one, my dad would disown me so you can rest easy."

"Hah!" His face flushed and he strode over to the window. "That's correct. Bloody Spanish heat, does this window open?" He prised it up and I felt a semi-relieving breeze flow through the room. "Doctor?" He asked a minute later and I turned around with the bed sheet in my hands.

"Yes?"

He looked at me with a hopeful expression and I knew what he was waiting for me to propose.

I smiled and held out my palm to suggest he should be my guest. "Don't feel like you need to be around me today, tomorrow, whenever. As long as we're in Barcelona, you can spend as much time with Dan

as you want, just so long as we get to see a few places together then
I'm happy." Because then it'd be just the two of us.

His face softened and he made an appreciative sigh. "You're
incredible."

I shrugged, "you kept your promise so it's time for me to give
something back to you. Have fun with your friend today, tonight
even, get drunk if you want, it's fine, I'll go to the beach
with Arwen."

"Yes." He thrust his fist upwards, a man easy to please. "Perhaps
we can all hook up later tonight? Hit a club or something?"

"Sounds good, I'll ask Arwen about it." I continued preparing the
bed, which was by far my least favourite household task but then I
stopped and slowly turned back to Gabe as my mind went
into spasm.

He was struggling with his own sheets and looked up. "Doc?"

"Were you..." no surely not. Surely he wasn't asking about Julia
and Arwen and lesbians and last night because he was afraid to leave
me alone with Arwen. "Never mind."

Because that would mean at least one of us was going paranoid.

———

HER HEAD JERKED FORWARD. "You've never had one?"

"No, gelato's an Italian thing, or so I thought." I stood on my
tippy toes, straining to catch a better look at the flavours on offer.
There were many. Not that I could see from this far back. "Besides, I
live in a cold country remember, we've not much use for ice cream.
You should try Scotland sometime and then you'll know."

"Oh crikey, you try gelato once and there's no turning back." Her
Australian expressions brought back memories of the long-running
soap opera, Neighbours, that I used to watch as a child.

"Is that a fact?" I stuck my head out beyond a particularly large
teenage boy but still couldn't see the flavours.

"Well, he certainly seems to think so. If you're not careful, by the
time you leave for home, you'll look like him." She held that
mischievous grin that somehow possessed no malice and showed her
white, perfectly symmetrical teeth.

I flicked her red braid upwards and it flopped straight back down
with a satisfying twang. "Well it hasn't damaged you, has it." Or your
figure.

"Ooh, was that a compliment? And do it again, please." She stuck her head closer and the blonde tumbled down over the front of her face, sending a pleasant cascade of peach washing over me.

"It was just an observation and stop that."

She straightened but the hair was still there, covering her face and then a red tongue poked its way out from between thick blonde tresses.

I checked over my shoulder, to a middle-aged couple in the queue behind, not impressed. "Arwen, that's gross."

She retracted her tongue then it came out again and then she was flicking it in and out, making perverted noises and I cracked up, tried moving her hair away but she was holding it in place with both hands.

"Arwen, that's so inappropriate." I slapped her lightly on the arm, conscious my hand remained for a little longer than what felt natural. "Coconut!"

"Huh?" She brushed the hair away to reveal her cheeky face. "Really? That's a poor choice, don't you think?"

I dismissed her with a hand. "Speak to the palm cos the face ain't listening."

She made a loud barking noise then bumped me with her hip, which sent me sidewards out of the queue.

I dashed back to her side. "Ok, so what *is* a good flavour then?"

She pointed to the display, which was slowly coming into view. "Well just look. You have Kinder Surprise, Oreo, Tiramisu, whatever that multicoloured thing is, all these exotic flavours and you go for boring old coconut?" She hummed and nodded. "On second thoughts, maybe something like vanilla would be more your thing."

I gaped and stepped closer. "Are you calling me boring?"

"Oh no, absolutely not, I mean, you did wade into the Gardon river. That's pretty hardcore." She was absolutely straight-faced but had to have been taking the piss with that one, it was never easy to tell. "And you did eat a snail." She gave me a thumbs up and winked.

"Right, now I *know* you're taking the piss and you've been doing that a lot, haven't you." My flip flop was touching hers and I reached out to pinch her forearm, she didn't move. "I'll have you know, I also ate cow brain and spontaneously drove the camper into a valley, not to mention..." I was about to say I'd also spent over three minutes passionately making out with her, which could be considered wild by anybody's standards, but managed to stop myself from venturing into complete inappropriateness at the last second, we were in the middle of a queue, after all, "...snail, I ate snail."

"You're right, Vanilla, you're pretty extreme."

My mouth plunged open again and this time she reached forwards with her finger to tickle my tongue and I closed my mouth in an exaggerated way. "Om nom nom. I'll eat your finger and you'd better *not* start calling me that."

"One vanilla?" The man behind the counter asked and we both cracked up in hysterics.

She stuck her palm out to silence me then fired off something in Spanish.

Immediately, I stopped laughing to scrutinise her and felt something stir right down below as I muttered something in baby language but wasn't sure what.

"Freya?"

"Huh?"

"What flavour?"

WE DAWDLED along the Passeig Marítim de la Barceloneta, the wide open walkway that skirted the sand. The beach was crowded and we pottered along the path in search of a more peaceful spot, which was probably unlikely to come into view for a while; it was early afternoon on a beautiful day and this was, after all, Barcelona, one of Europe's great cities. One would expect most tourist beaches this close to such a large city to be ruined with litter, beer bottles and all kinds of filth but from where we were, all appeared reasonably clean. Of course, actually walking on the sand might reveal different.

The gelato was everything Arwen had made it out to be. Feeling somewhat flustered, I'd made a hasty choice, going for a cup half filled with mint choc chip and half Starburst. I got real lucky.

"You have to try some of this pistachio." She said as we dallied past a pair of stray dogs.

I was about to say it was too late because the vendor was way behind us but I looked up to find her spoon already hovering near my lips. "Oh, um, ok." And in it went.

"Well?"

I closed my eyes and made a hum that sounded more sexual than intended.

She gently nudged me in the side. "And you were gonna go for vanilla?"

"No, I was gonna go for coconut." I nudged her back. "You really believe me to be vanilla, don't you? Well, perhaps I'll show you yet." And in the moment, I regretted not having a nickname for her.

But it wasn't lost on me that I was doing that exact thing to Arwen that I'd experienced several guys from my course attempt when they were trying to impress me. *Well, perhaps I'll show you yet* - Just like the time I told her I was training to be a doctor.

There was that guy, Oli Taylor who'd casually dropped into conversation that he'd just broken the javelin throwing record for the entire University of Edinburgh. Then there was John 'Briggsy' Collins-Briggs, who'd shamelessly let slip he'd achieved the highest microbiology grades of our entire year group. As it transpired, they'd both had crushes on me, Gabe had discovered that when they got drunk and told him. Extreme examples perhaps and thankfully, I hadn't yet resorted to blathering on at Arwen about my future as an emergency medical doctor and would strangle myself long before doing so. I simply wouldn't do it!

"Try some Starburst." I held out my spoon and without hesitation, her mouth enclosed around it.

She purred and licked her top lip. "Hmmm, that's really good."

A group of roller skaters were gliding in our direction and Arwen thread her hand inside the crook of my elbow to gently guide me out of their path but one of them noticed the Australian, his head fixing on her as he flew by and barging into his companion as he did. They both lurched forwards, arms swinging for balance and only managing to save themselves from a major accident due to some pretty good corrective skating. Angry Spanish was shouted and on they continued.

I covered my mouth with a trembling hand. "Arwen, how do you not cause more accidents?"

She barely flinched, probably used to causing pile ups. "What? They were drooling at *you*."

"Pah," I gestured to my friend's, well, everything, in that flowing yellow dress she was wearing. "Yeah, right."

Her face remained fixed and serious. "Frey, they were looking at you, at least Clumsy was, right before nearly killing himself and everyone else."

I gently shoved her on the shoulder. "You're taking the piss again."

She shook her head. "Nope. That's what the other pervert shouted, 'there's a redhead at the brothel, why don't you just get it out your system.'"

"Huh." I stepped back, unsure whether to be flattered or insulted. "Huh."

She closed the distance and her hand was on my arm. "You don't see it, do you. Awe," her expression softened, "you're a good looking girl, why wouldn't they notice you?"

"Because I'm standing next to *you*." I persisted.

"And I'm standing next to *you*." She persevered as I jerked upright and felt my pale face flushing, unsure what to say. She nodded up the path. "Come on."

And we continued for several minutes at the same dawdling pace, eating the goodness and making strange unconscious sounds as the sun demonstrated its power, joggers bounded past and tourists loitered everywhere.

It was something worth considering, that this dour Scot did not make friends easily, I was my father's daughter for sure, and often could be my own worst enemy, I'd proven that recently. I required time to feel comfortable around new people and even then I seldom opened up much. But there was something about Arwen that was beginning to bring a little something different out in me. She was playful, adorably immature, impossibly relaxed and in turn, soothing to be around, almost like a natural antidote to my stresses. I'd known some extremely high strung women, not for lack of reason in medical school, but short of a cross-country journey by car with Dan at the wheel, it was hard to imagine anything flustering this Australian girl. Even her walk was tranquillising, the way she leaned back, chin tilted up, arms barely swinging and just being around her, alone, had such positive transmitting effects on my mood. Near misses with roller skaters aside, just so long as she gave me no more, um, unfinished massages, which only produced the exact opposite effect, then I was unlikely to burst from an unsatisfied frustrating internal thrumming.

No, I really liked her. In fact, I could not remember a time I'd made friends with anyone so easily. Of course, the forced proximity was a major factor but had it been any other girl, I could not imagine feeling so comfortable strolling down the Passeig Marítim de la

Barceloneta, eating gelato with them right now, especially after last night.

"You've gone into deep thought." She pointed to an empty spot on the beach and we turned off the path to walk across the sand. "What are you thinking?"

I felt the satisfying shift of sand beneath my feet. "I was just wondering if your travels have made it as far as Scotland yet?"

She turned inwards and tucked a thick cluster of blonde behind her ear. "Is that an invitation?"

"Maybe."

"Well, maybe I'll look you up when I get there."

"Maybe you should." And I thought about all the places I could take her; Edinburgh Castle, the Isle of Skye, a whisky distillery, my dad's cabin on Loch Ness, even that thing on the Falkirk canal that lifts boats up and places them on the aqueduct above.

"Here's our spot." And I was brought back from my reverie by her hand pulling me down to the sand.

"Ah," I shook it away and knelt, surveying the vicinity. There were throngs of people along the entire stretch of beach, as expected, but at least here the groups were sparser, bringing a small feeling of privacy. There were hundreds of men, women and children all around us, lying on towels, some beneath giant umbrellas. From close, the waves surged across sand and children chased each other in the shallows. A volleyball game brought the occasional shout and the light patter of palms on beachball every few seconds and a man was striding along the beach, carrying a cooler and shouting, "Coca-Cola, beer ... Coca-Cola, beer."

I turned away, allowed the hair to fall over my face and coughed lightly as I delved into my bag for the towel, laying it purposefully over the sand, aware she was doing the same close by. "It's hot, isn't it." I rolled my eyes at my self-consciousness. "Oh, my poor Scottish skin. I'm not designed for this heat." I gathered myself, checked my back was still to her then lifted my dress over my head and continued to stare into the sand as I carefully folded the garment and then cancelled that out by stuffing it inside my bag. Now, in only a bikini and aware of my sudden discomfort, I delved for the factor 60, pulled it out and began applying it to my pale face, arms, sternum, belly and thighs.

"Here."

"Huh?"

But there was no time to be alarmed and I made a small jolt as, without warning, her hands were on my shoulders and I felt the delicious chill in contrast to the sun as she began working the lotion into my skin, moving in soft circles, up and down, side to side. She removed her hands and there was another squirt from the bottle, the sound of two palms rubbing together and then they were back on my waist and lower back before finishing in that little indent just above the point where the lower back meets the buttocks.

"Done. You can do me in a minute."

"Um, yeah, sure."

When I turned back, she was leaning over her bag shuffling things around, a copy of Women's Health magazine was strewn close by and a punnet of strawberries rested on the sand between our towels.

"Go ahead and help yourself." She said, like she had eyes in the back of her head. "I brought cherries too if I can find them."

I selected a strawberry and tasted the sunscreen on my fingers.

So casual and carefree, the act of applying sunscreen to a friend was nothing to her. She was Australian, all things considered, a country known for its low skin cancer rates and everybody else was supposed to follow their example.

I heard the zip and she returned, plonked down the cherries, grabbed the hems of her dress and I held my breath and angled away as she tugged it over her head. There was a wave of blonde in the corner of my eye and I went for another strawberry, keeping a hold of the stalk as I purposefully sucked out the juice. Something landed in my lap and I glanced down to find a bottle of factor 15.

"Oh, right." I flicked off the cap and squirted a large dollop into my palm.

She'd turned her back to face me and was presently using the contents from another bottle to rub over her arms. "Take as many cherries as you want. Aren't they just the best?"

I brought my hands down over the backs of her shoulders and felt a twitch from the feminine musculature below. "Strawberries, cherries, it's a hard choice." I moved my hands around those two blades, her scapulae, that protruded and oscillated beneath my fingers from the motions of her own hands as they smeared lotion into her skin.

"I'm used to the sun, in case you were wondering, which is why, despite being blonde, factor 15 is enough for me. Oh, look at that cute dog. Though I reckon it'd probably kill you, right?"

"What, the dog?"

Her head swivelled around and she made a humorous scowl. "No, factor 15."

"Oh, yeah, of course." I rolled my eyes, squeezed more lotion onto my palm and began slowly working my way down her back, pulling back the red bra strap to get beneath. "So, Arwen, you speak Spanish too?"

She made long strokes as she worked over her legs. "Yeah but my French is way better than my Spanish. My Spanish is almost non-existent, considering I've been working on it almost a year."

Christ. "You could have fooled me."

"Meh." She leaned forward to get to her toes, the conversation making the task feel much less tense for me, she had that ability. "The thing is, we Australians suffer the same problems as you Brits when it comes to languages ... oh damn, sand..." she made a few sweeping motions with her fingers against her leg and even futilely tried blowing it, "hate that ... never get it off me now. Anyway, it's not easy for us but it's great being able to practice at source. You finished?"

"Almost." I finished up around her lower back and where her hips broadened out almost insanely into that hourglass figure she possessed, which I thought was one of her best features. "Done."

She manoeuvred around to sit level with me and then, for a flicker, her boobs were under my nose before she managed to block them with her head as she leaned down to grab a handful of strawberries and then straightening at an angle to cram three in her mouth at once, stalks and all. With impossible flexibility, she reached up behind her back, finding the clasp of her bikini and undoing it. "Ah, the relief of release." She pulled her arms out and flung the garment atop her bag before positioning herself faced down on the towel and groaning. "Damn it, you get all comfortable and then realise you forgot your stupid book."

Like I said, the girl's lack of apprehension was infectious and, leaving my bikini top in place, I positioned myself faced down beside her.

WE STIRRED around forty-five minutes later when...

"Coca-Cola, beer ... Coca-Cola, beer."

"Shit! My bra, quickly."

I sensed her rise and when I sat up she'd already attached the thing and was busy thrashing her arm about like a madwoman.

"Over here," she yelled. "You want one Frey?"

I pushed myself up and blew sand off my lips. "Oh, um, yes if you're offering."

Her golden skin was glistening with a combination of lotion, sweat and sun. "Yes, I am off ... Yes, over here."

The man took one look at Arwen and ran faster, kicking up huge swathes of sand, eyes bulging. "Yes? Coca-Cola, beer, beer?"

"A great question, Frey?" She held up a finger and looked from me to him with that familiar mischievous sparkle in the eye. "Ah, are you sure that's legal here, drinking beer in public?"

"Yes, beer legal."

"Beer legal?" She smirked.

"Um, yes, beer legal." He was a short man with a humorous face, probably North African and exceptionally trim, doubtless from spending his days trudging across the sand carrying that huge cooler. Credit to him though, he seized the chance to ogle her cleavage the second she looked back to me.

"I don't know, Frey? I'm not so sure it's legal to sell beer on the beach." She looked back at him and finally, because we women like to compare ourselves to each other, and for no other reason, I copped a squint myself and immediately felt the flooding of warmth through my body, the clearness of her skin and the way the perspiration shined, their plumpness and the deep, rich crevice of her cleavage. Not surprisingly, she was more womanly than myself and I swallowed as I turned away to face the man, only vaguely aware she was still speaking. "What do you think Frey? Is it legal to sell beer on the beach? Or to even drink it? Especially to drink it."

"Yes, beer legal."

She grinned and I thought the man was about to pass out from the view. "Oh well, if you insist it's legal then I'll have two beers but they'd better be really chilled or I'm heading straight to the cops."

"Yes, yes," he beamed as she passed him the money and allowed him to keep the change. "You want open?" He asked, producing a grin and a bottle opener.

"Of course."

The man's hands were shaking and Arwen waited, amused, as the metallic utensil rattled against the bottle top. "I'm sorry, I try, one minute."

"It's fine."

Finally, the man succeeded with the task and passed the bottles down to Arwen, "thank you, you very beautiful," before nodding and backing away still gazing at her.

I shook my head and tutted. "Arwen, that man would have left his wife and kids for you." I'd seen some pretty obsessed guys in the past but that was bordering on the ridiculous. I knew blondes were rare in Africa but in Spain?

She handed me a bottle and raised hers for cheers. "He was adorable."

I clinked mine against hers and we both took a sip.

"How great does that taste on a day like this?" She grabbed a strawberry and sent it in after the beer.

"All the better for being illegal, hah."

"And now you've tasted, you've broken your first ever law, Miss Vanilla."

I slapped her on the thigh. "Oh, shut up, you. I'm not that vanilla."

"Oh, really? Then what other laws have you ever broken?"

Oh shit, she had me there. "Well, um..." I looked up to think but there was nothing.

She giggled, "I knew it, you're vanilla," and she held the base of her chilled beer bottle against my thigh.

I almost went into seizure. "Holy fuuuuuu ... oh, don't do that please." And feeling the necessity to instigate some sort of revenge, I again twanged her braid, the blue one this time, which was pitiful but about all I had the power to do.

The braid settled immediately under its own weight and then her mouth suddenly turned level as her eyes fixed on mine, pupils filling her irises, silence but for the distant waves and our breathing. She licked her lips and leaned an inch, two inches, forwards, tilting her head to the side as I felt a pulse in my head.

"I really like your braids." I tried to say but it came out more as a whisper.

She straightened and the smile returned. "I can do you one."

I put up a hand. "Oh, no, what would Gabe..."

But she was already on her feet and repositioning her towel to sit behind me. "It's cool, you'll look awesome. Gabe'll really love it."

I closed my eyes and slowly blew out air as I felt her knees taking to the sand either side of my bum. "Well if you really think Gabe'll really love it then really, I'll have it."

Her hand was on my shoulder as she steadied herself and my mind flashed back to the night before. "They're boho braids ... that's what they're called, just so you know."

"I think I've, um, I'm fairly sure I've heard of them."

"Oh?"

"Yes."

"That's what they're called."

"Yes.

"I like to do mine with fewer strands so they're less thick."

"Yes, that's what I love, um, like about yours."

"Then I'll do you one like mine."

"Yes."

"Shouldn't take too long."

"Good, I mean, oh." I squeezed my eyes closed and concentrated all my efforts on shutting the fuck up. Where was Gabe? I'd not heard from him since the hostel. Out with Dan somewhere. Not far away a dog caught a frisbee and ran it back to his owner.

Her fingers swept through my hair and I shivered. "You have such great hair, so long and shiny, an awesome colour too."

"I'm a product of the Scottish ginger factory," I said monotone. Had she resorted to taking the piss again? Let's face it, everybody usually did when it came to the hair colour of my countrymen.

"Well, I know what you're thinking and I'm not taking the piss and besides, it's not ginger, it's red, there's a difference and what's wrong with ginger anyway?" She blew at something and I could feel the long strands behind my head twisting and intertwining.

"Nothing, I have many ginger friends back at the factory."

She slapped me playfully on the arm. "Sorry, you deserved that."

And I wondered for what offence precisely. I pulled the punnet of strawberries closer and began feasting in earnest. "Would you like one?"

"Uh huh."

I held one up behind my head and then giggled as I felt her mouth close around it, taking the tip of my finger at the same time. "Oh, you are so gross."

"Careful, I have a freezing cold bottle right next to me. Unless you'd like it flat against your back then I suggest apologising at once." And I felt her knees briefly squeeze either side of my hips in a playful threat, *I have you and you can't escape if I so choose.*

I was quick to apologise. "Sorry, sorry, sorry, please don't." There was literally nothing worse. "I think an electric shock would be preferential."

She blew again and I shivered, felt the gentle tension and tugs of her fingers sifting through my fine red strands. "About halfway there." She stood and moved around to my front, coming to sit cross-legged on the space beside me atop my own towel.

I looked down, if only to get away, and in so doing received a front row ticket to the Arwen cleavage show. Averting my eyes to the right, I was gently tugged back to the left.

"Hold still."

Well, there was no escaping them now and she was definitely larger than myself, those two generous globes filling her red sequinned bikini top, a deep cleft separating the pair. What fascinated me though was the way her belly narrowed before broadening out at the hips. She was structured like a Renaissance sculpture, a mesomorphic somatotype, immaculately naturally proportioned, nature had played her a few favours for sure and let's not forget the starfish belly button ring for good measure. I squeezed my eyes shut but the image was still there and for whatever reason, the word that came to mind was intermammary cleft, the anatomical name for cleavage. Maybe that cold bottle would be appropriate right about now.

Her fingers came into view as she approached the tips of my hair, the backs of her wrists coming to rest on my knee as she continued to work.

"How did you get into dancing?" I asked after a brief period of silence.

She hummed and I wondered if I'd triggered some happy childhood memory. "It was Fred Astaire and Ginger Rogers, Gene Kelly, even Michael Jackson. I used to watch Singing in the Rain every morning before school. And Martha Graham, oh and Sylvie Guillem was an incredible ballerina. All I ever did was watch these people in videos and TV shows. We didn't have much money but eventually, my mum took me to dance classes, which were a relatively inexpensive hobby compared to some." She made a sweet noise, somewhere between a laugh and a sigh. "My friends were all playing video games and Mum thought I'd soon get bored of tap and ballet, just like the dolls and cricket but I didn't. I won my first dance trophy aged ten as my parents watched from the balustrade at the Sydney Opera House. Years later, here I am, a pro dancer and the best money ever spent."

It was hard not to get lost in her passion and obvious love for dance, her mum, for life, all whilst I'd spent the entire duration of her story watching her fingers twisting and weaving, my braid almost finished. Only about two inches remained at the tips, the entire braid not even the width of my little finger, which must have taken some serious skill and I lamented that in a couple of months I'd have to unravel it.

There'd been silence for a while and when I looked up from her fingers, she was already watching me, her bottom lip nipped between her teeth.

"Arwen..."

It took her more than a second to react, "oh," and she clapped her thighs and sprang up from the towel, "one last thing," and then she was bending over to rustle through her bag, returning to the same position a few seconds later, "it's a bead to add the finishing touch."

I saw it was a wooden bead, the same as what she had. "Oh, well if we're doing this, let's do it right."

"Exactly." She threaded the ends through the hole and slid it part way up the length of the braid.

"Arwen," I began, "is that why you like your own room? So you can practice your dancing in peace?"

"Uh huh, that and for my meditation, which you can't really do around a bunch of noisy, drunken Brits. No offence." She was tying the loose ends of my braid into a knot to hold the bead in place.

I shuffled, "can you show me how to meditate some time? I promise to be quiet."

"Of course," she grinned, letting go and the braid flopped against my leg, "all done."

I don't know, I couldn't be certain and didn't think it would last, whatever *it* was, but I was never the type to lie to myself. So I had to come clean, at least in my own head...

I had a crush on Arwen.

'WHERE ARE YOU?' I punched in the message and pressed send but that wasn't enough so after a few seconds I sent another. 'Not heard from you in hours. Are you both ok?'

"They could be anywhere, that's for sure, but if I know Dan then they'll be fine. He's surprisingly resourceful." Arwen didn't look worried at all, which was reassuring, but then she wasn't dating one of them.

I glanced around the heaving communal room of the hostel in a futile attempt at spotting them. Maybe they were here and hadn't thought to charge their phones? Actually, that didn't sound like Gabe, Dan maybe, but not Gabe.

"It's just that we were all meant to be hooking up to go to a club or something, Opium or whatever it's called." I sighed and felt the anxiety in my belly. "It's not like him, he's usually so conscientious."

A large group of lads strutted past, all dressed up with similar plans by the looks of it, white shirts definitely the common theme amongst them. The two at the back noticed Arwen and it was almost comical how their walks altered immediately, chests puffing out, chins up, crotches forward and almost bumping into the door as they crossed the threshold.

She was lounging on one of the sofas, one arm propped over the backrest holding a bottle of water and wearing her casual yellow dress again. It registered how relaxed she appeared, not to mention attractive. "You worry too much. They're in Barcelona. How about you do something else and before you know it, they'll have replied to your message."

It wasn't a ridiculous idea and I shrugged. "Like what?"

She leaned forwards and spoke like it was obvious. "Mingle."

"Mingle?"

"You're here to make friends, aren't you?"

"Um, maybe, perhaps, in a way, why?"

"So go make friends."

My head jerked forward. "What? I'm not so sure it works like that, it has to be natural." I glanced toward the exit. "What is it you're suggesting, that I go up to some stranger and ask them to be my friend?"

To my horror, she absolutely nodded. "Why not?"

I laughed, more from the lunacy of it, and stepped away, wondering if she was moon touched. "I'm sure if *you* went up to a group of people and asked to be their friend then the outcome would be somewhat positive but I'm not made from quite the same stuff."

"That's crap." She stood and seemed to hover in my direction, threading her hand through the crook of my elbow and pulling against me, it felt nice and horrible at the same time. "Aren't you here to do new things?"

"Well, yeah but..." she had me there and I wondered just how much she'd been reading my thoughts.

"But...but...but," she deliberately stuttered, taking the piss out of me again, "you never know, you may just be about to meet your best friend in the whole world."

"Yeah, right." I laughed and felt my resolve wilting, indeed, we were already heading toward a group of four at the pool table, two girls and two guys, one of whom was the very stereotype of the smelly traveller, and what would you know, but he was the one who clocked us first.

I received a shove on the lower back and jolted forwards, "hey, speak English?"

It looked like they were playing a game of mixed doubles and all four cues levelled as we stopped, my face probably flushing with some dopey imploring expression, *please don't hurt me.* An unfamiliar Spanish song blared from nearby speakers and people were either sitting or standing in the near vicinity, eating, talking or doing seemingly nothing.

The stereotype nodded and removed his brown fishing hat to reveal the squashed hair beneath. "Yes," he said cheerfully and gestured back to me, "you not so much."

I leaned back and smiled, "correct, I'm Scottish, my friend here's Australian." My heart was thudding and a drop of perspiration slid from my armpit down the side of my ribcage on the inside of my dress. "We just arrived and were wondering how you're all finding Barca?"

"I'm Samuel," rather than touch skin he simply waved with his free hand, probably because he was dating one of the two girls, no biggie, "we're Dutch, or rather I am, Luuk is, Floor too," finally he gestured to a girl with short blonde hair and tattoos on her forearms, "Karla's Canadian though." She waved from her perching position in the corner.

"Hi," I said in a high pitched voice and making a wave to encompass them all.

"Hi," Arwen repeated and I felt her finger tickling the side of my belly.

I tried to trap her hand with the underside of my arm as my body went rigid, Samuel's gaze flicking between myself and the troublesome stunner whilst one of his female companions, Floor, I think, the one with black hair stacked in an elaborate bun with some sort of metallic leaf headband holding it all in place, wrinkled her nose and curled her top lip to expose teeth.

Arwen spotted the threat at once and declared loudly enough for everyone to hear over the music, "I just love your tiara," and she unthreaded her arm and bounced straight over to the girl, whose demeanour flipped in a second.

In fact, I'd never before seen a human being completely switch manner so quick as Floor blushed, her hand moved to touch her heart and within a second they were animatedly engaged in a conversation I was not privy to, whilst all I could do was stand exposed and vulnerable, now without my wing, and wonder which version was the true Floor.

But I was impressed with Arwen, had that been intentional, identifying a potential enemy and turning her to putty in seconds. What was it Dan had said? That this free spirit would fit in with any group.

I rubbed my bottom lip, suddenly apprehensive for another reason, as my gaze ping-ponged from Arwen's backside to Samuel's face. She'd better not get too close.

Samuel said something but I didn't hear it.

"Huh?"

"You were asking about Barcelona?" He said again just as his friends, Luuk, and Karla ambled over from the other side of the pool table to lean back against it from my side, a sort of half-hearted attempt at appearing sociable.

I nodded and my senses seemed to heighten whilst, medically speaking, my body prepared to engage its fight or flight response, stupid as it was in 2017 but hey, I was engaging three strangers in a distant place and it was both scary and thrilling together.

"Yeah, Barcelona, what are the places you recommend?"

But they were all cool. Samuel did most of the talking, generally telling me to have fun walking around and discovering the city's masterpieces. They'd only been in Barcelona three days themselves but had already seen numerous buildings by legendary architect

Antoni Gaudí, which included the famous Sagrada Família. There were awesome live music venues and if we liked football, or even if we didn't, we should go see a game at the Camp Nou. There were so many art treasures, including a Picasso museum, that I'd never have chance to see them all. The old town and Gothic areas were substantial and I should get down there, lose myself amongst the cathedrals and enjoy the street performers and opera singers. He recommended the best tapas place in town, which he'd heard was where the locals went and didn't tell the tourists about. The big Sónar music festival was only days away as well as the city's major annual culture festival, the Festival del Grec. There were several fine parks they'd not yet had chance to see which, according to Luuk, was partially on account of spending the last few days intoxicated.

My attention was constantly shifting between the three travellers and Arwen, who was too far away to hear as she leaned against the partition, the other girl standing uncomfortably close whilst showing an intense interest in her braids, holding one between her thumb and finger and giving it extra special close up scrutiny.

My hand had spent the last minute clenching around that same partition railing and I asked who, if anyone, was dating who and Samuel explained that for his sins, he was in a relationship with Karla, the tattooed Canadian whilst Luuk, a light-skinned black guy whose dreadlocks came down to his jawline, had started seeing Floor when they'd met in Berlin.

"So, you're seeing *that* girl?" I asked Luuk, for no particular reason, as my eyes directed him to the tiara completely absorbed with Arwen.

He nodded, "yeah, kinda sort of." Whatever the fuck that meant.

Karla took her shot and apologised to Samuel for missing an easy yellow. "We're about to head off to a club but if we run into each other tomorrow then perhaps we can arrange to go for drinks."

"We discovered a really cool bar with a terrace overlooking one of the squares, great music and food too," Samuel added as he surveyed the mess his girlfriend had made of their game. "I'm not sure this is salvageable."

"I'd love that."

"We can discuss the usual travel bollocks, where we've been and where we're going," Luuk said with a playful smirk, "then we can all add each other on Facebook and part ways, never to hear from each other again."

"Awe, don't say that.' Arwen overheard as she pottered back to the larger group with the other girl tagging on close behind.

The tiara and I made eye contact, evidently disarmed and then some, and no longer perceiving either of us as a threat to her coupling with Luuk, held out her hand. "Hi, I'm Floor."

I stretched out to shake it, "Freya, and I'll try not to tread on you."

She exposed her teeth again, though this time it was more subtle and Arwen snorted as everything, including the music, fell silent and I wanted to crawl under the pool table.

Arwen gestured to Samuel and Karla, "I know you're all heading out but we have time for a game, don't we?" How had she known they were heading out? Had Floor invited her to a club?

"Yeah, guys, we can make time, I'm sure." Floor interjected on Arwen's behalf. She was taller than both Arwen and me, slim, with a feminine body and attractive face, sharp features, piercing eyes and big black hair held in place by a combination of elaborate bun techniques and the tiara. It looked good and suited her face and style but that kind of do was far too much effort. The group were already dressed and primped, Samuel's squashed hair excepted, and I had to admit that Floor would be turning heads tonight, wearing a sort of elegant black poncho over exceptionally tight fitting jeans.

Luuk smashed the black home. "We can now."

And the table was cleared, Luuk set up the balls, Samuel ordered over some shots, Floor annoyingly jabbered with Arwen at the far side of the table whilst Karla spoke to me about geocaching, whatever that was, and then the teams were divvied thus; Samuel, Karla, myself - Luuk, Floor, Arwen.

An hour, three games and many shots later, we declared a tie because, during the final play, we'd simply lost interest as the whole thing descended into one large drinking game.

"Right!" Samuel declared, slamming his cue upon the table and donning his fisherman's hat, "we really must go. Food first and then a club. Ladies, we'll be seeing you around."

We all hugged it out, Floor and Arwen doing that European kissing on the cheek thing and I watched, exhilarated as they filed out the hostel.

Arwen grabbed my hand and pulled me around to face her. "What did I say? You were remarkable. They loved you."

I was shaking and felt the need to sit. "I couldn't have done it without you, I mean, the way you dealt with that particularly difficult one, Arwen, you were awesome."

She waved it away but playfully propped a hand on her hip, breathing in the praise. "What, me? No, darling, it was all you. You just befriended a large group of strangers and Dutch ones at that, so you can chalk that bitch off the list." She beamed and rubbed my arm as a warm feeling of elation flowed through my bloodstream and then my bag started ringing from the chair.

I gasped, "it'll be Gabe," and dashing for my clutch, I fumbled with the zip to yank out the phone. It was him. "Gabe? Where are you?"

"Frey, I'm in a fucking cell." He said immediately, no greeting, and sounding panicked.

My belly lurched. "What?"

"We both are, in an area of the city called Sant Marti."

I squeezed the phone harder. "What happened?" Arwen, hearing my alarm, pressed her head against mine.

"Fucking gypsy is what happened ... tried nicking my wallet at the cash machine, or rather, the little shit *did* nick my wallet but Dan clobbered him and then another four came out from nowhere. There was a big fight and now we're here in a police cell with a couple of Russian guys who pitched in on our side."

"Oh gosh," I squeaked, "are you going to prison?"

"No, no, no, Dan says we'll be let out in the morning after we've sobered up and cooled down." He laughed, "they even have an English wing down here, there's quite a few of us and Dan says it's just like old times. I got my wallet back at least, minus fifty Euros, but I think I broke that gypsy kid's fingers ... definitely felt something snap anyway, so it was probably worth it in the end." He sounded slightly slurred but definitely alive.

My head swirled and I rubbed a thumb against my temple. "Gabe, this is a lot to take in right now. You're both definitely not hurt?"

"We're both alive if that's what you mean." Oh, Christ. "Look, don't worry about us. I'm sorry I couldn't speak to you before now but they kind of confiscated our stuff, this counts as my phone call but we won't be back tonight so don't wait about for Dan and me to get back. Enjoy Barcelona and I'll make it up to you tomorrow. Don't worry and I love you."

"I love you too," I said as the line cut off and I held the phone close. "Arwen? I don't know what to do."

"Come here." She opened out her arms and I stumbled into them, burying my head in the crook of her neck. "Don't worry, Frey, he said so himself, they're fine and this experience will turn out to be a good thing. He'll learn not to be so blasé at the cash point in future." As always, she was just so reassuring and I was so happy she was here, especially at a moment like this.

"He should have already known that." It was common sense. I inhaled her peachy scent with a sweet mixture of coconut from the suntan lotion and wanted to stay like this for as long as it didn't feel weird. "This has ruined your evening."

She laughed and I felt her hands stroking my back, strangely comforting. "This has not ruined my evening or anything else. I've been having a great time and it's just an experience, like any other. When he returns, he'll be a wiser man and will bore us to death with his stories and I promise you, there'll not be a thing he'd take back."

I nuzzled against her flesh. "When you put it like that..."

She brought me to arms' length and her blue eyes held that familiar mischievous hue. "And there's nothing stopping us from going out."

───────

I WAS FIRST out the shower, a necessity considering my body was still covered in sweat and sun lotion, I was sticky and could feel sand all over myself. Arwen took to the bathroom after me whilst I changed and applied my makeup in the peace of our dorm.

I hadn't brought that many outfits from home and only a couple of going out options, knowing it wasn't my usual thing and could easily buy new clothes on the continent at a slight discount thanks to the exchange rate. I was wearing an all-black outfit, one of those skirt short things, which I believe were called skorts. Above I wore a black shirt with a choker design and had the top two buttons unfastened but after studying my reflection, I released a third, exposing the smallest peep of the inner portions of my breasts. I rolled the sleeves up to my elbows, stepped back and surveyed what I saw, shiny red hair plush against black and big eyes that, despite Gabe's incarceration, held a happy shade of green. In fact, I dare say, I looked pretty damned elegant for a girl raised by the wolves.

I opened my makeup bag and went for the mascara just as the

door flung open, startling me and I whipped around as Arwen entered, clipping the floor with a pair of black high heels.

"Oh, holy fuck." It was a natural reaction to being both scared senseless and witnessing the wonder that was even now striding into the room.

"Oh, thanks, Honey," she joked, flicking a wave of blonde from one shoulder to the other. "Do I look that good?" She briefly caught my eye, made a small but noticeable misstep as her gaze flowed down from my face to my breasts before correcting herself and continuing towards the bed, glancing once over her shoulder as she did.

I made a strange nervous laughing sound, "no, I didn't mean..." the peach drifted through my sinuses and for whatever reason, I found myself unable to complete any sentence I might have been trying to say.

"You weren't expecting me out the bathroom so soon? I never take long to get ready." She glanced again over her shoulder and then turned sharply back when I caught her.

I swallowed and tried not to gawk too obviously. "Yeah, that was pretty fast."

In a matter of minutes, she'd managed to shower, dress and apply what little makeup she thought necessary. A low-maintenance hippy girl. She was wearing an all black two-piece outfit; a tight fitting skirt that cut off just above the knees and emphasised her best feature, those broad dancers hips whilst showcasing her incredible legs that seemed to glow from whatever she'd rubbed over them. It was the first time I'd seen her in heels and the enforced plantar flexion at the ankle joint made her calves pop most scintillatingly. Above she wore a bandage top with crisscross halter straps, exposing her arms and only the smallest glimmer of cleavage whilst below the breasts, the crossover design revealed the faint line between her abdominals where they met her belly button, which now possessed a green jewel dangling from a short chain. Her hair was stacked high, exposing her slender neck and the yin and yang tattoo at her nape with a single red braid flowing loose to rest against her sternum, making her look similar to how she had during our first proper encounter in the bathroom back in Bordeaux. Back then I'd barely paid her heed, not so now.

She was leaning over her bag and I'd been gazing at the curvature of her arse for, well I'm not sure for how long, but I swallowed and then realised I was still holding the mascara, so I tore myself away to apply myself fully to that task. There was the sound of Arwen smacking her lips together, like she'd applied lip balm and when I turned around, job done, I caught her eye again and she smiled before looking away.

I actually giggled on the inside because it was not like her to be cowed by anything, especially not me.

"Ready?"

———

THE LINE outside Opium stretched a long way from the entrance and we walked with arms linked towards the end, wherever that was. It was one of those moments you lived in slow motion because so many people were watching us, or rather Arwen, as we passed that my senses were elevated to some higher level of clarity. *Don't trip up, don't trip up.* Indeed, it was hard not to feel the pressure of such scrutinisation from both the men and women in the queue. I was sort of used to being ogled, I mean, it happened from time to time but never to this extent and it was obvious why.

The line, and it was long, hadn't moved a single inch as we continued making our way toward the back, wherever that was, and it was almost enough to prompt me to suggest going elsewhere but then we heard the patter of footsteps from behind and suddenly, standing in front of us, was a short, slender man with a goatee, one of those beanie hats and a stack of flyers in his hand.

"Ladies, are you coming to Opium tonight?" He backtracked a few steps as we continued walking.

Arwen applied pressure to my arm so I stopped. "We were but the queue's way too long. We aren't standing around for an hour when there're other clubs."

He held up his hands and spoke quick, evidently fearful we were about to continue on our way. "How about if I can get you straight in?" He spoke with a London Cockney accent and it only took a second to realise he was one of those people who stand close to bars and clubs, handing out leaflets offering free drinks to get you inside. Though this club hardly needed the advertising.

I shook my head, suddenly appalled. "She wasn't hinting at any favours." I gestured to all the poor disgruntled people who'd probably already been standing around for ages. "I don't think they'd take too well to having us push in front of them." And why? Just because Arwen had an ass like that?

He laughed and waved it away, "that's a good one, bird, it's called a guest list, you never heard of one?" I wasn't sure I'd detected an eye roll as he turned to my friend. "Listen, you just walked past the director slash owner who was happening to be loitering at the entrance, like he has every right to do. It's his patch of pavement, ain't it. He's the fat twat in the God-awful whistle and flute, and he told me to get you inside, do whatever it takes or you're sacked and so here I am, humbling myself before you, willing to prostrate myself if necessary but you *have* to come in. Ladies, what'll it take? Now, the usual thing would be to start low and haggle but the thing is, and this is strictly between the three of us, I could certainly stand to see the twat lose a few quid from the off, plus it increases your perceived value in his eyes. Your free entrance is a given. I can sort you out with a VIP pass and bottle of pink Champagne on ice and when I say Champagne, I'm not talking sparkling wine here, but something what actually came from Champagne which, as I've been reliably told, is a region somewhere in France."

My head was spinning but luckily Arwen had held her wits. "And do we get complementary nibbles?"

His face lifted at the lifeline. "You should see the menu we have, it's equal to anything you'll find in any of the typical three-star establishments in this city."

Arwen was already turning around. "In that case, lead the way, good man."

He performed some sort of a jig straight out of a bad Oliver Twist ripoff, hopping and dancing in front of us as we followed him back down the long line towards the door and I nudged the girl in the side.

"You are shameless." And indeed she was and it was a fact of life that some women could use their looks to get whatever they wanted. Like it or not but Arwen could do that and more without even having to try and why shouldn't she abuse that privilege if men were stupid enough to allow it.

She linked my arm again and pulled me close. "And you're too nice."

"But we were coming in here anyway," I whispered and felt her body convulsing in silent laughter.

There was an actual red carpet at the entrance but it was the four burly doormen in black suits and earpieces that drew the eye, each one of their gazes burning into us and I felt my arm squeezing around Arwen's as we followed the cockney beyond the admissions desks. There were three girls sat behind the tills and the stupid thing was that only one of them was working, the others sitting doing nothing and I knew they were intentionally slowing access to build up the line in order to make the place appear popular so more people would be attracted to the club, the scoundrels. Oh, those poor people.

We passed through a heavy velvet curtain and into a short corridor where couples were chatting in comparative quiet but I could already see how it opened out into a huge venue. "Follow me," the cockney reinforced because the crowds were appearing now and it was dark with laser beams and huge mirrors stretching from floor to ceiling and the techno music was so loud the floor shook and the vibrations made my ear itch. Two men stepped appreciatively back, eyeing Arwen from hair to arse and a Chinese guy actually filmed her on his phone - This would be a long night. There was probably over a thousand people already here, mostly crammed in on the large dance floor in front of the DJ's booth, who was jumping around waving his hand. We were walking around the perimeter and the cockney turned around, mouthed something I didn't catch but he was pointing up, which was easy enough to understand, before swerving and dancing up a flight of stairs adorned with red velvet coverings on the walls. People were lounging on the steps, drinking from bottles, relaxing, texting or else snogging the faces off complete strangers. I glanced back over my shoulder, to the strange modern-day mating ritual I wanted no part of, it wasn't me.

Upstairs the music wasn't as loud and the man turned to us again. "We're the only club in Barca what has five VIP areas. I'm taking you to the most exclusive. The other night Armin van Buuren was here." Whoever that was. He danced through another threshold, flashed his pass to a large man stood guarding the room, shimmied around a large fountain which, to my horror actually had live fish swimming around in it, and through another red velvet curtain.

My eyes widened.

We were on a rooftop terrace overlooking the Mediterranean and in the last of the twilight I could just make out the waves that gently rolled over the sand. Tranquil lighting provided a pleasant ambience, along with the pianist in white tux who slowly played with his eyes closed. There were several obscenely long sofas that curved around marble busts and three immaculately dressed waiters with chins held up, hands behind their backs awaiting the whims of anyone else who'd managed to catch the eye of their boss as they walked down the street. To my count, we were the eleventh and twelfth people here and although I'd truly enjoy having the chance to sit down and converse alone with Arwen, I wasn't so sure it was what we had in mind for a night out. Still, we were here and I'd enjoy it.

Our guide spoke to one of the waiters who then disappeared behind the bar that was staffed by a hunk of manhood pulled straight from a CK commercial. Our cockney guide then returned. "Ladies, your Champagne and nibbles are on the way. It's been a pleasure." At that, he jigged his exit and left me wondering just what was in it for them. Well, if some club wanted to grant free access and lavish freebies upon us just because of Arwen's rear end then they probably deserved to take a financial hit.

And since it was on my mind, I'd bloody well tell her too. "The things that having an arse like yours can do for your life."

She was turned into me on the sofa, her knee just barely grazing mine and she gazed down, twisting the end of her errant red braid. "It was not my arse but your face that did it." Oh, it was a lie, as well as the biggest display of insecurity I'd yet witnessed from her, for whatever reason. Indeed, her typical self-assured nature, no fucks given attitude was the trait I admired most about her, yet here she was bodily closing up and I was about to check if she was ok when there was an almighty crash from my side, forcing a jolt from us both.

Except it wasn't a crash, not really. "Your Champagne." It was in one of those ice buckets on a stilt, which the waiter pulled closer before placing two large Champagne flutes on the table. He then popped the cork, spilling nothing and filled the glasses before seeming to levitate back to his original position and continuing to stare into air.

"That's what you call walking with a broom handle stuffed up you." It was a good thing she'd said it before I'd taken a sip otherwise I'd have been snorting expensive Champagne everywhere. "You know you're born to be a waiter when you walk like that."

I slapped her on the leg and she responded by shuffling even closer so that our thighs pressed together, not an unpleasant sensation, and I marvelled at her shape and the visible line that separated her rectus femoris from vastus lateralis, wanted to touch it, her, but it would pass. I'd get over it.

"Arwen, we must drink a toast to something." Her name no long
sounded as funny as it once did.

"What do you suggest?"

"Hmm," I wanted to suggest toasting to friendship but bottled
"to Barcelona."

"Well, how about to friendship?" She said, smiling coyly.

All I could do was nod, half impressed, half ashamed. "Of cours
to friendship."

We clinked glasses and tasted the nectar and I allowed the fizz
flow over my palate before sending it back. Delicious.

"Arwen," I began, "do you think we'll still be friends after th
trip?" I felt myself sinking into the soft leather cushions and was
sure if it was the sudden taste of alcohol or something else. "I mea
I'm due back home by the end of September at the latest. You
either still be travelling or, I assume, will go back to Australia." Th
sudden realisation was like a huge kick in the...

Her hand made the small distance to take my own, whi
surprised me but it felt nice. "Of course we'll still be friends, Frey,
both have WhatsApp and you'll have to fight to stop me visiting y
in Scotland. I've always wanted to go snorkelling in Loch Ness."

My heart soared, not for any unrealistic, not yet fu
contemplated romantic whims that were sure to fizzle away just
soon I watched a Ewan McGregor movie, saw Gabe naked or v
parted from her but because what we had was a developing friendsl
with great potential and that was something I didn't wish to e
lose. "You do know Nessy's just a figment of some drunken saile
whisky induced imagination, right? I mean, what were the odds t
the one country that possessed some mysterious sea creature j
happened to be the very same that produces such a stro
intoxicating and addictive liquor?"

Her eyebrows dipped, "oh, don't say that, please. You're ruin
the dreams of an innocent child of yore."

"Of yore? You make yourself out to be older than what you
How old are you anyway?"

"I'm twenty-three."

"Same as me. When's your birthday."

"November 19th, yours?"

"October 22nd. We're quite close."

"We are."

"Yes."

"Yes."

We weren't holding hands properly, it was more like Arwen had slipped her fingers inside my limp hands that were resting in my lap but after half a minute, a wildly rough estimate, she pulled away and began to occupy them by smoothing out her skirt.

But what was I supposed to have done, interlink fingers and gaze softly into her eyes before leaning in for the kiss? And then what?

She again began to twirl her braid and despite maybe, possibly, almost conceivably, even hopefully suspecting what it might be, why she'd closed up again, I was about to ask what the problem was, when...

Shadows loomed over us and in unison, our heads tilted up to see a tall, well-built specimen of Spanish manhood in expertly tailored suit, tan, styled hair, gold cufflinks, expensive watch, polished black shoes, "hello ladies, my name's Alejandro," and an accent, "and I am the owner of Opium," and evidently full of it, the man hardly resembled the description given to us by the resentful cockney.

"Hello." We both said together, our voices rising in pitch. How we'd walked straight past him at the entrance would have been a mystery even two days before.

Without asking permission, he stepped around and occupied the pouffe, I guess he did own it, and only then did we notice the two underlings in suits standing apathetically behind holding walkie-talkies and Filofaxes.

He looked at me with piercing brown eyes. "You're very beautiful, what is your name?"

I straightened and felt my breasts pushing out as my eyes were drawn to his five o'clock shadow. "I'm Freya." I held out my hand, which he took and I felt the coarse skin from calluses, a weightlifter, it seemed.

"Freya, I'm happy to meet you," and I wasn't surprised to witness his next move and he turned to face my friend straight on as she did the same, a look of ravenous lust, of absolute burning fire in his eyes, "and you, Señorita? What is *your* name?"

Whether she knew it or not, she was doing the exact same as me, pushing out her boobs and I felt myself crumble being forced to witness this exchange, my eyes unable to look away, whilst his were fixed on her eyes, not moving, never moving. This was a rare man, no doubt, cocksure, arrogant, full of self-belief but perhaps with reason? What was he, mid-thirties and owning a business like this?

"I'm Arwen." She leaned forward, overextending to shake his hand and it was the first time I'd seen her supplicate to anyone.

"Arwen, Arwen," he repeated the name with warmth, "from Australia, it seems." He was still holding onto her with those eyes that refused to look away and the whole world evaporated as the only thing in existence were the three of us in this strange little bubble atop a rooftop bar overlooking the Mediterranean. "The moment I saw you, I knew we had to meet and now here we are, sitting together, in my bar on this heavenly evening." He pulled the pouffe closer, making it more comfortable for Arwen but didn't let go, never letting go. "I hope you're enjoying the Champagne, this beautiful city and, as a small token, my hospitality?"

She nodded and croaked, "yeah ... yes."

"As you can imagine, we get many thousands, tens, hundreds of thousands of women in this club but never have I ever seen..."

A woman, tall and dressed for business appeared, clipping the floor in heels and leaned over to whisper in his ear. It was the first time he'd taken his gaze from Arwen as his chin dropped but only a touch and he reeled something off in disgruntled Spanish. Arwen would likely have understood and despite it obviously being about the club, I hated that there were things being said that I was not privy to.

The woman again whispered into his ear, made an apologetic hand gesture and Alejandro looked back to my friend.

"I apologise but duty calls, Arwen, I have to cut this meeting painfully short but I must see you again." He delved a large manly hand inside his jacket and pulled out a business card, embossed, and handed it to her. "We must have dinner tomorrow night and I must find out more about you. Tomorrow night," he emphasised, "and there will be no interruptions. Enjoy the Champagne and my hospitality." The blood in my body was doing all kinds of crazy things and then he managed to pull his eyes from Arwen to address me one last time, "Freya," and then, with underlings tagging on behind, he was striding towards the exit but not before having to stop twice more as two beautiful women attempted to engage him, he humouring them with a kiss on each cheek before moving along.

Arwen was blinking slowly, mouth opened as her glassy eyes were pointed in the general direction of where the man had disappeared, a total look of befuddlement. Finally, an audible exhalation escaped her mouth and she examined the card.

"Alejandro Ruiz, Owner & Proprietor, Ruiz Ocio." His email and mobile number were below.

"Ocio?"

"Means leisure." She said monotoned.

"Right." So the smoothie probably owned more than just this one club I suddenly wanted to escape and I couldn't hold it in, I just had to ask. "Are you gonna call that man?"

She blinked and her wits returned, "oh, no, no, I don't even know the guy and it's obvious what he's after." She shuffled and placed the card inside her clutch, zipping it closed. "No, I'm not interested, nope."

"Excuse me, one moment." I stood and rushed for the bathroom.

———

I FUTILELY FANNED my face with a paper towel, having wiped away the tears and hidden the evidence, though the mirror revealed eyes still possessing a shimmer that would betray me and a defeated glare somewhere behind them, that would only disappear after an appropriate pick me up.

There was a knock at the door and I hastily turned on the tap, thrusting my hands into the jet.

"Vanilla?" She squeaked before stepping cautiously inside the small VIP bathroom, plush with decent squirty soap, hand towels, fancy mirrors, perfume and it was clean. "It would be easy to forget we're in a nightclub. Are you ok? You sounded upset when you stormed off."

I'd been smiling from the use of *that* name but my face dropped again. "Don't talk ridiculous, I did not storm off."

"You did storm off." She was enjoying this more than I was.

"I did *not* storm off, Arwen."

"Ok," she smirked, clearly not believing me and closing half the distance with a few heedful steps, stopping and then coming out with the big one. "Would you like me to tear up that guy's card? I'll do it, you just have to say so and..."

"No!" I whipped around and spoke fast, with instinct, perhaps even with some automatic thought for self-preservation, knowing that her offer to tear up the card was exceptionally loaded but I also suspected she could read my true feelings anyway, she wasn't daft, far from it. "Really, Arwen," I tried to sound as composed as possible, slowing down, breathing, maybe even pulling it off, "it's none of my business what you do or who you choose to date." Her eyes drifted down to my hands that were balling into tiny fists so I hid them behind my back. "He was gorgeous, you should at least meet with him to see if he's the real deal or if that alpha male thing was one big act."

Her face lifted and her shoulders quivered as she tried to suppress the laughter.

I stamped my heel on the tiles. "What? What are you trying not to laugh about?"

She took another pace toward me but I stepped away. "You really don't want me to see him, do you?"

My shoulders relaxed and I faced her square on. "I want you to be happy. *Gabe* and I *both* want you to be happy. If you're even minutely curious then you should definitely call him. Most women would."

Her eyes dropped and seemed to fix on my heels. "Ok," she rasped and was about to say something else but didn't.

"So..." I shrugged, smiling without the eyes.

"So, let's go dance."

SHE GRABBED THE CHAMPAGNE BOTTLE, filled our glasses, ditched the remainder and with an elaborate spin, danced through the velvet curtain.

All I could do was watch, powerless, shambling after her, as she twirled past the doorman, teased her arse inappropriately close to his hungry crotch before moving swiftly on, leaving him lusty, drooling and perplexed, to shimmy around the fountain in the most overly artistic way, blowing a kiss to the fish, dipping a finger into the water, leaning over and pushing off the stone, continuing, twirling through the now crowded upper level bar, grabbing the hand of the nearest man and falling into a salsa pose, swinging back up to press her breasts against his chest, spinning in his hands and sliding away with outstretched arms, leaving him gasping and wondering how much he'd imbibed, all in time with the music, as a hundred pairs of eyes fixed on this incredible dancing woman, a few diehards grasping for position and following as she gracefully pirouetted in the direction of the stairs, red braid flaring out from the g-force, clutching onto the bannister in the most artistic way imaginable, her entire body flowing like a wave from a stationary position, descending likewise as awed men and women stepped aside and cheered, reaching the landing and seamlessly phasing into a different style as the music changed to techno, her reaching out for my hand, me rushing wearily forward, grabbing her, being pulled through the parting crowd, further and further towards the centre, wondering what had happened to our drinks along the way, being pulled close, her hips grinding into mine, her hands on my waist, a small circle opening to encompass us, feeling dizzy, being spun, her eyes burning into mine, seeing us both on a big screen over her shoulder, the loud unbearable music shaking my brain, Arwen dancing with arms raised above her head, men and women filming on their phones, her twirling, grabbing my hand, guiding me away into the crowd, her returning and pirouetting, pointing at a man to join her, he so doing, my numbness, yet unable to look away, even for a second, feeling a tap on the shoulder...

"Isn't she incredible." It was Samuel, donning his fisherman's hat and holding a beer as his eyes bulged. "Where the fuck did you find her?"

Dancing with the angels. "France." I managed to pull my eyes away and saw Luuk, Karla and Floor all engaged in something between dancing and intensively watching her. Floor, in particular, possessed an almost deranged, entranced look, her tongue playing with the straw that poked out from her glass.

"There's a star in the house tonight." The DJ announced over the speakers to a big cheer from a thousand clubbers.

A slim, barbie stereotype attempted to piggyback off the attention Arwen was receiving and stepped in to dance alongside her. Typically good-natured, Arwen humoured the girl, even though she was so far out of her league and then another moved in, then another, and the circle spontaneously collapsed and then Samuel lurched forward because he'd been bumped from the side and I saw that it was Floor who'd barged past, yanked a tiny girl out of the way and shoved a path through to Arwen.

Floor opened out her arms and I saw the recognition register on Arwen's face, her mouthing, "hey," and then receiving an embrace.

The gap was closing up and then all I could see was Floor's extra tall frame shielding Arwen as she leaned into her ear, the strobe lights reflecting off the back of her tiara.

Samuel was saying something but there was no chance of hearing it, Karla casually bobbed her head, holding onto his hand and I looked beyond them for Luuk who, despite supposedly being involved with Floor, was dancing exceptionally close with another girl. Samuel's mouth touched my ear, "you fancy a drink?"

I was conflicted, wanting to get away yet needing to know what was happening with Arwen. I nodded and followed Samuel and Karla through the tightly packed bodies off the dance floor, which took over a minute and we waited in line at the bar. I turned back to scan the floor for my friend but she was lost, needle in a haystack.

Samuel's mouth was back at my ear, which was like having him literally shouting at me from close range. "It's two for one on bottles so don't worry about paying me back ... traveller's budget and all that but who cares."

I pulled a twenty Euro note from my bag and handed it to him.

"Um..." he shrugged but turned back to the bar and then Karla was standing in his place.

"I think my friend likes your friend." She screamed into my ear, observation of the century. "As if you couldn't already tell." Her hands were buried in the pockets of her baggy blue jeans as my stare fixed on the meaningless green swirly patterns of her forearm tattoos. She said something else but the only thing I made out was the word "Floor."

My head fizzed. How long was this drink taking? I reluctantly turned away from the dance floor, to at least try appearing more sociable but then the shapes of Floor and Arwen appearing in my periphery yanked me back. The bitch was holding Arwen's hand and leading her toward the booths at the far wall and I craned my neck for a better view just as a train of men wearing bright shirts strutted past. My eyes darted to and fro, found Arwen entering a booth and Floor squeezing in after her, at the same fucking side, a half dozen partitions blotting out any further view. The music was fucking awful.

My belly lurched, my heart flipped, my throat scratched and a bottle was placed into my weary hand - Beer.

I sank half in one go and Samuel began uselessly talking about something there was never any hope of hearing, Karla nodding along like she understood everything as time elapsed slowly, no movement from the booth, nobody entering or leaving whilst I fought the urge to run over there and see what the bitch was doing with my friend. But I wasn't *that* girl. At least I didn't think so.

I don't know how long past, forty-five minutes, an hour and a half, but at one point we went back to the dance floor then upstairs to the other bar for another drink and to have an actual conversation, not that I said much. Luuk breezed through at one point with a girl of a similar shade to himself, who couldn't keep her hands off his dreads, definitely not Floor.

"It's one of the hardest caches I've ever had to find but it's here somewhere, I know it is and I won't leave until I've found it." Karla slurped her drink. "There's meant to be a disposable camera in the box and the idea is that I take a selfie with it, place it back and then at a later date some other person can find it, develop the film and put the faces of everyone who found it on their blog. The usual problem is finding the thing but on this occasion, I can't even find the coordinates, which ain't a good start. I read they're painted on a building somewhere but I've been, I've searched and I cannot find them." She tossed a beer mat at Samuel, who rolled his eyes for my benefit.

I plonked my drink down, "guys, I'm not much fun tonight so I think I'm just gonna head off back to the hostel. It was nice bumping into you, maybe I'll see you all at breakfast."

Karla stood at the same time. "Oh, well, we'll walk back with you. We were about to head back anyway, weren't we Sambo?"

It was news to him but he stood and politely nodded and so the three of us left the club and as we approached the booth where Arwen had been, my entire world descended into slow motion as I prepared to witness the appalling scene that I was only just beginning to realise would hurt so much. What would I see? The back of Floor's head and a glinting tiara as she invaded my friend's mouth with her tongue, her hands hungrily roaming her body. But as we passed it was some other couple, a heterosexual one, of all things, who couldn't take their hands off each other. It was both a relief and an aggravation. A relief because I wouldn't have to see it, an aggravation because, well, where the fuck was she and what was she doing?

"If you see what looks like coordinates on any of these buildings then shout me at once."

"Hey, Piston, the poor girl doesn't give a crap about geocaching or helping you find your idiotic little box that's probably buried somewhere deep in a pile of cow shit." Samuel pinched her on the arse and she slapped him across the back.

"Oh no, guys, really, it's fascinating." It was a fifteen-minute walk to the hostel, which suddenly seemed like a long time to endure.

"See! And really?" Karla persisted, "you should come with me then."

"Oi, she's just arrived in Barcelona, why the fuck would she go geocaching with you when she could go to the beach, the casino or any of a hundred bars?" He playfully put her in a headlock. "Volunteering at an old people's home would be more entertaining."

She used her tiny frame to shove him off and playfully lashed out with a brown leather boot, precisely the type of relationship that was destined to last forever. "You insensitive prick. I was trying to offer her company after her friend abandoned her." And they'd seemed so nice before. She stamped away from him and began staggering beside me. "I know it's a cliche but there's many other fishes in the sea. Did I say that right? Anyway, you'll find another one."

I was quick to interject on that line. "Oh, no, we're not..."

"Is that the fucking coordinates?" She screeched in her Canadian twang, almost swiping me across the face as she pointed up at a building.

Samuel burst into laughter. "It's the phone number for a chiropractor."

And I conceded that if I didn't find *that* funny then something was definitely up.

I hugged them both goodnight and braced myself before opening the door to my, our, dorm but as expected, nobody else was home. I sat on the bed and spent a few minutes staring blankly at the wall whilst sipping a glass of water I'd brought up for the night.

It'd been a forlorn hope but a hope nonetheless, that maybe Arwen would have been waiting or even meditating and would have been annoyed that I'd disturbed her and we'd hug and say sorry and I'd probably cry and she'd see it and we'd talk into the small hours and I'd be vulnerable and possibly say something that might change my life forever.

But no.

Because she was with that other one. Probably in a hotel room where they'd have privacy.

I missed her. I was pathetic.

There was supposed to have been four of us in this room tonight but now, at three in the morning, I was the only one here. And I'd never felt so alone.

I brushed my teeth, removed my lenses, changed into a pair of shorts and t-shirt, switched the light off and settled into bed.

The traffic from outside was loud but I wanted the window open. I unlocked my phone, the light causing me to squint as it partially illuminated the room, I breathed and scanned through my photos, selecting the image of Arwen and me on the wall in Carcassonne.

"So beautiful."

I groaned and my belly stirred.

I opened Youtube and typed in 'Tiny Biggz,' selected the song titled, 'You Want Ma Money?' and squirmed as the video started.

The music was not my usual thing but for hip-hop, it wasn't all that bad and one could only be impressed by the production and scale. It took place at night, in the penthouse suite of a skyscraper as the bright lights of what had to be New York dazzled the viewer. The party was ongoing as the helicopter landed and as all the revellers stopped in awe, out strutted Tiny Biggz, sunglasses donned, despite it being dark, arm in arm with two girls. The breath caught in my throat as the image flashed over Arwen, dressed elegantly like she was going to the theatre. It was the first time I'd seen her without braids as she strode into the penthouse beside Tiny, who delved into his jacket pocket, pulled out a wad of dollars and began throwing them into the air. It cut to a closeup of his gold teeth, someone handed him a cane with a diamond in its handle, he pointed it at the two girls and for his amusement, they began sexy dancing with each other. A leather armchair was pulled up and Tiny reclined back as someone out of shot handed him a cocktail. Throughout the penthouse, a hundred girls were dancing but the camera focused on Arwen and the other girl, exotic looking, possibly Brazilian, as they pressed and rubbed against each other. Arwen leaned forward, exposing her abundant cleavage and I paused the video.

My breathing was loud in the quiet room and, holding the phone in my left hand, I slid the right down my body, over my belly, pubis and, spreading my legs a little wider, found my moist opening and bucked as my fingers glanced over my outer walls. I concentrated on my clitoris, pressing harder, breathing deeper, my eyes feasting on Arwen's face, neck, breasts but the girl on the screen was not the Arwen I knew and so I dropped the phone to my pillow, closed my eyes and imagined the Arwen beside the campfire, just us, nobody else, as we kissed and embraced in that special place, our Catalonian valley and the wind rustled the leaves on the trees and her hands were on my breasts and she was pleading for me to touch her, to touch her somewhere intimate and I brought my hand up beneath her dress and began to massage her folds and she sighed softly as our lips could not bring themselves to part. Suddenly I was again in Barcelona and my back arched from the bed as my arm tensed and I could feel the explosion building from deep within, that same suppressed explosion that had been humming inside of me since Catalonia, since she first laid her hands on my back, since we shared that incredible kiss. My breathing intensified and there was mumbling from somewhere close and I heard the beep from the keycard and I wrenched my hand back, turned off the light from my phone and laid still.

The door creaked open and there in the threshold, enveloped in orange light from the hallway, stood Arwen.

My heart soared and thudded and screamed all at once. Who was she with? That awful girl? I couldn't watch but neither could I close my eyes, even though the strong light hurt.

She stepped inside, paused. "Frey?" She used her foot to close the door but left a tiny crack to enable her to see. "Are you there?" She was alone, most definitely alone and I felt a rare euphoria surge through my body.

"Arwen," I whispered.

"Ah, there you are. I was searching everywhere for you. You had me very worried."

I let out a silent whimper. "I'm sorry."

"Me too, Vanilla, I'm very sorry."

My pillowcase had dampened with tears. "Arwen?"

"I won't turn the light on. I think we need to talk."

"Yes."

"We'll do it tomorrow."

TOGETHER, Arwen and I came down for breakfast as the usual heads turned to scope out the Australian dancer. Samuel, one head among a crowd of travellers, waved at us from a table his group were occupying by the window but it was the scowl from hell, bestowed upon me by Floor that felt awesome this morning. I was perhaps rightly beginning to suspect my name might have been raised during their private conversation of the night before and what I wouldn't give to have a transcript.

"Looking good," Samuel declared to Arwen, who'd come straight from the bedroom in her dressing gown. I loved the way she didn't give a damn and still looked better than anybody else in the building and beyond. The hair on one side of her face was a disordered mess but other than that she looked perfect.

We approached the buffet and required three trips to bring back toast, cereal, muffins, ham, cheese, coffee and freshly squeezed orange juice. When we finally took our seats, Floor shuffled away from us, just enough to be noticed and in response, Luuk, who doubtless thought she was shuffling towards him, casually propped an arm over her shoulder.

"Damn shame there's no bacon, sausages, hash browns, baked beans, mushrooms," Arwen remarked as she scraped butter into her toast. "Heck, I could even go for some of that black pudding rubbish you Brits eat."

My smile lifted even further at being addressed out of everyone and Floor's top lip pulled back to reveal her teeth, bright, shiny and menacing. But there was something more than threatening, unsettling even, behind Floor's eyes as she continued to bodily ignore the two of us. Not that I cared right now. She'd forgone the tiara this morning and her hair was kept in a ponytail of long black that draped over one shoulder to rest at her midriff.

Samuel leaned forward and pointed his fork at Arwen. "You know, it sounds like the two of you would seriously enjoy coming along with us on the Camino."

Karla, mouth full of food, made a strange noise and sprang forward beyond her boyfriend and from where I was sitting it looked like her head was sprouting out from his shoulder. "Yes, you have to come and do the Camino with us. We'll be wild camping every night and using a stove to cook bacon and sausages and all that good stuff you just said."

"Easy girl, easy." Samuel restrained her with the back of his arm then looked back to Arwen. "She gets keen, that is, until she gets bored, as you've probably noticed with her present hobby, searching sand dunes and people's gardens for small boxes filled with shit. But the offer's there if you fancy it."

Arwen put down her toast. "The Camino? I must admit, it's always been on the list." She rubbed her chin as my body made a swift involuntary jerk towards her. "Hmm," was she actually considering leaving us? "No." She finally shook her head. "We just arrived here and have barely even scratched Barcelona's shiny surface. There's just too much I want to see here first."

Karla flopped back and Samuel held out his palms. "Well like I said, the offer's there. We're not likely to leave Barca for a couple of days yet and we'll be on foot, so even if you change your mind you could probably catch us up. All you'll need is a cheap tent and ready supply of bacon, eggs, sausages and all that other stuff."

The Camino de Santiago was a religious pilgrimage to the shrine of Saint James at the cathedral in Santiago de Compostela, North Western Spain. Technically speaking, the pilgrimage could begin anywhere but the route from Barcelona was an emerging one with tourists and took you through a number of interesting spots. Ultimately, it would involve a lot of walking, from here, about seven hundred miles of it, but added to that there'd be good food, camping, interesting sites, friendship and quite possibly an experience never to forget. The problem for me was that knowing Gabe and his aversion to all things religious, he would most certainly be against the idea, even if it was treated simply as a long walk through the centre of Spain and I had an inkling Dan wouldn't be too keen either. Arwen, on the other hand? All I knew was that it was a great relief when she turned them down.

But I felt the strong need to reinforce Arwen's refusal. "Besides, it's kind of in the opposite direction to where we're most likely heading next. We were thinking down the coast; Valencia, Granada, possibly Madrid."

"Madrid's straight west." Floor mumbled testily into her coffee.

"Yes, you're correct, Floor." I smiled at her, intentionally pronouncing her name as that thing we walk on rather than how the others were saying it, *Floo-er*.

Luuk leaned over and spoke with a surprisingly effeminate voice for someone so tall with dreadlocks. "To where you're *most likely heading* next? You don't have a rough idea?"

Arwen tipped a spoonful of sugar into her coffee and then gestured to me with the implement. "Well there's more than just the two of us to consider, that is if we're sticking together after Barca but we're travelling with two other guys you've not met."

Floor now turned back to a more central position and although she was filling her mouth with cornflakes, it was easy to see she was scrutinising the details.

Samuel shrugged and looked over his shoulder. "Really? Bring them down. Where are they?"

I coughed into a napkin and, patting me on the back, Arwen

answered in my stead. "Well, Dan and Freya's boyfriend are kind of in jail right now."

There were confused blinks and scratches of heads all around, Floor in particular perked up, a dozen questions all at once forming in her mind.

I cut her off. "Oh, Arwen, they're not in jail." I glanced back to the others. "No, they're in a police holding cell and are due back any moment." Where were they?

"But you have a boyfriend?" Floor predictably asked.

Ordinarily, I might have ignored her but the others were all looking at me for an answer. "Yes, Floor, I have a boyfriend."

Her gaze switched from me to Arwen and back to me before deigning to occupy herself by continuing with her breakfast.

The piston sprang forward and I almost spilt coffee. "So, Freya, you're really not..." Oh, Christ.

I had to act quickly on this one. "...No! Karla, as I told you last night."

She shrugged because doubtless the memory just wasn't there and Arwen gave me an expression of something between amusement and total confusion. By the looks of it, she had her own questions.

But if this was a taste of what was to come after whatever Arwen and I were still to talk about then I couldn't be sure how things would go when Gabe and Dan returned and had questions of their own.

And as of yet, I hadn't even done anything.

I fanned my face with a napkin and then Karla was back, directing a question at Arwen.

"And this *Dan* guy, he's your boyfriend?"

She shook her head and swallowed a mouthful of toast. "No, no. We're just really great mates."

I liked them, well, most of them, but it was a relief when they cleared away their plates and we were able to watch them through the window as they crossed the road and plodded into the distance with huge backpacks slung over their shoulders.

I blew out air. "Shower and then we'll do the same."

Though not with them, only us.

THE GOTHIC QUARTER.

And had I been alone then I'm sure the buildings, plazas, markets, museums, the Roman walls, secluded medieval alleyways, a temple and even a Baroque church covered in shrapnel holes from an explosion during the civil war would have been a lot more bewitching in the moment. However, there was a problem.

Arwen was wearing a white plunge cropped shirt, treating me to a little more cleavage than yesterday, the lower edges of which were tied together to reveal her tight midriff and the jewel she wore in her belly button. As if that wasn't enough, she also wore the tiniest pair of denim shorts I'd ever seen, showcasing those Goddess pins whilst the white and light blue colours totally complemented her golden skin. It had to have been intentional, the little minx, and several times since leaving the hostel I'd caught her making sly knowing glances from the corner of her eye. Yes, it was intentional, she knew what she was doing and it was turning my head to mush. Not only was it hard to concentrate on the ancient buildings, stonework, arches and the rest, it was damned near impossible to take my eyes off her.

And I was far from the only one. The square was humming with tourists, most of whom were subtle about it but there were those less so, and I saw several people casually filming her on their phones.

"Don't you just love these little alleyways?" She asked in all seriousness as we walked around the narrow stone slabbed back passages of the Gothic Quarter, a labyrinth of winding streets and hidden squares with a complete absence of vehicles. Dress us in clothes from a bygone era and we could have been in some other age.

We emerged in Carrer del Bisbe with its fantastic Neogothic-style bridge that linked the Catalan regional government with the presidential residence and Arwen pulled out her phone that she'd somehow managed to squeeze into the pocket of those devilish shorts.

"Selfie?"

"Of course."

She held it in an outstretched arm whilst I shamelessly seized the opportunity to rub against her, threading my arm around her waist, experiencing the smoothness of her exposed flesh and pulling her close. She brought her left arm around to do the same and I felt her fingers sink into my hips through the skirt I was wearing, a complete thrill.

"Ok, ready?"

"Uh huh."

Our cheeks crushed together which forced a squashed smile from me, not my best photo but I reasoned that like me, she was trying to get more than close and every second, every graze of contact felt beyond description. It was certainly a different selfie to the one we'd taken in Carcassonne.

"Oh, no, we didn't get the bridge." She declared with mock dismay.

I gasped with similar pretence. "Oh damn it, best take another then."

She brought the camera back and, drunk in the moment, my hand innocently pressed flat against her right bum cheek.

She giggled, stuck it out for my enjoyment and then her free arm was back around my hip, pulling mine into hers.

I shook my head, "no, no, that pigeon's all blurry, better do another."

"Oh, well, if we absolutely must."

This time I casually slipped my hand inside her back pocket which, due to the lack of material, not to mention the substantial portions within, wasn't easy but I was more than willing to take a hit trying. If this was how it felt to be intoxicated with aching lust then I never wanted the feeling to end.

My name is Freya Argyle. I was supposed to be a dour Scot, descendent of old Highland gentry, raised on oats and lawn croquet, sensible to the point of being intolerable, I spend my nights studying, my entire life is planned and predicted.

Yet here I was, in Spain, cuddling up to the most beautiful *girl* I'd ever seen and I couldn't understand any of it.

We arrived on Las Ramblas, which according to the tourist brochure, was the most famous street in Barcelona. There were theatres, government buildings, the city hall, market stalls absolutely everywhere, so many flower baskets covering buildings, lampposts and even the ground that the place resembled a garden. At the far end, framed by the sea and visible from way back stood the Christopher Colombus monument, pointing west, atop a two hundred foot high plinth.

Though truthfully, it was all a haze. I knew it was all there, I just barely noticed any of it and neither did I much heed the thousands of locals and tourists and everything else that buzzed in our periphery. It was almost like Arwen and I existed in our own little world and nobody else was allowed in. There were shapes and blurs that moved and buzzed all around us, adding to the ambience as we plodded down Las Ramblas but if they noticed two young women, we didn't notice them.

Though this level of self-awareness comes at a price. My senses had heightened to such absurd levels and I was experiencing this moment with such unfamiliar clarity that my heart was pounding extra hard from some kind of natural counteraction to the vast quantity of dopamine my brain was synthesising. Every action has an equal and opposite reaction. It couldn't last forever but in the here and now, I most certainly was existing in some kind of higher place, almost like I was looking down at myself from above.

"We're shrouded in trees," Arwen stated to herself and I wondered if she was experiencing the same because, sure enough, we were. "I find they can turn even the loudest of streets into a haven for the soul." The backs of our fingers were brushing together as we plodded so lazily it'd take an hour to reach the monument. "And the birds that fly here for the summer to make this street their home ... don't you just wonder where it is they came from? And where they'll go next?" Our little fingers linked together. "Can't you hear them? I saw a parakeet earlier and up there I can see a crested tit." She was referring to the tree behind me but I didn't turn to look because we'd stopped and turned into each other, our flip flops making contact on the stone tiles, my knees literally quivering, our little fingers still entwined. "If you listen hard, you can make out the waves. Isn't that something, the way sound travels? Would you like to hold my hand?" She asked in the exact same casual tone of the birds and the trees and the waves, like it was nothing, that it wasn't taboo, that this next small step wasn't really monumental and life changing at all, that it was simply a natural progression for us, that it was the next logical stage in our relationship.

And in no way had it been a surprise, I'd known it was coming and nodded without hesitation. "Yes."

It was hardly a big leap forward to hold her hand from where we already were and our fingers seamlessly interlaced, though despite the relative ease of it all, I couldn't stop my knees from shaking and she felt it all the way up my fingertips.

"Are you nervous?"

"Yes," I whispered.

"Would you like to let go?"

"No."

Her smile broadened and the reality of being so close to Arwen and her unearthly beauty could only ever have made me tense, timid and shy like I'd never before experienced. But all these emotions were part of whatever this was, and I wouldn't have had it any other way because to remove the anxiety is to remove the thrill. And it was a thrill. And despite Arwen doing her best to make this gentle for me, I still knew there were implications not far ahead, major implications.

But in this moment, I would not think of that, of what was to come. I just wanted to enjoy the now.

Her hand was smaller than what I was used to, her fingers thinner. Her skin was certainly smoother too. But I'd never before experienced this kind of rush from the mere act of holding a person's hand - That was the main difference. Was it because Arwen was a girl or because the girl was Arwen? Or both? As we continued down Las Ramblas, my main preoccupation was, what next? And it was this unknown that provided the biggest thrill of them all.

"I love all these cute little market stalls." I knew I was speaking to take the attention away from the fact I was holding Arwen's hand, yet conversely, I didn't want to think about anything else. "The colours of all the apples and oranges look so much deeper in Spain. Awe, look at those." One stall was stacked with wooden animal carvings though, in truth, I wasn't really that interested.

Her hand squeezed mine. "Tell me, do you have any siblings?"

"Um, yes, a brother and a sister ... oh, look at that." I tugged her in the direction of one of those tapas bars, of which there were many, though this place had a huge window display of exquisite looking nibbles. "Arwen, it's snack time."

She cast me a glance from the corner of her eye but didn't argue and we approached the counter, filled a large plate with various tapas dishes, ordering coffees as well and found a table in an isolated corner.

"Have you seen this?" I selected a tiny hamburger, about the size of a two Euro coin. "It's adorable, I almost don't want to eat it." I crammed it down my mouth regardless. "Oh, are you any good at that?" I was referring to the five large prawns, whole; heads, tails, everything.

"Obviously," she smirked, "I'm Australian, you can bet I've had practice peeling these bad boys." She plucked one up and twisted its head off, peeled away the skin and slid off the tail, all within five seconds.

I slapped the table. "Wow." I shouldn't have been surprised she'd be good at that too.

"Pfft, try it." She pushed the dish toward me as she placed the prawn in her mouth. "It's so good."

I smiled with sympathy at the four little faces staring back. "Um, ok. Oh, bloody hell."

"It's easy, here." Evidently sensing my trepidation, she grabbed one at random and passed it to me. "Don't be afraid of it. Just twist its head off." She was right, of course. It was pathetic to wince at such a thing, given how much I loved meat and I was aware of the whole, *if you eat meat you should at least kill an animal once in your life* argument, just so I could experience all of its consequences and implications, yet all I had to do here was peel an already dead prawn. At least this little fishy had a full and happy life before it was caught, sigh.

I made a strange whimper as I held it in both hands, closed my eyes and began to twist, feeling it separate.

"There, now use your thumbs to prise apart the skin from beneath." She was reaching around me to offer instruction, her chin nestling delightfully on my shoulder and she hummed as I opened the skin from underneath. "Hmmm, good, well done, you got the legs as well, hmmm, how good is that."

I'd become more excited by the sounds she was making than by the prawn but wouldn't let on about that little perversion. "And the tail? Teach me."

Her hands, as I now discovered, were not there to give me pointers but instead to connect around my midriff and I was now locked in a cosy embrace, her chin still resting on my shoulder. Her voice descended to a groan directed softly into my ear. "Just pinch the tail and pull out the prawn."

My head swivelled to meet hers. "Like this?" And away it came.

"Like that."

I brought the prawn up and felt her jaw press lightly against my shoulder as she opened her mouth and began to chew whilst making delightful little humming sounds. It was so funny and I couldn't stop myself from giggling and I clasped my hands around hers, closed my eyes and simply melted into her embrace, only to let go when her tongue flicked out to lick my earlobe.

"Ewww, Arwen." I slapped her on the wrist and turned gently

towards her, her lips already waiting for mine and they connected as I inhaled the peach from her hair and her clutch around my belly tightened and we both opened out our hands to clasp each others' tight. It was an awkward position for my neck but I couldn't bring myself to shift from her envelopment, body, everything. It was the kiss I'd craved ever since Catalonia, only this time it was completely voluntary by me, by her, this was us, what we both wanted and I squeezed her fingers, felt her do the same as I hummed and gently rubbed my back against her breasts as she pressed them back against me.

My mobile phone blared from my bag, startling us both.

"How's that for timing." I heaved for breath, stroked her forearm, wanted to ignore the bothersome device but finally retrieved it from my clutch. "Oh…" it was Gabe and I felt a wave of guilt wash over me, something I was not in the frame of mind to consider right now. I knew it was coming and I'd have to deal with it eventually, just not now, I wanted today, just one day with Arwen, just to see. And shit, were they even now rambling Las Ramblas and the rest of the tourist spots in search of us? My heart sank, even as Arwen was holding onto me.

"Gabe?"

"Frey, I'm so sorry…"

"What?"

"Fucking gypsies!" He growled. "I tell you…"

"What," I shook my head, "Gabe, settle down and tell me what's happened now?"

"Fucking gypsies is what's happened. Can you fucking believe it but they're still there, outside, waiting for us to leave … bastards sure know how to hold a grudge and the police are less than useless. Apparently, they're too short-staffed to escort us safely back to the hostel, can you believe that? Told us they're not a fucking taxi service. Well fuck them, fuck the EU, and thank God for Brexit, is all I can say."

"Oh gosh, you must really have hurt that boy's fingers." I sighed and felt Arwen's vibrating chest stifling laughter. "Gabe, you've served your time, can't you just walk out?"

"No, we can't, weren't you listening? There's at least thirty of them just hanging around. Even Mikhail and Bogdan are refusing to leave without an escort."

"Um, who?"

"The Russians, the Russians. I won't be long, there's another phone down the hallway." The last bit sounded distant. "Listen, Freya, you and Arwen, do your thing, again, and I'm sorry. I'll make it up to you, I promise. Down the fucking hallway." He shouted.

"Gabe!"

"They've promised that if those walking dysgenics are still loitering around in the morning then they'll designate someone to drive us back, so we're *definitely* released tomorrow, first thing. I'm sorry, Doctor, I love you."

"But..." the line cut out and an involuntary exhalation left my mouth, leaving me somewhat stunned.

"Now, there's a side to Gabe I could grow to like." Arwen absolutely burst into hysterics and I slapped her on the arm. "Oh, shucks. What shall we do without them?"

"Arwen?" I gaped. "You are terrible."

She shrugged, didn't seem disappointed in the slightest. "It's a tragedy. How shall we occupy ourselves?" And at that she absolutely squeezed my thigh, sending a wonderful shiver all the way up my spine to culminate in my shoulders. And she felt it too and smirked with triumph. Oh, the effect this girl had on me and she was barely even trying, of that I was sure.

I shifted to a more comfortable position and cupped her face in my hands, bringing my lips to meet hers. She leaned into me and her hands were in my hair as our breathing increased in intensity and our tongues clashed. I was overwhelmed with the desire to explore her incredible body, to slip a hand inside her plunge shirt and cup a breast but, suddenly aware of a couple entering with their three young children and not wanting to get too touchy-feely in public, I pulled away, devastatingly hard as it was. Living an uncharacteristically dangerous life I may now apparently be doing but deep down I was still that dour Scot and if I'd feared Arwen might have been offended, I needn't have worried, she understood. I was new to this. I had no clue what was happening.

"I think I need some fresh air," I groaned into her ear and, taking her hand, we left to emerge back onto Las Ramblas.

I wasn't sure how long we'd been inside but the change in heat was evident and Arwen pulled me over to the right and into the shade to continue toward the monument that loomed ahead. Some shops had closed for the siesta and the throng of people had diminished though there were plenty of gelato places still open and we stopped to fill our tanks, Arwen going for cherry, whilst I made a point of choosing stracciatella. We sat on a shaded bench to enjoy them, happily sharing each other's flavour whilst she spoke so casually about all the places she still wanted to see.

It was impressive, that such a young girl could arrive in Europe, all alone and with nothing but a long list with no logical order to go by, no idea of how she would get from one place to the next other than by using her charm and loveliness to hitch rides with fellow travellers. Such was the girl's confidence that clearly, a minor thing like not having a plan had never fazed her. My mind was mathematical and scientific whilst hers was artistic. I like having at least some idea of what's happening today, tomorrow, next week, ten years from now. It was a major difference in our personalities, the way we thought and how we viewed the world. Yet here we were, somehow together, getting along so well, feeding each other ice cream, holding hands, exchanging saliva. No, she was not fazed and never had been intimidated, not by being alone on the other side of the world and certainly not by me.

I was also amazed by just how casual Arwen could be. Here we were, two girls, caressing, fondling, getting close for the first time and whilst I was anxious and so many other things I had yet to come to terms with, she was so relaxed. I knew she was Australian, true, and they had a reputation for being unflappable but there had to be more to it and I just couldn't hold my questions back any longer.

"I'm not your first am I?" I asked as we arrived at the giant Colombus monument. "I mean, woman, I'm not your first woman ... not that we've even done anything yet ... and not that I'm taking it for granted that we're going to do anything but you get the idea ... ugh, kill me now."

She stopped, opened out her arms and gave me a look that suggested I was adorable, "cuddle me this minute."

Which I was, adorable and vulnerable, like a virgin suffering badly through her first major crush, which happened to be for an older, far more experienced friend. I was used to being in control, always in control, knowing what was expected, how to please him, how to handle him. Now, I was so far out of my depth it was terrifying. Yet I couldn't stop even if I wanted, which I didn't. And as I lost all control over my feet and fell into her open arms, peeping into her big, warm blue eyes as I did, I knew just why I couldn't stop. It was different, it was exciting, it was thrilling and yes, it most certainly was terrifying.

"You want to know my sex story, don't you?" And she was so soul-destroyingly beautiful too, which kind of helped.

I nodded into her shoulder and felt suddenly insecure for what she might say. Was she into guys as well as girls or just girls? Or, like me, had she assumed she was only into guys? Somehow I doubted I was *that* great, to turn her over to the dark side just because we kissed by a campfire. Nope, I wouldn't be taking credit for that one. Ok, just shut up and listen. "What I'd like to know is, have you always been into women?" My voice came out muffled against her neck.

She released me from her squeeze, took my hand and we continued the short distance towards the statue, coming to lean against the giant plinth. "You're looking at me like I have some major secret to divulge. Really, it's not that interesting." Boring was good and her words soothed me some.

"But it's interesting to me." Truth is I was almost giddy for info on this girl and found myself turned into her at a right angle, my brain blotting out the pigeons and pedestrians and tour buses lest I miss any small detail.

She leaned into me and slipped her hand between the plinth and my hip, concealed to the world as she whispered into my ear. "Of course, I love women." And I distinctly felt a squeeze of buttock.

"Well, duur, like I couldn't already tell from the way you kiss me." My hand was resting between my abdomen and the indentation of her midriff and was holding onto the knot she'd tied at the base her shirt.

"You know, the way you kiss *me*, it's enough to think you were only ever interested in women."

Or one woman in particular. Whatever my situation might be, it was clearly more complicated than the lightness she was making of it.

She shrugged, "I dunno really, I've never given myself any labels and never would, I don't care for them. To call myself a *lesbian* would be to overly simplify what I am and would be expected to conform to. The truth is, I don't give it a great deal of thought. I am attracted to who I am attracted to."

"As I'm beginning to find out for myself." I squeaked, only now realising my breasts were crushing against her arm.

"I've always felt women were beautiful, right from the time I was a child and I'd watch them dance and do incredible things with their bodies. So, if you were expecting any major life-changing moment when I suddenly saw everything with clarity, then I'm sorry, I don't have it. It's always been there. And of course, I will admit, I've had relationships with men too. Why should I rule out fifty percent of humanity just because of their gender? And that works both ways." She sighed heavily. "The problem is, I've never managed to find that same level of connection with men as I have with women. Honestly, for whatever reason, I turn their brains to mush."

I giggled, totally loving her swagger and crushed harder against her. "Oh, I have no idea why that might be."

She grinned, "if I were being honest, I wouldn't completely rule out being with another man in the future but when my head is turned by a beautiful looking person, ninety percent of the time, it's a woman. So sue me. And if you were thinking I've bedded everything under the sun then I'm sorry but you're gonna be disappointed." She nodded and I felt the relief flow over me. "So, there you are."

What had I expected? That a girl who'd toured the world with a company of fit, toned and talented dancers had engaged in endless meaningless sexual encounters? I was relieved to discover my fears had proved unfounded. Doubtless, she'd had opportunities, she looked like *that*, after all, but I was ecstatic to learn she was better than that, as if I hadn't already discovered by how I'd previously underestimated her.

It was a two-mile walk to La Sagrada Familia, which we began at our usual almost none moving pace as we held hands and simply enjoyed being alone with each other. We had to come back on ourselves to get there and eventually it became clear that during the morning, we'd missed Barcelona's most famous attraction by only two blocks, which meant even more walking to get back to the centre and then another reversal would be required to return to the hostel. The perils of not having a plan, à la Arwen, not that I cared one bit because it gave us additional time to enjoy the walk, the beautiful weather and each other.

"It's not just the brains of men you turn to mush," I said, risking the triggering of her ego by alluding to her earlier crack.

Her eyes flicked up, "you're talking about Floor?" She got it. "Yep, I see what you mean." Oh, the arrogance but I loved it.

"Arwen, she's gorgeous." A bit of a predator, yes, but definitely gorgeous and certainly with her own unique style that made her quite the interesting specimen.

She was quick to allay my concerns. "She's attractive, I won't lie but she's nothing next to you." She made a delightful deep purring sound as she leaned in and kissed my neck, somehow managing to awaken some dormant spot and causing my entire upper body to lose itself in spasm. She grinned in triumph and all I could think was that if she could literally turn me into a quivering wreck from such small acts of intimacy then what was she capable of when unleashed in the bedroom? It didn't bear thinking about and neither was I certain I could even handle her.

"Arwen..." I trailed off after recovering. What was there to say?

She bumped hips and squeezed my hand. "Where were we? Oh yeah, she's nothing compared to you and besides, in case you hadn't noticed, she's presently sleeping with Luuk and God only knows what else, which is hardly attractive and to top it all off, that girl was literally throwing herself at me." She rolled her eyes at the sky. "Some women, honestly, it's not a turn on when it's that easy."

Was that why she was interested in me, because she saw me as a challenge? During our first few encounters, I wasn't exactly falling at her feet and there was Gabe too, to throw that extra sporting element her way. I was realistic and aware Arwen was out of my league, there had to be some reason she was into me, at least for the moment, when there were girls like Floor around literally throwing themselves at her. I knew I was just being insecure but the fears were there regardless, I had a history of not giving Arwen the benefit of the doubt and felt ashamed when I should have been exhilarated. Of course, a large part of all this was likely due to that other factor - Gabe.

I couldn't help it. No matter how much I tried to keep it out, he was always there in the back of my mind and whilst, for the present at least, a large part of me wanted to explore what was happening with Arwen, to see what it was like, to ravage her body, to have her ravage me, there was always that other part that hoped Gabe would appear, to stop this now before it got out of hand. I'd already crossed more than one line, I knew that. Arwen and I had kissed, more than kissed, we were getting close and comfortable and it could only inevitably lead to one place. But more than what had already occurred physically between us, we were also developing a deep connection and the further that went, the less I would begin to feel for Gabe and that was the thing that scared me the most.

"Um, Frey?"

"Huh?"

She frowned at me. "What the heck are you thinking about?" And then she saw the look in my eyes and her mouth turned down, almost like she'd made a good guess and got it right but didn't mention it, just stepped back and jerked a thumb over her shoulder. "It's just that..."

I looked up and there, looming behind her was La Sagrada Familia. How the fuck had I missed that? My eyes widened, my lips parted and the breath hitched in my throat. "Oh, my..."

"Are you sure you're ok?" Her back was turned to the wonder so she could concentrate on me, her hand on my arm. "Freya, we're here. Back to planet earth."

I shook it off, blinked and beheld what had to be the most beautiful building in the entire world. Anything less and I could not have pulled my eyes away from the girl. How could it be described? Other than that the angels had decided to spend one hundred and fifty years painstakingly crafting, inch by inch, stone by stone, their masterpiece, a gift to the world, for no reason other than that they could. The angels were showing off, for sure.

Arwen and I stood back, in silent contemplation for a long time, as we perched against a wall and held hands. I noted that thus far, it was the one place we'd been able to be together, alone, and inconspicuous, invisible to prying eyes. It was almost certainly my paranoia, mixed with heightened senses that made me assume we were always being watched, two attractive young women getting close, whilst my boyfriend, and possibly others, were not too far away. I was not usually the type to seek out danger or any type of discomfort but I'd be lying if I was to say there was not a certain element of perverse enjoyment to it all, and that I couldn't explain. The tourists swarming around were entranced with the building's magnificence, as were we, but I was also aware of the high probability of being spotted cosying up with Arwen by one of our foreign friends.

I tugged her hand. "Let's get dinner."

———

"I CAN'T WAIT to see them in their orange jumpsuits." The shameless girl sipped on her white wine.

"Arwen, you are intolerable." Yet still, I hated that the table was so large that all we could do was hold hands from across the candlelight.

She stroked my little finger with hers. "I will make jokes for as long as I'm so hungry and the longer I wait the more vicious they become." She snorted, evidently struggling to suppress the laughter. "From my understanding, they have form here, don't they?"

I giggled in turn and nodded. "I can confirm they've previously served time together and for pretty much the same offence."

"Those two hardened felons. Well, as they say, that's how it starts. Today they're getting into fights and tomorrow, Doctor Gabe's carjacking trucks and making cross-border gun runs."

I slapped her on the wrist, or rather, I tried but she caught my hand. "You're trying to wind me up, aren't you." It was a struggle to stifle the laughter.

In response, she wiggled her eyebrows before leaning forwards just enough to expose some more cleavage.

I made a strange exhaling noise as my eyes feasted on them. "Arwen..." the little tease. She was trouble, oh, how she was trouble.

She sat back with a smug expression, she knew it, the little minx, and our hands slipped apart, freeing mine to imbibe more wine, which I needed.

The seafood paella arrived in a giant pan, still sizzling from the flame. The smells, the colours, the way it all looked, it wouldn't last long given we were both so hungry after a long day exploring. There were mussels, calamari rings, salmon, what had to be octopus and of course, more prawns, half of which I spooned onto my plate.

"Are you sure you can handle them, Doctor?"

I banged my fork against the table in acknowledgement of her jibe. "I'll have you know, it was only this lunchtime that you taught me." I knew I'd inevitably eat heads and legs, ugh but I felt the urge to make some sort of come back. "Are you sure you've got enough there?"

She was piling rice onto her plate, a total overload of carbs. "Meh."

"If you're not careful you'll pop right out of those shorts and I'll have to carry you home." A scenario that appealed greatly.

She stopped mid shovel and looked as shocked as I'd yet seen her, I finally managed it, and she went for her clutch and pulled out Alejandro's card. "You know, I still have this."

"I'm sorry, sorry, sorry." I rushed to say, wanting to reach over, to take it, to feed it to the pigeons that were strutting about my feet.

We were in one of those outdoor restaurants that were

everywhere in this city, our table being on an old cobbled street tucked away somewhere in the Old Town and it was warm, pleasant and, but for the other diners, peaceful. There were several restaurants, all small family owned places that lined the cobbles and not far down the street a violinist had just set up and started playing.

Over the flickering candle, I gazed at Arwen, the mood phasing from jokey to something else. "You were supposed to be meeting with him for dinner tonight."

She returned my gaze and spoke softly. "Looks like I had a better offer."

Something danced inside of me. "Last night, you asked if I wanted you to tear it up..."

She was turning the card between her fingers. "And you told me not to."

"Does that offer still stand?"

She raised the card to the candle, held its corner to the flame and I watched as it slowly began to burn before being discarded without ceremony into the ice bucket. Her face remained neutral, she didn't give a shit.

I felt a fresh wave of relief and something else I just couldn't explain, a beautiful feeling, almost like being reborn. The paella tasted so good but then, in that moment, anything would have tasted amazing and I didn't care if my prawn peeling was so bad that I ate legs and God only knew what else.

"Freya, I want you to tell me about your family."

I instinctively looked away, down, up, back to the floor and scratched my ear. "How's your paella?"

There was the clatter of knife on table and then her hand was grabbing onto my wrist. "Freya, I want you to tell me about your family."

I flopped back into the seat and retracted my hand as my arms dangled by my sides. "Arwen, I'm not sure I..."

"You have a brother and a sister," she said as a matter of fact, "they're your family and I want to know about them."

How did she know? How could she see so deep inside of me? I gulped wine and contemplated whether there was any way out of it, or maybe I wanted her to know, to know everything about me.

"Your brother?" She asked so calmly, our food ignored for now.

I exhaled and smiled warmly at the thought of Lachlan, who I hardly got to see these days. His red freckly cheeks and constant smile, his strong hugs and love for all living things. "Yes. I have a brother. He's called Lachlan and I love him very much." I was playing with my bread, pulling out wads from the roll, balling them up and squeezing them in my fingers, looking down, feeling her eyes on the crown of my head. "Lachlan ... Lachlan's been in a wheelchair ever since the age of nine." My voice wavered and I glanced back up to find Arwen's reassuring eyes.

"What happened?"

I sighed as a sheen fell over my vision. "It was snowing, my mother lost control of the car, skidded off the road and into a wall." I shrugged, felt hopeless, and even though I'd long since accepted everything, it never made telling the story easier, which was why I was happy few people ever asked.

"Freya, I'm so sorry." The sheen was mirrored in her own eyes.

"I barely remember him not being in a wheelchair, possibly a few vague memories running up the stairs but that's about it."

And then I went on to explain the rest. How my brother had no use of his lower body, partial damage to the brain and how it had almost certainly triggered my desire to study medicine. "It turned into a thing I'd always say to him, to make him happy, that I would one day become a doctor and help him."

She applied pressure to my hand. "You made a promise to him?"

"More than a promise, it was a pledge and so far I've stuck to it and I will continue to fulfil it."

She nodded, "I know you will."

I continued to explain how my mother had blamed herself for the accident because she'd not ensured he was wearing his seatbelt, how she'd fallen into a depression, month after month of lying in bed, aimlessly wandering around the estate grounds, getting drunk in bars, gambling at the casino, not eating, creeping outside at night onto the snowy grounds in her dressing gown and walking into the pond, my dad finding her the next morning.

Arwen brought her chair around the side of the table so that we were now positioned next to each other and she grabbed ahold of my forearms. "I can't imagine losing my mother like that at such a young age, I'm so sorry." She made long soothing strokes up and down the length of my arm and I couldn't help but feel incredibly close to her.

"I was three. My sister, on the other hand, was six, so naturally, she took it a lot harder than I did."

"What's your sister's name?"

I took a breath. "She's called Lizzie."

She sensed my anguish from saying her name. "There's more, isn't there?"

I nodded and dabbed at my eyes with the edge of the tablecloth.

"Here." She rustled through her clutch and within a second there was a pack of tissues in my hand.

"Thanks." I sniffed, wiped my eyes and blew my nose. "Oh, Arwen, I still remember the day. I was fifteen and boarding at Fettes College when I came back to Inverness for the holidays, my dad was sitting on the stairs, stern-faced, and announced that I was now his only daughter, that the ungrateful one was no longer a part of the family and that it was now only the three of us."

"Oh, good gosh, Freya, that's terrible." Her grip on my forearms tightened and it felt so comforting. "Why? What did she do?"

I made an involuntary exhalation that came out almost as a bark. "Only my dad knows for sure and he's never said. When I pestered him for answers he shouted something about marrying someone and running away."

"Really, where?"

"Gibraltar."

Her eyes jerked up and I knew she was trying to think where it was. "Spain?"

"Technically not." And I abruptly left it at that, lest she suggested doing something stupid, like finding her. "I've not seen her in eight..." I couldn't complete the sentence and broke down in palpitations.

Arwen brought her seat as close as it could get and pulled me into her breast as I heaved and sobbed against her, in public, which was not me at all.

"I never even got to say ... goodbye ... I just ... miss her so much." It was a subject I'd never felt able to discuss with Gabe, indeed, he'd intentionally avoided it.

She made soothing sounds and I felt her hands tenderly rubbing my back as my nose nuzzled against the upper portion of her breast, her scent causing an inebriation even deeper than the wine. "I'm glad you told me," she whispered, "and you know I'm here if you ever need me for anything, anything at all."

"I know that." And I pulled myself away, to look into her big blue eyes, and as they fixed on mine, I'd never felt closer to any other person as I did to her in that moment. In that moment, I wanted nothing other than to be close with her, closer than I'd ever been with anyone else.

Indeed, to be with Arwen, to have her be with you, was to be the only person who ever mattered, or existed, such was her attentiveness and warmth and I wondered where such a gift came from. Maybe it was solely down to the deep connection developing between us? All I knew was that if I'd previously had doubts, there was only the one remaining now. And it was that one doubt that stopped me from taking her there and then, here and now.

And then she astounded me by proving absolutely everything.

"You're holding back because of Gabe." She spoke with restraint, which I could see was taking a lot of willpower, because her hands were even now on the verge of becoming indecent, rubbing my waist, ribcage, arms, as everything else in the vicinity, wherever we were, evaporated into nothingness.

I moaned into her neck. "How do you do it? Arwen, I just wish..." I trailed off, hopeless, what could I do? I wasn't *that* girl. I was supposed to be decent.

"Freya, babes, I think you're the most beautiful girl I've ever seen." Her words were like sonnets from the angels. "Believe me, I'd like nothing more than to take you back to our room and just see what happens but I'm not the one tied down. Listen," and she placed her palm flat on the inside of my thigh and I wanted to melt into her, "it's your call. I'm not putting any pressure on you, ever. I'm perfectly happy to be your friend for life." And then she pulled away, her hand, her body, and in that awful second I'd never felt so lost, so forlorn, so hopeless that my arms reached out of their own accord and pulled her back, I wanted, needed her hand on the inside of my thigh, and that was just for starters.

I heaved for breath and groaned into her ear. "Then let's see what happens."

It was a miracle the waiter happened to be approaching because I didn't think either of us could restrain ourselves much longer.

He noticed the half-finished meal. "Everything ok with your dinner?"

"La cuenta, por favor." Arwen spoke, not taking her eyes from me.

"Si," and he produced the bill, Arwen and I both taking out more than enough money and handing it over, standing on wobbly legs and leaving without waiting for whatever change was due.

My hand had never left hers and now we strode down the narrow cobbled alley, the slick discharge from between my legs announcing its presence, my belly vibrating with frustration and exhilaration both. Tables from all the restaurants were arranged in such a way that there was small room between them and the medieval walls, made yet more cramped by the uncountable pedestrians and it was irritating having to stop and wait for endless lines to file past. We were at least a forty-five-minute walk from the hostel and by the end I'd be ready to burst.

"That's some grip you have." She had to speak up through the throng. "I'm not going anywhere, not for anything."

"Sorry," I turned around and gave her my best apologetic glance, "I'm not sorry really. This is going to be the hardest walk of my life." I was also aware that for a change, I was leading her, and I had to look back over my shoulder to hear what she was saying.

She didn't say anything but instead pulled a face and leaned forwards, exposing that damned cleavage and suddenly it was as though my underwear had been put through the wash, they were that damp and bordering on becoming uncomfortable.

"Stop that, you," I demanded, even though I loved it, I think.

There was an alley that I suspected led to Las Ramblas and freedom, or at least a fast road back home but more importantly, it was free from the crowds and so I tugged on her arm and dragged her down it. Of course, there was another reason this dark passage was so appealing.

I spun around and grabbed her by the hips, pulling them into mine with a sudden force. She was probably expecting it, which was why her hands were already clasping my buttocks and she didn't wait to bring her lips to mine as they pressed together with a rare intensity and passion, our mouths open, tongues clashing, the noise from the crowds a distant murmur. I slid my hands around her back and seized those generous buns, pulled them into me and felt the muscle harden as she clenched them and our kiss broke off as we fell against each other in hysterics.

I put my hand on the wall for balance and shook my head. "Christ, I think this is going to be an experience unlike any other."

"Don't you know it." And she probed for my neck, finding a

special spot below my earlobe with her tongue and I almost lost all sentience, thank God for the wall, as my legs almost collapsed beneath me.

I had to push her away, though even that was difficult. "Arwen ... we need ... home ... so far."

Uber!

I remembered that thing and managed to find the capacity to pull out my phone and access the app.

"Oh, what the fuck?" No Uber in the area, or all of Spain for that matter. "Fuck! Get with it, damn country."

She giggled and forced herself back onto me.

"You're really not helping." I panted, my feeble hand failing miserably at pushing her away, succumbing instead and pulling her close. "Need taxi." My squashed voice tried to say into her mouth and her face nodded against mine.

Yet it was difficult to pull myself from her and I instead surrendered for several more minutes, my hands devouring her boobs through her plunge shirt, the knot that would free them only inches below, it was the first time in my life I'd so much as made contact with another girl's breasts and they felt so large and heavy in my small feminine hands. It was also the first time another girl had so much as touched mine and she now squeezed them in a way that felt different to how I'd become familiar. Her hands were smaller, which made me feel fuller, and she was gentler, though I suspected that was because she was still teasing me.

Something scuffed from up the alley and a young couple, similarly lost in themselves, were making slow progress towards us, just as well really.

"Come." I tugged her away and tasted blood faintly on my lips.

She interlaced our fingers. "Back to full speed ahead, huh? Man, you have a powerful kiss."

"Not usually," I muttered as we passed the couple and shortly after emerged on Las Ramblas where the crowds were again thick but at least I knew where we were, kind of.

A row of taxis were lined up where the pedestrian zone ended and I'd never been so relieved to see the distinctive black and yellow Barcelona design. I dragged the girl up to the nearest one, yanked open the door and bundled her inside.

"Oh, for the love of..." she stared open-mouthed as I slinked in after her, closed the door and leaned between the seats to speak to the driver.

"Straight to the ... oh fuck." I turned back to the girl with an expression of horror. "Where are we staying?"

She fell sideways and banged her head on the window, her barking laughter deafening within the taxi's confines. "Serves you right for being so horny."

I slapped her on the thigh. "Pray he doesn't understand you and you're hardly helping." I turned back to the driver, an elderly Spanish guy. "It's a large hostel somewhere after La Sagrada Família, if that helps? Oh, and it has a big glass door."

He shrugged and began running through a list of places he knew by heart, none of them sounding familiar until he said the name Rock Palace, I shouted in the affirmative and then we were finally moving.

Except, as it transpired, even at night, Barcelona barely moves and we immediately hit traffic. By this point I was biting my lip, my clenched fist trembling out of sheer frustration, trying to remain as decent as possible, even as Arwen began tickling the inside of my thigh with her thumb, taking advantage and knowing I was not the kind of girl who could react in the present company.

I continued to glare straight ahead and hissed. "You're dead for this."

"Uh huh, and what else are you going to do to me?" She breathed hotly into my ear and I could only close my eyes, count to one hundred and think of Scottish Highland Cattle, the cutest of all the world's cattle, with their horns and the way their hair fell over their eyes. We had them on the estate and I used to love sketching them when I was a child, the beautiful docile beasts. "Are you thinking how it will feel when I have you naked in our room?" Make that two hundred, stupid traffic, and a large group on a stag party sang as they crossed the road in front of us, one maniac hunching over our bonnet to sing a chorus of some song I couldn't decipher before running to catch up with his mates. "How about when I'm teasing your wet folds with my fingertips?" Three hundred, and I shivered, the car moved at a pace I could probably outrun, indeed, two night joggers were gaining on us beneath the streetlights and they had to swerve out the path of an elderly woman with a dog. Her hand was moving further up the inside of my leg, which was exactly where I needed it, just not in the back of a taxi cab and I pressed my hand down atop of hers to prevent it from further exploration, about the hardest damned thing I ever had to do. "You're wet for me, aren't you?" Her breath was so hot in my ear and she hummed, shifted in the seat so that the leather squeaked.

I clamped my eyes shut, thought of that class we took on medical ethics and how I'd very nearly fallen asleep.

Her hand made another playful push north, forcing me to press down even harder and when that proved futile, I took her hand and placed it back in her own lap but then the fingers in my armpits began, interrupting my previous thoughts on the case for and against euthanasia, of all things to be thinking of now, and instead I clammed up and fell into her, furious yet laughing.

I'd never found another human being to be quite so irritating, majestic, annoying and exhilarating all at the same time and she was absolutely loving it. I suppose I was myself, on some levels, but for a girl who had absolutely no clue what I was supposed to be doing once we actually got back, I was sure in a hurry to get there.

There was gridlock again as we approached La Sagrada Familia but even I could find the way back from here. "Keep the change." I had the money ready in my hand and he looked at me with a bushy eyebrow raised obscenely high on his head.

Arwen translated and he nodded and then I shoved the door open, grabbed the girl by the wrist and tugged her out onto the pavement from where she stood, feet and hands together, the latter clasped beneath her chin as she gave me a goody-goody expression.

"Ah, back to being coy and submissive now, are you?" I asked in astonishment, secretly loving every second, "don't think you can fool me after that display, you want it just as much as I do, if not more." No, I doubted that was true.

She blinked and her eyelashes never looked so long, her face so innocent or her voice so sweet. "Want what as much as you? I thought we were going back to drink cocoa and tell ghost stories."

I thrashed my arm into the air. "Why are we still standing here?" Especially when the hostel was only a couple of minutes away.

She shrugged and we both laughed, again linked our fingers and began at a pace toward the Rock Palace Hostel, which was now mercifully in sight. We both ran the final stretch, shouted at a group leaving to hold the door open so I wouldn't have to waste time finding my keycard then we were through the door and feeling the beautiful chill of the air conditioning on our skin, repeatedly pressing the button for the lift and torturously waiting for the bloody thing to arrive.

I caught her eye from across the few inches of air separating us, a knowing look emanating from hers, of what we were about to do, a mutual understanding. But what could she see in mine? Excitement, elation, outright fear? Everything up to this point had happened so gradually it was hard to pinpoint a moment that had profoundly changed our relationship. But what was about to happen in our room...

It was about to happen.

And it *would* change things.

It was not too late to back out but one look at her reminded me of why I had no intention of doing so. No, I wanted to experience this, whatever *this* was, with her, Arwen. No other girl, no other person, just her.

Evidently, having sensed my change in mood, she remained in contemplative silence as we entered the lift, the only contact our hands, the door closed and we began moving up. My heart thudded hard as the door opened and we began the short walk to our room and I noticed how neither of us had the keycard ready.

"Oh, one moment." I delved into my clutch and brought it out, slid it through the mechanism, saw the green light, heard the satisfying buzz and pushed the door open.

The room was large with only the two of us present and I stepped over to the window to close the curtains, taking a breath and a moment for myself before turning slowly around, tucking a wad of red behind my ear and beholding the Goddess standing watching me.

"It's ok, just let me take care of you."

I nodded and croaked. "Ok. Thanks." And I'd never felt so vulnerable yet so safe, which was absurd.

She was still a few steps away and her hand slowly moved down towards the knot, her eyes never leaving mine as she gently pulled at the ends and the sides of the shirt separated. The parts that had been rolled up and made into the knot were creased and she removed one arm from the sleeve followed by the other before discarding the shirt to the floor.

She was magnificent, truly a dancer's figure, a lifetime of training sculpting the body she possessed as she grinned, so confident, in only those damned denim shorts and white bra, which made her breasts appear even larger and fuller than they had on the beach when she was wearing a bikini top.

My knees were actually shaking and I had to take a half step back, to where my bed offered stability, to ensure I wouldn't buckle under my own weight and God only knew how perverted and deranged I must have looked. Ok, breathe and get a grip.

She began to dance, just gently swaying her hips to some tune she was humming, and even though she was barely trying, she was still completely captivating. Her hands moved up behind her back and when she turned around I could see her fingers working the bra clasp, it unhooked, she unthreaded her arms one by one even as she continued swinging her hips, the bra was flung over her head to land somewhere close, she inched back so that the peach and Aloe Vera grew gradually stronger and then turned slowly around.

I let out an unconscious audible exhalation as my eyes were drawn to that spot where those deep undersides met her ribcage, which in anatomy, we call the inframammary fold, though why I'd be thinking that now just went to show how mushed my head was.

She shimmied closer, grabbed my hands and pulled them over her breasts. "Yeah, see, there it is, babe, I know you've been wanting this all day." I just loved her confidence and her eyes closed as she did some belly dance thing, slowly inching nearer and closing the angle at my elbow.

Meanwhile, I'd lost most cognitive function. She was large, very large and my small feminine hands could never hope to seize the lot, not that I didn't try and enjoy failing and it was a thrill like I'd never experienced to feel the heavy weight of a beautiful woman's breasts in my grasp and I continued fondling and caressing and playing and feasting until her body was pressing so tight against me there was no room for further manoeuvre.

That was when she physically removed my perverted hands, "I think you've had enough fun with those … for a short while, at least," and pressed her lips to mine and we locked in a passionate embrace for time unknown whilst my hands had to settle for exploring the smoothness of her back, squeezing her buttocks and becoming lost in her hair.

Throughout, I was fully aware that my entire body trembled and she must have felt it too but I wouldn't have changed any of it. Yes, I was anxious and so nervous but that was such a big part of what was making this event so arousing and then I kicked off my flip flops.

Our breasts had been crushing together and she leaned back an inch to slip a hand between us and I trembled for a different reason as I felt her small hand enclose around my breast to begin kneading in earnest.

"I love these, you have the perkiest breasts." She whispered into my ear and then her hands were moving down to the hems of my dress. Instinctively, I shifted to help remove it but she shook her head. "Hey, I said I'm gonna take care of you."

I nodded, "ok," and then she was slowly lifting the dress over my head and I saw her in a haze of yellow, there was the distinct smell of static and then she returned to beautiful clarity once more.

Her gaze immediately lowered and she wasted no time in reaching around to unhook my bra. I felt the sweet release of tension and as she leaned back, I held my arms out to enable her to remove the garment.

My arms instinctively wanted to pull back in, to clam up, I was wearing only a damp pair of underwear, after all, but all I needed was one look from her to be reassured that she more than liked what she saw.

She stepped back to admire me and her pupils noticeably dilated as she bit her bottom lip but she couldn't stay away for long because she came forth again and we locked in another embrace of passionate kisses, our breathing hot and intense, my hands gripping her tiny waist, hers lost in my hair.

We pulled away to breathe and I could only look down to marvel at the sight of our contrasting skin tones, my pale freckly Scottishness against her golden Ozzy tan as our breasts smushed together. She had small areolas, as did I, and both our nipples were hard and erect. I knew I wasn't as womanly as Arwen but from how she was soon back on my breasts, I figured there were no complaints.

She placed a hand behind my back, "lie down," and gently guided me to the bed, the other never leaving my breast and as I manoeuvred down, she came with me.

To witness her boobs hanging over my eyes as she took position was a million times better than any sight I'd so far witnessed this trip and as she came to rest on her elbows, my breasts were flattened out, whereas hers were plump, round and felt heavy as they came to settle over mine.

Our lips connected, slow at first then fast and with extreme verve but always with our tongues tangling with the other. One of my hands was lost in her hair, clutching chunks of blonde or else winding a braid around my fingers, the other had somehow found its way inside the back pocket of her shorts. Meanwhile, her hand was still devouring my breast whilst the other, only now, was beginning its slow descent down my body as it nestled between us, ribs, abdomen and finally, the outside of my underwear.

"Wow, you are really wet." She panted as I caught the fire in her eyes.

I heaved, "it's all you ... you," I gave up and then jerked uncontrollably because her fingers, through the thin fabric, had glanced off my clitoris.

She grinned devilishly, "are you sure you really want this because once I go in, I ain't coming out again."

I'd started nodding before she'd even finished speaking and then her mouth was back beside my ear.

"Just relax, Frey, and I promise you an experience you'll never forget. I've got you." Her breath, her words were so hot and I never doubted she *had me*, I trusted her entirely. "Close your eyes."

I obeyed and there was the creaking of bedsprings as she rolled to the side, something rustled, a zipper and the sound of friction, which had to have been her pulling off those damned hindering shorts. Then her arm slid between my head and the mattress and her lips were back on mine. I could tell she was lying on her side and then her thigh moved across my abdomen and I was correct, she had removed everything and I was powerless to prevent my hand from sliding down and clutching her exposed buttock. She began gently thrusting her hips into me as she squeezed my breast harder and worked her kisses around my neck.

On cue, my body went into spasm and then I heard the ocean as my earlobe disappeared inside her mouth and I was only prevented from clamming up entirely due to the weight of her thigh across my body.

I could tell she was smiling into the crevice between my neck and shoulder, where her mouth came to rest as her hand searched down my body until it slipped inside the tight elastic of my underwear, over that thin strip of red and then I bucked when, for the first time in my life, another woman made contact with my most sensitive spot.

She made soothing sounds, "you're ok," and then she was back, her two fingers slipping across, around, up and down my knot but always gentle. My heart pounded so hard, I swallowed excess saliva, my breathing increased, she applied more pressure and said something about not believing how wet I was, which was undoubtedly true. No other person had ever succeeded in bringing me to climax, I often struggled with that task myself and indeed, my last attempt had been interrupted by the very girl who was even now on the brink of making me explode. She'd seemed so confident, I'd had my doubts it was even possible, but fuck, there was most definitely something building inside of me, my belly twisting, brown swirly patterns forming in the darkness, yet more saliva with an added tint of something salty. She knew I was close and began thrusting her pelvis harder into me, no, she wasn't thrusting, but rubbing herself against my hip and she confirmed what she was doing by letting out a loud gasp right next to my ear.

I opened my eyes to find her already gazing at me, her cheeks and skin at the bridge of her nose flushed the sort of deep red one wouldn't think possible for a blonde and then she winked.

"I'm sure you don't mind me getting some too, cheers for the help." She stifled my laughter by pressing her lips against mine, her hips began to pulse, her thrusts so hard I thought she'd push through me.

And then I felt it brewing from the pit of my stomach like a ball of fire that kept growing. She sensed it too and pushed her mouth hard against my neck, my hips thrust up and she pressed down harder, faster and then her thigh was squeezing against me as we both exploded as one, gasping for air, our sweat running hot and cold both, stars and sparkles flashing in our vision, her arm locking tightly around my head as she pulled me in panting and we both lay shaking in each others' arms.

After a minute I was still out of breath. "I had no idea my hip could do that."

She sighed, "you're probably wondering how I first discovered I could bring myself off like that."

I slapped her on the thigh. "Probably abusing the refrigerator."

She slapped me back and gaped, "oh, so this is the all-new Vanilla, is it? Got a touch of zest now have you? You cheeky sod."

"And after you made me, um, *go* for the first time."

"*Go*, huh?"

I felt suddenly embarrassed and averted my eyes. "I mean, no other person has ever been able to push me over the line like you just did." I was not the type who could usually discuss this sort of thing.

"And don't make fun of my terminology, I'm a prude and you know it."

"Well, not anymore." Her shoulders quivered from what I took to be laughter. "Not after that." She turned back into me and propped her head up with a hand. "Are you fucking serious? Whoa, talk about a delayed reaction but ... surely Ga ... I mean, surely you've gushed before?"

I shook my head and frowned, "at least now I know there's nothing wrong with me." All thanks to her.

"Oh, trust me, there's absolutely nothing wrong with you," she said emphatically and was quick to say it. "Crikey o'Reilly," she shook her head in wonderment, "now I almost feel bad for teasing you so much these last few days."

I pushed myself up, threw one leg over her belly and straddled her, pinning her down by the wrists. "I fucking knew it. And you've been getting off on it too! The massage, your bloody outfits, the massage..." I said again.

"Hmmm, I like this," she bit her bottom lip, pushed her hips gently off the bed and I went up with them, "don't pretend like you didn't love it."

I shook my head, unable to stop myself from grinning hugely, the girl was incorrigible. "I'll have you know it was extremely frustrating at the time."

She was still lifting me off the bed by thrusting up with her hips and I marvelled at their power even as her eyes feasted on my breasts that I brought temptingly over her mouth. "Hmmm ... so, you were gagging for it ... I'm glad to have offered you some assistance, feel better?" Her voice was low and husky and before I had chance to respond, she overpowered me in one swift motion and within the blink of an eye, we'd exchanged positions.

"Oh, how did you..." but now there was a Goddess straddling me, which sent a fresh wave of euphoria shooting through my veins and prompting me to purr with lust.

She took her cue and manoeuvred atop of me, began kissing her way down my body, furnishing extra attention upon my breasts, my nipple that'd hardened to such a point inside her mouth, her tongue swirling around and that strange popping sound that comes when the mouth is released.

She ran her kisses down my abdomen and her feet dropped off the edge of the bed to land on the floor, her hands circled my thighs, coming to rest upon their insides and pushing them further apart to expose my throbbing cleft to her eyes.

Her humming and my settling back, full of anticipation yet uncertain what to expect, how it would feel to have a woman's tongue inside of me, her mouth enveloping my jewel and then that final line was crossed and I no longer had to wait or wonder as something wet and flexible slipped along my outer walls, my hips making gentle circles, her mouth enclosing my bud, sucking, pinching between her teeth, making swirly patterns with her tongue, switching to my passage, delving within, returning to my pearl, slipping two fingers inside, rubbing whilst sucking and all the while I heaved, and perspired and made strange mewing sounds.

Perhaps it was wrong to make comparisons but this felt smoother, without the irritation of stubble, and she worked with far more enthusiasm, like my juices were giving her energy instead of draining it. She possessed a greater stamina, her tongue seemed not to tire and she instinctively knew what pressures would bring me to the brink without overdoing it. Though the reality was that because I'd only experienced being eaten three times in five years, making an accurate comparison was difficult.

And not only had she already made me gush once but she was about to make me gush twice and I lifted my head from the pillow, and caught her eyes from across my supine, quivering body, her winking, my inability at suppressing the inappropriate laughter even as I threw out my arms to grab a fistful of sheets, her head bobbing up and down, the occasional smacking sound of escaped air, her elbow pumping as her fingers searched ever deeper before sliding out, over and over, a flash of light, a deep explosion, my crying out, her mouth clamped hard around me, her hand clutching my thigh, her tongue lapping at whatever juices were spilling out from me and my holding out a hand for her to join me on the bed.

I could only glare at her with blurry unfocused eyes, rub them, blink it away as I gasped for air. She brought her forehead to mine and we lay in silence until finally, we pulled the sheet over us and fell asleep in each others' arms.

SHE SNORED into the back of my neck.

It wasn't every breath when the noise would splutter from her nose, more like every third or fourth but that didn't make it any more tolerable.

For the thirtieth time, my eyes followed the swirly brown patterns painted on the wall, a kind of circular maze with Barcelona's landmarks you had to find.

I was lying on the edge of the small bed, the covers kicked off my legs due to the heat, one of her hands was nestled behind my head, the other draped over my ribcage so that every now and then, whenever she twitched, a finger would graze my breast.

Outside the roar of exhausts penetrated the windows, they'd never ceased, throughout the whole night they'd revved but now they had a different tone because there were more of them, rush hour was about to begin and the light was already seeping in through the small crack between the curtains.

One side of my mouth was stinging and I could taste the blood from my gums that I'd spent the last hour, two, three, or maybe longer chewing and biting. There was also the faint taste of wine still on my palate and I'd slept with my contact lenses in.

Fun, experiences, memories, to be able to say I'd lived - Those were the things I'd wanted from this trip. But fucking a girl was, without question, taking things far and beyond what was acceptable.

Gabe.

I loved him and he didn't deserve this.

She wheezed and snored into my neck, her finger twitched against my breast, so I took her limp hand and removed it from my person, flung it so that it came to rest on her leg before toppling off and landing back on my knee.

She stirred and I gently lowered my legs to the floor, grabbed a towel, some clothes and my toiletries before tiptoeing to the bathroom. The hostel was silent save for the almost deafening whir of the air conditioning.

I glowered into the mirror, hating what I saw, "you're supposed to be the rational one," and last night I'd been inebriated and emotional after that woman had dredged up all my family crap. "That was not you, you're a junior doctor, don't throw it all away, you are *not* your stupid sister, remember why you're doing this." Whatever the fuck had happened, had been happening, yesterday, the last few days, could not continue, the consequences would endure far beyond this mere summer. Work, career, Gabe, my entire life was supposed to start proper and I stared into my cold, emotionless eyes, "don't fucking throw it all away, Freya, *don't*."

And then I saw it, the braid obscured within a pile of red and so I grabbed it, tried to undo the knot, became impatient, rustled through my bag for the scissors, snipped off the end, threw the bead and hair down the toilet, flushed it away, returned to the mirror and speedily unravelled the braid.

I spent a full five minutes cleaning my teeth before heading for the shower, searching each cubicle for shower gel, retrieving three half-filled bottles, using the lot, washing my hair, ripping the mosquito band from my wrist, the same with the one on my ankle, watching them slither down the plug and thirty minutes later emerging to consummately dry my skin.

I dressed in a plain white skirt and blouse, applied new lenses, no makeup and slipped my feet into my flip flops before grabbing my things and exiting, creeping quietly down the corridor, as forlorn as it was because now doors were slamming all over the place to add to the shouting coming from the floor above. I slid my keycard through the mechanism, the red light flashed green, it clicked, I took a breath and pushed open the door.

"Morning." She was in the process of applying her gown and beamed, forwent closing and tying the cords and bounded straight over to me, exposed breasts leading the way.

I twisted away at the last moment, clutched my belongings into my stomach, stalked over to my suitcase, dumping the lot inside and began rustling for my bag and phone. I was hungry and wanted to eat.

"Babe, what's wrong?" She followed me over, her voice possessing the smallest hint of alarm, of being choked up.

I ignored it, mumbled something about breakfast, found my bag and coiled the strap around my hand.

"Excuse me, I didn't catch that?" She was closer now, her voice louder.

I stood but looked away, to the light beam that shone through the curtain crack and the thousands of dust particles it revealed, which was frightening to see what I'd been breathing in. "I'm going for breakfast, I'll probably see you about."

"Ok, stop!" And then her hand was around my arm and I wrenched it away, skirted around her to get to the door but she'd anticipated it and was backing up in that direction, her hands clutching at the hems of her gown as she pulled the sides across each other and tied the cords. "Freya? What the fuck has happened? Speak to me! Your hair..." she gasped, the choke again rising in her voice.

I continued to stare into the floor, her toenails were painted red, which I'd never before noticed, "excuse me, may I pass please."

She was flush in the way of the door, her hand rubbing at her arm. "No fucking way! Not until you tell me what's wrong. Look at me!" She pleaded and then sidestepped, blocking me, when I tried to dash past. "Freya?"

I exhaled and spoke after a few seconds pause. "You let me do it, you took advantage, you put me into an emotional state asking personal questions you knew I was uncomfortable with." My voice was calm and completely lacking in emotion and I'd raised my glance but only to stare at the door over her shoulder. "You spent the last week travelling with Gabe and look what you did. What did that sweet man ever do to hurt you? And for what? Just because you have an ego that insists you can have whoever you want." I barged past and cringed when my arm made contact with hers. "Now, excuse me please."

"Freya? I..." her voice cracked, was high pitched and lacked belief, "I..."

But I was out the door and calmly closed it behind me.

———

IT WAS ONLY a few minutes after sitting with a big heap of breakfast when a white and blue police car pulled up by the hostel entrance and two weary-looking, bedraggled ex-felons exited and dragged themselves inside.

"Gabe?" I called out across the dining room, the few heads that were up turning towards my excited voice. I stood and ran to meet him halfway, throwing my arms around him and sinking into his embrace.

"I should start assaulting more children." He squeezed me hard, his stubble scratching my face, and carried me part the way towards the coffee stand.

"Maybe just the thieving ones." I was floating backwards and saw Dan trudging in through the door, his hair all out and free-flowing, eyes automatically scanning the room for...

Gabe put me down and shook out his arms but was tactful

enough not to call me heavy. "Not much sleep," he said instead, as though that explained his lack of physical strength.

"Of course," I beamed, "you made it most of the way so drink up," I grabbed the largest mug available and filled it to the top with coffee, black, no sugar, just the way he loved it.

"Cheers." He grabbed the mug and sniffed, took a sip, gazed at me like he always did and pushed up his glasses.

"What did you do to those?" My face scrunched up because his frames were all bent and wonky. "Oh, no, Gabe, did they hurt you?" My hands found their way to his forearm, interrupting its task as lever in bringing the coffee to his mouth and spilling some over the side.

"Careful." His jaw clenched briefly before softening. "They didn't hurt me much because..."

"...Because Gay Boy proved he's even more adept at running than I'd previously thought." Dan's Yorkshire accent boomed from close, where he was stacking a plate full of pastries, toast, ham and everything else.

Gabe shook his head, "don't listen to him." Closer inspection of his face revealed the faintest sign of a periorbital hematoma, like he'd been punched but not very hard, possibly by a child, in the eye, which probably explained his glasses.

"I think you got off extremely lucky, here..." I grabbed his hand and tugged him over to our table, "sit, I'll get you some breakfast."

I did and a minute later returned, pulling my chair closer to Gabe.

Dan sat back and regarded me with hands in his lap. "Do we usually eat just the three of us? Where's the blonde?"

I grabbed a croissant from my plate and dumped it on Gabe's. "Sorry, I forgot to get you one of these ... Dan, how was prison?" I gave him a quick squint and decided he wasn't too bruised. "I'm glad you're not hurt."

"What?" He looked from me to Gabe and back again. "Can you not see my face?" His mouth slackened. "My lip, my eye, my beautiful hair?"

I looked briefly back and shuddered, grateful he'd neglected his earlier enquiry but right then the woman herself traipsed in. Dan caught my eye glaring over his shoulder and twisted around, throwing out his arms and shouting her name.

She'd been heading towards the coffee but stopped, caught my blank stare and glanced from us to anywhere else, probably searching for our Dutch and Canadian friends but they weren't down yet, so she slowly made her way over to our table, aiming for Dan and scuffing her feet several times on the way. She was dressed in pyjama bottoms and a t-shirt but as for any other details, her state, I was too engrossed in my food to ascertain.

I shuffled closer to Gabe, turned into him and concentrated on making an odd ham sandwich between two pieces of cold toast, occupying my hands by thickly spreading mayonnaise over the meat. I didn't even like mayonnaise.

"Easily the best sight in Barcelona, right here." Dan declared loud enough for the people three tables down to hear.

"You've been in prison so I hope you're right." She muttered and I was vaguely aware of her standing, arms dangling at their sides as I took a large bite of sandwich. She made a quiet coughing sound, "um, Freya, may we have a word please?"

I exhaled angrily through my mouthful, making a gesture to the food at my fore, "can't you see I'm busy?"

But she didn't move and her solemn face was liable to crack at any moment and who knew what would happen then? If there was one thing that was hard to predict, it was a recently spurned lesbian. Why risk Arwen, in some overly emotional state, screaming out accusations in the heat of the moment? No, there was no choice because she'd asked to have her little word even as Gabe's hand was nestling in my lap, which was a low blow and it incensed me. She had me and she knew it.

So I swallowed my food, casually pulling out my seat, "excuse me one moment, Gabe," and moved my hand lovingly over his shoulders in a gesture for Arwen's benefit and thankfully both guys were far too concerned with their breakfasts to pay much heed to us.

I led the way out the dining room, down the corridor and into the ladies as Arwen's light feet pattered close behind. The cubicles were all empty, we were alone and I stood in the room's centre, turned to stare bodily at her and folded my arms across my chest.

She stood a cautious distance away, the smallest hint of wetness glowing in her eyes and I couldn't say why but she appeared physically smaller than at any other time I'd known her. After a moment of silence, she held out her palms with a hopeless questioning expression.

"Well?" I demanded, "I'm not a mind reader, what do you want?"

"What do I want?" She asked faintly, "Frey, can't we discuss what happened?"

"What happened?" I asked, glaring hard, cocking a brow.

"Last night."

"Last night?" I shook my head, "nothing happened last night. Did you not just see me out there? That was my *boyfriend* you saw me with ... you know, *penis*!"

Her lips parted and the whites of her eyes were prominent. "Freya?"

"And that other guy, you know, *Dan*, the one you've been teasing and leading on for weeks..." my foot tapped against the tiles.

She brought her hands into her solar plexus, "I have never led on anybody. Freya, what happened with..."

I stepped forward, startling her, "listen up, because I'm only saying this once. I'm Gabe's girl, you hear me, and don't you even think about telling any tales about what you imagined happened last night or any other time. Gabe would only believe me and Dan's his best mate. Who do you think he'll believe? You're the odd one out here and don't you ever forget it." My arms had briefly unfolded and I jabbed a finger in the direction of her face. "And what do you mean by demanding I speak with you in private when I'm with my *boyfriend*?" I emphasised the last word.

She was hunched over and flapped a pitiful hand, "I just needed to speak with you." Because she knew I was compelled to accept when Gabe was right next to me.

"Well, that was a dirty trick and don't you ever do it again." I wanted to leave right then and there but she'd just started to cry. "And pull yourself together, will you, I don't want either of them thinking anything's amiss because there isn't ... nothing happened and nothing ever will." I skirted her and grabbed ahold of the door handle. "You've got mascara on your face. Clean it off before you return."

I made my way back to the table, smiling, trying to remain composed and reclaimed my half-eaten sandwich.

"Everything all right?" Gabe asked.

"Of course."

Arwen returned a couple of minutes later and to her credit, to my eyes at least, she appeared to have it mostly together, and I was looking for signs she might crack. She'd wiped the black gunk away from below her eyes, which I assumed she'd also dashed with water.

She was almost smiling and walked with an upright gait. All was fine apart from her feet which seemed to drag a little too much for comfort, and the fact she was aimlessly approaching us and not the buffet table.

I turned closer into Gabe and there was an odd silence as both the guys glanced briefly at me, which gave me the impression Arwen was doing the same but then Dan cut the tension I was sure I could feel.

"Well, go grab yourself some food and sit, woman, you look like you're starving ... and you couldn't fetch me another of these, could you?" He asked, holding up a pain aux raisin, "and it might be an idea to stock up for the day ... free buffet and all ... would be daft not to take advantage, no?"

"Right," and then she was moping towards the food, Dan's vision burning a hole through her pyjamas.

He pinched his thumb and two fingers together and kissed them loudly, turned back to us and dropped his head. "One day..." he said when he looked back up, "if that's not wife material then I don't know what is."

It was too risky, there was no way in hell we were about to have a cosy breakfast for four and so I crammed down my sandwich, sent the coffee after it and had to thump my chest to stave off the approaching indigestion I could feel beginning to burn. "Gabe, let's go, it's about time we saw some sights."

His hand had been reaching for some toast but was diverted when I stood and pulled it away. "What? We only just arrived ... Arwen just arrived. Sit and eat your..." he stopped because whatever food I'd had was now in my bag and I now began wrapping his pastries in napkins, ignoring his silent protests, filching them and stowing the lot in my bag.

"Move, Gabe! Dan said, take your food with you." It was a slight embellishment but the same principal and I glanced up to check on Arwen's progress.

She was standing somewhat stooped, waiting for her toast to pop and even now the man beside her was checking her out.

Gabe was still gaping up at me, eyebrows turned down, glasses wonky. "We just arrived."

I made an impatient sigh, "yes, you said but if we don't go now then the bloody queue at the Casa Milà will be too large and we'll never get in. You promised to spend some time doing what I wanted and now, after your long absence, you're about to keep that promise, so get up." I tugged on his arm and he succumbed, standing and shaking his head but after being absent for two full days, I had him and he knew it.

Dan was too busy smirking to intervene on his friend's behalf, "have fun," and doubtless wasn't completely against the idea of being alone with the woman, which was convenient for me too.

Arwen had popped her toast and was now collecting her condiments so I was quick to snatch up my bag, as well as Gabe, and jerked him towards the exit.

As it turned out, there was no queue at eight in the morning and Gabe wasn't happy and neither could the Casa Milà's unconventional, bizarre 'open quarry' appearance placate him.

"There could have been queues and maybe there still will be." I shoved him over the threshold where we paid the admission fee, "anyway, you owe me big, mister, and no fighting today, no fighting the rest of this trip, no fighting the rest of our lives, ok?"

His eyebrows raised above the frames of his bent glasses. "The rest of our lives, huh?" He pulled me in and his arms clasped around my back, suddenly placated. "So that's how you really feel is it?"

"Of course that's how I feel, don't you?" My face squashed against his collar and he inhaled my hair but then pulled back because the ticket guy was watching and we both laughed before continuing into the building.

And what a building.

If the exterior had been unconventional then it was nothing compared to inside. It had originally been intended as an apartment block and many of the flats were still occupied but that didn't matter because it was the building itself that was the attraction and perhaps Barcelona's finest example of Antoni Gaudí's genius, or madness, and attention to detail. Everything was unusual, from the door designs and door handles, stairs and chimneys to the gentle curves of every wall, the attic and its incredible arches and brickwork. We spent half an hour on the roof, looking out over the city, from where we had an incredible view of La Sagrada Familia.

Gabe took a few photos of the distant church. "From one Gaudí to another. We should go there next."

"We could but I already went."

"You did, huh, with Arwen?"

"The Magic Fountain ... we could go there." I was quick to suggest.

"Hmm, I hear the shows are only Thursday through Sunday and only in the evening." His eyes snapped up. "You any idea what day it is?"

"You know, I have no idea," I giggled, "that's what prison and travel does." But a quick check of my phone revealed it was Tuesday, which ruled out the fountain for a couple of days at least.

As it happened, there were more immediate concerns because Gabe's bent frames were causing irritation to the skin around his nose and so we found an optician that promised a one hour repair service, which turned into two, and was hardly how I'd envisioned spending my first day alone with Gabe in Barcelona but there was no getting around it because without them he could barely see the hand in front of his face.

When that task was finally completed it was time for lunch and we found a bench in a small park from where I began pulling out the food from my bag.

"You sure you wouldn't rather find a nice tapas bar somewhere?" He was inspecting a croissant as he unwrapped the napkin from around it.

I unwrapped mine and blew off bits of loose pastry. "Well, we have all this food and there's that little thing called our budget," which I'd been meaning to mention, except, he'd been absent, "and that reminds me. I know it wasn't your fault but the last few days I was left very close to destitute."

He bridled ever so slightly but his expression was quick to ease and I guessed he felt bad for leaving me with so little money and no means of obtaining any from our Epic Euro Trip joint account. He patted me on the knee, "I'm sorry, Doctor. How about we go to the machine and withdraw you a little something."

I coughed into a closed fist, "well I was thinking, because it's a joint account, how about I look after the card. It's just that..."

He turned sharply into me and scowled, "you don't trust me?"

I held up my hands, spilling pastry scraps over my skirt, "no, no, no, of course, I do but for two days you left me with no means of accessing our money and..."

"You know, you do have your personal account and your credit card." His glance was hostile and so was his voice and I didn't like it one bit.

"I'm sorry, yes you're right." I rubbed his leg and bit into my pastry and after a minute raised the subject again. "But you know, Gabe, that's beside the point, I shouldn't have to go into yet more debt by raiding my personal account when we have a joint account with savings that are half mine."

"Which is why I offered to withdraw some money to give to you," he said impatiently.

I shuffled, "yes and I thank you for that but wouldn't it be better, you know, just in case, if I held onto the card and..."

He threw down both his croissant and pain au raisin, prompting a charge from a dozen nearby pigeons who began fighting over the large unexpected prize.

"Gabe!"

He raised his voice, "and what if the local gypsy vagrants try snatching your bag? We're in Barcelona, Freya, and they're every-fucking-where." He jabbed the faint bruise beneath his eye as though that made the point for him which, I suppose, it did.

Because let's face it, if anyone tried to snatch my bag, they'd probably succeed. Gabe had been lucky but only because he had back up. Put simply, why risk giving me the card when Gabe had already proven he could protect it and so I apologised for causing a spat, we had a nice little make up kiss and shortly after we were at the cash machine from where I was handed two hundred Euros.

"Don't go crazy with it," he said with a stern face, "we're on a bloody budget, don't forget."

"I know, there's no need to be so tetchy. Honestly, Gabe, am I no longer a frugal Scot just because we're travelling?"

He nodded acceptance and then we decided to spend the afternoon at Parc Guell, which meant taking a taxi through the city and that was fine planning because those who'd taken the bus then had an uncomfortable kilometre long walk up a steep hill on a scorching hot day and by the looks on the faces of the long files of tourists, they were hardly enjoying the hike.

The park was another wonderful demonstration of work by Gaudí, which lay atop a huge hill overlooking the city. It had originally been intended as a holiday home development though due to low sales, it was turned into a monument instead. The park area was large and we spent an hour walking amongst the trees and wildlife though it was the monument zone itself that was the real reason for coming. The best way of describing it would be a fairyland filled with colour and incredible beauty and it didn't matter where I pointed my camera lens, there was a ready photo just waiting, from the tiled benches and animal mosaics to the grand stairway and towers, and everybody walking around carried huge smiles, which was infectious.

Gabe and I took several selfies from what had to be the best lookout point over Barcelona, with a clear view of the long beach and the metropolis that verged right on to it and it was whilst enjoying the vista when he pulled me in close and pressed his mouth to mine, slipping his tongue inside, grabbing a bun and scratching my face with three-day-old shadow.

"You make me so fucking horny," he groaned into my ear, "and it's been too long since I've taken you. I think we need to get back to our room and think about lunch only after..." he left the rest unsaid.

I heaved against him, "after?"

"Those two will be out," he said as though it was obvious, "so we have sex now whilst we have the room to ourselves then when we're done, we go for something to eat and hope they're still not around even after that."

It wasn't the most romantic plan in the world but, considering there were certain things that needed forgetting, nay exorcising, it was probably a necessary one.

I grabbed his hand, "let's find a taxi."

———

THE RIDE TOOK a little under half an hour, half an hour of Gabe touching and fondling and caressing me borderline indecently, the driver periodically clocking my eyes in the mirror and shaking his head with the occasional tutting sound.

"I thought that journey would never end." He took my hand and led the way inside before repeatedly jabbing the lift button in a way that was eerily familiar.

It was six in the evening, which meant most people were out seeing the sites, eating or drinking and the hostel was quiet save for a line of new arrivals at the front desk.

We entered the lift and when the doors closed, Gabe wasted no time in pinning me against the side, his hand tugging my hair, crotch grinding into me, kisses slavering my neck, "I'm gonna fuck you so hard," stubble scratching the same, other hand squeezing my breast harder than I'd ever known him do it.

The lift opened, he tugged me by the arm, produced his keycard, slid it through the device, red light flashing green, mechanism clicking and shoving open the door.

"You!" Came the voice.

I was pushed in first and saw Dan stomping straight over, hair unbound, face wild and red, eyes puffed and threatening. My heart thudded, filling me with a sudden rush of adrenaline, my eyes widened but mercifully he stopped a few feet before barging straight through me.

Gabe saw it and thrust an instinctive arm across the front of my chest before placing himself bodily between us. "What the fuck, Dan?" His hands were on Dan's shoulders now as I backed into the corner, unable to open the door and flee due to the lack of available space. It was certainly one way to kill the mood.

And it could only mean one thing.

Dan knew!

I knew it at once. And now he was about to tell Gabe and my life as I knew it was over.

My mind rushed to find an escape, it was instinct, self-preservation, and in the few seconds they were shouting, whilst Gabe struggled to keep Dan at a distance, I managed to knock up a few desperate excuses.

She's lying. She's crazy. I didn't do it.

But before preemptively blurting anything out, I was able to calm and control myself just enough to remain quiet, to be sensible. I still didn't possess the facts, was it really so bad as the worst case scenario my mind had instinctively thrown up?

"Mate, settle the fuck down, that's my girlfriend your shouting at." His voice was high-pitched and quivering. Poor Gabe, he must have been terrified, not to mention the fact he'd been thrust into the middle of this, and all because of me. "What the fuck has she done?"

"What has she done?" Dan jabbed a finger to within an inch of my mouth, his eyes so white, "why don't you ask *her* what she's done?"

"Oh, God, please." My knees were quivering and had the wall not been there, I could not guarantee I'd be standing. But this was the absolute worst thing imaginable. Clearly, he knew about Arwen and I and now, backed into a corner, figuratively and literally, I was supposed to confess to make things easier on myself. Did he really know?

Luckily, Gabe spoke before I got the chance, "because I'm asking *you*, you're the one who's upset, so why don't you tell me why."

"She's gone, that's what she's done!" He rushed forward again but Gabe was ready.

"Will you give us some space ... back the fuck up and let's talk about this."

But really? She'd gone? If that was true then I had no idea what to make of it, not right now when I couldn't think properly. There were so many questions but how to ask them when Dan was in this state?

There was a brief merciful silence as Dan's nostrils flared and Gabe almost dared lower his arms.

"Right. That's better." My man breathed, "now, by *she*, you clearly mean Arwen."

"Really? She's gone? Where?" I jumped in, "and why?"

Dan's left eye narrowed and I knew he assumed I was acting the innocent. "Perhaps you could tell me?" He continued, his rage having subsided almost as soon as it had blazed, his chest shaking, head drooping and he wobbled over towards his bed at the far side of the room to perch on the edge, holding his face.

I breathed and felt at least a little relieved because I was beginning to suspect Dan didn't actually know all that much. Certainly, Arwen had not blabbed about what the two of us had done in this very room only the night before.

"Are you all right?" Gabe asked me and I nodded and then he looked back to his friend. "Mate?"

He made a strange sigh that sounded full of anguish and I felt for him. "She went all weird not long after the two of you left. She cried at breakfast ... wouldn't tell me what the fuck was the matter. I thought I'd take her out for a few drinks, work on her a bit, and then she'd tell me what was wrong but I never got the chance." He was speaking to the floor, the occasional word coming out as a palpitation. "I went up to shower and when I found her again, her bag was packed. She said she just couldn't stay anymore, that she wasn't welcome and that she'd decided to do the fucking Camino, whatever the fuck that is. She told me goodbye, that it had been incredible and maybe one day we'd meet again."

Oh, fucking Christ! I thought as I took a deep breath and the influx of oxygen enriched my every muscle. She'd actually gone and done it. And indeed, her bed was bereft of all her things.

"Dan," I croaked, fearing my voice might provoke him again but I just had to know, "what exactly did she say?"

"I just told you what she said," he grunted, "and the next thing I knew, she was wheeling her bag outside and there were four others, a smelly looking tramp, an unimpressive midget, a Bob Marley wannabe and some reject from the Rocky Horror Freak Show with a grin wide as a grand piano." Which had to have been Floor. "I begged and wept, made a tit out of myself in front of a roomful of people but she left anyway."

And that was when it really hit.

Or rather, dropped out the bottom.

She'd gone.

And now she was with Floor and the others.

But what of it?

Arwen had done the one thing I never asked or expected and now, it looked like I was completely in the clear. My infidelity would never be discovered. And what a weight off my shoulders. I exhaled deeply and must have smiled because Dan caught my eye and straightened, pointing at me.

"It was her." The accusation came with another rise in tone.

"Whoa," Gabe interjected calmly, "why are you blaming Freya for this? From the sound of things, Arwen never even mentioned her." Although Gabe didn't sound too convinced of that himself and if he didn't know, he doubtless suspected I at least had something to do with Arwen ditching us for another group but that he felt compelled to do the protective boyfriend thing. I had to convince him though, and so I put my hand on his shoulder and leaned into him as a physical gesture of showing thanks for backing me up.

"Who fucking else could it be?" Dan held out his palms whilst pinning his shoulders in a raised position. "She was the only one with her these last two days. The two of us were detained, it can only have been that bitch." He shouted across the room then his head dropped hopelessly. "I fucking loved her."

Gabe had silenced and I knew he was thinking it all over so I was quick to preempt his conclusion.

"Dan, don't you remember saying Arwen would leave us one day and join another group?" I spoke soothingly and was careful with my choice of words. "Well, I'm afraid it looks like that day's come, she found what she considers to be a better group, probably with a nicer motor and she ditched us. It happens, Dan, don't beat yourself up over it."

Gabe met my eye and nodded, "yes, that ... that sounds quite reasonable. Mate, as hard as it is to hear, it's not all that surprising, is it?"

Dan was shaking his head and sniffed but didn't say anything.

Right now, Dan needed to be around friends and so I made the suggestion that the three of us should stick together, maybe go out for dinner but he wasn't hungry and so instead we went downstairs to mope and lounge about the communal room. Regardless, Gabe ordered in a large batch of tapas and in the end, Dan's portion went to a brace of starving young travellers from Germany and we just ended up playing pool whilst keeping a watchful eye on Dan as he fell into a silent despair, missing easy shots and getting angry with himself. A movie was playing on the screen and we watched the second half of that and only afterwards did Gabe pull me aside. If I had reason to believe he'd quiz me about Arwen then he surprised me by raising a different subject.

"I'm thinking now might be a good time for us to slink back upstairs..." he waited for me to catch on and when I didn't, "...you know, for sex."

I straightened, caught off guard by the proposition and my glance moved to where Dan was sitting on the window ledge, staring blankly into the street as the last remnants of daylight revealed the people passing by. "What about him?"

He shrugged, "he's too busy checking all the foreign faces for Arwen ... doesn't sound like she's coming back though ... pity for him ... he was a bit obsessed but he ain't about to do anything stupid if that's what you're afraid of." He brushed up close. "But if you're worried he might barge in then I'll have a word with him, tell him not to, he'll understand. It's been sooooo long and you're not helping, walking around in this fucking dress," he plucked at the hem, "I want you right this very moment."

After a second, I nodded, remembering the exorcism I probably needed, "right."

Gabe put the plan to Dan and a few minutes later we were back in our room, I was thrown face first against the door and Gabe commenced grinding his crotch into my buttocks.

His hands were simultaneously fumbling with his zipper, tearing into a little foil packet and slipping the dress straps from my shoulders - Who said men couldn't multitask?

"Fuck, this thing won't open ... hold on."

And then I jolted when something crashed against the other side of the door, "Gabe?"

"Fuck off!" He called and something in Spanish was returned, "fuck! What do you want?"

"English?" Came the masculine voice, "my keycard is flashing the thing but the door won't open."

Gabe's face screwed up as he grabbed a handful of his black hair and tugged. "That's because I'm trying to fuck my bird against it," he spat through gritted teeth.

"I think there might be an internal lock, could you turn it for me?" It was the voice of an older man.

Gabe was actually hesitating but it was a no-brainer for me. It wasn't happening when someone was trying to enter the room.

"Just let him in, Gabe." I straightened my hair and slipped the straps back on as I pottered over to my bed and sat.

Gabe, flushing obscenely red out of frustration, which seemed to bring out his black eye, unlocked the door and the man, who was evidently Arwen's replacement, stepped cautiously inside, hauling one of those vintage brown leather suitcases. There was a big gash in the wooden door, where I assumed the suitcase had been dropped and we watched in silence as the man heaved it inside, blinked, and then hauled it atop the spare bed, the very same where only last night, Arwen had made love to me.

He was a big man, probably around sixty, wearing a white shirt pushed out by his belly with large wet stains under the arms. His face was covered in three or four days of stubble and his eyes possessed only sadness. He lowered himself onto the bed, surveyed the room, the lockers, the dust, the one window, the angry company, and sighed before unstrapping his case and began sifting through his belongings.

Then, to our surprise, Dan walked through the still opened door, not that it made any difference now, and blanched as he stepped in the air trail left by the newcomer. He prised the window further open then returned to his bed from where he joined us in studying the man as he began pulling out garments, a bible and other papers before spreading them around. In the moment, I almost thought I could read Dan's mind - *What kind of a substitute is this?*

I decided to break the silence and make the man feel welcome. "Hello, I'm Freya and these are Gabe and Dan."

He looked up, "oh, right, hello, I'm Juan," and then went back to his clothes. I tried.

"Right then," Gabe said in an authoritative voice, "this city has been a complete disaster ... might as well decide where we're heading next." He was looking at Dan as he spoke and to my surprise, I didn't even care whether or not he continued travelling with us, he needed friends right now so either way really, although I wouldn't push it too much.

"Where do you have in mind?" I asked, trying to include Dan but he just continued staring blankly ahead.

Gabe shrugged and adjusted his cargo shorts. "Down the coast would be most logical; Valencia, Alicante, Malaga, hmmm, excuse me?" He gestured to the old man, "you're Spanish? Where would you suggest?"

The man was slow to realise he was being spoken to and rubbed his bristles, his bed now displaying a large array of clothing and, amongst other things, a frying pan, dish and a few utensils. "Oh, um, I don't know."

"Well, where are you from?" I asked, for whatever reason intrigued.

"Here ... Barcelona."

Gabe snorted, "travelling far?" I could have clouted him.

But I was even more curious now. "Um, isn't this a youth hostel? As in ... meant for travellers?"

His chin lowered and he rubbed his eyes. "Cheaper than hotel."

Very true and judging by his appearance and demeanour, I now had the impression he'd been kicked out by his wife and had no intention of further venturing into his personal business. So he wasn't a traveller, let's leave him be.

Then, for the first time in a while, Dan spoke. "You got caught, didn't you?"

I shook my head as the man baulked and looked from me, to Gabe, to Dan. "Let me give advice to you young people ... the next time your wife say to stop chasing other woman, you listen."

Chapter Six

ANDALUSIA

*I*t was a long and lazy seven days journeying south, clinging to the coast as much as the roads would allow as the sun baked us alive and opening the windows seemed not to alleviate the temperature within the camper. We spent nights in Valencia, Alicante and Murcia, though the latter was heavily industrialised and looked nothing like the brochure and it was good to get away, to find the next place, wherever that might be.

For the first time, it genuinely felt like we were on the road, that we were travelling like we were supposed to and could go anywhere, that we were free, that the world was ours and the pressures of home were so far behind they might never have existed. The country was large, the roads surprisingly clear and the company relaxed. I was alive.

We saved money by parking the camper and spending the nights under trees or overlooking beaches, buying low priced food from supermarkets and cooking it on the stove, drinking tea or cheap alcohol and whiling away the evenings seeing whatever sites the town we happened to be had to offer or else relaxing, reading, chatting and playing cards or games on our mobile devices.

"Some say it's the most beautiful city in Spain," I was reading articles about the city we were heading as we cruised at an easy sixty along an empty road and I raised my voice for Dan in the back, "have you heard of Malaga?"

He barely stirred from his position lying down on the bench, facing into the wall as he always did, from where he stared into his phone. "I've heard of it."

The girl leaving had changed him. Where before he'd enjoyed being the life and soul, now he spoke only when spoken to, and even then it was only ever to mutter a few words. That was apart from when he was busking, which he did almost daily, setting up in busy streets and singing the classics he said paid the most, though I couldn't help noticing they were all sad songs and imagine my surprise when he began handing over enough funds to cover his third of the fuel. Though upon returning to the camper, it made little difference where we were or what magnificent scenery and views we passed, Dan would always spend the journeys lying down, sleeping or staring blankly into that small screen. It was like he'd given up any pretence of interest in travel and exploration and took each day only as it came, just getting through it with as little exertion as possible. The reason for his melancholy was obvious and over the course of the week, three or four times, his phone would chime and he'd perk up unexpectedly, though only briefly, and it was an easy guess who'd messaged him.

I didn't ask, even though I was curious myself, what she was doing, where she was, how she was. And over the long hours, as I gazed out the window at the mountain ranges, there was much time for reflection.

I'd been worse than a bitch.

I'd grown to like that girl an awful lot, respected her, revelled in being around her, truly enjoyed her company and, had we met at university or anywhere else, there was little doubt we'd have been lifelong friends. But the magical, far removed from real life experiences of travelling through Europe had severely warped the dynamic, the natural order of existence, the normal boundaries of friendship and what was acceptable. For me at least.

I'd been under a spell. I knew this because I could still feel it working inside me. It was the adrenaline of freedom and after a lifetime of regimented discipline, of boring study and high expectations, I'd received an extra large dose of freedom all at once. Added to that a captivating woman, alcohol and the final ingredient, an opportunity, then it had all come to a head.

I'd been wrong to blame her because it was not all her doing. We'd connected on a rare level, I'd felt truly close to her and in the moment I'd truly wanted it. And she was good. So very good.

And then I'd panicked because I'm not a lesbian.

No, it was just one of those experiences, which I'd thought I wanted. But now, at least, I could look back and know I'd done that one truly crazy, or stupid thing and rest easy knowing it hadn't completely fucked up my life.

I'd been lucky there. Anything could have happened. We could have been caught, she might have blabbed or a million other things might have occurred to mess things up for my future.

Of course, I regretted the way things were left but I'd had no choice. It was the nearest I'd ever been to breaking up with someone and, as it turned out, I was terrible at it and yes, I'd miss her friendship but it was impossible for anything to have developed between us.

On reflection, it was for the best she was gone.

But I would miss the girl. Perhaps not as much as Dan, but I'd miss her and now, as I marvelled at the Mediterranean just metres away, I found myself smiling from the memory of her changing our burst tyre. I'd remember her fondly and one day, she'd make some lucky girl happy.

We were only half an hour from Malaga, outside a small town that went by the name of Rincón de la Victoria, which lay on the southern coastal road and where a hill provided an amazing view of the beach below, we pulled onto a patch of grass and parked the camper for the night.

It was what we often did because who wanted to sleep in the camper on a busy city street when we could easily choose the scenic option instead? This way the nights were pleasant and we could roll into our destination first thing in the morning and have the full day to explore before hitting the road again in the evening.

There was, however, one problem with this approach and, at eight in the evening, I swatted at one of them now.

"I thought Arwen gave you a mosquito band?" Gabe was futilely blowing at the air and cursing that the buggers dared enter our camper.

"She did," I slapped at the air around my face, "but I didn't like the smell and you know, they snap real easy."

"Still, we could do with some of them now. How well did it work? I was bit five times by the fuckers last night." Indeed, there was a large red blotch on his neck and he was becoming increasingly irritated by them. "I should text Dan and tell him to pick up some spray at the supermarket."

"I think they work on some people but not others."

"Huh?"

"Bloody mosquito bands."

He clattered against the counter top and let out a girly shriek. "So they're useless then because mozzies bite some people and not others and they're certainly getting me and not you." His face was red now and his side parting had dislodged.

I shut my Kindle and rubbed my temples, "Gabe will you settle down, you'll do yourself a bloody mischief," and trying to concentrate on some family named Stark moving south was an impossible task with such distractions. I'd been told the book was good, and there was apparently some TV series doing the rounds, which had missed me completely but still, it was escapism and there'd never be a better time for it.

"That's easy for you to say," he said something else but it was lost on me as he bounded through the open camper door to the outside.

He returned five minutes later, evidently having found a shop because he was now furnished with a box of mosquito repelling incense sticks. He lit them, wafted his hand about the air, sniffed and hummed. "I swear, they get worse the further south you get but let's see what this does."

"Gabe, your forehead?" I recoiled at the sight of another large red patch that had appeared from nowhere.

He checked his face in the mirror and swore, again ran from the camper and returned a few minutes later with a small tube after apparently having been to a chemist. "And there was Arwen with a simple wristband." He rubbed some cream onto his forehead. "That's what I've been meaning to ask ... did the two of you have an argument or something? A bit weird she'd just up and bugger off like that."

My face was buried in the Kindle and I didn't look up. "It's not weird at all, Gabe, how are those smelly sticks working?"

He fanned at the air about his face in a way that reminded me of Kelly Atkins and how she'd done the exact same thing when her boyfriend dumped her, though Gabe was sniffing the air and had a different expression. "They seem to be working so far ... fingers crossed ... smell nice at least."

"They do." Now please some silence whilst I read.

It was less than a minute later when the clipping began and my eyes darted up to see he'd crossed one leg over the other and was cutting his toenails. The shards were landing on the carpet when there was a perfectly good outside right in front of him.

He noticed my angry glare, "I ain't going out with those bastards swarming around. In here, I have my protective barrier, I'm safe."

"Whatever," I exhaled and shut the Kindle, one day I'd finish chapter one. "Gabe," I began, thinking now might be a suitable time to broach the subject, "Malaga ... well, when we get there ... it's only a two-hour drive from Gibraltar and I was thinking that maybe we could go there after?"

He frowned, "Gibraltar?" Snip. "I've heard there're monkeys there?" Snip, snip.

"Yeah, so?"

"So, my allergy." Snip.

"So, don't go near them then, problem solved." I shook my head in exasperation. "Really, Gabe, there are cats everywhere and you deal with them all right," I'd heard some pitiful excuses in my time but that one really took the biscuit, cake and muffin all in one, "and it was only back in Dinan when you suggested that very thing yourself."

"What?"

"Our first night here."

"Huh?" Snip. He looked up and his eyebrows dipped, pulling the rash down his forehead. "Doctor, what are you talking about?"

For a moment, I could only stare in confusion. Was he playing the village idiot all of a sudden? I spoke slow and deliberate, just for him. "To see my bloody sister! Who lives in Gibraltar! Remember?"

Snip, snip, snip. "Oh yeah, you're probably right. Yeah, we could do that." Snip. "Come on, Dan, how long do you need, I'm dying of thirst here."

Since Gabe was hungover, the next morning I drove the camper into the city. Malaga was indeed everything I'd hoped for. It had that special something that couldn't be explained but after giving it some thought, I reckoned it was probably the way the beautiful birds tweeted from the trees on the main promenade, how everything looked so spruced up, even though the place was ancient and indeed, the harbour looked like it had only just been finished with outdoor bars and restaurants all appearing so shiny, the asphalt with barely a discarded piece of gum to tread on and the benches and posts with fresh coats of paint.

We found a place for breakfast and sat at a table beneath a large marque as the morning sun established its heat and the harbour's water shone abnormally blue. There were huge yachts moored sporadically and I couldn't guess as to their value. We ate ham and eggs over a diced potato base with extra strong coffee.

"Just what I needed," Gabe croaked from beneath his sunglasses, his breath still reeking of last nights beer. His arms were now covered in red marks from mosquito bites, to add to the collection growing over his face and neck, though for whatever reason, they'd chosen to ignore me completely. I'd told him to find some Aloe for them but, typical man, he didn't think his complexion was bad enough to warrant it.

Dan was leaning back in his seat, hands clasped behind his head, having not spoken a single word all morning.

"Do you fancy coming to the Botanical Garden with us?" I felt the need to include him more than ever. It wasn't yet at the stage I feared him wandering the streets alone but who could say where things might lead?

He shook his head. "Thanks but no."

"How about the Alcazaba?" I asked, referring to the eleventh-century fortress that adorned all the postcards.

"I'm thinking I'll just head to the beach, maybe check out the historic centre later and find a nice spot to play some songs."

I hummed, "maybe we'll catch you at some point."

The Botanical Gardens had been built in the mid eighteen hundreds and combined the forest with grand estate gardens not unlike what you'd typically find in England. As it turned out, they were indeed built by an English woman and her Spanish husband and I wondered how many of the birds that perched in the trees had come from my country since some of them, the redbreast robins especially, looked so familiar.

Gabe was crouching near one particular sweet bird whilst making tweeting sounds to entice it to come closer and I'd never known any wild bird dare approach a human like that. I guess it was Gabe's karma and since the universe was at peace with him, I thought now would be the ideal moment to again mention a certain topic.

"That thing we were discussing last night?..."

He raised an eyebrow that seemed to agitate the growing red splodge on his forehead, "mosquitoes?"

I squeezed his hand and giggled. "No silly, Gibraltar. You do remember when I told you my sister lives there?" He remained silent so I continued. "Anyway, it's just that we're so close and I've not seen her in so long, I really shouldn't pass up this chance and I honestly think you'll love her..." I finished in the hope he'd pick up where I left off and he did, after a while.

"How can you be so sure I'd love her when you haven't seen her in so long?"

I let go of his hand, "because she's my sister, you have no choice."

He gave me a funny look as if to suggest my reasoning was stupid and that maybe I was daft for wanting to see my sister for the first time in so long. The truth was that only a week ago it was the last thing I'd wanted but I don't know, something had happened in the meantime and I wasn't sure what exactly. It doubtless had something to do with my sudden proximity to her and therefore an opportunity presenting itself but I also thought that Arwen triggering Lizzie in my head had a lot to do with it too. I still wasn't a hundred percent sure I wanted to go through with it, and would likely even lose my nerve when the time came but right now it felt like something I had to do.

"Don't you look at me like that," I finally told him, "and while we're at it, I didn't appreciate how you acted so indifferent last night. She's my family, why am I even having to persuade you?"

He raised his voice, startling an elderly couple who were admiring the nearby flowers. "Because she abandoned you and your family. What kind of sister does that? Honestly, your family..." he stopped suddenly and shook his head.

For a moment I couldn't speak. "My family? What of my family? You met my dad and said you adored him and tell me, what could my brother possibly have done to offend you?"

His mouth twice opened to speak but he bit down so hard on his bottom lip that it turned white. Finally, his face softened, "I'm sorry, of course, I love your family and that includes your sister. We should visit her."

I beamed and took both his hands in mine. "Are you sure? Because if you're not we don't have to."

He laughed because he knew there was no way out of it now. Didn't I have the best boyfriend?

And then it hit me.

Because the day after tomorrow, I'd see my sister.

"BARCELONA, IT AIN'T." He picked up a pebble and threw it at the sea but it fell short.

I shook my head, wanting to ignore his bad mood. "How would you know, you barely got to see it."

"And I'm supposed to lie on this?" He adjusted his towel for the third time and began ransacking through his bag for, I assumed, some sunscreen. "And you know that wasn't my fault."

"Well personally, I prefer this beach to Barcelona." Which was true, not that it appeased him. The thing is that sand sticks to your skin the minute you apply sunscreen and after the slightest breeze you're covered in the stuff. At least with shingle it isn't an issue and neither do you have to worry about nearby volleyballs landing splat on your face whilst you're supine.

He pulled out his factor sixty and began plastering it over his legs. "It hurts to lie down and my back's already in pain. Would it kill you to do more of the driving?"

I sighed and spread my own cream over my legs, arms and front. When it came to beaches on a hot sunny day, I'd trust the Spanish and on this day, the beach was crammed with locals. As for his remark about driving more, I'd been doing at least half but such a thing was hardly worth arguing about, not when all I wanted was to enjoy being with Gabe on a beach, something that, despite its simplicity, we'd never done before. "I'll be happy to do more driving."

He nodded, "good," and handed me his sunscreen, turning his back to face me, "would you mind?"

"Of course," I squirted a dollop into my palm and began lavishing it over his back, noticing he'd been bitten several times at the base of his neck, "would you please find a chemist and get some hydrocortisone, for me?"

He grunted acknowledgement and after finishing, I kissed him on the back, handed him the bottle and turned around for him to return the favour.

"Thanks, Doc."

And when his hands never came, I turned back to find him already lying on his front, eyes closed.

I was so incensed, all I could do was squeeze the bottle as hard as I could to prevent myself from throwing it at him and even then, I still came very close. Instead, I settled for silently mouthing something I'd never before called him, flattened my towel across the shingle and lay upon it, faced down.

"Beer ... Coca-Cola, beer ... Coca-Cola." The nearby voice woke me.

I stirred, not knowing for how long I'd been sleeping, opened my eyes and found Gabe was already sitting up, waving his arm for the man to approach.

"Over here," he called, "Doctor, you fancy a beer?"

"No, thanks." I was still angry, seething even and readjusted my nose, trying to fit it comfortably between two large pebbles.

"Si? Beer ... Coca-Cola?"

"Beer. No, no, just one."

Someone mumbled something and there was a jingle of coins.

"You want open?"

"How else am I supposed to drink it?"

I shuffled and scratched at my back, which had begun to itch.

There was a clink, shortly followed by that familiar eruption sound, "awe, Señor, I so sorry."

"The fuck?"

"Please, I sorry, I get you another."

"You soaked my fucking shorts."

I opened my eyes and scowled into the pebbles.

"I sorry, here, I open another," clink, "I sorry, here."

"A hard job ... walking up and down all fucking day, yet you can't even do that without drenching your customers."

"I say sorry, Señor. Have nice day."

I pushed myself up and glared at him, "Gabe, what has got into you?" The man was bounding down the beach towards a new group lying on the shingle. "Since when were you ever so mean to poor," I didn't know what the man's job title was so I couldn't say it, "well?"

His jaw set upwards. "The man was a buffoon and he drenched me, look," he brushed at the stain on his brown cargo shorts, "and I'll smell of beer now."

I didn't say that he already did and instead shook my head hopelessly. "So? You can put on a fresh pair back at the camper, no harm done. Why are you being like this so suddenly? The Gabe who got me through university never treated people like that." Not once. And I was beginning to worry what was happening to him. And why.

He took a large gulp from his bottle and threw another pebble.

"Sometimes ... sometimes it just feels like the whole world's..." he squeezed hard around the neck and tapped the base against his knee.

"The whole world's...?"

"Nothing, never mind. I'm fine, don't worry."

"Well, if you won't tell me, I can't help you." I put my hand on his arm and he moved it away.

"I don't want your help. I just want to relax."

We stayed another hour without saying a single word to each other and when it was time to leave and I moved my arms, I definitely felt an unfamiliar chafing sensation all over my back so that the simple act of slipping on my dress was like being set on fire as it unfurled down my body. As for my bag strap, I wasn't about to risk that digging into my flesh, so I settled for winding the cord around my hand and carrying it.

Of course, I knew what had happened but didn't give a shit and hoped I still wouldn't give a damn once the pain became truly terrible and even when we stopped at the chemist to purchase some hydrocortisone for Gabe, I still forwent buying moisturiser and anti-inflammatories.

THE NEXT DAY, Gabe surprised me.

Despite the boys engaging in yet more late night drinking, he was awake before I was and it was the smell of bacon and eggs drifting through the camper that brought me to.

"Coffee," he placed the mug on the small pull out table to my side, "breakfast won't be long." There's nothing in the world quite like waking up to the smell of strong coffee and a cooked breakfast whilst the sun pours in through the open windows. He pecked me on the cheek and returned to the stove.

I had to blink and rub my eyes because not only was he cooking but he'd also showered and shaved so that there was no facial hair to conceal the ever-growing bites and subsequent allergic reactions that covered his face and neck. But after the disaster that was yesterday, if he was turning over a new leaf then I wouldn't argue.

He was grinning whilst flipping a bunch of mushrooms and that was when I noticed what he was wearing, jeans instead of cargo shorts, a white shirt and pair of black shoes, of all things.

"Hey, are you feeling ok?"

He knew what I was referring to and opened out his arms to encompass himself. "Just because a guy's travelling, does that mean he can't dress nice?"

I was still regarding him with narrowed eyes until finally dismissing it, "it's just not like you, that's all." It kind of suited him though, in a way, I just wasn't used to it and had to think whether it was my birthday, which it wasn't, then I realised the reason for his madness. "Run out of clothes, huh? That beer guy trash the last of them? Don't worry, we'll find a launderette. Where's Dan?"

Gabe set the food on a plate and to my astonishment, brought it over on a tray complete with a single Gazania flower, the very same I'd told him I loved back at the Botanic Garden. "Enjoy, my love," he kissed me on the cheek and sat beside me, "Dan said he had a good day yesterday so he set off early to play some songs and yes, I took that from someone's garden, cos I know you're wondering."

This last was because I was sniffing the flower and still gazing at its bright orange and red beauty. I shifted against the backrest because my back was itching terribly, which reminded me of our arguing the day before but today was a new day.

I bit into a rasher of bacon, which crunched most beautifully. "Aren't you having any?"

"I, um, I'm not hungry this morning." He patted me on the leg and went to stand in the open door from where he spent several minutes staring out at the sea that crashed against the cliff face below.

I finished the breakfast and silently approached him from behind and he was startled when I placed my hands on his shoulders. "Are you all right? Gabe, you're shaking." I stepped back, my hands taking his forearm instead.

"Am I?" He shrugged, his pale skin revealing no evidence of having been in yesterday's sun. "It's fine, I'm fine, don't worry."

"Something you've eaten, fish perhaps?"

He'd taken a beating from the mosquitoes but they wouldn't cause him to shake. Sunstroke? No, the symptoms would have manifest sooner. He could tell I was trying to make a quick diagnosis and raised his voice. "I'm fine, Freya, don't look at me like that. If there was something wrong, don't you think I'd know?"

I backed away, "ok, ok. I love you and was rightly worried, that's all."

His arms opened. "I'm sorry, I shouldn't have snapped, it's just ... it doesn't matter."

After a small hesitation, I fell into them and sniffed the fresh cologne of something yummy. "How could I be mad when you cook me breakfast? And I hope you won't boil in these clothes."

He brought me to arms' length. "You know, since I've put on a shirt, I was hoping you could wear that red dress I love. Did you bring it?"

I nodded, "of course."

Half an hour later, I was driving the camper into the city and after parking, we walked the short distance to the Alcazaba, arriving just before midday. Alcazaba was the Arabic word for citadel, which it most certainly was, an incredibly large castle structure surrounded by two ancient walls atop a hill right in the centre of the city. Opposite the entrance, there was a Roman amphitheatre, closed off to all but the dozen cats that had made it their home. The Alcazaba itself was far more of an impressive attraction than the two Euro entrance fee would have you expect, with so many nooks providing surprises around every corner, beautiful gardens, Moorish wall designs, art, artefacts and lookout points providing the best views over the city, from where I could see an enormous cruise ship moored at the marina and an endless file of slow walking people trickling from it.

Although worth it, some of the slopes were extremely steep and I took care to walk in shadow whenever I could. My back felt like it was being scratched by a cat every time I moved my arms and my bag strap chafed like fire to the extent I was now severely regretting yesterday's tantrum. There wasn't much to be done with sunburn, other than keeping it moisturised, out of the sun and riding it out whilst hoping you don't develop melanoma. In the meantime, the pain must be endured and I kept a tight grip of Gabe's hand, if only to prevent him from putting his arm around my back, not that he tried, or even said very much, whilst I reflected on the logic that if we Scots were meant for the sun then we'd probably have it more than two days out of the year.

After a couple of hours at the Alcazaba we went for tapas and coffee, followed by a wander around the fantastic shopping area that, whilst outside, had decorative draperies hanging from one building to the next, covering street after street so that we were shaded by artwork. The pleasant breeze that swept up the Calle Marques de Larios was like heaven in the heat, not that Gabe appreciated it.

I stopped and turned into him, "Gabe, you're sweating."

He nodded, "well it's a hot day and I'm wearing jeans," he checked the time on his phone, which had to have been the fourth or fifth occasion in the last ten minutes he'd done so.

"Somewhere you need to be?"

He dismissed my concern with a hand then used the same to take my own and led me through a tangle of narrow, drape covered streets, his hand noticeably cold, clammy and trembling before we emerged in the open and found ourselves standing in a busy square.

Despite its small size, the cathedral entrance was nearby, which suggested this was actually an important historical place and indeed, the crowds reflected that. Nearly all the cafe tables were occupied, a flock of pigeons darted from one building to another and from the fountain, the gentle strums of a guitar were just audible over the ruckus.

"Oh, how beautiful." From the postcards, I recognised the square as the true centre of Malaga.

Gabe cleared his throat, "it beauty and full of musical over there."

"What?" I squinted as he pulled me in a ragged path towards the fountain and music.

A crowd had gathered around the musician and no wonder, he was good, and the fountain was so pretty and someone tossed a coin into its shallows followed by another in the guitar case and the atmosphere was so pleasant and I readjusted my sunglasses and what the fuck, but the musician was Dan and the reason I hadn't noticed was because he was wearing a tux.

I stepped closer and my head jerked forward. Yes, it *was* him and he looked so clean and even his man bun was tied up, which was a surprise and why was he wearing a tux to busk in this oppressive heat? Then I recognised the song.

> "Gotta go, go, go,
> I said yo, yo, yo,
> Gotta go, go, go,
> I'm ready, let's get it on."

It was by that someone guy, the one who wore the cool hats and then Gabe's hand slipped from mine and people were jostling and turning to stare at me.

"You're my beautiful lady,
Let's do something crazy,
Hey baby,
What you say you marry me?"

I was still watching Dan, who was grinning so much some of the words were coming out flat and he nodded at the space near my feet and I twisted around to see Gabe not where he left me a few seconds before but a few paces away, down on one knee.

My chest thudded as the significance of the moment struck, there were flashes of cameras, a woman squealed and Dan continued to play as he stepped into the gap between myself and Gabe, who now had to shout above the music.

"Freya, my Doctor," he swallowed, his skin white as paper but for the red blotches covering his face, "ever since after we met at first when we were at university all those five years ago, I knew that I thought I would want to marry you one day ahead into the future," he wobbled and I feared he was on the verge of passing out as a bead of sweat dripped from the tip of his chin, "well, there it is ... oh..." he delved into his pocket and pulled out a small black box, dropped it, clawed it back and opened it.

Someone gasped and there were more flashes as I was distantly aware a few dozen people were filming the event. With good timing and a flourish, Dan finished playing and now there was only silence and I could do nothing but glare at the diamond ring being presented to me.

By now, I was beginning to sweat myself and I coughed, stepping forward, any pain I should have been feeling all across my back temporarily numbed.

Gabe wiped his free hand across his forehead and shook off the drops. "Oh, I was meant to say ... will you marry me?"

Louise Shilton - That's who came to mind. Her boyfriend had interrupted a lecture on the nervous system to propose in front of a packed out theatre and at the time, I'd thought that was a damned idiotic way of doing it. She'd said yes and, to the best of my knowledge, they were still engaged four years later.

"Doc?" He glanced wearily about the large crowd that had just become a whole lot larger, blinked and I guessed the sweat seeping from his forehead was stinging his eyes, though his lenses had steamed up so bad it was hard to see them.

I scratched the back of my neck, and what would you know, the searing pain hurt like bloody hell, which caused me to wince and someone to my left made a barking noise.

A man said something in Spanish, a few people laughed, and then I heard some English in an American accent, "boy punching above his weight," and then, "don't worry, it'll soon be over, son."

"Doc? Frey?" And there he was, so close, yet I'd never felt so cut off from him than these last few weeks. Why would he choose now to propose? Not just here and now in a packed square in Malaga but now after feeling so distant, now after I'd cheated. "Frey?" He pleaded, his shirt absolutely wet through. At least now the cause of his earlier symptoms was clear.

"Well? What do you say to the man?" Dan asked as though the answer was obvious.

I'd been stunned and Dan's booming Yorkshire accent from so close knocked the clarity back into me. In the moment, all I wanted was to end Gabe's suffering, to give him the answer he expected, the answer that would end his discomfort and allow him to walk away with his head held high. There'd be time to think about it later, because I was not the woman who'd turn him down in front of his best friend and so many others.

And damn you, Gabe, for putting me in this position.

"Gabe," I stepped forward and grabbed his hand, "yes, I'll marry you." Now stand up.

Feeling the tug from my arm, he stood, yelping out in triumph and embraced me in a soggy hug and I felt the sudden influx of heat flushing through him. "I was so nervous, I thought you were gonna make me wait forever." He laughed into my ear and spun me around as Dan began playing Celebration by Kool And The Gang. "And I've got another surprise coming."

"Oh?" I relapsed back into a stunned state as people came out from the crowd to shake Gabe's hand, pat him on the shoulder, throw money into the fountain for our luck and even pose for photos...

...Because apparently, I was engaged.

———————

"YOU WERE SUPPOSED to try it on when I proposed, silly. Here," he took my hand and slipped the ring on my finger, "I couldn't wait to see it on you. Suits you, don't you think?"

It was gold with a single diamond, modest and beautiful, not over the top yet neither did I think he'd scrimped and I worried about him getting into yet more debt, though I wouldn't mention it now.

More than the ring, however, it was the Gran Hotel Miramar that worried me because it was a five-star hotel and we had a sea view. It was an unnecessary expense yet I felt unable to even gripe about that, he was so happy and I couldn't bring myself to be a killjoy, not on the day I'd agreed to be his wife and that thought felt so ... well, I wasn't even sure yet.

"I know what you're thinking but we were always intending to spend at least one night in luxury, I just brought it forward, that's all, and what better night than tonight, aye?" He pulled open the balcony door and the fresh sea breeze flowed in. He inhaled, "get a load of that air. You know what this calls for?" He was bouncing towards the minibar now, "let's see what we've got ... ah, just the job," he pulled out a bottle of Champagne and had to move his head closer to the price list glued to the fridge because his glasses were removed on account of them badly needing a clean, "we can justify it tonight, one bottle, maybe two, and don't worry, they're only fifty Euros."

"Sure, why not." I was still standing by the door but now stepped inside and dumped my bag on the table before peering into the bathroom, which was incredibly plush with a large assortment of soaps, gels and freshly cut flowers.

I was engaged to be married.

And for whatever reason, the one thing that came to mind was the last thing that should've been there.

Arwen.

Where was she now and what was she doing? Was she still traversing Spain or had she given up five miles down the road? Was she still with Floor and the others? Were they sleeping together? And why was I even thinking about her at a moment like this?

He handed me a glass that fizzed, "to us and our future."

"To us and our future." I agreed, clinked his glass, sipped and felt relief from the alcohol going straight to my head.

He held the menu in his other hand. "We'll be having only room service tonight and I'm thinking something extremely Spanish and exquisite, maybe some chocolate mousse for dessert and you know where that's going." He leaned in and with Champagne cold lips, kissed my clavicle before working his way down toward my cleavage.

"A waste of good mousse ... careful, you'll spill." I backed away and he laughed.

"Well, we can't waste good mousse, not that it would be wasted."

"What's Dan doing tonight?" I glanced across at the balcony, as though doing so would provide the answer.

He snorted, "well, he ain't staying here if that's what you're thinking."

"It's just that I've got the camper keys. His things are in there and where's he staying?"

He shrugged, "he's earning money now, he'll probably just book into a hostel, who cares? Hah, he'll be the best-dressed guy wherever he ends up." He opened out his arms to encompass the room, "we're here, forget about him and let's just enjoy." He downed his glass and because mine was already empty, refilled both, handing them to me, then dived onto the large bed and despite his playful mood, his lips turned down and his eyes lost the sparkle of only a moment before. "You really had me worried there for a moment, Doc. I wasn't sure you'd say yes."

I perched on the bed's edge and handed him his Champagne. "Well ... did it have to be so public?"

He sensed my agitation, nodded then slapped his forehead, "d'oh." It was an odd response but I wouldn't press him on it when there were more important things to discuss.

"Gabe, we have to talk about this."

He patted the space beside him. "Let's take a tumble first. You know what that little red dress does with my ability to think straight. If it's a coherent conversation you're after then best leave it till after."

I shook my head, "I'm sorry, no we can't, this is important."

He patted the bed closer to me, his fingers stretching playfully towards my thigh. "Hey, come on. I want to give my fiancée a nice, passionate ploughing."

"Ugh, is sex the only thing you ever think about?" I shifted away and then his hand slashed through the air and there was a loud smash from the other end of the room. I jumped and needed a second to realise he'd thrown his Champagne glass, which had smashed against the far wall.

"Gabe, what the hell has got into you?" I leapt up and paced into the open space. "Why did you do that?"

He sprung up and faced me from across the bed as a sudden gust lifted the curtains and made them flare inwards. "*Ugh*, did you really just say *ugh*? And what do you fucking think is wrong with me? You've been frigid as fuck ever since this whole trip began." He ran his hands through his hair. "Why, why can't we have sex? Answer me that!"

My faced clenched up and I turned around, whipping up my dress from the back, the movement striking me with sharp pain. "Because, Gabe, my *considerate* fiancé, somebody was too selfish and thoughtless to protect my skin after I did the same for him."

For a moment he just glared wide-eyed at my back, which was red, unsightly and peeling and if that didn't cure him of the horny monster then nothing would. His mouth slackened, "no ... you're blaming me for that?"

"Uh huh, and it kills to even move, why do you think I've been shifting about so awkwardly and carrying my bag by the strap? And you never once asked if I was ok." I shook my head, "honestly, Gabe, you don't notice these things yet I'm the one who's neglecting you?" And as I yelled it, I finally understood what the problem was, or at least one of them. "You take me for granted, Gabe. You've barely considered my feelings this whole trip." I thrashed a hand through the air as someone shouted from the next balcony. "You never used to be like this. Back home you were always so wonderful but now? I don't know what's happened but you just don't consider my feelings anymore. You drink all the time, you're aggressive, you get into fights, you get arrested, you throw your glass in a rage and I worry where it might lead next. Gabe, we've lost something and it scares me."

He stamped onto the balcony, angled his head around and shouted, "mind your own fucking business," before slamming the door closed and scowling, "you're blaming me for everything? Do you have any idea about the pressure I've been under and..." he was about to say something else but cut himself short and I could tell he was frustrated about whatever it was.

"Gabe, we've both been under pressure, why do you think we're here now?"

He bared his teeth, "no, you don't get it."

"I get that you've been anxious all day about proposing but you've not been yourself for just as long as we've not been *ploughing*, as you so articulately put it." I waited and hoped he'd tell me what the problem was but he just remained silent. "Well?"

He exhaled and glanced at the wall, to the shiny wet patch with lines dribbling towards the floor and the shards of glass scattered over the carpet. "Why didn't you just ask me to apply your sunscreen? I'd have been happy to."

I threw my arms up and the pain made me regret that but clearly, I wasn't worthy of knowing what was going on between us. "Should I really have to? You ought to be looking out for me. I didn't even have to ask Arwen, she just..." I bit my tongue.

His head jerked, "Arwen?"

"Sunscreen, Gabe! Marriage," I was quick to mention, "there's that little thing called residency approaching and I'm sure I don't have to tell you we have specialism after that. We'll have other things to worry about when we return home. Do you really think now's the best time to be considering this?" I was a lot calmer now and my sudden mentioning of marriage had eased his demeanour also.

He breathed and casually pulled out a chair at the table, patting the other seat for me to join him. "Of course, I've given it more thought than you'll ever know."

I dragged myself over and sat, eyeing the kettle and thinking a nice cup of tea was probably in order for this conversation.

He read my mind, "I'll get it."

And when he returned and we were both calm, we engaged in a rational conversation like two doctors rather than two brats. We spoke about our residencies and the likelihood of being separated, possibly at opposite ends of the country because it was quite feasible that I'd be in Brighton whilst Gabe would be stuck close to my dad in Inverness, or vice versa, or a dozen other possibilities and what would that do to our relationship then?

From across our tees and a very nice hotel pen and notepad, I reached across to take his hand. "I know you'd like to be near my dad but what good would that do us?"

He shuffled, "that's the beauty of us being married, we'd be a special case and could request to be kept together for the sake of family."

I laughed and almost sent tea down the wrong pipe, "don't leave us much chance to breathe do you?" I continued laughing but his expression remained neutral, he couldn't have been serious. "Hang on, hang on. That scenario would depend on us getting married before making the decision."

And still, his expression remained stern, "yup."

I gaped, "as in ... within two months from this moment?"

He nodded, "don't you just hate long engagements?" Fuck, he was totally serious.

I blinked hard and shook my head several times, "you want a quick wedding just to ensure we're not separated?"

"Hey, you said yes, you agreed to be my wife and I want to spend the rest of my life with you. I see no point in putting it off."

I was still trying to fathom his rationale, it was completely out of nowhere. Being engaged was one thing but talking about going through with it so soon really brought it all to the fore.

"Think about it, Gabe, it's not very likely we'll be separated, our choices will overlap somewhere so there's no point in panicking and going through with a rushed wedding only to find we've been accepted to the same residencies, so can we please calm down here?"

That at least was statistically true because we'd spent hours discussing our options and had both made certain to choose the same towns and even in the unlikely event nothing matched up, we could simply pick up the phone and cause bloody hell. But even that scenario was unlikely because we'd both opted for emergency medicine, one of the most underserved fields of medicine in the country, which gave us another advantage. Put simply - We would not be separated. And again, I tried to impress this upon him, and that even if we were parted, it was still no reason to jump into a quick wedding.

We went round and round in circles, discussing, arguing, debating this one point until darkness arrived, we ordered room service which, despite it being exquisite could hardly be enjoyed and then finally, I said something in the heat of the moment.

"Gabe, it's just so much pressure out of nowhere. You're pressuring me to marry you the minute we arrive home and all after proposing in a way that pressured me to say yes."

"What?" His mouth fell open to reveal the churned up squid rings within and he made an odd sound swallowing in haste, "you didn't mean it?"

I rubbed my arm, "well..."

His skin had turned white again and he was quick to interrupt, "wait, wait, wait ... let me ask this some other way. If I had asked you in private, for example, in here tonight, what would you have said?" The hurt on his face was painful for me but I had to be honest.

My arms were pulled in close as I unknowingly rubbed them and I had to force myself to meet his eyes. "I think that after these past two weeks, I'd have asked for time to think about it." And that answer told me so much and after his face crumpled, with immediate tears flowing from the slits in his eyes, as weak as I was in the moment, I was quick to follow up. "But if you'd have asked in Dinan or Bordeaux or Edinburgh, I'd have said yes without thinking."

He snorted into a napkin and seemed to take hope from my addition. "Then let me ask you this ... are we engaged or not?"

Chapter Seven

SOMEWHERE IN TUSCANY

$\mathcal{I}$t took twenty minutes. Twenty minutes for the builders, tilers and carpenters to drive their vans and pickups back down the dusty path that meandered towards the gate of the Giordano Vineyard before the goods wagon filled with wine heading for Siena could finally get out. And when it did there was another altercation between the drivers at the gate, insults about their mothers, threats about what would happen to their daughters and then all was forgotten, temporarily at least, as they went about their business.

Alberto tugged at the long grey hair at the back of his head and grunted at his daughter. "One day, this infernal wine shop will be finished and we can get back to normal." He closed his eyes, tried to remember what normal was and pined because his life would never be normal again.

Alessia, ever with hands on hips, watched as the three trucks ground slowly back up the path, and dreaded the process having to be repeated again when the wagon returned. "We need to widen the path, tarmac it." She waited for the drilling to cease before continuing. "We need to modernise."

For a while, Alberto didn't speak. She was right, of course, it would make certain things easier around the vineyard but modernism was not what Vino di Giordano was supposed to be about. They traded on tradition and little had changed in over four hundred years. They made premium wine at Giordano, some of Tuscany's best, they produced less but sold for a higher price and when the tourists arrived, that's what they wanted to see and taste - Tradition.

That was yet one more thing to stress Alberto. All the other vineyards were welcoming tourists and taking their money but the Giordano Vineyard had never bothered with it. "We just make wine here." Alberto always said but now that his daughter was involved, they'd taken on more and more and now this formerly peaceful part of Chianti was a constant grinding of saws, banging of hammers and bickering of men and women. He'd wanted none of it but had foolishly allowed himself to be persuaded because, let's face it, men did not say no to his daughter.

"How long until the squatters arrive?" Alberto asked during a rare lull in the din.

"Ten days and they're tourists, not squatters."

"Same thing, just ask any Florentine. Will we be ready?"

Alessia hesitated and groaned when the tiler's pickup broke down halfway up the path, obstructing both the builder and the carpenter. "We'll be ready."

Alberto doubted it as much as he doubted the regional government's ability to make good use of his taxes and then what of their reputation when hundreds of obnoxious Americans, camera-happy Chinese and impudent French arrived to find the place amidst typical Italian chaos.

"We need to modernise," Alessia repeated, "we need to widen that path."

"And add a road gang to the madness already around here? And what of the expense?" He tugged again at his hair. "Sometimes I wish you'd have gone to England with your woman, it would have been better than having you both around here, making my life a living hell. At least then I'd have peace. Where is she and what is she doing?"

"My English is abysmal, Pappa," Alessia began jogging down the track towards the broken down vehicle and shouted over her shoulder, "and you know what she's doing."

Alberto puffed out his chest. Yes, he knew and he watched with pride as the angry workmen fell silent and began to swarm around his remarkable daughter as she popped the front of the pickup and began probing around inside. There the distant sound of an engine firing, Alessia wiped her hands on a rag but long before she could see her father admiring from a distance, he'd turned around and gone.

DAYNA CLOSED her eyes for a few brief moments of solace, the fan's rhythmical whirs gifting calming relief from the stifling Tuscan heat as she thought of her village in Dorset that was never anything like this. Would she ever get used to the heat? When she opened her eyes it was still there, the countdown on the screen in large black type - Ten days.

There were emails to deal with. Enquiries from people as far away as Australia, Canada, Russia and even one from Djibouti, wherever that was. Was it really a traditional Italian vineyard? How much for a ticket? Are there discounts at the shop for taking the tour? Are there wheelchair facilities? Is there a meal that comes with the price? Then there were receipts from local tour operators who'd sold five tickets, eight tickets, another for twelve tickets and they'd deposited the money minus their commission.

There was indeed a meal that came with the price, at least, Dayna hoped. The intention was to serve traditional Tuscan fare but Dayna was having problems with the suppliers, indeed, they'd yet to find a catering manager the whole lot could be dumped on. Yet another thing that needed doing.

Then there were other staff members. The girl they'd hired for the shop had since met a man from Venice and without notice, gone to live there and two of the vine hands were constantly creating problems over various disputes long built up over time.

Ten days.

Then the boy growing inside of her kicked, Dayna caressed her belly and again closed her eyes to allow the fan's soothing whirs to bring peace as she gently blew out air through her mouth.

The familiar patter of footsteps increased in volume and then Alessia's arms were enveloping Dayna from behind to rest upon her swollen belly.

"You don't have to check on me all the time, what could have happened since an hour ago?" Dayna pressed her cheek against Alessia's and held her hand atop of hers.

"On the hour every hour for two fleeting minutes. You know I can't stay away. How's our boy? Wait! Don't answer yet." Alessia angled her head around so she could kiss Dayna and as always, what was intended as something short became drawn out and intense. "Ok, speak."

Dayna was still whirring but not from the fan. "He kicked again and you missed it, again."

She swore in Italian and swore again. "This fucking workload. I miss everything. You'd better not be stressing! Leave that all to me." And Alessia was stressing, even if she tried and failed to hide it from Dayna.

"I'm all right, no need to worry. How's progress?"

"A joke." Alessia repositioned and perched on the desk, her browned thighs in those damned shorts that always fizzed Dayna's mind so temptingly close. If only there was time to take her upstairs, to undress her, to lay her on their bed, to spread her legs and lose herself in her essence, to come back up only after she'd exhausted herself and her tongue. It had been a while and Dayna missed it, craved it.

Dayna suppressed a shiver. "And Alberto?"

Alessia's jaw clenched, not because of her father but because of her mother. "Same. He is who he is. Puts a brave face on for me. Wouldn't know anything was wrong."

It had been the job of Alessia's mother Maria to travel Italy in search of new outlets for Vino di Giordano, a responsibility that had always kept her away from home for long periods, most of the week, every week, often weeks without returning, to visit restaurants, to cultivate new relationships, so to speak, a task she'd evidently been better at than anybody knew, though if the amount of new business she'd procured had dwindled then there was a very good reason for it. Maria had only been caught because the wife of the Milanese restaurant owner she'd been sleeping with for so many years had followed her all the way back to the Giordano Vineyard, all three hundred and thirty six kilometres, which had to be a record of some sort, and presented the video evidence to both Alberto and Maria, a day that Dayna would forever remember.

Thirty-five years of marriage. And now the divorce settlement was about due, Maria would see out her years in a large house overlooking Lake Como whilst the vineyard was on its knees and everybody left behind was on the verge of breaking. If the tours and wine shop failed then nobody who remained had a future.

Ten days.

And the entire vineyard was a cacophony of deafening madness in the hottest summer Dayna had known, where new workers could not be found and those that existed were disappearing, when they were almost a million Euros in debt and the bankers were sending letters and the vineyard patriarch was losing the will to carry on and a baby was only a few weeks away.

It was just another year at the Giordano Vineyard.

But at least nothing else could go wrong.

"IT's because there is sin living under your roof," Goro insisted as he fanned his face with his hat, "all the delays, terrible workers, rotten grapes, lost business, your wife and now your impending bankruptcy."

Alberto had been occupied with the grape press, turning the lever attached to the great wheel that crushed the fruit and allowed the juice to pour out into the cask. It was labour intensive and exhausting but, as Alberto had argued with his daughter, traditional, which was why her beloved tourists would come in the first place. She'd nodded and succumbed to his point, which was a first for humanity and perhaps a miracle to rival that of Christ's resurrection.

Now, Alberto let go of the handle, wiped the sweat from his forehead and took a moment to catch his breath. It was a job for younger men but they were short of staff and so Salvo was needed in the vines. Alberto restrained his rage at the impudence. "So you keep telling me, Goro, but what would you have me do, kick my daughter from her home? She's all I have in this world."

"Not your daughter but her trollop and then there will be no more sin on this vineyard."

Alberto rubbed at the coarse flesh on his face and considered his options. But what could he do? He couldn't lose Goro because he'd take his two brothers with him and then what? The man might be the son of a goat but, for whatever reason, was well liked amongst the hands and Alberto could not risk open rebellion by having him turfed from the grounds. As for Dayna, Goro could find one of those goats and do as he pleased because she was staying. And neither was Alberto convinced enough by the fool's superstition to do anything irreparably rash. It was always the problem with hiring folk from Calabria, they always brought with them their extreme version of Catholicism and Alberto worried about the extent to which the man had been preaching his poison to the others.

Alberto managed to remain composed. "You'd have me remove a pregnant girl from her home?"

"And what is that she's carrying but the spawn of the devil?" Goro came closer and sniffed at the air above the juice. "It's rancid and there's talk amongst the hands ... talk that perhaps your rancid luck will be visited upon them. Last week, Bartolomeo's daughter was narrowly missed by a car and Matteo's wife grows senile."

"You blame old age on this vineyard?"

Goro seemed not to hear Alberto's scepticism and raised his hands to the sky. "Thank the Lord that the car missed and that sweet Dorotea still has her wits, for now at least, but it's a warning ... a warning from God about the sin in this place. You must purge the vineyard of the sinner so that our harvest might not be rancid, that our livelihoods might not be lost, so that our children are not mown down in the streets, so that our women do not lose their minds and," he looked down from the ceiling to Alberto, "so that our wives are not taken by other men."

Alberto removed his hat and threw it to the ground. "Get off my property before I turf you out myself." He shouted and moved towards him, wheezing, the broken vessels in his face flaring. "Take your brothers and whoever else wants to go, take them all, we're better off without your poison." He shoved the man who backed away.

"Think about what you're doing Alberto, where else will you find good hands in high summer? Who else will pick your grapes?"

"I don't care, now get out." Alberto pushed the man all the way to the large opened doors of the building from where the sun roasted down upon them. "Take your things, go, and never return."

Goro spat into the dirt, donned his hat, turned and strolled down into the vines.

Alberto watched until the man was out of sight, caught his breath and returned to the grape press. The first few turns were always the hardest but the rage burning within was so palpable it was as though there was nothing in the barrel and the juice flowed from the spout like water from the bathroom tap.

The sweat poured from Alberto's face. "How dare you mention my wife ... my wife ... loved her the moment we first..." a sharp pain shot through his body...

And then he twisted from the machine, his withered hand clutching at his chest, his face reddening before finally, his legs buckled beneath him and the stone ground hit hard.

Chapter Eight

ALGARVE

Nervous.

How else could I describe how I felt?

I'd not seen or heard from Lizzie in eight years and today I would spring a surprise.

Would she recognise me? Yes, of course, she would. But would she be happy to see me? Logically, there was no reason why she wouldn't but I was still nervous. Fate had dropped this one opportunity into my lap and so I could not tempt providence by ignoring it, I had to go and whatever happened happened.

How would she take being surprised? What would she think of Gabe? After what she'd experienced at the hands of our father, would she feel justified in taking an instant disliking to him or would she hold no malice towards me for being favoured?

And who was the man she'd married? I'd been so preoccupied with how she'd take me showing up that my own concerns, fears and questions had taken secondary preference.

Gabe wiped at his eye and yawned from behind the wheel and I placed my hand on his knee.

"You're exhausted, why don't you let me drive?"

He waved it away. "I'm fine, it's only a short drive." Which was true compared to some of the mammoth runs we'd done this trip, a mere two hours, though it was only two days before he'd specifically requested I did more driving, yet here I was offering and being turned down.

We were both exhausted. After all, I'd accepted his marriage proposal only the night before though, despite what Dan thought, it was not due to fireworks or the wearing out of bedsprings that we were both yawning like newborns and it was probably the only time in history an acceptance of an offer of marriage had resulted in nightlong bickering. I hoped it wasn't an omen.

Gabe had been unable to drop the idea of a snap wedding and try as I did to convince him it was completely unnecessary, he wouldn't listen. No, he'd only doubled down and listed his reasons that ranged from the logical to the absurd and we'd finally gone to bed and two hours later were still awake, him seething with frustration, me shifting from sunburn, which only exacerbated his frustration, which in turn fed the terrible soars that kept me awake and then we arrived for breakfast to find Dan had somehow managed to blag and bluster his way into the five star buffet on our ticket and wasn't there just a five star smile upon his face when we dragged ourselves in looking like death. And then he'd regretted slapping me on the shoulder.

"Yep and now my arm's bruised, you violent fiend," he again cursed me from the back, to which I tiredly and wordlessly responded by showing him my shoulder and that shut him up.

We were travelling southwest along the AP-7, a fast toll road sufficiently far from Spain's southern coast to provide any view of the Mediterranean. Instead, the land was mostly barren with mountains covering the horizon until we approached those mountains and then tunnels that seemed to stretch forever would send us beneath them, which explained why the tolls cost so much. Still, the road was busy in comparison to some of the other toll roads we'd experienced, bypassing Marbella and other British strongholds, which possibly explained it. And here we were heading for Gibraltar, an actual British possession the Spanish would forever object to.

We passed the exit for Marbella and, as the sun dazzled me from the left, a sudden increase in the morning temperature prompted me to open the window a crack and I leaned against the glass and shielded my eyes to stare into the middle distance of bland brown hills as the rhythmical noise from the road was peaceful and soothing. I closed my eyes...

...to wake and find those bland brown hills had morphed to a greener shade and, wiping the crust from my eye, I checked on Gabe to my right, his face expressionless as Dan slept in the back.

"You fancy stopping for coffee? Looks like we could all do with some."

He shook his head, "I reckon I'm ok but we can stop if you fancy some?"

"Meh, I was thinking mainly for you, I'll survive." I turned away and read up on the history of Gibraltar, how we could occupy ourselves there, these mythical monkeys and whether we could expect problems crossing the border and, just so long as we didn't leave our British registered vehicle unattended on the Spanish side, we could envisage few. But naturally, the proximity brought my thoughts back to Lizzie and I experienced an odd combination of exhilaration and trepidation.

I stared at the green hills to my left, the sun no longer dazzling my vision then checked into the back, Dan still asleep on the bench and the bright sun that cast its beam into our camper from behind. My mind went into spasm, like something wasn't right but I couldn't think what it was and I glanced over at Gabe who was staring straight ahead with the same expression he always had when giving something his full concentration.

An overhead motorway sign stated we were now on the A-381 and although that meant nothing to me, I knew it was a different road to what we'd been on before I'd closed my eyes and fallen asleep, a road looked like a road, after all.

For how long was I sleeping?

I sat in silence as my fogged mind tried to work things out and after five minutes a big blue sign approached in the distance. As it neared and the text became readable, I saw what it said – Cadiz, 40km.

I scratched my head and wondered why Gibraltar wasn't yet signposted. And where was Cadiz anyway?

I pinched my bottom lip and then the three lanes split into twelve as the toll booths approached, and that was when it finally hit because the six leftmost booths were signposted for Cadiz, the three in the centre going straight to the nearby town of Jerez de la Frontera, a place I'd never heard of, whilst the three booths on the right headed for Seville.

Mucus built in my mouth and my hand began to tremble because Seville was on my list and I knew it to be located considerably further north and west of Gibraltar. I'd had no reason to suspect Gabe had intentionally missed Gibraltar, after all, why would he have done such a thing and even now, I still couldn't believe it was possible and needing physical confirmation, I pulled out my phone and checked our location on Google Maps.

The blue dot pulsed outside the town of Jerez de la Frontera, seventy miles or ninety minutes past Gibraltar and then a fog passed over my vision. For how long was I asleep? It had to have been two hours at least and I was angry at myself, as well as circumstances but most of all I was incensed at the bastard sitting to my right.

"You couldn't pay the machine, could you?" Gabe dropped the card into my lap as the camper slowed to a stop.

I was too enraged to even object as I unconsciously took the card, pushed it into the machine's slot and the barrier lifted.

"The card's still in the machine," he said after I left it, "don't leave that or we're fucked."

I leaned out again, reclaimed the card and his palm was held out ready to take it back. I handed it over and finally found myself able to speak, "why are we here?" My voice came out as a deep grate.

He gave me a look as if to suggest I'd lost my mind, "um, because I drove here."

"We were meant to be going to Gibraltar, to see my sister, remember?"

He paused and looked up with a dopey expression, "oh yeah, clean forgot about that. Oh well, I think we'll find Seville better anyway, no harm done."

So that's how he was playing it, by pretending to be dumb, when it was only at breakfast I'd spoken for a full ten minutes about wanting to climb The Rock with Lizzie.

"Don't look at me like that," he continued as he drove through the gate and changed into second, third, fourth, "mistakes happen. I've had Seville on my mind because I knew it's where we both wanted to go and where we'd have been heading now anyway had you not sprung this sister bullshit on me at the last minute." *Sister bullshit?*

"So, you're claiming this is a mistake?" I sounded weird, scary even, like a demon had taken possession of my vocal chords.

He shifted and sounded defensive. "Are you claiming I did it deliberately?"

"If you didn't do it on purpose then prove it, turn around and drive back to Gibraltar." I heard Dan stirring from behind but didn't turn around to look.

Gabe opened his mouth to speak but decided to take a few extra seconds to consider his words. "I think we're a little too far beyond it now to bother ... go see your sister some other time and besides, that last toll cost nearly thirty Euros, not to mention the fuel."

For a long moment, I was too incredulous to speak and once or twice he turned his head to check if I'd let it drop but no, I was still glaring into him and seeing nothing of what I thought I'd always loved.

"So you did do it on purpose. This is why you wanted to drive so you could plead ignorance and drive right past it."

Dan approached and stuck his head between the two front seats. "What's up? I thought we were going to Gibraltar?" And by that, I could at least deduce this was not something Gabe had concocted with his friend, who appeared to be just as ignorant as I was. No, this had undoubtedly been an opportunistic change of plan because, for whatever reason, my fiancé did not wish to meet my sister.

Gabe ignored Dan and addressed my earlier point. "Well it serves you right for falling asleep, doesn't it." He raised his voice, his earlier defence now turning to attack, blaming me for this but his statement brought the logical conclusion.

"You saw me sleeping and decided to drive straight past Gibraltar." I accused as I watched carefully for his reaction but he just squinted at the road ahead, changed lanes and shifted into fifth.

I turned bodily away, knowing the truth even if he wouldn't admit it. All the pieces fit except for the one about why he didn't want to meet Lizzie. Not that it mattered now.

Because we were heading for Seville.

And that changed things.

IT WAS OFFICIALLY the hottest city in Europe and easily one of the most beautiful, not that I got to see a great deal of Seville, despite spending three nights there.

It's not that I was 'sulking,' as Gabe put it but rather thinking through everything and I did so alone, as the boys explored the city, leaving me in a small camper park a mile out from the hustle and bustle where other campers settled and shared wine, food from barbecues and tales of their travels.

I didn't need long to realise skipping Gibraltar was probably for the best because why would I want to introduce my sister to Gabe anyway? And that thought was a revelation. Though soon after thinking it, I'd backtrack and feel bad but then Gabe and Dan would return to the camper after midnight, wake me up drunk and I'd feel it all over again.

Gabe repeatedly denied that missing Gibraltar had been intentional but I didn't believe him. After five years it was easy to tell when your boyfriend was lying but I didn't bother questioning him on the reasons. What was the point? He was still denying it and, to my surprise, I found myself caring less and less about his excuses, which was another revelation. Indeed, I found myself caring less and less about what he was doing at all, even if such a rumination came and went with my ever-changing moods.

At one point I toyed with the idea of jumping on a train and heading to Gibraltar solo, even taking off with the camper whilst they were on one of their all-day benders and leaving them to pick up the pieces but I lacked the spirit to do anything that crazy. I feared I'd get halfway there and then regret it, turn back and look like a damned over emotional bloody fool and besides, the last thing I wanted was to see my sister after all these years only to have Interpol on the lookout for me.

One evening, whilst sharing a burger and beer with a middle-aged couple from Germany, I spent considerable time staring at my ring, wondering how a future with Gabe might be.

Something had changed, either with him, myself or both of us and I wondered if it had been a bad consequence of travelling and, for the first time ever, being away from the environment where we grew and became used to each other. Had that altered our relationship? It was one possibility. Though in all likelihood it was probably a combination of a range of things.

Would our relationship return to normal after arriving home and we were able to engage in the sort of routine we were used to?

And even if I had that guarantee, would I want it?

Maybe we'd simply run our course and the cracks were finally exposing themselves. But if we were to end things, what would that mean for the last five years? Would all that time have been wasted? Did it even matter?

For the best part of three days, I thought about all these things until the time came when we left Seville and drove straight west, crossing the River Guadiana to arrive in the Algarve region of Southern Portugal. From the reading I did, which was later confirmed by what I saw, the beaches were some of the most incredible in Europe, with perfect clean sands and shallow waves that rolled so fast yet so gentle that your feet were constantly awash as you strolled along the surf.

And I walked alone, flip flops in hand, hat donned and usually in the early morning or after the sun had set so that my shoulders were not further aggravated.

I'd never seen so many campers than in Southern Portugal. At times, it seemed like every camper in Europe had descended in this one place so that the locals, screaming from behind their wheels, would lose patience at the sight of every slow-moving foreigner and I saw several near collisions on long narrow straight roads. Along the entire coast there were so many camper stops offering full facilities at low prices that we spent an entire week travelling only a few miles as the beaches became better and better the further west we ventured. There were no major cities to speak of, only small towns spread out, and I saw many new build houses and apartment blocks, most probably holiday homes for the continent's middle classes as the population expanded faster than the infrastructure was able to cope and I lamented that this place of incredible natural beauty would inevitably soon be lost forever.

One night we followed the map and drove to the south and westernmost tip of Europe, a road through craggy landscape where the only thing that grew were strange shoots and bushes that burst up through the rocks, a place that had been considered sacred ground since the Neolithic period, a place where the Romans thought the sun set larger than anywhere else, where it sank hissing into the ocean, a place that marked the edge of the world, a place called Cape St Vincent.

We were far from the only ones with the same plan and we parked amongst the many other campers on the edge of a cliff that overlooked the Atlantic. It was twilight and the waves crashed against the rocks far below. The night was cloudless and to look up was to see the stars like no other place. It was almost like this spot had been made for contemplation and introspection, and to stand at the cliff edge was to look out on the world.

It was the moment in the movies where a person in deep trouble comes back from the brink after having made a major discovery about themselves, though the truth was I made the discovery days ago.

It was the discovery of why, no matter how hard I tried, nothing with Gabe seemed to work anymore. And I truly had tried. But my relationship was failing regardless. And it was failing through a combination of three things; Gabe, providence interjecting on our behalf and myself. And I was wrecking it both consciously and unconsciously.

And even though I'd made the discovery, I'd held out from acknowledging it. Perhaps I'd wanted to be certain or maybe I was too afraid to admit it because if I was to once again embark down that path then this time, it would not merely be for the summer, but forever. The rest of my life.

The consequences of falling in love with a person who was far from suitable, whatever that even meant, would almost certainly mean I'd find myself in the same position as my sister. Lizzie was cut off from her inheritance but more than that, she was cut off from her family.

I loved my dad, as pigheaded as he was, but he'd already lost so much and he did not deserve to lose me as well.

But if I married Gabe, I knew I would never be happy.

I was in love with a person who was not suitable, a person who would cost me my inheritance, the security that came with it and the two people I loved more than anything else in the world.

But I was in love with Arwen.

Not that it mattered because she was gone, I'd never see her again and I had to accept that. Now, as I stood atop the cliff edge, the Atlantic thrashing at the rocks below, all I could do was wonder where she was, what she was doing and who she was doing it with.

Ever since this road trip began, I'd been challenged, asked questions, flipped over and turned inside out. Europe had tripped me so hard that it was impossible to be sure of anything anymore.

I don't know for how long I stared blankly out into the abyss as the last of the day's natural brightness phased to black and the only visible light came from the stars and the rotating beam from a far-off lighthouse. I was waiting for a sign, any sign, something from Providence, any message which, my logical mind knew, was futile.

They say that when you're ready the answers will find you but I don't know what I was expecting because in this moment of contemplation and introspection, nothing happened and neither did Gabe, with a fear for the safety of his fiancée, bother leaving the camper to check how I was doing after all this time standing on the edge of a cliff.

Save for the constant churning of water, there was nothing. No sign from Providence to tell me I was on the right track and nothing came from the void to tell me I was completely crazy.

I yawned and plodded back to the camper. There were torch lights flashing from where I guessed people were heading over the rocks to find a spot to toilet. Some of the campers were lit, two or three with people sitting on chairs beside opened doors as they ate cheese and drank wine into the night.

Gabe and Dan were doing the same and as I approached, their conversation fell silent and I knew they were discussing me and my recent moods. Ignoring them, I stepped inside, tired, and went straight to my backpack to find my nightclothes and I rustled through the mess that was my things, couldn't find what I needed, continued, chucked clothing out and still couldn't find them and in a fit of impatience, I picked up the bag and tipped it upside down.

Amongst the clothing and toiletries, something heavy thumped against the floor and I stooped to retrieve it before holding it to the small intermittent light from the beacon to read it in the dark.

It was a wine bottle, still full, corked, with a deep punt at the base and fancy script that read Château Haut-Brion from Bordeaux.

I'd forgotten all about it.

And as I collapsed onto the bed, I knew one thing.

Providence had given me a sign.

———

SO MUCH FOR TRAVELLING.

It was like we'd discovered the Algarve and had no intention of ever leaving, to explore what the rest of Europe, or even Portugal, had to offer. Though in reality, it wasn't quite like that.

Gabe loved it down here and had quickly managed to learn basic Portuguese but did so at the expense of having to spend long hours sleeping in the camper surrounded by a protective shield of incense.

Dan was still just as bummed out over Arwen as the day she left almost three weeks ago but at least the town of Portimão provided him with a place to make money busking whilst drinking low priced alcohol to dull his melancholy. I could tell he was messaging Arwen by the way he reacted on the rare instance she'd ever reply and on more than one occasion, I had to physically prevent myself from enquiring about her.

My skin had peeled and recovered and now I'd had my little tantrum, I was more careful about covering my Scottish skin whenever I was out in the sun, which is what I spent much of my time doing.

I was unhappy. More so than at any time in my life. And the long lazy days only provided time to reflect on my mistake.

I'd been with, albeit painfully briefly, the most wonderful person in the world. Not only wonderful but funny, intelligent, worldly and incredibly sexy. After a bad start, we'd found ourselves clicking, however that had happened but it did.

That this person was a woman was still uncomfortable for me, incredibly uncomfortable in fact, but I couldn't help it. I'd never thought of myself as one of *those* women and had it not been for Arwen, it was doubtful I ever would have. What that meant, I had no idea, and the thought of having to introduce Arwen, or any other girl, to my friends and family as my girlfriend struck me down with fear and a lot more besides. I don't know, it had all come from nowhere and I'd had little time to get used to this new idea of myself. In fact, all I knew for certain was that I missed her more than anything.

She was always there at the front and back of my thoughts, the whole time and I spent such long periods staring blankly into her photo, watching her music videos and replaying our time together in my mind that I worried I'd make myself sick.

I could only ever eat small amounts, despite the food being so delicious and sometimes I could eat nothing at all.

Gabe, Dan and I did spend some time together as a group though it was mostly for breakfast in the camper and the occasional futile dinner at a restaurant though conversation was mostly absent and the subject of what to do or where to head next was never broached. It was like we'd developed a group fatigue and now we'd found a place we could lounge about in comfort, we'd lost all desire to explore though in truth, what good is exploration when everybody's miserable?

It was this misery, exacerbated by long periods of solitude that finally forced a decision upon me. Though my making the decision came about indirectly and with a little help from an unexpected source in a moment of despair filled madness, which is hardly the time to be making life-altering decisions but what could I do? A bottle of wine from the heavens had spoken.

By this point, it was only out of necessity that Gabe and I were sleeping in the same bed, though always with a large gap between us. One night I awoke to find him snoring on the floor, and another, when I was still lying awake at one in the morning, I crept outside and made the short walk into the town of Lagos, soon afterwards finding myself in a bar. It was most uncharacteristically irrational behaviour and evidence to my mind that I was not right in the head.

"It's port around here, isn't it? I'll have whichever you recommend." I told the barman, a tiny slip of a man who looked too well groomed to be real. It was moderately busy, though hardly late by Portuguese standards and Born This Way by Lady Gaga was playing on a diminished volume.

"True but if you'd like to experience my country then we're trying Ginja." The girl took the seat to my side and spoke some quick Portuguese to the barman who began preparing the shots. "Trust me, you'll love it."

"I will? What is it?" I turned to briefly appraise the newcomer and let out a mini exhalation, perking my eyebrows in appreciation.

"Morello cherry liquor." She had the sharp features of a typically attractive girl from the Southern Med, dark skinned and black haired with bits of red infused into it and all styled in a grungy look. She was wearing a white sleeveless vest and had tattoos of roses and mystical animals covering both forearms. I'd have put her at maybe a few years older than myself and definitely a looker in good physical shape. "I'm Neves." She held out a hand and I took it.

"Oh, I know that one, it means snow, and I'm Freya."

"You're Nordic?"

"Not a terrible guess. My name certainly is of Nordic origin," I nodded and felt her thumb stroking my hand, "but we Scots commandeered it." I considered her for a second. "You're understanding me ok? I don't mean that as an insult but, you know, Scottish..." it came out as a babble and a Scottish babble at that but she grinned, still holding my hand.

She spoke softly because, I guessed, she could easily tell I was terrified. "You're easier than that movie Trainspotting and don't worry, I'm sure you're not all like that."

I laughed, half with relief and half because I was so nervous to be doing something like this whilst lamenting that even now, after all this time, people still thought of Trainspotting when hearing the word Scotland. Forget modern medicine, the inventor of television, the microwave and ATM, whisky, golf, bagpipes, tartan and caber tossing no, it's all Trainspotting. Damn, I was really nervous.

The shots arrived and after clinking glasses, we sent them back.

"Well?" She looked at me with expectation.

I licked the residue from my lips, "absolutely delicious. I'll be taking a bottle back for sure."

She told the barman to keep them coming, a good idea. "So tell me, Freya, how is it that I'm able to find such an attractive young lady sitting all alone in a gay bar at this time of night?" If she'd thought I was some innocent foreigner who'd accidentally stumbled in and was looking for any sign of surprise on my part then she didn't find it. Fear, perhaps, but not surprise.

"To be honest, I ... I don't know, I think I just felt compelled to have a look." My seat was on a rotating axis and I felt just able to swivel it a few degrees towards her.

She did the same and ran her gaze down my torso and legs. "Spontaneous?" This was in reference to the fact I was in my shorts and t-shirt, which said 'Hug Me' on it, and was bereft of all makeup including contact lenses. If I'd found myself drawn to this place then I'd subconsciously ensured I was looking as far from presentable as possible, though Neves didn't seem to think so.

I laughed, "literally just got out of bed."

"Can't sleep or early riser?" When I didn't answer she filled in the gaps. "I see. You can tell me if you want? What else is there to do and the longer we speak the more Ginja we get to drink." The next shots arrived, this time we savoured them and she continued to smile as she waited for me.

"I've had a few bad nights." I sighed and almost put my hand on her leg, a habit from the last girl I was this close to. "In fact, I very nearly came here last night and the night before." Which was true. I'd walked past the place on several occasions and each time had failed to make it beyond the paving curb.

She nodded slowly in recognition like she understood the subtext to my words though I was sure my demeanour also gave it away. "We've all been there," she touched my arm to make the next point, "we lesbians anyway." And then she also registered my discomfort at being called *that* word. The truth was I didn't consider myself one of *those*. "Ah, you really are way back in Narnia."

I laughed loud at that one, "way back in Narnia? That's hilarious and you amaze me with your ability to have a two-way conversation with yourself."

Her hand had never left my arm and now we were facing each other straight on. So this is how it felt to enter a gay bar and meet a woman who liked women. No harm had come to me so far, though what had I been expecting? The girl was friendly and chilled enough and the conversation, so far, had been without pressure.

She was studying my hair and her hand left my arm so she could feel a few errant strands of red between her fingers. "Did you really just get out of bed?"

I nodded, "I wasn't joking, which is why I'm totally flattered yet confused you're finding me attractive."

She again ran her gaze down my body, "because you look *that* good in your pyjamas, so you have to be worth getting to know."

I brushed some red behind my ear, "thank you, that's kind of you to say," and something I needed to hear right now and in a fit of hysterics, I almost broke down and blabbed all my problems, only managing to stop myself because she'd turned again to the barman.

She spoke Portuguese, some port was poured and two glasses were handed to us. "I'm not liking the lack of privacy around here, let's find a booth."

My heart rose into my mouth and it was clear where she wanted this to go but she was already striding towards a quiet booth in the corner and for the first time I could see how tall she was, with slender legs in tight fitting jeans and I had to admit, I admired her confidence. It was never like this with men, at least not until they'd become accustomed to me, or in Gabe's case slept with me, because the chemicals turn mens' brains into an incoherent mess. But Neves had it together, which made me wonder just how practiced with this she was, though in the moment, I couldn't be certain I really cared anyway. I was lonely, hurt, confused and here was a girl, a stranger, showing me some interest.

It was one of those circular booths, dimly lit by a low hanging lamp and the leather seating squeaked as we slid around from opposite sides, coming to meet in the centre and either by accident or design, our thighs squished together and she didn't move to correct that.

My arms were pulled inwards as I clammed up and I reached

nervously forward to take a sip of port. "I like your hair." I told her and received a smile in return.

"I like your figure," she returned, "I noticed you the minute you walked in and wasn't about to let someone else say hi first."

I looked down and to the side, without thinking tried to tuck more hair behind my ear and found nothing loose. I coughed, "so, tell me about yourself." Please be normal.

She drank some port and, recognising that I needed the pressure taken off me here, went into a long relieving monologue about how she'd taken a law degree at the University of Coimbra and then settled into a job making pastry at a small local bakery, how she'd hoped for something more but the economy was bad, even for lawyers, how she was one of two sisters, the other being straight and married with a baby on the way.

I began to open up, little by little, possibly because Neves seemed absolutely normal. What had I been expecting? And the conversation became gradually more two-sided as she asked about my travels and I spoke mostly about Carcassonne and Barcelona, ensuring to omit details about my travelling companions and if she was curious about who I was with, she knew better than to ask.

My head swirled from the port and we spent a few moments watching the other couples in the bar.

"This is your first time in one of these places, isn't it," Neves said as a matter of fact. "Are we all as frightening as you imagined?"

I blushed and felt like a fish out of water. "It's all very interesting, I must admit."

The place was extremely relaxed, though I put that down to it being a Portuguese rather than a gay bar. The lesbian couples outnumbered the men and not a single person was dancing, instead, everyone had paired off and sat in similar booths to ours, in deep and cosy conversation or else kissing. It was all very peaceful, even if to my uneducated eyes, some of the couples looked incredibly mismatched, though I recognised I was probably being unfair. Was that how people would look at Arwen and me? And then I squeezed my eyes shut and slowly exhaled, guilty I was thinking about my Australian but being unable to help it.

"I'm sorry," she began, "I can't be this close to you all this time and not do this..." and she gently turned my jaw towards her and then there was the taste of port as she pressed her lips to mine and her hand was lightly tugging my hair before sliding down, grazing a breast and coming to rest on my thigh. I needed a while before moving my hand from my lap to her leg, and despite being in the moment and enjoying her kiss, her touch, it was nothing like being with Arwen. That I was kissing someone else and it felt like I was being unfaithful not to Gabe but to Arwen said so much to me, though I couldn't be sure if that was because Neves was a woman.

Our tongues touched and her hand slipped under my shorts to rest against the flesh high up my outer thigh and with a hard passionate finish, she pulled away, licked her lips and hummed, arching her back and pushing her breasts against my arm. It felt good but not the same.

"Now that was enjoyable." She readjusted herself and the leather squeaked. "Listen, I've pretty much already given the game away that I'm attracted to you so there's no harm in going for broke here," she continued as my head fizzed, "my apartment's a five minute walk away ... if you're interested? And just so you know, I make the best breakfasts in Lagos."

Well, it was there if I wanted it, a human touch, to feel needed, to be taken by a woman who obviously knew what she was doing. And to look at her was to see an attractive woman, except I felt no attraction for her.

And why was that?

Was it because she was a woman or because she wasn't Arwen?

She saw my hesitation, "Freya? Are you all right?" Her hands touched my forearm. "If I came on too strong, I..."

"No, no ... I ... I mean, you're lovely," I heaved and my chest quivered and then I couldn't prevent the tears from cascading from my eyes and I was so embarrassed that I had to turn away, "I'm sorry ... so ... so sorry." I began to slide out from the booth because I wanted to run, somewhere, anywhere, to curl up, to hide but I felt her hand on my shoulder and froze.

"Freya," her voice was warm and caring, "you can't go anywhere like this. It's fine. Please, stay, tell me what's wrong."

I hid my face under my hands, "you don't want to know."

"Oh yes, I do." Her arm was around me now and how could I not return to her?

I slid back and breathed, wiped the tears, tried to meet her eyes and couldn't. "I'm sorry for ruining your night."

She pulled me in and began patting me on the shoulder, much like how a parent would tend a crying child and if she'd wanted me a minute ago, I doubt she did anymore and it was a small mercy that I was in no physical position to be able to look up and see her disappointment. "You have not ruined my night." She lied.

I needed a few minutes to dry my face and settle myself whilst she passed me tissues and made soothing sounds into my ear.

Did I really come to a gay bar as a cry for help?

Well, if one thing came from this whole episode, it's that I could no longer refer to myself as the rational one. That title could go to Lachlan and probably even Lizzie before myself, which showed how bad things had become.

"If you're ready, I'm here to listen."

Oh, where to begin but I unloaded it all, everything, the pressures of life, the trip, Gabe, Dan, meeting Arwen, developing a major crush on a girl, my infidelity, panicking, being a horrible cow, making the biggest mistake of my life, her leaving, the inevitable breaking down of my relationship with Gabe, his bloody proposal, my accepting, experiencing a delayed reaction to Arwen leaving, even that bloody bottle of wine that fell from my bag, until finally, with nowhere else to turn, I'd come to the one place I hoped to find a friend. "I really fucked up and I just miss her so much." She almost got a word in but I spoke over her. "I feel like I discovered the best thing that ever happened to me and didn't properly appreciate it, I treated her like crap, and forced her away because I was a selfish coward and now she's gone and I'm only now realising I might have thrown away my only chance for happiness," I scrunched up another soggy tissue, "I just feel so helpless."

She snapped her fingers and a bottle of port was brought over.

"Oh, I'll get this," I went for my bag but she dismissed me.

"No chance, you're a guest in my country," she paid the man and poured the sweet red liquid into our glasses, "and I owe you because after hearing that, I feel much better about myself."

"Huh?"

She grinned, "because I thought I was losing my powers but it doesn't sound like you're much of a dyke to me." Seriously? That's what she took from the story of my ordeal?

"But..." I stammered.

"I've still got it and that's a relief." She flicked her hair from one shoulder to the other and saw my stupefaction. "Oh, relax, I'm joking."

"You are?"

"Drink." She pushed the port closer to me and I took it and drank. "Listen, you're an intelligent woman, which apparently is no barrier to getting yourself into a mess and yes, you've been a bitch to two people and in return, you're getting it back." She shook her head, "listen, I'm no believer in karma. I don't think good things happen to good people just by sitting around and waiting for it to happen and neither do I think bad shit happens either. What I do know is that you've cheated on this Gabe guy, which means your heart isn't in it and every minute extra you spend with him is two minutes wasted."

"Mine and his."

"For a doctor, you catch on quick. Are you sure you're not knocked up too?" She smirked and I slapped her on the arm. "You know, it's not too late to take this to bed," she said with a straight face.

"I..."

"Relax, I'm half joking."

"Um..."

"Freya, you're too easy," she grinned again. "Look, I can't tell you what to do but if it were me, I'd break it off with the man and go find the woman. Is it really rocket science?"

I squirmed against the seat, "but how can I be sure she won't just laugh in my face?" It's what I would do and probably enjoy it, though Arwen was not me, even though she loved laughing and often at other people's expense. I didn't think she'd take pleasure in my misery.

She shrugged, "it's a possibility and if it were me, I probably would and it'd be deserved," great, and now that makes two of us, "but if you're serious about this Arwen girl then she's probably worth the risk of being laughed at."

Which meant I had to find her and beg for forgiveness.

Something in my belly sank. "I have no idea where she is." Come to think of it, I didn't even have her number although Dan did. Attempting to obtain it would raise questions though that was hardly my most pressing concern.

"You sure like to throw up obstacles to what's actually pretty simple. The logistics are for you to figure out, that's beyond my pay grade as a friend, or whatever we are."

"I hope we're friends," I said and meant it.

"We're hardly likely to ever see each other again after tonight," which was sad but a fact of life, "and all I got to show for it was a kiss, nice as it was."

I turned the port glass in my hand, "maybe you should not be so quick to dismiss karma. You can't be so sure the universe will never reward you for being a good person." I was beginning to sound less and less like someone who'd studied mathematics, science and medicine and more like one of those artsy types, someone like Arwen.

"Freya," and then a lesbian I met in some gay bar in Portugal spoke the words I would one day frame and place in a position of prominence, "the universe rewards us every single day. We're here. We have free will to do whatever we want but only for a very short time. The biggest crime in existence is to waste it."

———————

IT WAS whilst strolling through the surf, flip flops in hand when from behind pattered the soft steps of feet on sand and I turned to see Gabe running towards me. I waited for him to catch up and when he did he was panting for breath.

"You really need to get yourself in shape." I told him before continuing.

His complexion had improved since he'd been exiling himself from the mosquitoes, though him being outside this late in the evening was a risk. "Freya, we need to talk." It was said with the kind of tonality people used when it was something important, something like a breakup and indeed, he'd foregone using my pet name, even going so far as saying my name in full, which he seldom did unless he wanted my attention.

I raised an eyebrow. "Sounds serious."

"Of course it's serious, it's about us."

The waves were of that typical Algarve sort, small yet rapid and they felt so gentle and soothing on my bare feet. "You've left it a long time. We've barely spoken since Seville and now, suddenly you want to speak with me, whilst I'm enjoying a nice walk along the beach? What happened?"

He ran his hands through his hair, which was the longest I'd ever seen it. "I'm not proud of that but I've had a long time to think about things."

"You're not the only one," I said, looking straight ahead at the long empty stretch of sand. It was the evening after I'd met Neves and I knew what had to be done and as horrific as it would be, I felt strangely at peace with it. My relationship with Gabe was over, even though, for now, I was still wearing his ring.

I'd spent the entire day ruminating over the details. After five years we had shit to unravel, things like living arrangements, placements, bank accounts, mutual friends, property and several other such things that would be better left until after we arrived back in the UK and I'd briefly entertained the idea of leaving the breakup until then, as grotesque as that sounded.

But no. As Neves had said, wasting your one life on earth may be a huge crime but it was an even bigger one to waste that of someone else, and someone you loved at that. It needed to be done despite the fact we were on holiday, which was far from ideal timing yet it was also necessary if I was to separate from the group to find Arwen.

Though from Gabe's tone, I half wondered if he was about to get in there first which, I'd admit, would be a relief.

"Freya, I want to make things right between us."

That was a shock and I was suddenly incensed, catching even myself by surprise. "I have absolutely no desire to make things right with someone who continues to lie to me."

He knew what I meant and we both found ourselves stopping. "I'm sorry, I regret what I did and I admit it. I didn't want to meet your sister and when you fell asleep, I held my breath and continued." He was looking defiantly at me. "I don't know what I was thinking … I mean … what did I expect would happen, that you'd wake up and not realise? Agh, this whole trip…"

I felt my facial muscles softening. "Well thank you for finally admitting what I already knew but why didn't you want to meet my sister?"

He looked down and I followed his gaze to see he was wearing his trainers and even now the waves were washing over them. "Because … agh … because your family…" he shook his head, "no, that's not true, I'd have no problem meeting your sister, ordinarily."

"Your feet, Gabe, and you're not making much sense."

"Oh, I don't care, not right now and I'm trying, ugh." He blew out air and was doing his best to maintain eye contact. "It's just that, I've been under so much pressure."

"Yes," I drew out the word, "as you said before. We've both been under pressure."

"No ... I've been thinking about this a lot and nothing will be right again until I just come out and say it."

Well, he certainly had my attention now. "Say what, Gabe?"

He closed his eyes and took a few breaths. "That stupid proposal. I was under pressure to do it because of your dad."

I blinked, "I'm sorry, my dad? What's he got to do with anything?"

He threw up his arm. "It was his idea. More than just his idea, he was practically threatening me to do it and I caved because, quite honestly, he's your dad and he terrifies me."

I'd lost all feeling in my face as the blood drained from there to go where it was needed, my legs to power a flight response. But I would not run from Gabe. "My dad threatened you to propose to me?"

But already, such an idea was hardly difficult to envisage. No, it was something my dad was most definitely capable of demanding but to actually hear it spoken from Gabe was something else. I didn't want to believe it but it explained so much.

He nodded, "I went to see him a few days before leaving."

"You went to Inverness?"

"Yes, it was that day I told you I was going to see my parents."

And he went on to explain how my father had implied that unless he agreed to marry me, and did so quickly, then he'd do whatever he could to ensure we broke up, his primary weapons being to make Gabe's life a misery and threatening to cut me off like he had Lizzie.

"And you believed all this?" I asked unnecessarily, knowing what my dad was like.

"Of course," he pushed up his glasses, "what could I have done? I didn't want to lose you and I didn't want you to be harmed like your sister. The only choice I had was to propose and do my very best to convince you to have a snap wedding."

And again, I listened as the evening heat felt cold against my skin and I wasn't sure whether to be angry, disappointed, relieved I was finally learning the truth or what. How we were supposed to get married by October, move into a house and have children before my career would prevent us from doing so.

I recalled that evening at the expensive hotel in Malaga. "That's why you were trying so hard to convince me to marry you so quickly." The pieces were beginning to fit and Gabe nodded.

"I didn't just suddenly turn crazy, you know, and I'm pretty sure all this hanging over me has been making me sabotage everything. I mean ... ugh ... I'd gladly marry you, theoretically, but I'm just not sure now's the right time. A long engagement perhaps..."

"Now isn't the right time." I agreed and felt my head spinning. I needed a drink.

"You're wanting a drink, aren't you?" He grinned, how did he do it? "Let's find a place."

We found a nice bar tucked away off a side street and after taking our seats, Gabe ordered for us both - In Portuguese.

I readjusted myself, "Gabe, that's very impressive."

He shrugged it off, "it's only the very basic stuff but I'm learning. I'm not sure what I'll use it for after leaving but it's fun."

I hummed, "well, it's always good to have a second language," and went for my bag, "but at least allow me to pay."

He quickly waved it away, "oh, no, trust me, I insist."

"Um, ok."

The bar was busy and the customers were all locals. I could tell because they were mostly drinking beer from those small glasses called caña, which held a little less than half a pint, whereas we Brits ordered full pints usually. Except right now, of course, we'd ordered port, which I was beginning to worry I was taking too much of a liking to.

We were sitting in a booth with a noticeable space between us, far enough so that it would be a stretch to hold hands. I couldn't help but think how my dad interfering had unwittingly destroyed the relationship he was trying to cement but it was brave of Gabe to finally come clean about everything and the truth was that I admired him for it. Given no choice, he'd agreed to my father's unreasonable demands and had suffered from their consequences, and he'd done so all for me. After learning all this, it pained me that it may have come just a little too late to save us. I still had to do what was necessary. Sometimes life could be so unfair.

"Oh, what am I going to do about that man." I blew out air and would have cried had I not been so numb and all cried out. There'd have to be a conversation with Dad eventually and I couldn't see him being happy come the end of it. Though the best course to take would be to delay speaking with him whilst everything was still in flux, despite feeling a strong urge to phone immediately and demand he stay out of my love life. The truth was, I had no idea where I'd be or even who I'd be with next year, month, week or even this time tomorrow.

Gabe held out his palms. "He's only doing what he thinks is best for you. It wasn't hard to see he'd do anything for you and your brother, including murdering anyone who brought you to harm."

"Anything except butting out of what doesn't concern him." I shuffled closer, "and after everything, you're still backing him up?"

He shrugged, "he's your dad. I don't like it but I understand."

"You're too kind to him," all I could do was shake my head, "are you not touching your drink?"

"I'm, um, I'm trying to turn over a new leaf."

My own glass had been on its way up but port suddenly tasted very off. I pushed the glass away. "So how's..." I began but he spoke at the same time, "sorry," again, we both said together and laughed. "You go." I finally managed to say.

He bowed his head then looked at me. "Freya, I'm so sorry but there's more."

"Oh God," perhaps I was too quick to reject my drink, "what now?"

His cheeks were turning red and it was a struggle for him to raise his chin. "Freya, my love, I've been lying to you since the day this trip began."

I squirmed but couldn't pull my eyes away. "Lying? What do you mean?"

His shoulders hunched, causing his chin to lower and he had to physically pull himself back up, to hold my eye. "We have considerably more money than what we saved."

"What? How?" And what did that have to do with him lying to me? Clearly, I needed more information and I sat, waiting patiently. "Gabe?"

"Ten thousand pounds to be exact." His fist was clenching atop the table. "Freya, I demanded the money because I was angry, I thought he might respect me more if I made some sort of a big demand, and I felt that I deserved it for what he was asking of me ... I have no regrets about that. What I regret is keeping it from you, for making you suffer and sacrifice beyond what was needed when all along I had the means." He cleared his throat and fidgeted with a coaster, all whilst my body numbed. "Like I said, I've been sabotaging our relationship ever since this trip began and part of that was punishing you for what your dad was demanding of me."

My saliva tasted salty, we'd both been sabotaging this. "Ten thousand p..." I could barely finish the words. "All this time? Money? Is it really so important to you?"

He was quick to hold up his hands. "No. It's nothing compared to the person I've had to be without these last weeks. I miss us and I want to make things right. I've told you everything now and I'm willing to accept the consequences of my lies."

I collapsed back into my seat and the air seeped out from inside the cushion. Was he suggesting I was supposed to hand down some kind of a punishment? Because I had one.

"Gabe," I slipped the ring from my finger and slid it across the table, "I'm sorry but it's for the best."

To my astonishment he didn't cry, he didn't frown, he didn't even speak. He just looked at me with a kind of defiance. "I deserve it but I'll win you back."

I jumped when his phone rang.

"Excuse me," he pulled it out and checked the screen, "it's Dan ... great timing as always." He answered, "yo?" His face was solemn and serious as he listened, "what, now? Right now? Are you fucking serious? It's seven in the evening."

"Gabe?"

He nodded, "ok, we'll be right there."

"Gabe, what was that?"

"Doc ... um, Freya, we have to go to Lisbon right now. Are you coming or not?"

*T*he guitar and Dan's singing were loud within the small confines of the camper as we raced along a fast toll road and he revelled in working annoying rejoinders into the lyrics every single time I enquired upon the nature of this mad two hundred mile dash north to Portugal's capital.

"Dan, will you just answer the bloody question," I demanded for the tenth time, "why do we have to be in Lisbon so urgently?" And why now? He'd been as good as dead for weeks and now he was transformed and not only that but for the first time, he'd selected our destination, all man of culture suddenly.

He continued his annoying strumming and sang the response, "I just had a craving for some Belém custard tarts," it was just so infuriating, even more so because it didn't rhyme and wasn't funny in the slightest. But he was back. And that made me happy. Although to look at a map, Lisbon was our next logical destination anyway, so I doubt making the choice had taxed even his brain that much.

"I'd forgotten how annoying I always found you." I stuck out my tongue and in response, he humped the air.

I was sitting in the passenger seat beside Gabe whilst carrying out my usual research and caught a whiff of my odour as I did. It was coconut from the sun lotion, with a large infusing of sweat. I'd been at the beach most of the day and had bits of sand I could feel all over my skin so that I really regretted not sparing the two Euros to take a shower at the beach facilities. Of course, at the time, I'd assumed we were poor. Not so, as it turned out, and the more I thought about that betrayal, the more let down I felt.

The truth was, I didn't begrudge him any of the money, not after what my father did, although I was extremely perplexed he'd kept it a secret from me. I recalled all those times he'd been profligate with our funds, caused me needless anxiety, the major effort it was to be granted any funds for myself and how he'd made me feel completely unreasonable for requesting any. That I could never explain and it was that which hurt the most. And what's more, none of that had anything to do with Arwen and had I never even met the girl, Gabe would still have been lying to me, and over money, of all things.

How could I forgive that?

This bloody trip...

Yes, we were still travelling together, for the moment at least. This Lisbon adventure had been last minute, which had left no time for either of us to make alternative arrangements and besides, so far, everything was still completely amicable though there was no saying for how long that would last.

"Gabe?" I asked and he glanced over from behind the wheel. "Are you all right?"

He smiled and nodded. "Don't worry about me."

At least he was taking it well, for now anyway, and a little less drama around here wouldn't be unwelcome.

It was a little before ten in the evening when we crossed the Vasco da Gama, the longest bridge in Europe which spanned the Tagus and a short while later Gabe impressed us all by squeezing the camper into an impossibly tight space directly outside the Lisboa Central Hostel. Things were looking up. And then we discovered that because it was Saturday evening, parking would be free until Monday morning.

"The rich get richer, right Gabe?" I remarked and he simply shook his head and turned away.

"Right!" Dan declared, "if you don't need my contribution, I'm off."

"What? Where?" I was still on the verge of bursting and now this was most intriguing.

"None of *your* business." He said, placing emphasis on the 'your' like I'd done something wrong and he scooped up his infernal instrument and dashed off down the street.

"Do you have any idea what he's all about?" I asked Gabe, who was gathering the bags together. The hostel was right beside us and I could see, not surprisingly, that the place was packed out, with a bright communal light, flickering screens and people drinking, standing and ambling around inside.

"My guess is he's gone to the train station. I think someone he knows is arriving or something. Could you wait here and look after the bags? I'll return for you and the rest after I've checked us in."

"Sure, why not." I watched him walk off with a bag in each hand and feeling completely deflated, I reentered the camper, sliding the door shut and poured some bottled water into the kettle, flipped the switch, dropped a tea bag into a mug and stood waiting as the water slowly began to hiss and bubble.

The door slid open.

"Give me chance to have a cup of tea, will you?"

"Is that any way to greet an old friend?" The voice.

I spun around and gasped. "What the fuck?"

The blonde hair and braids. "I didn't think you'd be happy to see me but I was expecting a little better than that."

"Arwen?" My mouth was opening and closing and God only knew how dumb I must have looked. My voice barely came out, "what?" Seriously, what?

She stepped inside and reached behind to slide the door closed, not once taking her eyes from me. It was everything I ever wanted but something had changed, I had that feeling immediately. She still looked just as soul-destroyingly, one in a billion, so insanely perfect you just wanted to tear your eyes out beautiful and it took everything I had not to collapse into her arms and declare my undying love for her right here in the camper. But seriously, what the fuck was she doing here?

For the briefest of surreal moments, she seemed to be taking me in as her eyes moved slowly over me. Had I changed much since we were last alone in that bathroom back in Barcelona, where I'd stupidly broken her heart? Physically, I was slightly more tanned with longer hair, a plus, though the last few weeks my nutrition had taken a lesser priority, oh and I had bags under my eyes too, a more recent development and definitely a minus. Though mentally and emotionally...

"Since we're back in the same city," she finally began after folding her arms, "I thought it best to get this out of the way." Her voice was different or at least it seemed so to me and her tan was deeper now.

She was wearing her tiny blue denim shorts and a plain white vest, so simple yet devastating, and to look at her was to lose the ability to breathe. "Our secret's safe. I just wanted you to know that. Gabe won't ever discover anything from me, so you can rest easy. But since we've apparently done a circle and met in the middle ... well, here we all are ... in Lisbon. And just so you know, I'm not doing this for you but for Dan, my friend, who I miss." Her words were hurtful but hardly surprising and not undeserved.

Behind me the kettle was boiling and hissing and, irritated by the noise, she scrunched her nose so that the cute little thing wrinkled up. "You gonna turn that stupid thing off? I saw your boyfriend struggling with two small bags, I'm guessing he'll be back soon so let's get this unpleasant yet necessary confrontation over with."

That was the first sign, right there, and I felt the smallest crack of a smile form on my mouth and she must have noticed it because hers turned down in equal measure.

I was about to tell her that Gabe was no longer my boyfriend when something scuffed outside, Gabe or a pedestrian perhaps, she instinctively turned her head to the sound and I saw a new braid weaved into her hair at the back, this one green to add to the existing red, blue and pink.

I was still unable to form a sentence, indeed, to think was impossible and her head jerked forward as she raised a probing eyebrow.

"Don't have much to say for yourself, do you?"

"Dan?" I managed to squeak.

"He thinks I'm arriving at the station but there was an earlier train from Coimbra. I tried to grab him just now but he was too fast. Unlike some people, Dan appreciates me." That there was another unintentional morsel thrown my way. She may have been trying hard to appear indifferent but she couldn't help it with the jibes, which were lifelines for me. She was hurt, still, and I wanted nothing more than to make it all perfect. And I would, or so I dared hope.

I took a single step forward and her arms quickly unfolded to pull on the handle so that the mechanism clicked and the door flung out from its catch, devastating, and stopping me mid-step.

"You accused me of having an ego, which is true, and you'd have one too if you had an ass like this," even now, "but you're selfish and I was just a curiosity, an experiment, because you're boring and have led such a sheltered, uninteresting life. You used me for a kick and that's much worse than anything I did." That hurt, probably because there was so much truth in it and she half twisted to leave and my heart screamed but then she turned back to look at me. "And you were very wrong to blame me entirely for what happened."

Yes! She was right and I needed to tell her so, that I was sorry and would do anything to take it all back. "Arwen, please, can we just..." I dashed forwards and saw Gabe standing across the street, looking both ways as he waited to cross.

She'd seen him too, "like you said, pull yourself together, we can't have Gabe thinking anything's amiss."

I squinted at the vague memory of my own words being paraphrased against me. She remembered all that?

"Arwen? It is, isn't it?" There was laughter from outside as I remained standing limply in the camper. "That about explains it then. It's really good to see you, ugh, big hugs." There was a pause. "But, didn't you see Dan?"

"I'm on my way to find him. Thought I'd say hi to Freya first ... poor thing looks worn out and starved. How are you anyway?"

"Oh, yeah, you know, fine. You're staying here I take it? We should all go for drinks tonight ... be like old times again?" His hand was patting blindly around inside for the bags and in my daze, I shoved them towards him.

"Maybe we can, Gabe, maybe we can. Ooh, you got those?"

"Um, I think so ... a bit heavy ... Freya's got something weighing a tonne in this one."

"And that's why she's so lucky to have such a big strong man as you."

Oh, the little minx but I concentrated all my being into scrutinising Gabe's response. Was he about to do what I didn't have the chance for myself and tell her we were no longer together?

There was the scrape of feet scuffing on paving, "ah, now..." a pause, "um..."

"Anyway, Dan's gonna be angry if I don't intercept him, I'll catch you in a bit."

"Oh, yes, ok."

And that was that.

Because apparently, Arwen was in Lisbon.

GABE and I waited in silence on a rooftop bar called Topo, which overlooked the Mouraria district of the city and had the São Jorge Castle looming in the near distance, providing a splendid ambience with soft music and a view lit by the city's night lights. If only I was in a state to enjoy it.

For the fifth time in as many minutes, Gabe checked the time on his phone, sipped his soft drink and muttered something under his breath. Then finally, just when the silence was becoming painful, his face shot to life, his line of sight pointed straight over my shoulder and I whipped around to see Dan and Arwen walking over, arms around each other, as they threaded a path between tables and sofas.

They were both beaming as they took seats facing Gabe and I, and whether intentional or not, Dan chose to sit opposite me so that Arwen was furthest away at a diagonal.

I coughed and shifted, which prompted a snide sideward glance from Dan and in my paranoia, I could only assume he still suspected, rightly, I had a little something more to do with Arwen's leaving our group than he knew.

"Was it worth coming to Lisbon or what?" He declared and shifted around to lean against the wall so that he was facing Arwen and I was cut out.

Arwen dragged her chair around to face Dan but did so in a way that did not exclude Gabe and now she was closer to facing me, though so far she hadn't so much as looked at or acknowledged me, despite the fact I was finding it hard to look both at and away from the girl.

"Boy could hardly leave me alone but you sure feel loved walking over those mountains, hitting an accidental hotspot and having thirty or forty messages all tumbling in at once." She rubbed Dan's arm, the grin on his face was something to behold and all I could do was ponder whether that was a dig at me, who'd done little but think of Arwen these last weeks, even if I'd not attempted to contact her.

"Jesus," Gabe said, "you're not even exaggerating."

She shook her head. "I sure felt loved."

The waiter arrived and asked if we'd like to order drinks. Gabe gestured to his nearly empty glass and, in Portuguese, ordered another soft drink. The waiter puckered his lips in appreciation, glanced at Arwen and exhibited the usual look of derangement I was so used to seeing. She arched her back, which caused her boobs to push slightly out and I lost all feeling in my legs as that familiar thrumming began to stir in my belly because Arwen commenced a conversation in Portuguese, ordering tapas for the table, or so I assumed. The waiter then looked to Dan.

"Ok, I'm giving this a go," he cleared his throat and rubbed his temples before surprising me and totally impressing Arwen by labouring through something vaguely resembling the native tongue. The girl was willing him on, correcting him on a couple of words and Dan insisted on starting again from the beginning because he wanted to get the whole thing right, whilst the waiter was good-natured enough to humour it. The word Sangria was easy enough to work out but from the sound of it, Dan was changing the recipe to his own specifications.

"Leave out the apples and add more sugar and brandy." Gabe helped for my benefit before he and Arwen cheered when Dan finished his order.

Finally, it was my turn, "beer please."

There was an extended silence until, mercifully, the waiter broke it by saying, "ok," and leaving as I felt the heat rising. Back in Barcelona, I'd cruelly called Arwen the odd one out but now it was me.

Gabe broke the tension, "so tell us about the Camino?"

She turned to face him and her eyes swept over me so fast I was unsure whether it actually happened. "It was really fricking awesome. What could be better than a seven hundred mile cross-country trek with awesome company? No offence, Freya. Oh, it was one big adventure, exploring, camping, feasting, making good friends and seeing sites all over the place, cities like Zaragoza, Burgos and León. Oh, and let's not forget Santiago itself," she grabbed Dan by the arm, "you have to see it. There's nowhere else like it on the planet and I'm not even religious."

"What about your feet?" Gabe enquired.

She dismissed his concerns by flapping a hand then propping it on her hip, all nothing can faze me. "Oh Gabe, thanks for the concern but I think I can handle it."

My brain was already chewing over the details and I could tell Gabe's mathematical head was doing the same. I was glad he enquired for me. "Seven hundred miles? It's been what, four weeks, a little less?"

She shrugged, "who's counting, babe?"

Giving her the benefit of the doubt and calling it thirty days would mean she'd have to have been walking from anywhere between twenty and twenty-five miles each and every day, no days off. Stopping in those cities would take time off the thirty but I already knew Arwen had spent time in Coimbra, which was not even in Spain but the middle of bloody Portugal. I was beginning to smell the bullshit even if nobody else could and my wishful mind was starting to throw up hopeful scenarios where she'd had a bust-up with her Dutch travelling friends and ditched them, Floor particularly, maybe even taken a bus ride or twelve and left them burning in the hot Spanish sun. It was wishful thinking, for sure, but there was something she wasn't telling us. So far, our Dutch friends had not been mentioned and, to the best of my knowledge, they weren't even here with Arwen in Lisbon and I was beginning to dare hope that my earlier fears of Floor and Arwen being together as a couple were unfounded.

"Any other fine places you recommend we see?" I finally spoke up and for the first time since her arrival, Arwen and I made eye contact.

"Yes, Freya," she said so formally I didn't know what to make of it, "I recommend visiting Porto," she continued in the same tone, another Portuguese city.

Now I was feeling mischievous, "I hear it's beautiful but quite large, how long did you say you spent there?" I wondered if I detected the smallest, faintest twitching of her left eyelid.

"Only two nights, Freya, you see, I had the Camino de Santiago to complete, which pretty much ate up most of the last month." She was on to me and the funny thing was that she lost the formality and instead used a slow cautionary tone, whilst watching for my reaction. She knew, or at least suspected I was sceptical of her claims and I made a deliberate show of leaning back in my seat, interlacing my fingers, nothing else needing to be said as her eyes, most satisfyingly, narrowed further.

I don't know why I did it, perhaps to provoke a reaction, good or bad, because anything was better than being ignored by the girl you were in love with, even if she went straight back to ignoring me after. I had to do something.

But there was no way, no way I could envisage *that* group completing a seven hundred mile trek through Spanish mountains in what was probably only twenty-five days, with backpacks weighing them down, repeated stops, setting up of tents and visiting sites of interest. Karla was another factor, with her short legs and constant diversions to dig up every geocache within a fifty-mile radius. And that's not forgetting Floor, who I hardly took for the type to enjoy getting dirty and squatting it out on that kind of a trip. No, there was more to it, I was convinced of it now and after thinking it all over, when my blank stare regained focus, Arwen was still watching me and had to quickly look away.

The drinks and tapas arrived and I had to endure Dan's constant innuendos involving Arwen and his plans for their future together, tongue in cheek as it was, even though we all knew it was exactly what he wanted. It was the sort of thing Arwen should have been discouraging, not that it would do any good regardless, not with a guy like Dan, and especially not after he'd been so long apart from our mutual obsession. Instead, Arwen enjoyed it more than what was sensible, though the occasional sideward glance at me whilst it was happening made me question her motivations.

"I have gifts," she announced later, sifting through her bag, pulling out a small bottle-shaped object in wrapping paper and passing it to Dan.

His eyes widened as he seized the gift and began unwrapping in earnest to reveal a bottle of Lea & Perrins Worcestershire Sauce. "Oh, my Christ, where did you get this?"

She shrugged, "I actually bought it in Lisbon, there's a British expat shop in the Madalena district."

He was already unscrewing the top as I prepared to blanch, "you have to take me there," and then he sent it down, imbibing almost half the contents in one go and wiping his mouth with the back of a hand. "You'll make an excellent wife for me one day." And the thing was that coming from him, it didn't even sound weird.

She returned to her bag and wriggled uneasily as she handed me the wrapped present. "It's for you *and* Gabe."

"Ah," I shifted a little myself, unsure how to respond and Gabe cleared his throat as I shook the gift, a flat square object, quite light and I began to remove the paper that only now could I see had the words 'Mr & Mrs' printed all over it.

Shit.

I peeped up to catch Arwen's eyes snapping from me to Gabe and when I looked down again, I found myself holding a picture frame. I turned it over and saw what it was. It was one of those box frames with our forenames connecting over the word 'Engaged' in Scrabble letters.

She smiled from the mouth, her bottom lip trembling so subtly. "I'm so happy for both of you," her voice sounded choked too.

Gabe rubbed the back of his neck and it was suddenly hot on this rooftop. "Oh, Arwen, I'm sorry about the, um..." he began and I felt it a duty to finish for him.

"Arwen, we actually broke up," I spoke as earnestly as I could.

Dan immediately burst out into laughter, almost spilling everyone's drinks when he tipped back in his seat, and stealing my attention from the girl. It occurred to me that it was likely Gabe hadn't yet told his friend the news, which was quite understandable, it had only just happened and was still sinking in for us both.

"Not quite the reaction I was expecting but it's a funny joke." She swiped a large cluster of blonde out from her eyes before glancing at Dan who was still struggling to contain himself.

"It's not like you, Freya, to make jokes and you said it so serious." He had to untie his man bun to deal with the many strands that had fallen loose. Dan had obviously filled Arwen in on the gossip as to our engagement but had not thus far been privy to our breaking up and therefore neither had Arwen.

"*Our secret's safe*," is what she'd said in the camper, "*Gabe won't ever discover anything from me.*" She'd known and bless her, wanted to protect me despite the turmoil I must have put her through.

Gabe tugged on his collar as I concentrated on the meandering floor patterns and neither of us were smiling.

"What the fuck?" Arwen suddenly cried out. "You're fucking serious?"

Dan's face flipped into a grimace as his eyes bulged out. "He is, he's serious."

The present was still in my hand and I stared blankly at the 'a' in 'engaged' and how it connected with the last letter of my name. "We ... um ... it's true, guys, we broke up."

Dan shot forward. "Fucking when?"

Gabe coughed, "earlier today."

Arwen came level with Dan. "You never told me."

I had to look up to see she was speaking not to Dan but to me. "Well, you didn't give me chance."

"I did but you were too awestruck by my presence to spit it out, literally." Oh, that little minx. "Perhaps you didn't think it was important enough to tell me?" Her voice came out as a squeak, quite unlike anything I'd ever heard from her because she could barely believe the news, and I didn't care that the people on the nearby sofa were watching us because that was another lifeline. She truly cared and I needed to speak with her this very minute.

My hand had balled into a fist of its own accord and I spoke through clenched teeth as I was literally shaking. "I think it's time for a bathroom break." I jerked my face in the direction of the ladies room to suggest that she should join me.

I probably should have glanced back instead of striding straight off because ten minutes after I'd entered the bathroom, she still hadn't arrived. Perhaps she hadn't noticed my little nodding signal? No, of course not.

I was still shaking when I stomped back, Gabe was holding his head, Arwen was grinning at me, which hardly helped, and then Dan shouted loud enough for too many people to hear, "did you drop a kidney?"

I retook my seat and had to bite my tongue, I was that liable to blow and all whilst she smiled so smugly, not because Gabe and I had broken up but because she had me and she knew it and was fully intending on prolonging my misery for her amusement.

Why?

Did we have nothing to discuss? To straighten out? To get off both our chests? All I needed was a few miserly minutes alone with the girl to explain myself, my position, everything. If she was playing some game to frustrate me then it was working and over the next hour, I sat patiently, waiting for the moment when she would inevitably need the bathroom, but alas, that moment never presented itself because, as it transpired, the girl had a bladder like a bloody football.

It amazed me how she could flip from incredulity one minute to indifference the next, that in one instant she sought clarification as to my status with Gabe and the next couldn't care less. How much of it was an act and how much was her way of further frustrating me as punishment?

But I would get my opportunity, I was determined about that. I just hoped that when it arrived I could keep a clear head and not fall to pieces like I had in the camper.

We left the bar and walked back to the hostel. It was a strange walk home, where Arwen and Dan were animatedly catching up on what they'd missed, whilst Gabe and I lingered a long way behind struggling to make conversation.

But I knew which room was Arwen's, on account of watching her walk through the door, and she pulled a face directed at me as she closed it behind her.

Thirty minutes, I told myself, and I'd be banging on that thing and I cared not if I interrupted her meditation or anything else.

I lasted less than ten and almost kicked the door in frustration because through it, I could hear Dan serenading the girl with a little help from the guitar string *I'd* purchased for him.

But I'd get her tomorrow.

Just try stop me.

I WAS downstairs early for breakfast, showered, makeup applied and dressed in an attractive casual white and red flower print summer dress I'd purchased in the Algarve. Perhaps I was too early, the only other people awake being an older couple who were checking out but I couldn't risk not grabbing my moment with Arwen so I had to be here.

I'd thought it all over, exactly what I needed to say, rehearsed it in my head and so I hoped it would make a difference when the time came to apply it.

As it was, it was Gabe who arrived first, which obviously meant I'd again have to wait, wait and bloody wait and my coffee rippled in the mug as I brought it to my lips.

"Doctor ... sorry, Freya, we haven't spoken much since yesterday," he sat with a large plateful and a coffee.

I straightened and rearranged my mini croissants and pain au chocolates around my plate. "That's because you've spent all this time lying to me."

"Yes, and I will always regret that. You know that's not me but we need to discuss the rest of this holiday."

"You'd like to know if we're still travelling together after everything?"

"Well aren't we?" He was quick to ask.

"The camper, Gabe, you paid for it with this ten thousand, didn't you?" I'd had time now to think about that as well as a few other things.

"Well, yes, I did."

"So tell me, how much is left?"

He squirmed, "of the ten thousand, pretty much nothing," he saw my stern expression and was quick to elaborate, "the camper cost six thousand and we've used up the other four, give or take." It sounded reasonable enough though I couldn't be sure whether or not he was telling the truth and that was the whole problem. Though assuming, on this occasion, he was being truthful then that left our original five thousand budget untouched.

"I want my half of our savings, Gabe, and not a penny less, either on a card or in cash. Give me that and then we can discuss the rest of the holiday."

He nodded and said nothing else, not then and not before Dan and Arwen arrived together several minutes later.

Dan had been in his bed when I awoke and so I assumed he'd been kicked out of Arwen's room at some point during the night and had been good enough not to wake me like on so many other occasions. When I rose, I'd been surprised to find him already awake, stroking a ginger cat that lazed and purred atop his sheet. "She belongs to the hostel," he'd whispered, not wanting to disturb her, "and I've named her Freya," and I'd wondered if that was his way of insulting or forgiving me. There were times men could be just as perplexing as women.

"It seems like forever since we all last had breakfast together." Arwen now stated as she opened a mini box of cornflakes and I concurred, it was too long ago. She was wearing that red jumpsuit I'd last seen in France and it was a necessary struggle to keep my eyes occupied elsewhere. How nobody had yet spotted me gawping was a mystery, though that was probably because everybody else was doing the same. She was a distraction for sure.

Dan, obviously sensing the building friction between Gabe and I, suddenly raised his voice. "Whatever it is with the two of you, you'd better sort it out and quick."

I shook my head. "Some things aren't as simple as that, Dan." I caught Arwen's eye from across the table and neither of us looked away until Dan yelled again.

"I don't give a shit. Listen, Miss Logic," I jerked at that, "you bagged a bloody doctor, so don't fuck it up and you, you four-eyed moron ... you bagged a bloody doctor, and a slender redheaded one with nice tits, so don't fuck it up. Don't make me lock the pair of you in the janitor's closet until you sort it out, whatever it is."

Arwen was making herself small and although the pair of them were pretty tight, there was at least one subject she'd kept from him. No, Arwen could be trusted, which was more than could be said for anyone else around here.

But it was times like this that I understood why people 'came out,' if only to stop others from interfering. One swift declaration that I was in love with Arwen would put an end to it all and let the pieces fall where they may.

And why not do just that?

This was not some weird phase I was going through, I knew that now, and I most certainly did love that stupid girl. The problem was that when those fragmented pieces settled, they'd be scattered far and wide and no amount of glue would ever stick them back together again. No matter how much of a disaster this holiday had been for my relationship with Gabe, I had no desire to see him hurt. And besides, my love life was no business of Dan's or anyone else's.

I wanted to change the subject and was about to ask Arwen how she intended to spend the day when my attention was taken by movement in my periphery.

No.

They were here, or at least two of them were because even now, Samuel and Karla were walking towards us, or more specifically, Samuel was creeping towards Arwen with a hushing finger held to his lip but Arwen noticed my glassy expression, turned her head and yelped with delight, shoving away her chair and skipping across the room to embrace the pair of them.

I liked both Samuel and Karla but seeing them now really brought the bitter taste out in my coffee as I scanned beyond them in anticipation of the other two emerging any second. Both Dan and Gabe held questioning expressions, Dan, in particular, being unable to look away from the activity as the screeching diminished and a more subdued conversation began from a distance. Dan no doubt had them pegged and would know they'd be her Camino buddies and I wondered if he felt like I did, that the girl he craved was slipping away because she had other friends now. Clearly, they must have bonded.

After a few minutes, Arwen brought them over, the newcomers recognising my familiar face first.

"Hey, Freya," Karla said, not needing to stoop to offer me hugs from where I sat, "it's so awesome to see you again," which sounded genuine enough but then, why wouldn't it?

Samuel merely nodded. "I really recommend Coimbra if you've not been yet," he spoke to us all, his usually friendly self in fisherman hat, "historically, it's the university city, like your Oxford or Cambridge, Freya. I tried to tell Arwen that one day wasn't enough but you lot arrived and so we got ditched."

So, the news was that Arwen had been with the gang, or at least two of them, up until yesterday and I noticed how Dan perked from the news that they were ditched in favour of him. He'd spent the last minute studying the pair but now stood and used his height advantage to look down on Samuel as he held out his mitt. "I'm Dan."

"Samuel," he took the palm, winced from the crush and tried to let go but found himself unable to retract, "it's nice to meet you," he reinforced when finally, he was able to take back his limb.

Arwen nudged Dan in the side, "we're going to Belém if you're interested?"

He shrugged, "Belém?" Then the recognition hit him, "you need a whole day to buy custard tarts."

Samuel answered for her, "it's not just the custard tarts but the Torre de Belém."

"Which means tower," Gabe helped.

"We're both massive fans of that style of architecture," Arwen said and Dan's eyebrows dipped with scepticism.

"Oh really? And what style would that be?" He directed the challenge to Samuel, evidently believing the guy had ulterior motives and I quickly fired a text to Dan to explain that Samuel and Karla were in a relationship and that he should stop being a jerk.

Samuel didn't even flinch, "that would be the Portuguese Manueline style."

Dan had no answer to that and then his phone vibrated, he checked the message and subtly nodded in acknowledgement.

"Are you coming or not?" Arwen repeated.

"Uuum, I don't think so," passing the chance to spend the day with Arwen was evidently easier now he knew Samuel was no threat, "but bring me back some custard tarts. They're at least one thing I miss from England."

"Me too!" The Piston yelped and everyone's head turned to look at her.

"You're not going with them?" I enquired.

Samuel shook his head. "If it's between old buildings and geocaching, there'll only ever be one winner."

Dan coughed and Arwen beamed in my direction, "Freya, you should keep her company. You always said you fancied giving geocaching a try. Now's your chance."

I felt my facial muscles slacken as I shot her an angry glare that I had to quickly cover up. I'd said nothing of the sort and she knew it, the little minx, and I lamented the inability to drag her out into the corridor and tell her so, along with other things.

The Piston shot suddenly forwards, hands clasped at her solar plexus. "Oh, you should so definitely come. Nobody ever comes with me, it'll be so much fun."

I glanced apologetically at the girl, "I really would, Karla, but it's my first day in Lisbon and I was kind of hoping to explore the sites."

"Well that's what geocaching's all about," Arwen intervened, helpfully, with more than just a little sparkle in the eyes, "walking around the city, following GPS signals, or whatever, and burrowing for the hauls, right? You could both totally do that whilst exploring Lisbon."

What could I do? She got one up on me and I then had to endure the remainder of my breakfast with her triumphantly grinning from opposite, whilst all I could do was promise to get her back at some point.

I soon realised, however, that I'd been wrong to so readily dismiss geocaching and by default, having to spend the day with The Piston. Sure, my outfit was wasted and yes, she repeatedly chastised me for having the desire to wander off from the signal, or whatever it was we were supposedly following, whenever there was anything of interest to see but there were positives too.

Karla was an easy target, innocent as she was, and as long as I could direct the conversation towards more interesting subjects, then knowledge could be attained.

"So, how many hauls did you dig up during the Camino?" I asked as my attention was stolen by a beautiful quaint little street with old shops and a tramline running straight down the cobbles.

"No, no, not there, it's this way," she tugged me away from where I'd wanted to go and onto the adjacent boring street with nothing of interest. As it turned out, The Piston could be a little too assertive when it came to certain things. "The Camino? Only three, not many."

"Is that all?" I tried to sound disappointed. "Why?"

Her face was full of concentration as she stared into her phone. "Because, Freya, people get bad tempered. Are you paying attention? Left at the end of this street then we have to go north by northwest."

"Really? For how long?" We were heading away from the centre now, from the things I wanted to see.

"Until I say, Freya."

I decided not to interrupt whilst she simmered down and she used the time to talk about geocaching, Samuel and geocaching, all as the girl's short legs barely moved. It truly was a strange hobby for such a plodder and yet more evidence against Arwen's Camino tales. Karla might have been capable of walking faster when not staring into a phone though I doubted it.

"Arwen was wrong to call it a haul," she said with a serious tone a few minutes after we'd turned left, "as were you back there."

"What?" I asked, not knowing what the heck she was referring to, though the mention of Arwen's name focused my attention.

"Before, at breakfast, she called it a haul when it's a cache. She was wrong about that. You too."

I couldn't help grinning. "Well, did you ever offer to take her along with you? How else is she supposed to learn about it otherwise?"

"She came! Everyone did! And she still can't remember obvious terminology." This was most interesting and uncharacteristically catty of Karla and I remained quiet whilst she rambled on, in the hope she'd eventually drop a tidbit of juicy gossip, which meant having to endure and sift through the useless crap first, entirely geocaching related. "And it was one of my best ever caches ... in Zaragoza. I had to get down on my hands and knees and pull up a tonne of weeds but it was worth it because someone had left a crushed coin with the word *geocaching* engraved on it. I took it and replaced it with a Lego man and then Arwen started laughing and said she couldn't take it anymore." She shook her head from the unpleasant memory. "That was when she told us she was taking the train and everyone ended up following her."

"Hah." It came out much louder than intended, which prompted Karla to show her teeth. "Sorry." I considered it for a second. "Hang on ... train to where?"

"All the way to Santiago de Compostela," Karla snarled.

And there it was. The lying little minx. Oh, but what now of all Arwen's tales of traversing mountains and meadows and streams whilst camping in the wilderness, of making lifelong companions and eating fried breakfasts, of singing Kumbaya around the campfire and visiting strange and wonderful sites, of dancing with nature as the sun sank over the horizon. As it turned out, she'd done little more than geocached her way only as far as the first major city, Zaragoza, which Google Maps confirmed was less than two hundred of a seven hundred mile journey. And poor Karla was still upset over it.

"Let's find this cache," I said softly and in return, she absolutely beamed.

"Looks like it's somewhere over there." She nodded up the street, a mere residential one at that, which was hardly a scintillating introduction to this strange hobby. Still, I'd go along with it for Karla, I liked her. "They were sharing a tent most nights."

My heart thudded. "Who?" I half yelped as my throat backed up, as if I needed to ask.

"She was, with Floor." My worst fears were confirmed in a tone almost like we were taking a gentle stroll on a quiet street, which we were, even if my surroundings suddenly lost all clarity.

I had to take a breath, "Arwen and Floor were sharing a tent?"

"Not far now and why are there so many parked cars around? Some geocachers have no imagination. Huh? Oh, yes. Well, most nights, for two weeks or thereabouts. I only know because they argue a lot and we hear it through the tent. Nobody can understand them because it's always in Spanish but other times it's in English and your name gets mentioned and Luuk says Arwen's only doing it to wind her up."

I didn't know whether or not to take relief from that last bit, though there was one question I just had to ask. "Karla, are Arwen and Floor in a relationship?" As soon as I asked, I regretted it. Not because I feared Karla might suspect my reasons for asking but because I didn't know how I'd cope with the truth. Surely, if they were a couple then Floor would be with the rest of them in Lisbon, yet to the best of my knowledge she wasn't and even though I was afraid of the answer, I couldn't look away.

But Karla just shrugged, "dunno, they don't tell me anything and after Zaragoza, I don't speak much to Arwen, not until she apologises." Which was hardly helpful and only threw up more questions. But if they were sharing a tent then either they were in a relationship or were simply ... I could barely bring myself to contemplate it.

I exhaled loudly, prompting a questioning sideward peep from Karla. It was all driving me mad, though the truth was that after what I did to her, I probably deserved it. I just hoped Arwen wasn't enjoying my misery too much.

———

IT WAS one of the better hostels.

In my limited travelling experience, there weren't many that organised evening socials with cheap food, drink and music so that travellers could mingle. Usually it was left up to chance and you'd converse with the occasional Scandinavian or Brazilian in the laundry room but here, because you only needed to pay three Euros for a glass of wine, which they'd happily fill to the top, there were now dozens of travellers in the communal room with more trickling in every few minutes. I was still on a budget and it was an inexpensive way to spend an evening.

The Piston and I had only just arrived back and after spending an entire day with her there were few things that sounded better than a glass of wine and together with Samuel, we loitered by a large fish tank whilst I tried not to watch Arwen too hard as she happily distributed Belém custard tarts from a carrier bag, like she needed to do that to be popular. Apparently, they were the reason to come to Lisbon and I was curious as to their taste.

"I'm sorry about before," Karla said after taking a sip of beer, "I get tetchy looking for geocaches."

I pulled my eyes away from Arwen, who was held up by a tall guy wearing a bandana and who leaned too far forwards, unable to look away as the pastry rested forgotten in his hand. "I wasn't in the least bit offended." I reassured her. "If anything, I found it amusing. It's good to have hobbies you're serious about," or so I assumed.

She examined her keyring of a tram, which apparently were big in this city, if I ever got to see it. She'd taken it from the cache and replaced it with one of her patented Lego men and I'd had to think of my breakup to keep from laughing. She was still wearing her jeans, covered in filth from when she had to crawl beneath a parked car and through a puddle from where there was a loose cobble, under which was buried the cache and she'd remarked how it was her new favourite.

The communal room was gradually filling with more people, one group from which headed straight for the bar before beginning a game of air hockey and I scanned the room for Gabe and Dan but reasoned they were most likely still out busking.

Arwen noticed me from beside her bandana and, unable to resist the mischief, skipped straight over, leaving behind a poor infatuated soul whilst struggling to maintain a straight face. "How was your day geocaching?"

Karla turned away with a "humph" and I knew there was no way I could give Arwen the satisfaction of knowing she was under my skin, at least not with this.

"We had an incredible time, right Karla? And I can't thank you enough for suggesting it." I grinned, thrusting out my chest and her eyes narrowed. "There's a geocaching society in Stirling and I'm thinking of taking it up when I get back."

"Is that a fact?" She asked with a sceptical tone. "Then I'm sure you'd love to do it again tomorrow, right?"

"Are those Belém custard tarts?" I didn't wait for her invitation and thrust my hand straight into the bag.

"Why not help yourself."

I pulled one out from the many cartons she'd bought and as it was, they weren't all that dissimilar to the egg custard tarts that were popular back home, though these were sweeter with a much crispier pastry.

"Would you like one, Karla?" Arwen offered with a smirk.

The Piston was leaning into Samuel and the back of her head twitched.

"That's a no." Samuel clarified.

Arwen jerked her head in the direction of the bar. "It's thirsty work, being the most popular person in the room, I'm off for a drink."

Finally my chance. After patiently waiting for an excruciatingly frustrating time, I had to risk indigestion by hurriedly scoffing down the tart and I'd only taken the first step when my attention was stolen by a figure dressed in black hobbling through the door. She was tall, she was striking and she had a style I'd never seen anywhere else and seeing her prompted my eyes to commence rapid blinking.

Because Floor was here.

And despite her apparent difficulty walking, which raised yet more questions, or perhaps answered them, she still made a beeline for Arwen, seeking her out only as quickly as someone with an obsession could.

She was dressed in her usual black, a blouse that showcased her slender arms and skirt that almost covered her feet so that I could only just see the special shoe she dragged across the floorboards. Her black hair was loose to frame her striking features, having evidently ditched the stupid tiara and that was when I noticed the braid and my heart thudded.

That was supposed to be one of *our* things, even though, in a moment of madness, I'd unravelled it and washed away the last essence of Arwen.

Now Floor had a braid.

And although the next minute had the potential to hurt me deeply, I couldn't turn away because all my questions were about to be answered.

I held my breath as Floor tapped Arwen on the back, she turned around and, despite my watching closely, I was unable to witness Arwen's reaction due to Floor's head blocking the view, though what happened next could in no way be misinterpreted.

They kissed.

It was only a quick kiss, on the lips, closed-mouthed but I saw Arwen's smile now, dwarfed by Floors as it was but then Arwen's eyes snapped across to me and I jolted and froze, caught, unable to look away, despite feeling an ache like I'd never experienced. One side of Arwen's mouth turned down but then she centred back to Floor, cupped her jaw and pulled her in for another, longer kiss as her hand slipped into her hair from where she began to wind Floor's solitary braid around a finger.

I knew what she was doing, even understood it, that she was trying to make me jealous and succeeding pretty well at it. But what the fucking hell was she playing at? What if Dan had been here? Sure, I'd hurt her but had she lost all subtlety and decency over the last few weeks?

Finally, their lips parted but Floor clung to her arm, totally besotted, and pressed her boobs hard against Arwen and knowing I was still watching, she returned the gesture by crushing against Floor.

"There's supposed to be a good cache in Belém. We could do that tomorrow." Karla chirped from my side.

Over the last few seconds, a group of three male travellers had subtly shifted closer to the two women and again, Arwen and I made eye contact through the gap between them but I couldn't tell what was going on behind her eyes. It was like she was conflicted but I couldn't explain it.

"The geocaching forum said it's one of the best in Lisbon."

Arwen sipped from her wine glass and held her teeth at the rim then Floor flirtingly pulled her arm down and began nuzzling her neck. Arwen's eyes again met mine but this time Floor noticed she wasn't receiving her crush's full attention and she followed her gaze across the room and I was startled to be met with the most chilling moment of my entire life.

Floor made a double take, her eyes bulging and fixing on me, and she whipped back on Arwen who stepped away and then they both commenced exchanging rapid hand gestures and angry facial expressions.

I had no idea what to think, on one hand it was funny, on the other confusing, and my head fizzed so hard that I needed to sit down to process things.

"What do you reckon? We could set out after breakfast and be back in time for tomorrow night's party." Really, the girl was beginning to resemble a one-dimensional character from a bad romance novel.

"Yes, novel."

"What?"

Why had Floor reacted like that? Obviously, she was surprised to find me in Lisbon, which meant Arwen hadn't told her I was here and judging from that look of sheer poison, it was easy to surmise Arwen had given her reasons to hate me which, I supposed, was a good thing, I think. Not that it discouraged Floor because she now took Arwen's hand and tugged her towards the couch.

I turned into Karla, if only to avoid Floor's constant menacing daggers as she continued to demonstrate her possession of Arwen, all whilst I had to endure the obvious subject from Karla. I glanced over her shoulder and saw that at some point, Luuk had arrived and was now speaking with Samuel.

It was all too much and the heat didn't make it any easier. What did Floor know about Arwen and I? She'd been given reason to hate or perhaps fear me though I just couldn't picture Arwen blabbing the sensitive details to another person, she'd already promised it was our secret. By far the worst thing though was having to watch the two of them together and although Arwen was hardly instigating anything, she was far from discouraging it. And why was that? Did Arwen like her or not? If she didn't like her, why were they kissing and snuggling on the couch? And did my being in the room affect how things were playing out? Ugh, if she'd wanted to hurt me back then she was succeeding.

My mind was a mess and I hated it and if I didn't get a few minutes to speak alone with her soon, I was likely to lose my mind. No, I had to take a chance and fuck the consequences, I no longer cared.

There was a door situated between myself and where Arwen and Floor were seated and it wasn't like I needed to pretend much, as I wobbled in that direction, which drew both girls' attention, and the tears flowed easily as I screwed up my face. I almost bumped into one man holding a pint glass and then staggered as I passed through the doorway and into the empty corridor where I crumpled against the wall, sobbing and waited.

I received my reward after only two minutes.

Her hand touched my shoulder. "Frey?"

What good is making a person jealous if they're not there to witness it?

I spun around, she was alone, and I seized the opportunity, "gotcha," as well as her wrist and pulled her into the laundry room, locking the door and standing square in front of it as imposing as I could.

Her mouth plunged so far open I could see a filling, so she did possess at least one physical flaw. "Of all the..." she was lost for words and I wondered if I detected the slightest hint of admiration on her face. "You can cry on command? Are you sure medicine's the right field for you?"

I finally had the girl where I needed her and what little relief I might have felt was now overcome by everything else. Added to that was the recognition that this was the moment I was supposed to say everything that needed saying and as predicted, my mind had gone to crap. There were also four or five washing machines spinning ferociously and the noise was horrendous but I was hardly in a position to negotiate such trivialities.

She was still in her red jumpsuit and God, she looked good, so good I knew I'd be incoherent again and now she stepped forward and stood arms akimbo. "You must have gone completely mad. Do you really think that woman will stand for this?"

And it was there, in her words, her tone, her eyes, that I knew it at once and I unconsciously took a step towards her, she didn't move, as I silently mouthed the words "that woman," and I couldn't help but smile, almost weep with joy. Floor was nothing to her and nothing Arwen now said would convince me otherwise. And she came to me! I'd fled the room and she'd come to find me.

"I don't give a shit about that woman or anyone else." I declared as I feared I'd fall apart. This was it, this was the moment I'd dreamt about and now, as she stood and waited for me to speak, I knew this was the moment that could change my entire life. Ok, Freya, just speak from the heart. "Are you trying to make me fucking jealous? Because if you are, it's bloody well working so just stop it." Ok, that was perhaps not the best thing to say, but it was certainly from the heart.

She blew her knuckles. "You knew what you had."

I involuntarily exhaled at that, yet it was exactly the kind of response I should have expected, that coming from anyone else would have sounded ridiculous though somehow Arwen was able to pull it off so easily.

"Yes, I did," I began hopelessly, "and I still do, I know exactly what I stupidly threw away but please, you're playing with fire out there. What if Dan had seen the pair of you?"

She flinched at that, it wasn't what she wanted, to hurt him and it was the only time I could recall she didn't have an answer. Instead, she changed subjects, to annoy me again, "tell me, how was your day with Karla?" She asked with the kind of sexy smirk that could have made me melt and reminding me of all the mischief she'd earlier caused, that she was still revelling in.

I shook my head and laughed, which I didn't want but couldn't help. "You do know it's physically impossible to walk seven hundred miles lumbered down with that girl, right? You might have fooled Dan and Gabe but you can't fool me. All you did with your scheming was unwittingly give away your bullshit Camino story."

Her mouth twitched but there was geniality behind the eyes. "I don't know what you're talking about."

I stepped forward, both appalled and amused she was persisting with this line. "Oh, stop it, Arwen! Karla already blabbed it all. I know everything about Zaragoza and the train and..."

She lunged and suddenly I was pushed back against one of the dryers, her hands in my hair and she paused, perhaps to check for my reaction but I had no objection, and then her lips were hard against mine, her tongue forcing its way inside my mouth, her hands seizing my hair, tugging, the dryer's deep vibration ricocheting through my body to resound against her, my hands quickly seizing her breasts, her hips grinding forcefully into mine, the taste of blood on my palate, the throbbing way down in my depths and the explosion of relief flooding my veins. It was the sensation of weeks of hurt coming to the most beautiful, sudden, powerful and blissful end.

She pulled away and ran her hands down my body to slip her thumbs just inside my waistband, not to tug down my skirt, horrendously, but to pull herself casually into me as her tongue slid across her lower lip and her enlarged black pupils refocused.

We both heaved for breath as my mind hazed.

She bit her lip, "how've you been? And tell me the honest truth or so help me God."

"I've been like shit," I panted.

"Good! You deserved it."

"I think I needed it."

"You did."

I took a second to gather my wits as we both held each other in seeming realisation of the moment. We needed each other, there was no doubting that now and there was no reason for anything to remain in our way.

"Arwen, we need to talk about..."

And at that she pulled away and there was nothing I could do, no way for my quivering legs to catch her as she darted for the door, unlocked it and disappeared, to once again leave me questioning what the fuck was happening, where I stood with her and what game, if any, she was playing.

I waited several minutes to gather myself before leaving and when I opened the door I didn't immediately see Floor standing in wait and there was a flash of anger as the girl, who was several inches taller, pushed me back inside. She locked the door even as her other hand remained around my collar and the musty scent of unknown spices was overpowering.

"What do you think you're doing?" I screeched with a defiance I wasn't sure I felt. My heart was pounding hard. There was never a time in my life I'd been handled in such a way and my instinct was one of rage, even if my rational side knew not to lash out but attempt to control the situation. The girl was obviously volatile and had reason, not wrongly, to suspect something.

Why did drama follow some people wherever they went? Ah, of course, because she looked the way she did. I just hoped that Arwen would prove worth it.

Floor let go, now that I couldn't escape, and she made a point of tilting her chin down to meet my eyes. "Are you following us around, bitch?" Came the well thought through accusation masked as a question.

I exhaled and shook my head, "last I checked, I was here before you."

Her top lip curled, "this place, bitch. You're following her around like a little puppy dog." Obviously, it was untrue but she sounded so menacing that I feared doing anything to provoke her.

"I think Arwen's free to do as she pleases," which was absolutely true and I noted how Floor's eye flickered from the mention of the girl's name.

She leaned even closer and seemed in two minds whether or not to touch me again. "Listen here, you stuck up cheating little ginger bitch. If I ever so much as catch you looking at her again, I'll tell your wimp of a boyfriend your little secret."

The breath caught in my throat, which I hoped was the only physical reaction I gave up because she had to be bluffing, had to be, and I didn't want her to detect anything that might have revealed how right she was. For one, she hadn't even met Gabe, to the best of my knowledge, and Arwen wouldn't have given me up, I knew that and the fact Floor thought Gabe and I were still together only confirmed that to me. She was obviously paranoid but knew nothing for sure, other than that Arwen and I were, or at least once had been great friends, which was evidently enough to provoke this woman given we were all back at the same place and she now had a rival.

I stepped back and my heels touched the wall. "Hang on one minute. If anything was going on between Arwen and I, which it isn't, but even if it was, wouldn't telling Gabe then free me to see her in the open?" I hoped she didn't discover we'd already broken up because that would only make her even more paranoid, perhaps not unjustifiably. "How would that help you then?"

Her eyebrows dipped, her lips twisted to the side and I could have laughed at having so easily confused her, if only I wasn't feeling so threatened. She really was a beautiful woman, or would have been without that deranged glint behind the eye, which took everything away. Then her hands were back around my collar and the musty spice was stronger than ever.

"Listen bitch, she's my girlfriend now, so just stay the fuck away, or else."

It was another half hour before I returned to the communal room, where the music was now louder, after having first sat on my bed contemplating this most bizarre of evenings, staring at the wall, out the window to the nearby view of the São Jorge Castle and finally to my backpack crammed into the corner by the lockers. It was a fleeting thought, to put all this behind me, just go, be a doctor, try make myself ecstatically happy. But it went almost as soon as it arrived.

I'd been threatened by a bitch and to run would give her too much satisfaction.

And satisfaction was exactly her look right now as she lounged back on the white leather couch, cocktail in hand, my girl in the other.

I was thirsty and in need of alcohol myself and I had to skirt the room to avoid them but found myself unable to look away regardless and from a distance, it was easy to see Floor with her arm draped over Arwen's shoulders like some precious possession as she whispered in her ear.

I ordered a white wine and at once tasted why it cost so little as the bitterness introduced itself to my palate but I didn't care and I skirted back the other way, towards the air hockey table and, finding no familiar faces, leaned against the wall and endured a Katy Perry song crackling out from the cheap speakers.

Floor pulled her attention away from Arwen to scan the room but I looked away before her eyes could settle on me and a few minutes later when I checked back it was Arwen who found my gaze. She lacked her usual sparkle, instead there was something else, sadness perhaps and I'd have given anything to know what she was thinking. Why she was doing this to me? Then our eye contact was broken when Floor guided her back with a hand on her jaw and their lips touched and Arwen lifted her hands over Floor's head to lose them in her hair.

I had no time to consider the implications because my attention was stolen by Dan and Gabe who were now standing just inside the door, stock still, eyes agog as the revelation of what they were witnessing struck.

I actually had to blink, wipe my eyes and squint across the length of the room to be sure it was really them but there was no mistaking Gabe's wavy side parting and glasses, not to mention Dan's guitar and man bun that now bounced as he bounded the short distance in Arwen's direction.

Her head jerked back in recognition as I held my breath and Dan halted, having covered only half the distance, took another step, stopped, turned, flung up his arm and stalked out. Arwen threw Floor's arms away and ran after him as I felt my wine spilling over my feet.

Gabe now spotted me from across the room and, his nose leading the way, threaded between the other travellers and strode over.

"She's a lesbian? Did you know that?" He made a clicking sound, "never did hear her speak much about men ... not short of opportunities, for sure." His speech was slurred.

"Didn't stay long off the alcohol then?" So much for turning over a new leaf.

He shrugged, "I'm on holiday, it's not like I'm a big drinker, I'll give up when I get home."

"Whatever," it wasn't like I'd even asked him to give it up in the first place and besides, it was no longer any of my business, "did you go to the bank?"

He was gazing with a goofy glassy expression at Floor who was striding across the room to where she found Luuk and Samuel. "Not a bad looking girl that. I bet Dan's gonna be conflicted. A lesbian though? Assuming she is. I mean, I had no idea."

I exhaled loudly, "the money, Gabe, did you go to the bank?"

"Huh?" He delved into his bag, "oh, yup, here it is, two and a half big ones and you can count it if you don't trust me."

I doubted he'd descended so far as to screw me out of my own rightful money and so I took the notes and stuffed them into my bag. "Thank you for doing that."

"It was nothing, I'm serious about regaining your trust, in fact, I

was kind of hoping that perhaps now we could discuss us?" He
continued but I found my attention wandering to other places because
they knew now and I wasn't sure how that would change things.

Dan would be upset, not just because it would put an end to his
hopes of being with Arwen but because, I guessed, she never felt able
to tell him herself and he'd feel betrayed by that. They were close,
though evidently not close enough but then that was her business
and I guessed that right now she'd be trying to explain to him that
she wasn't, in fact, a lesbian and just liked who she liked because she
was who she was and rejected the label and all labels. There's nothing
to tell, she'll say, and whether Dan would accept that explanation was
anyone's guess.

"We could go north to Porto like Arwen suggested and because
she's already been, she won't want to go back so getting rid of her will
be easy. Mind ... she's probably travelling with those other people
now but I'm kind of getting bored of Portugal so we could just cut
east, head to Madrid but Dan's talking about getting a plane to one of
the party islands, Ibiza or Tenerife ... speak of the devil."

Dan was stomping towards us, his hair free-flowing and flaring,
but then changed trajectory and instead aimed for the pool table
from where he snatched the cue straight out of the hands of a much
smaller Japanese traveller who mouthed a half-hearted protest before
scurrying away. Samuel, Luuk, Karla and Floor were all nearby to
witness the minor exchange and all backed away towards the wall as
Dan angrily racked the balls and I recalled how our Dutch
companions might already be wary of Dan after learning about his
two nights in a Spanish prison.

Arwen traipsed back in, her face grim, but only made it a few
steps before walking back out and I had a feeling this most surreal of
nights was about to become even more unusual.

"Fuck it," I said aloud to myself and headed straight for the tapas
to spend several minutes indulging in unknown quantities of
interesting nibbles; cod balls, dates wrapped in bacon, clams, meat
croquettes and tiny cuts of toast with pesto, of all things, and of
course there were Belém tarts too.

"Karma got her," it was Karla who almost made me choke, "she
tries being nice to me now her friend isn't but still no apology so I
told her to fuck off."

"Karla!" I rebuked her, "please don't sneak up on me like that."

Indeed, Arwen was back and was hovering between groups and

finding nowhere to settle. She was keeping a distance from Floor, perhaps sensibly, and on two occasions, Dan moved away when she tried to approach him. In addition, Karla had apparently told her where to go and she was keeping away from me as well. Now, Arwen was sitting on a stool by the bar drinking wine alone with an expression that kept everyone else away as she rapidly tapped her phone screen, I guessed to send messages to Dan.

What else could I do other than play air hockey and so Karla and I began a game whilst Dan and Gabe played a match of doubles pool against Luuk and Samuel, which at least was a relief they were getting along. I'd thought too soon, however, because Dan began an argument with Luuk over the legitimacy of a shot, the latter backing down probably due to Dan's supposed reputation as a criminal. It was only when we'd finished air hockey that Karla and I approached their game and found they were playing for money, fifty Euros that awaited the winners beneath a glass, and because the game had been made interesting, a crowd had gathered for the sport.

I wanted to go to Arwen, if only to show there was still someone in this city who was thinking about her but for whatever reason, I hesitated and knew it was because she'd kissed Floor in front of me. What had become of her tonight? If she was having problems then she'd brought them on herself but still, on at least three occasions I had to physically stop myself approaching, but if she wanted me then I was here, always.

"Foul shot!" Dan shouted at Luuk for fumbling but I'd seen the shot, which had been so bad he'd missed the cue ball entirely, so technically it wasn't even a foul.

"How can it be a foul when I made no contact with the white?" The dreadlocked Dutchman yelled back and leaned over the table to attempt the shot again.

"My advice is don't play for cash when you're too drunk to hold a cue." Dan let it slide and strutted around the table and because he was concentrating on the balls, almost clattered into Arwen who'd suddenly appeared at the corner.

"Dan, can we please have a moment outside?" Her voice was so choked up she was likely to burst into tears from the slightest provocation.

He blanked her completely and I don't know how she managed to keep it together as she backed up to the wall, found Floor close by and sidestepped several paces away from where she continued to sulk.

I touched her arm, "Arwen, are you all right?" I'd never seen her like this and just had to check on her.

She sniffed and nodded appreciatively but I knew she was lying.

"Fucking hell!" Dan shouted at my ex. "Get a new pair of glasses you fucking blockhead."

It was the first time I'd seen Gabe playing pool and as it turned out, he was about as useful as Luuk, which had prompted Dan to verbally scold him in front of everyone. I didn't like it one bit, not so much Dan, but more the way Gabe allowed it to happen, to be spoken to like that and doing nothing to defend himself, which reminded me of the incident in that French cornfield just outside of Carcassonne and how, at the time, I'd been so disgusted.

I crossed the floor to where Gabe was looking down at the floorboards, for some reason thinking it was still my business. After all, an injustice was an injustice. "Are you going to allow yourself to be treated that way?"

"Well, I've had a lot to drink, Doc, um, Freya, so my aim's all askew," he smoothed back his hair and glanced at me helplessly, "and we're playing for money so it's kind of understandable."

What could I say to that? Absolutely nothing was the answer, so I threw up my arms and stamped away, exchanging a mutual look of disdain with Arwen, and I wondered what she was thinking, not just about this sorry display but everything.

There was a cheer when Samuel potted the black, he collected the money from beneath the glass and handed half the winnings to Luuk who then commenced dancing at close range in front of the losers. I held my breath because he was taunting them and under the circumstances, Dan was liable to do something stupid but mercifully, Samuel had the foresight to pull his friend away before offering to shake Dan's hand.

"Well played there, close game."

Dan held back, "double or quits."

Samuel hesitated, "I think it's probably for the best if we just quit whilst we're ahead, things are getting a little heated in here."

Arwen used the intermission to again approach Dan. "Hey, could we please have a word, I'm really sorry, I should have..."

"Fuck off!" He turned his attention back to Samuel and raised his voice, "if that twat's gonna dance like that in front of me when he's as

EURO TRIPPED 281

bad a player as that then he can at least play again for double or quits."

Luuk pointed his cue at Gabe. "I'm not as bad as he is."

"Then you're on for double or quits." Gabe retorted.

It was on, though not before even more alcohol had been brought over to fuel the fire.

Dan twisted open a fresh bottle of Lea & Perrins Worcestershire Sauce and, to Luuk and Samuel's utter disgust, sank two thirds in one shot and where the previous game had been loud with the occasional joke, now it was silent but for the music as all players gave their full concentration so that there was a palpable increase in tension.

I didn't want to be around for the outcome but like a bad car crash playing out before my eyes, I couldn't look away regardless, and now there was one hundred Euros, no small amount for travellers on a budget, awaiting the winners.

The game was evenly matched and around halfway through, Floor slinked closer to Arwen but she moved away from her and nearer to me and then Floor moved between us, coming so close to me that I had to back away to keep a distance. It was pathetic, stuff I could never remember having to deal with even in my teenage years. Floor had been drinking cocktails all night and I'd left my wine just in case I was again threatened and had to be alert.

That was when I noticed Arwen but what really caught my attention was her expression. She was smiling but it was a smile filled with sadness, but more than that, it was the way she was looking at each of us, Dan, Gabe, Floor, Samuel, Luuk, Karla, myself. She held her gaze on me the longest and I saw the tear roll down her cheek and I'd never before seen Arwen looking so fragile and so lost as that moment and never before did I so badly want to reach out to her.

But my attention was wrenched away by a roar when Dan slammed the black home. He snatched up the money and gave Gabe a high-five before the two of them positioned themselves strategically close to Luuk and commenced their little handshake celebration routine.

After enduring a mere ten seconds there was a loud crack.

Everybody stopped to look around, stunned, and then found Luuk's foot embedded within Dan's guitar that had been propped against the wall. He tried pulling his foot out but it was tangled in a mass of mangled wood and strings and Dan, needing a second to comprehend the horror, grabbed his pool cue, screamed and lunged for Luuk, only to find Samuel, who was still holding his cue, in his path, and I had to spin away as there was an almighty crack of wood followed by screaming.

Gabe dived into the melee from the side as my skin turned cold and the two male receptionists were approaching far too slowly and as I willed them to be quick, my eyes refocused to the movement behind them because Freya, the ginger cat had leapt up onto the front desk and amidst all the mayhem, she alone remained cool.

Arwen trundled past with her bag.

My heart jumped into my mouth and without even thinking, I dashed for the door and as I passed the cat, I knew that if God existed, he was with us in animals.

"Wait! Please, wait." I called after her and she stopped but didn't turn around. Her face, I recalled from a few moments before, she'd been looking at me for the final time. I stopped in front of her, blocking her path and screeched. "You're leaving?"

She nodded and the tears were streaming down both cheeks. "Can you blame me? This isn't me, I can't deal with it. The stress ... I don't do stress."

No, just cause total chaos and run.

But I was not losing her again. "Will you wait?"

She sniffed and wiped at her eyes, "what?"

"Promise me you'll still be here in five minutes."

She nodded without thinking and I ran back into the hostel, I only needed three minutes, and returned with my bag and something else. I jingled the keys in front of her nose and was so relieved when she laughed and spluttered her tears all over me.

"Are you fucking serious?"

"Quickly," I told her and we were both in hysterics as we ran across the road to the waiting camper, opened the side door, threw in our bags, slammed it shut and jumped into the front.

"Frey?" She looked at me with an expression of complete astonishment but she was no longer crying and that was good enough for me. "Have you gone insane?"

"Oh fuck!" I shook my head and laughed again. "I don't know, probably yes."

"From this moment on, I can never again call you Vanilla."

My hands were digging into the wheel and I turned to look at her, her face, her, Arwen, sitting beside me and although I was so terrified, I knew I was doing the right thing, the only thing I could possibly have done. "I'm sure you'll come up with something else." I turned the key and the engine fired up. There was almost a full tank of fuel.

She giggled, slapped the dashboard, bounced in her seat and screeched. "But Frey, where are we going?"

I was still gazing at her and couldn't look away because in her eyes I was seeing exactly how she felt about me and I was sure she was seeing the same in my own eyes, a look of hopelessness, of vulnerability, that we'd unwittingly placed our entire lives' happiness in someone else's hands. "Anywhere, I don't care."

Yes, it was a mess. Yes, I'd completely fucked up my entire life. And no, right now, as Arwen and I left Lisbon in a stolen camper, I didn't give a shit.

What a summer.

Chapter Ten

IBERIA

The first night we'd been full of adrenaline and made it almost as far as the Spanish border before finally pulling over to sleep in a national park. We awoke to bleak ranging hills, marshland and low flying birds cawing all around us and within ten minutes we were moving again.

By this time, it had hit. What we'd done.

It wasn't the mere act of having taken the camper that caused consternation but that I'd burned my bridges, that I'd split from the group, alone but for Arwen. Once the adrenaline had worn off and there was only hours of empty road ahead, there was time to think about that.

It was not how I wanted to leave things with Gabe and Dan but what had been the alternative? They were acting like childish thugs and the woman I loved had been running out the door.

Still, there was not one bloody thing I'd change.

By midday neither of us had yet received contact from anyone, which either meant nobody missed us, they hadn't yet discovered we'd absconded or they were presently spending time in an Iberian cell, to which at least two of them were becoming accustomed. There was also frequent periods, driving through the mountains, that we had no signal, which might have been a factor.

I worried about how Gabe might take things after discovering what I'd done but I tried to push those thoughts away. I'd made my decision and now had to own it.

It took most of the day to reach San Sebastián close to the French border and by that time I most certainly was aware of the split-second, life-changing decision I'd made only the night before.

"Still no idea where we're heading, huh?" Arwen was sitting opposite with her plateful of tapas.

I shook my head and wondered if this was how Thelma and Louise felt. "I thought you were used to drifting?"

"I am but you're not." She peeled a prawn in about three seconds, sent it down with a mouthful of beer and gestured to my plate. "Not touching yours?"

"Just the prawns. You may have them if you want."

She took them and I marvelled at her lack of anxiety, typical Arwen, just going with the breeze, even now. "Are you sure you'll be ok? Doing this, I mean. You're used to structure and order and now you don't even know where you'll be tomorrow."

I stared blankly forward, "I'll have to adapt," and rubbed my ear.

"Well, don't feel bad about borrowing the camper. From what you said, it's yours just as much as, if not more than his." She waved around the empty bar. "Do you see any police? He's not about to dob in his ex-girlfriend for borrowing the camper and even if he did, they wouldn't give a shit."

"He can have it back when we're done with it." Because, at the very least, he knew where I lived and would probably have things to say if and when he ever saw me again. How would *that* conversation go?

She leaned back and considered me for a while. "You really surprised me last night. I still can't quite get over it. You! The girl with the perfectly folded underwear in her backpack, even after all this time on the road. How long's it been?"

"We left in early July so it's been a little over six weeks now and you've been looking at my underwear?"

"Well, I hope that by the time you get to six months, your bag more resembles mine or I'll be seriously worried, and of course."

My sight refocused on her. "Six months?" I was playing with what looked like a meatball skewered onto a slice of French loaf, quite bizarre. "I have to be back home, doctoring awaits me. So at the absolute tops, I have another five weeks of delaying life and then that's it forever."

Arwen's eyes dipped and as the gravity of that statement struck, we both spent several minutes in silence.

Is this how it was supposed to be, Arwen and I finally being alone? I still couldn't believe I was able to stare across the table at her, just the two of us, no interruptions or obstacles or brick walls or men or anything, as she required a full minute to peel her next prawn.

That we were both subdued was perhaps to be expected, we'd both just ditched people who'd been extremely important to us and so far she'd not once mentioned Dan by name, as I hadn't mentioned Gabe. Though subdued we both still were and after the painful awkwardness that was last night sharing the pullout bed, I wanted to do something to at least attempt to bring back what we had in Barcelona, to feel close to her again.

I braced and reached over to take her hand and to my relief, she didn't pull away. "The other day ... when you turned up at the camper..." my lips pressed together and my head swirled from the memory, of finding her again only to be left helpless.

"Your face," her smile lifted, "talk about being stunned."

I coughed lightly, "yes, well, those things you said..."

"Couldn't get a word in, could you."

"Pretty much like right now." I squeezed her hand and she rubbed my leg beneath the table, it felt so nice yet frustrating at the same time, this was important. "Arwen, I wanted to say that those things you said were true. At first, I did consider you a curiosity..."

"...Because you've led such a boring life." She cut in and seemed pleased with herself.

I nodded, "I'm agreeing with you, I've led a relatively boring life and yes, you are, um, what we did was by far the most thrilling thing I've ever done..."

"...Or will ever likely do." She was enjoying this a little too much.

I shifted against the seat, "perhaps. But I want you to know that's not the reason I'm here with you now."

Her mouth levelled, "go on."

I'd thought deeply about my next words, whether or not they should be said, whether or not I'd ever get the chance to say them at all, and assumed that if I ever did, the moment could never be as magical as I'd dreamed. "I'm here with you now because I haven't been able to stop thinking about you." There it was, I'd just placed my heart in the hands of another woman, and a drifter at that. So much for being in control, Freya.

"Obviously." It was the answer I should have expected, which unfortunately did not precede us hurriedly undressing each other, as in my dreams. She tilted her head, which was at least something. "And why is that?"

Because I love you, I wanted so badly to say but just couldn't. It wasn't due to the risk of further inflating her ego, which was one of the things I loved about her, but because I knew I just couldn't cope if she didn't feel the same, it would crush me.

"What happened between you and Floor?" I blurted out instead and immediately cringed at my insecurity. She did this to me.

Her head jerked. "Floor? You want to know about Floor?"

I looked down, "not really but yes."

"Ok, if that's where you're taking this." She blew out air. "If you truly want to know, I tried to escape her evil clutches as soon as Zaragoza, it wasn't because of the geocaching, that was just a bonus really. How was I to know the whole lot of them would end up ditching the Camino to follow me? I made a few enemies that day, I can tell you, and that Floor girl was one seriously clingy woman." She spoke with her usual swagger, the same that coming from any other person would have been impossible.

I shook my head. "But you did escape her, she didn't make it to Lisbon until the night after you?"

"Which just goes to prove my point. Even with everything, I lasted no more than a day as a free woman and that was only because she was laid up in a hospital two stops back with blisters. What kind of idiot does the Camino in heels? And they have the gall to blame me for ruining the experience, not The Piston with her constant stopping to root through people's compost heaps and not Floor who wouldn't have lasted another minute anyway, even after buying walking boots. We got to Porto and I took my chance ... a fast train to Coimbra and on to Lisbon, freedom."

Such fun she must have had, it explained much and eased many of my concerns but if all that was true and Arwen felt nothing for Floor, she'd still used the girl to make me jealous, though that would have to remain one of those things I'd just have to let go and forgive. It was I who'd broken her heart in the first place.

I hesitated with the next bit, I didn't want to come across as being anything like Floor. "Karla told me you were sharing a tent."

She shrugged half-heartedly, "we did after the second night," she admitted straight up, to my surprise. "She discarded her tent on a Catalonian hillside because, she said, too many bugs had found their way inside, a lame excuse, and she denied it was for ulterior motives.

She couldn't share with Sam and The Piston and she's constantly bickering with Luuk, so..." she trailed off, sighed and began grazing my hand with her thumb. "Look, I'm not denying nothing ever happened between us, I know you're not so stupid to believe that, but it was never anything more than kissing and that was only because I was hurt and pissed at a certain Scottish doctor."

And I believed her. She could have done the easy thing and chastised me for believing anything Karla had said and denied the rest but she didn't.

"She threatened me back in Lisbon."

Her eyes widened to reveal her large blue eyes most beautifully, "what?" And that reaction told so much about how she felt about me, at least, I hoped. "When, where and what did she say exactly?"

"It was in the laundry room, soon after you left me. She was basically using her height to threaten me and said she was your girlfriend now."

Her head jerked forward. "The absolute rotter. Oh, Frey, it's not true," she insisted, "the total, absolute rotter. I should go back there right now just to kick her arse."

My eyes softened, "unfortunately, it's a little too late for anything that drastic but I suspect she'll be spending the next few weeks living in her own painful purgatory."

"Yeah, but still. Did she hurt you?" She asked this last hurriedly.

I shook my head. "Anyway, it's you I'm more bothered about right now," my grip tightened around her hand, "and I know *I* hurt *you*, Arwen, and I've still not had the chance to properly apologise for what I did," my words came out strained, "I'm very sorry for the way I treated you. It was the single biggest mistake of my life."

She clamped her eyes shut and her chin wrinkled, "I thank you for that," and when her eyes opened they were suddenly cold. "She was a rebound, I guess, I've never done rebounds but then nobody has ever dumped me before you. If it could even be called that..." she said the last as an afterthought. "I want you to know that I've been feeling like shit this last month, as I'm glad you have too, you deserved it."

"I deserved it..." I repeated monotone and defeated.

"Yes you did and I want you to know that although I thank you for apologising, I cannot forgive you." Her hand slipped from mine and it was devastating.

"I..." my mouth moved but I couldn't speak, "you cannot forgive me?" I finally managed to croak.

"Because you're selfish." She spoke with purpose whilst holding my eyes and I knew she believed it to be true.

And why not? It was I who'd cheated on Gabe for a bit of excitement. No, that wasn't true. I'd certainly felt for Arwen, even if I didn't know how much at the time. But I'd certainly discarded her like a piece of rubbish the morning after, just to make my life easier, so I wouldn't risk losing my doctor boyfriend and the status that came with that. And deep down I knew that I'd put up with far too much and held onto him for longer than I ought to have for the same reason.

I was selfish, at least when it came to the big things. Was I really different to most women in that respect? Or most men for that matter? I was human. We each have to look out for ourselves in this life because nobody else will.

"You know, that was the most possessive woman I've ever come across," she began, I suspected because she knew I was having difficulty with the truth she'd just spoken, "she's the exact opposite of you. Would it kill you to be just a little bit possessive?" Selfish but not possessive, I'd have to take that for now. "Life's all about balance, you know? All you do is study and now you've totally gone off the deep end. Grand theft auto ... what next?"

My smile returned. "I could learn to be a little more possessive."

She slapped the table, "good."

"And, Arwen?"

"Yes?"

"Thank you."

After leaving, we pitched the tent on a low clifftop overlooking the Bay of Biscay, where gulls had gathered in anticipation of treats and not too far away, luxury liners and small boats approached the port of San Sebastián. It was the first time this trip I'd used the tent and needed to employ my boot to hammer the pegs into the hard ground whilst Arwen pumped with her legs to inflate the mattress.

She faced away and her braids danced with every thrust of her thighs, blonde hair perturbed against her back in a beautiful contrast against golden skin, the way her back tapered down to an impossibly slender waist to broaden out at her dancers' hips. I'd missed that body and I longed for it.

I swallowed and hammered in the final peg, entering after her and zipping up the flaps. The faint scent of peach mixed with Aloe Vera was stronger within the cramped confines and there was shuffling by us both as we fumbled with our bags.

"This might help." She turned on the light from her phone and the interior illuminated.

"Thanks."

"No problem." She was facing away and her elbow pressed into my neck as she pulled her t-shirt off over her head. "Whoops, sorry."

"Sorry." I had to push my bag towards the flap for some small room and, also facing away, I removed my blouse, quickly peaking once over my shoulder to admire the way her scapulae moved beneath her flesh.

"Could really do with some more room in here." Her voice was sweet and quiet.

"Yes, some more room." I pulled on a t-shirt and turned to face her as I knelt and even through the air mattress, I could feel the hard ground beneath my knees.

Her bra was red and the strap pressed into her flesh. A fresh smelling t-shirt was pulled over her and she fanned out her hair before reaching up to tie it into her usual nighttime bun, her single red braid left free, the sinews in her arms just barely visible.

I coughed lightly as she played with the mosquito band at her wrist. "Oh, the sleeping bag."

"Yes."

It was down by the flap and I had to gradually manoeuvre myself around to fetch it and then more of the same to bring it back and during the shambles, there was no stopping my feet from rubbing all over her thighs, belly and arms.

"Sorry."

"Sorry."

I cringed as I unrolled it and straightened down the edges, a completely unnecessary endeavour. It was a two-man bag and thus far only Arwen had slept in it back in Catalonia.

"An old friend says hi."

"Excuse me?"

I shuddered, "um, we can get in now ... that's if you're coming inside."

Her eyes widened and I heard the sharp intake of air as I realised what I'd said and I could have burst into tears right then and there.

"Arwen, please say something," I yelped.

"The zips at your side, Frey." Better than nothing.

"Oh," I slid the zip all the way down, opened out the bag and from there, navigating ourselves inside was a major exertion with more apologies whenever a foot or an elbow or an arse touched something it shouldn't have. I didn't think last night's awkward pain could be beat, yet here we were.

I zipped up the bag, turned around and found her already facing me.

"Goodnight, Frey."

"Um, yes, goodnight, Arwen."

There was a moment, perhaps less than a second, when I saw the hesitation but then we both acted as one, moving our heads closer and there was a quick kiss on the lips.

She turned away, curled up and the light went out.

———

THE BACON, eggs and tomato sizzled from the small portable stove as I dashed them with pepper whilst to my side, Arwen agitated the cafetière before pressing down on the plunger.

We were sitting in the tent flaps on the edge of the mattress facing the sea and two large vessels that slinked their way out towards the Atlantic. The morning sun had not yet appeared from the direction we'd soon be heading.

"Coffee," she handed me a mug and sipped from her own as she brought her feet into her body and wrapped her arms around her knees. She was still in her t-shirt, the one that said *L ♥ve Sleep,* which strained to contain her breasts, and to have her this close whilst she was wearing it was a distraction. It wasn't cold but still, her arms were covered in goosebumps, I hoped, though doubted, from sexual arousal.

I crammed an egg and half the bacon into a bread roll and handed it to her. "Breakfast."

"Ta." She bit into it and the yolk drooled down the crust, "oh dammit," and flicking her wrist, a strand of orange goo was flung into the grass. "Anyway, what happened to your feet?"

I stirred and readjusted myself, "my feet," I said monotone.

"You were never so cold in Barcelona. You get bad circulation all of a sudden?"

"I doubt it." There was nothing wrong with my feet or my circulation.

She sniggered into her food and I knew she was playing with me, "well at least *they* got some action last night, huh?" Yes, action.

I shifted again, "so you were kicking me because they were cold? Is that the line you're taking?"

She didn't answer, just struggled to keep the laughter contained and I wanted to drag her back inside the tent and punish her properly but what could I do?

I studied her and bit my lip. "Say, Arwen, your cutis anserina is exposed."

She straightened and looked down, "my what? Where? How?"

I was about to take a bite but couldn't and when I began laughing she slapped me on the arm.

"You'd better tell me what that means this minute."

I had to put my breakfast down. "Do I really arouse you that much?"

Her eyebrows dipped most comically. "What the heck are you talking about?" And she grabbed my arm, which was also covered in goosebumps, though not from the cold and I stopped laughing and there was silence and her hand was still there and my gaze lowered to her lips as she did the same but then she removed her hand and wiped the spot she'd been holding. "I got yoke on you."

I leaned back on the mattress, "yep," breathed and deigned to eat my breakfast and then there was a succession of vibrations from the pocket of my shorts. "Oh shit, I think a hotspot just found us." I had a feeling what it was, indeed, I was surprised it had taken this long and pulled out my phone whilst bracing for the inevitable abuse. There were several messages and twenty-six missed calls.

'Hey, did you and Arwen hit a club last night? You still out? Or did you come back and go somewhere for breakfast? I think we just missed you.'

'Just let me know, we're kind of worried here.'

'It's lunch and you're still not here?'

'Ok, now I'm getting really worried. Where are you?'

I was reading them out to Arwen, who was silent, as she leaned into my shoulder.

'Those Belgian losers say they don't know where you are either and neither does anyone else at the hostel, will you just fucking call to say you're ok, this is most unlike you.'

'Fuck! Someone's stolen the fucking camper! My passport's in there.'

'Freya, did you take the camper? If so, where are you? Is Arwen with you too? Are you ok?'

'WhatsApp says you ain't even getting these messages. You have no idea how worried I am.'

I turned to Arwen, "tell me we did the right thing."

She wasn't smiling, "we did, of course, we weren't sticking around with that lot any longer but, in retrospect, perhaps we could have left a note at reception."

I stared at the screen, "he'll see the little ticks on the app and know we're not dead."

She nodded, "let's get moving."

She drove and we headed east, which was the only way we could feasibly go, crossing the French border within minutes and then traversing the Northern Pyrenees in the direction of Toulouse. We had no real destination but of course, that was the point, and I remarked how I was now living life the same as Arwen, like a nomad, as thrilling as that was, for a few more weeks at least.

"You're right," I told her.

She glanced across from behind the wheel. "Of course I am but about what specifically?"

"I'll send a text to let them know we're both ok and that they should just enjoy the rest of their holiday without us, although I'm sure that'll open the floodgates."

She nodded and I sent the text, though because of the mountains, there was no signal.

"They'll get it when they get it, I suppose," and I propped my head against the window.

An hour later we hit another hotspot and a barrage of messages and missed calls came through all at once. I read them out.

'You did take the camper! You STOLE it!'

'The hostel showed us the CCTV, there's no denying it.'

'You fucking bitch!'

'Doctor, I'm so sorry, please come back.'

'Just got your text and how can I enjoy the holiday with no camper? You fucked up everything! If I ever see you again...!'

'How am I supposed to get to Porto now?' I squinted at the screen. "I thought they were going to a party island?"

'I fucking hate you.'

'Forget what I said, I didn't mean it, I love you.'

'Ok, this is getting really fucked up now, we already know Arwen's a dyke but that Belgian Flower girl's saying that you're one too.'

'Freya, tell me it's not true.'

'Oh my God, I just had a terrible thought ... Are you the reason Arwen left our group? Why? Is it because you turned her down or did you actually cheat on me?'

'Flower says you did!'

'We haven't fucked in weeks!'

'You fucking bitch!'

'I'm gonna tell your fucking dad and see how you like that.'

"Arwen, what a mess this is." There were several more messages but I couldn't bring myself to read them and instead, I shut down the phone and began tapping it against my leg.

She scratched her neck. "Sounds like he's in a state, for sure."

"Why am I feeling so bad about this? After the other night, they don't deserve my thoughts and sympathies."

The pair of them were becoming increasingly intolerable to be around, and that was before the culmination of violence, but still, it was probably no way to have left things with them, Gabe especially. I sighed and could feel my heart beating unusually fast but then all I had to do was look to my right for a reminder of why I was doing this, putting myself through it all, everything. I never supposed coming out was easy, but this?

She peered at the road. "It's something I've had time to think about myself. I don't know ... you already broke up with him so how much do you owe him, really? But the decent thing would at least be to call him and..."

"And say we're together?" I anticipated her with a yelp. "How would that make things better?"

She regarded me with a stern expression. "That's not what I was about to say, Freya, because we're *not* together. Just say you've gone travelling with me because, quite honestly, that's all we're doing. And then say they're both jerks and you felt threatened for your safety. At least then he'll know you're alive and can, hopefully, move on."

"Easier said than done," I muttered and she tutted in response and then for a while I went into a sulk as I thought about her words, her adamant and disheartening words. After ten minutes, I felt the need to broach an earlier subject and only after speaking did I realise the unfortunate yet apt timing, which pretty much proved it all. "Do you really believe I'm selfish?" I clamped my eyes shut, turned away and heard her sharp exhalation. I was stupid.

"I don't think there's much more for me to add here, Freya, do you?"

But I wanted to give us a try, a proper one, Arwen and I, which meant doing whatever needed doing. "I will call him and tell him everything if that will prove to you that..."

"...You don't need to devastate him, he doesn't need to know you had a meaningless fling with another woman just to prove a point to me."

"It was not meaningless, Arwen!"

"It was at the time!" She grunted and I hated it. "*Selfish* maybe was the wrong word but you certainly don't give a shit about other people's feelings ... the way you told me to fuck off out of your life..." she made a high-pitched yelping sound, "but forget me for a moment, what about Gabe? Sure, he may have turned out to be a violent drunkard on a downward spiral but after five years, I'd think he deserved an explanation before taking off like that ... with his transport, not to mention his heart. Look, I don't care necessarily, it's your life and it's your camper too and he probably deserved it on some levels but it was *your* relationship and if you'd do a thing like that to him after five years then what else would you do to me?"

For too long I was stunned and could say nothing, I'd never seen her like this. And she was right. "The guitar string ... I didn't buy it for Dan, I bought it because I wanted to hear some music."

"Which means you've never done a damned thing for anybody in your life." She looked across, hummed and almost smiled. "Well, at least you're honest."

"I have that."

And that meant I had to change, starting with Gabe. One call, say goodbye, mail his passport and move on so I could have a chance with Arwen. A simple plan.

Then we were both shaken when my phone rang and Gabe's image flashed up on the screen.

It was a split-second reaction with no thought put into and I'll never know how it even happened but I threw the bloody phone straight out the open window where, I assumed, it smashed into a million pieces.

And the most frightening thing was, I was supposedly training to be a doctor.

Chapter Eleven

CHIANTI

On the road from Toulouse to Provence, we passed Carcassonne in respectful silence as we gazed at that place that held memories for us both, spending a night on a marsh with a hundred flamingos just outside of Toulon, short stops in Cannes, Nice and Monaco, where Arwen was propositioned by a fat billionaire with a yacht moored on the Med, crossing the border into Italy, passing through Sanremo, onto Genoa and north to Milan, where Arwen was approached by several people calling themselves fashion scouts because we were stupid enough to spend too long in the wrong part of town, Lake Como and over the Swiss border where the prices terrified us into returning south, Verona and the supposed balcony from Romeo and Juliet and realising that if we travelled any further east, we'd miss the rest of Italy, which couldn't be allowed to happen, coming back on ourselves to head south, Bologna, the incredible Florence with its art and museums and architecture and Michelangelo and da Vinci and old bridge and palaces and onto Pisa. By now we were deep in Tuscany with its endless rolling hills of grapevines and winding roads and beautiful medieval towns until, quite by accident, we passed the one place that rivalled Carcassonne's majesty and stopped.

"We've found a base." Her little finger curled around my own as we ambled slowly, oh so slowly, up the ancient cobbled street, narrow as it was with the buildings either side reaching up at least five storeys, making you feel small and inferior because they were so old. "And it's about time too."

I had to think how long it had been since we left Lisbon and decided it was probably around two weeks and in all that time, we'd not spent more than a single day in any one place. "Agreed, I'm tired of all the driving."

This type of a holiday was not possible without an infinite amount of driving but still, I'd had enough of it and fancied an extra day or two somewhere special. Who'd have thought that two women travelling together could be so hard to please and not even Milan, Florence or any place between Portugal and Italy had felt satisfactory.

That was, until we arrived in San Gimignano, deep in the heart of Tuscany.

Built on a hill, the town was famous for its many tall towers resulting from family rivalries over the centuries. When normally rivals would declare war, here they'd merely tried to see who could build the tallest tower and the result was the beautiful town we now intended on calling a base, for a few days at least.

We were enjoying morning coffee in Piazza della Cisterna and watched as the usual tourist flocks followed guides holding flags or symbols or teddy bears on the end of long sticks. I glanced around the square and looked up.

"You're trying to count the towers?" She was leaning back in her seat, devilishly cool in sunglasses as our legs touched beneath the table.

Some of the towers had collapsed over the years due to earthquakes and I didn't want to miss any. "In this square, I think there's seven." I sipped my coffee and enjoyed the sensation of her bare flesh so smooth against my own.

For two weeks we'd been alone and what an experience, being able to finally have her to myself, just Arwen, no bullshit, a chance for us to get to know each other and see how we were together.

But the last two weeks had felt different to before, weirdly different.

We were close, for sure, I felt closer to Arwen than I ever had and there were the occasional sparks of what we had in Barcelona.

Back in Monaco, she'd made a point of cuddling up closer to me to "overwhelm that creep's eyes" that she could still feel crawling over her body. That fat, disgusting billionaire, who I'd recognised from the news, had offered Arwen fifty thousand Euros to spend the night on his yacht and she'd laughed in his face even as her nails were digging into my palm.

"Please say you'd never allow me to do anything like that." Shortly after, she was absolutely shivering in my arms as I snuggled up and felt conflicted, appalled yet so turned on and privileged to be the one allowed in this girl's presence. She'd looked up suddenly and for several minutes we'd enjoyed one of our more passionate embraces as our mouths pressed so hard together I feared I'd melt into her. Unfortunately, the camper had been parked across town and even if it had been close, we were in the middle of a busy city and when we finally did find a place to pitch the tent for the night it was too late, she was cold again and once more I had to endure that frustrating thrumming from deep inside, something that only Arwen had the power to satisfy.

But then, there were also the occasional exhibitions of what we had when we first met, though in reverse, of my getting under her skin. Long drives made her tetchy, as did my inability to peel prawns, no matter how many times she tried to teach me the skill. My supposed cold feet were a constant problem and it was always my fault if she had to go more than two days without showering. "I can't share a sleeping bag with you tonight," she'd say and I'd sulk into the night wondering if there was something else behind it. I'd sometimes watch as she practiced her dances whilst she listened to the music from her headphones and that was fine but as soon as she began meditating it became a problem. "You're putting me off, why don't you go find a gay bar somewhere for an exorcism, you're looking at me like I'm the last woman on the planet."

And I'd told her I went too, when in reality I was sitting on a park bench balling my eyes out.

It was a new side to Arwen, she was human, as it transpired, and the realisation she was not the Goddess I'd always assumed came as an incredible relief because it made me less intimidated to be around her. On the contrary, she was exceptionally flawed, just like anyone else, yet was so in the most adorable of ways, evidence yes, as to my love for her.

She muttered in her sleep, though never anything of coherence and the one time we ran out of coffee I worried she might cause damage to my person. One night we made the mistake of going to a bar, a regular one, and she'd been approached by so many horny men that the final unfortunate soul was told to "fuck off," before, in exasperation, she dragged me out by the wrist. That night I worried my poor legs would be bruised so badly by her kicks that I'd left her in the tent and gone to sleep in the camper and the next morning, I awoke to find her beside me in bed, our legs tangled together.

We bickered all the time, over matters large and small but always, it was with an undertone of sexual tension, even if she never felt ready, or capable, of seizing me and doing as she bloody well pleased.

I was beginning to get a taste of what a lesbian relationship was, just without the sex, which I absolutely craved. It was a constant rollercoaster of ups and downs, of not knowing what the fuck was happening and never being sure which of her actions or moods were intentional or not. Still, to spend a single day with Arwen was more interesting, thrilling and indescribable than five years with Gabe.

Yes, things were different now, I'd hurt her and I was paying for it. No matter what I did, evidently I was unworthy. She didn't wish to make herself vulnerable again, which is exactly what I'd become in her stead. I'd learned my lesson but what difference did it make? And I reasoned that she'd long ago made up her mind that I was good enough only as a friend, not as a girlfriend, and that was the most devastating realisation in the world.

I sipped my coffee and watched her do the same, her big blue eyes never leaving the pamphlet.

"It's a tourist trap, is what it is. There's so much to do, we're here in the peak of summer and won't we just pay hand over bloody fist for everything." Italy, as it turned out, wasn't much less expensive than Switzerland and Arwen was always complaining about the price of food.

I smiled because she was using my expressions now. "Something relaxing, perhaps?"

She hummed, "that rules out the Museum of Torture and Execution, of which there are three in this one town, can you believe that?"

I wasn't quite sure what to make of that. "Um, not really my thing but I'm sure there are castles and more towns just like this."

She squinted into the small brown sheet of paper and whatever she was reading must have been good because she held up a finger to silence me. "There's a hot spring about a hundred miles away, a village called Saturnia, where we can bathe out in the open. Everybody looks so happy."

I sighed, "too much driving, maybe another day. Personally, I'd settle for an early night with some wine and you in the camper or tent, I don't mind."

She looked up and licked her lips. "You say you still have that wine I gave you in Bordeaux? It's supposed to be delicious."

I nodded, the truth was I'd been waiting for the opportune moment to drink it with her as it seemed like the right thing to do. "I still have it."

She pulled a funny face. "It's red though."

"So?"

"So." She mimicked my Scotch accent perfectly and I rubbed her leg beneath the table. "We're not in Bordeaux anymore, we're in Chianti and here they make *white* wine." She said as her eyes snapped up to the wall over my shoulder.

"You're guessing, aren't you. You don't know squat about the local wine."

She flicked the pamphlet. "Which is why this wine tour will be the perfect way to learn all about it."

I squeezed my eyes closed and felt the fatigue take control of my body, Italian coffees were so small in comparison to what we got back home and the one I'd just finished had barely any effect on me. "If it even matters about drinking *local* wine just because we're, well, local, then surely we can just buy a bottle or two from a shop, some food and maybe watch a movie on your tablet."

She wasn't listening and now her finger was back to silence me. "It says traditional."

I shrugged, "so?" I mimicked her Oz accent just as perfectly as she did mine.

"And we get a free meal included in the price, so the jokes on Italy." She saw my blank expression. "Really, Frey, you go to Belgium, you eat chocolate, you go to Germany, you eat sausages, you go to Poland you … doesn't matter, but when you come to Tuscany, you take a wine tour."

I conceded with a nod and took her hand. "Ok, ok, we'll do it. I'm sure it'll be great." And I wanted to make her happy. "But I need another coffee first."

It wasn't far away, about six miles east before the town of Poggibonsi and we had to park the camper on the road because of the large iron gate that blocked access to the dirt track that led towards the building, or rather, bomb site at its pinnacle. There must have been work going on because I could see the huge piles of rubble, workstations with discarded tools, wheelbarrows and several vans and trucks.

I frowned and wanted to return to San Gimignano. "This can't be the right place."

She waved the pamphlet in front of my face. "It is and look, there are people up there."

They looked like workmen to me, rather than tourists but Arwen wasn't discouraged and the intercom crackled when she pressed the button.

"Pronto?" Came the woman's voice after a short wait.

"Siamo qui per il giro."

I gaped at the girl as my entire body unsteadied. I shouldn't have been surprised. "Italian too?"

She held up a hand to silence the intercom, as daft as that was, and turned briefly to me, "Freya, it's pretty much the same as Spanish, French and..."

The intercom crackled but nothing was returned.

"If you say so."

We stood still for a few minutes, stupidly exposed to the late August sun as I tapped my feet and stared forlornly at the camper with its curtains and privacy. "Gordanno Vineyard? Am I saying that right?" It was impossible to tell how many similar vineyards we'd passed on the way, but there were many, any one of which would be happy to take our money if this place didn't open the gates.

"It's pronounced Jee...or...danno. Say it."

"Giordano."

"Right."

"Well, I reckon that maybe Miss Giordano's coming down personally to open the gate for us." I joked, even though it wasn't funny. "Seriously, let's just go. Bordeaux doesn't sound so bad right now, does it?"

She was about to speak but then there was a loud buzz and we both jumped.

And then the gates slowly began to open inwards and before us was the empty dirt track with what I could now definitely see to be workmen sitting idly around at its summit.

We'd arrived at the Giordano Vineyard.

"WE'RE one of the oldest vineyards in Tuscany to have been run continuously by the same family." The tour guide grimaced because we were facing the steep ascent back up the slope toward the large barn at its summit and she took a deep breath in preparation. "Strap yourselves in for the charge. Where were we? Ah yes, the Giordano family has been making wine through war, pestilence, plague, revolution and numerous repossession attempts by the bankers," she laboured with every step as the two of us fell in close behind, "but we're still here."

That was our cue to smile so we did, after having spent the last fifteen minutes strolling through the many rows of vines and being told about the unique type of grape they grew in Tuscany and that Giordano wine was superior to most because of their strict inspection process, which meant having to scrutinise every single grape.

Arwen's face betrayed her lack of interest which, given this tour thing had been her idea solely, prompted me to assume that either she'd had a different romantic view of what a Tuscan vineyard would be, or else had simply wanted to get tanked up on the produce.

We reached the barn, which turned out to be a factory, and had all kinds of fancy, yet very old winemaking apparatus and hardware, most conspicuously the twelve giant wooden tanks lined against the wall that had to contain the fruits of the vineyard's labour.

The tour guide's name was Dayna and when she'd greeted us, I'd been surprised to hear an accent from the south of England. We'd had to wait twenty minutes in an unfinished reception area with loose wiring and sawdust strewn across the floor and soon after her arrival, she disappeared again, we guessed to use the bathroom. Now, she excused herself once more, whilst Arwen and I were left alone amongst the vats, and returned a few minutes later, face flustered, and directed us to a large oak cask with a wheel and lever attached to it.

"This is the grape press and is where every drop of our wine passes through, where we separate the white winemaking process from the red winemaking process." She had to shout above the hammering and sawing that was coming from somewhere nearby. "The grapes go in here, we turn the wheel to crush them and the juice flows into this tub. Because we make white wine, we have no further use for the skins, which are required only for making red wine."

"Ok, yes." I nodded, feeling the need to show I understood.

Dayna was one of those stereotypically beautiful petite blondes, or except she might have been with a few good nights' sleep in her. She had a soft face but it was buried beneath a hard exterior, with the first sign of lines appearing beneath the periorbital puffiness, or eye bags, which were displayed prominently on what I put to be a girl in her late twenties or very early thirties, though in truth it was hard to tell. And oh yeah, she was liable to pop at any moment.

"Seriously, why isn't she reclining back on a comfy couch right now?" Arwen took a moment to whisper in my ear whilst Dayna was taking a sip of water and cooling her face with one of those foldout fans she'd been carrying from the outset of this tour. It was a good question though none of my business.

"The press is presently full of grapes so let's give it a whirl." She manoeuvred herself over to the handle attached to the big wheel and alarmed, Arwen and I both dashed forwards to preempt her.

"Ooh, let me," I called, "I've always wanted to try this," which was a lie and I gave it a few turns, which required considerable effort and was rewarded by a stream of juice that began to flow from a spout at the base, straight into a wooden tub with wheels. "Arwen?"

She took over from me and the juice flowed with even more vigour.

"You're probably wondering why we use such antiquated methods," Dayna continued above the added noise of hundreds of squelching grapes, "and that's because here, we're traditional."

There was a squeaking sound and Arwen and I both turned to see a man in a baseball cap wheeling into the warehouse a large contraption with four long tentacles and pincers for hands. "Where do you want the Agbot?"

Arwen smirked and nudged me in the side as Dayna's cheeks flared. "Over there." She pointed in the direction of a closet and stepped in front of us in a futile effort at cutting off our line of sight. She shook her head and managed to meet our eyes after the man had disappeared. "We, um, we've had a recent staff shortage."

She again excused herself so that after almost an hour on the tour, we'd barely learned anything, not that we could blame her personally, just whoever it was making her work in this condition. But it gave us time to leave the barn so we could relax under the shadow of a tree and admire the beautiful landscape. It wasn't just the vista but also the four-hundred-year-old mansion that acted as the Giordano family residence, wherever they were. Regardless, it was certainly large with three floors and impressive with its timber frame, intricate stonework and window shutters.

Dayna now strolled out from that building as she clutched at her lower back like women in the late stages of pregnancy often did and I felt for her. "If you'd like to follow me, it's lunchtime."

We were taken through to a small canteen with three long wooden tables and benches to accommodate sixty tourists at least, except today it was just the two of us. The walls had yet to be plastered and the wiring was visible between the joists, while the light fixtures hadn't yet been screwed in and the air possessed that distinct smell of wood shavings.

Dayna handed us menus and after placing down a carafe of water, proceeded to fill two wine glasses from a bottle with an elegant label. "This is our Panizzi blend, featuring a seventy-five percent Vernaccia di San Gimignano grape as you saw, perfect for lunchtime. We recommend it with the ricotta and spinach tortelli."

Arwen ran a finger down the three item menu, "I think I'll go for the wild boar pappardelle."

I nodded, "sounds good, make that two."

She sucked in air, "ah, I'm afraid we're out of that."

Arwen looked back to the menu, her gaze flashing over me as she did. "In that case, I'll go for the tordelli versiliesi, I've no idea what it is but it sounds good."

I flipped the menu and found the other side was written in English. "It's beef ravioli, which means make that two."

Dayna bounced once on her toes, "might I suggest the ricotta and spinach tortelli?"

Arwen's eyes happened on mine again before switching to Dayna. "You're out of the ravioli too, aren't you."

Dayna nodded but kept her smile. "Two tortelli, I'll tell the chef." She disappeared into the kitchen, which left us to finally sample the famous Giordano wine.

Now, I'm no wine expert but I know what I like and I most certainly did enjoy the dry fruitiness of this Panizzi blend.

Arwen sipped hers and her eyebrows lifted appreciatively. "At least something's working around here."

"Oh, she's working, all right, in fact, it's beginning to look like she's the only one around here who is." This was because I was leaning back on the bench to peer into the kitchen and I could just make out Dayna's backside and elbow as it moved rhythmically back and forth and I whispered to Arwen that it was apparent that Dayna was also the chef.

"What? Noooooo." She stood to lean over the table, gifting me with the most heavenly view of her cleavage, I went for more wine and gulped it back, and she retook her seat and shook her head. "I feel for the woman, of course, but all I really care about right now is that whatever it is she's making is delicious and fills me up."

As it happened, we had to wait thirty minutes for lunch to arrive, and when it finally did the ricotta and spinach tortelli was only about average and neither did it fill us up, but then what were we expecting? I tried to tell Arwen that it was only lunch and we'd get something more substantial for dinner.

"I'll just be glad when this tour's over. It's no wonder we're the only fools here, it's been a disappointment." Her face scrunched up in that cute way I loved but I had to agree with her.

"We'll pig out in the camper tonight with a film ... sound good?"

She didn't have chance to answer because Dayna was back and from there we were escorted through a side door in the main residence and down a flight of stone steps that led into the cellar. It would be the final call of the tour before finishing in the shop, which Dayna had earlier been eager to tell us about.

"Do you own the place?" Arwen joked but I don't think Dayna heard.

We passed through an arch and I gasped because I could now see the many hundreds of oak casks stacked up, either on large wooden frames or atop of each other. "Wow," I said, involuntarily, "who'd have guessed all this was under that house?"

The air was thick with a deep mix of wine and oak, which made it harder to breathe and the room was barely lit by the few aged lanterns hanging from the walls, bestowing a definite sense of history, as well as claustrophobia.

Arwen was pottering around of her own accord whilst I remained further back, closer to the way out with Dayna.

"These days, most wine is aged in stainless steel barrels," Dayna began, "but ... but of course, being traditional, we do things the old-fashioned way, ageing our wine ... ageing our wine for up to a year, allowing for an extremely slow oxygenation process as the air seeps in through the oak. Doing so also improves the colour, texture and taste of the wine." She fanned her face vigorously and held onto an upright and then Arwen reemerged from the shadows, traipsing back in our direction.

"It's kind of stuffy down here, don't you think?"

Dayna took a step back and Arwen waved an arm in the direction of the cellar's deep recesses.

"I went down as far as I dared ... almost felt like suffocating. I'd hate to be the guy charged with finding the Dom Pérignon 1975."

"Our wine..." Dayna began.

"I remember that one time I accidentally locked myself in my parents' chest and I swear, by the end I was hallucinating weird animal creatures." She jerked her chin into the void, oblivious to whatever discomfort she might be causing her companions. "Now, I'm hoping that was an apparition and not a rat I just saw down there."

Dayna had stepped further away and I felt it necessary to cut my blundering friend off, cut her off with absolutely anything.

"Dayna, I have to ask, where's everybody else?"

She let out a howl and staggered, hunched, to the foot of the stairs and clutched the bannister with both hands and I rushed to offer my assistance, putting my arm around her back so she knew I was there.

"Oh gosh, Dayna, was it that hard a question? I've got you, let's get some air."

She transferred some weight to me and I had to readjust my position to cope.

"Freya, you're the worst tourist ever." The ditsy one remarked from behind and I scowled over my shoulder.

"Oh, shut up, Arwen and help."

She did, by carrying Dayna's fan. "No worries, we'll soon have you outside in the fresh air."

Dayna panted and managed to tell us that outside was too hot and that we should take her to the office inside the residence.

"Oh fuck!" Arwen and I both said together as we entered. The house was impressive, my immediate attention being drawn by the huge oak beams and wooden rafters holding up the high ceiling, the exposed stonework and fireplaces, the tapestries and tasteful furnishings, lanterns and candles, archways and stone flag floors, the sheer size of the interior and that it was mostly open plan but for a few rooms.

We now helped Dayna into one of those rooms, which turned out to be a small, cosy office.

We placed her down in the seat and she waved a hand in silent gratitude. There was soft music playing and a large fan whirred from the desk.

"You need to take it easy," I told her, my tone sounding harsher than intended though perhaps that was no bad thing, she shouldn't be doing what she was doing, taking tours, cooking, almost turning wheels attached to medieval contraptions and dealing with Arwen. "Your employers can't make you work like this, when do you go on maternity leave?" If Italian laws were anything like they were in the UK then she should have been excused by now.

She laughed, which was hardly the response I expected, and sank back into the leather whilst slowly blowing out air. Her face was flushed and I hoped she wasn't about to make things yet harder for herself.

Arwen had been standing close by her side, blocking the breeze from the fan, whilst making the occasional apprehensive glance at her belly. "Would you like me to call the father?"

Dayna shook her head, snatched the fan from Arwen's hands and proceeded to flap it near her face. "Mother," she panted.

Arwen met my eyes with a smirk, "she's not feeling very well," then leaned towards her with a hand on her arm, "yeeees, soon you will be." She grabbed the phone from the desk. "What's his name?"

Dayna heaved, her fingers clutching the armrest and jerked her chin towards the ceiling. "Upstairs. Two floors. Second door on right. But..."

"Easy." Arwen beamed, slamming down the phone and leaving the room. "I'll do that now."

I nodded at Dayna and smiled awkwardly whilst she sat and stared back at me. "Um, can I get you something, some water?"

She shook her head and I listened to Arwen's feet stamping up the stairs as I awkwardly perched against the desk, trying to occupy my eyes without coming across like I was prying too much, to what looked like a staff rota on the wall and the large crosses struck through most of the names, the dead and dying plants, the many packs of Kit Kats and the large half-eaten jar of marmalade. There were also four photo frames turned to face the wall.

There was a knock, followed by a more insistent one a few

seconds after. Dayna and I were both staring absently at the roof and
there was another knock, which was immediately followed by screams
in Italian. Arwen gave as good as she got and shouted something
back, the exchange continued and Dayna winced as she slid down in
her chair, something heavy banged against the door, Arwen shouted
again and then she was thumping back down the steps.

Arwen walked in and threw up her arm. "I don't think he, she or
whatever's in there's coming down."

So what was there we could do? We could leave and not think
anything more of it but neither Arwen or I were that bad as people.
We'd been in the vineyard grounds for anywhere between two and
three hours and seen only the one worker breeze through with an
agricultural robot. There were no women and nobody else in this
huge place, save for a few contractors banging with hammers and
they were unlikely to be of any use, if indeed we were even needed
ourselves. It just felt like we ought to remain behind, for a short
while at least, it was the decent thing to do.

We suggested going through to the main room and Dayna,
apparently feeling better, led us through and we each took separate
couches, Arwen and I checking the time on our phones every few
minutes, the only sound some rhythmical strumming from a
grandfather clock in the corner. It wasn't merely the Giordano
winemaking process that was medieval.

"Are you sure you're all right?" I asked again.

Dayna nodded and sighed, "I'm sorry for giving such an abysmal
tour, of course, I'll refund you both the full price of admission."

We both waved our hands to dismiss such nonsense, even though
a full refund was probably justified. "Oh, no, no, don't worry about it,
we had fun."

"Right," Arwen agreed and nodded towards a space out of
Dayna's hearing range.

I stood and walked over and Arwen pulled me in closer by the
shoulder to whisper into my ear.

"I think we can probably leave now, she's fine."

I glanced across at Dayna, who was lounging back on the couch.
"You really think? I'm worried about leaving her alone."

She shrugged. "There's someone else upstairs, it might be a
woman, I'm really not sure but there's definitely something up there,
in full existence. Whenever she or it decides to come look after
Dayna is another matter but it's not our responsibility." She tutted

and had to speak above the hammering and I worried Dayna might overhear. "That was quite a greeting she gave me, Frey."

I recalled our very first encounter. "Now you know how I felt."

Arwen scrunched up her face as my attention was taken by a row of picture frames on the mantelpiece that had all been turned away to face the wall. There were more on the windowsill likewise but then I noticed three together on a table in the corner and all were visible and I had to squint across the room to see that the images were of a man in his sixties with grey hair and an affable face. So far, they were the only photos I'd seen that weren't bizarrely turned away, the table also possessing flowers and those small candles you light in church.

"Frey?" Arwen prompted me.

"Um, I don't disagree, we probably do need to get moving."

There was a succession of bangs followed by an odd hissing, which caused even Dayna to perk, the noise stopped and a few seconds after the man from before, in red baseball cap, paced in from the outside and spoke to Dayna. "It was Fabio," he held his hands out in an apologetic gesture, "he put a nick in the sewage pipe ... bit of a spills but honestly, it under control, in case you can taste the stink."

"Salvo," Dayna grimaced as she tried pushing herself up and Arwen and I rushed over to help, as unnecessary as it turned out to be, for we were worrying too much, "how many times? I speak Italian." This was spoken in Italian, which Arwen hastily translated for me. It was a strange reaction to the news, aye.

Salvo removed his filthy hands from the back of the white leather couch to shrug, "I try learn English for I next trip."

Dayna rolled her eyes and waved him away.

"Wait," I called on Salvo and he stopped before reaching the door. I wanted him to wait behind long enough for Arwen and I to safely leave the property.

Arwen caught on quick and grabbed ahold of my blouse cuff. "We'd best be off then."

I was already moving and thinking of an early dinner and the wine we were having tonight, Bordeaux or Tuscany, I didn't much give a shit, and whether that would be enough to finally put the animal back into Arwen. "No need to show us out," I called over my shoulder and was horrified to see Dayna already shuffling towards the door only a few steps behind us.

"Well, thanks so much for coming, it's always nice to have a fellow

English girl around the place," no correction required, "although I hear they're producing wine down in the south now, Surrey and Kent, ah well, good luck to them. Ooh gosh..."

We'd reached the door and for some stupid reason, I found myself twisting around even as Arwen gave a couple of quick but noticeable tugs at my sleeve. "Thanks again."

Dayna blew the strands of loose blonde away from her face, "it was our pleasure."

"Yep," Arwen had to reach around me to pull the door open.

Dayna leaned against the wall, only a few inches from the opening and wiped her forehead in a display, "say," she panted, "I know this is out of left field and I don't mean to be a nuisance but since you're here, I don't suppose you wouldn't mind just helping out with a couple of things?"

My mouth jerked, again Arwen tugged and made a strange whimpering sound, Salvo had disappeared anyway and Dayna looked so sweet, vulnerable and distressed.

I wanted to cry but what could I do?

———

"How did this happen again?" Arwen pointed her pruning scissors at me and I had to step away from her wrath.

"A few hours won't kill us and it'll be a big help to her." I snipped at a small bunch that looked ripe and tossed it into the cart.

She loosened her collar and took a big step into my space, which ordinarily I'd have welcomed. "Why did you bloody stop? We were at the bloody door, staring out at freedom, you daft drongo."

My gaze dropped towards the dirt and I pinched at the skin between my eyes. She was right, kind of, I should have kept moving. "There's no need to get so worked up, Arwen." Usually, I loved the very rare occasion she was in a bad mood because I adored the way her face expressed itself, even if I'd never tell her that but this felt different, she was angrier than normal and I'd done it to her. "Besides..." I stopped myself and continued pruning, hoping she hadn't heard.

"Besides?"

"Oh, nothing."

"Whatever."

And I felt a grape bounce off my head.

The besides had been that I could sense something was wrong here, don't ask me how, it was just one of those things, woman's intuition but it was there and I was curious about whatever it was. Anyway, divulging it to Arwen in this mood was only to risk triggering the girl so I put it to rest and out of my head.

We were working downhill, taking a row of vines each, snipping away the ripe bunches and chucking them into the large cart we had to drag along with us every step of the way. It became progressively heavier so that I dreaded the prospect of heaving it back uphill when it was full, towards the barn where presumably, someone else would check our work and send them through the press.

"Hey..." Arwen hissed as though there were nearby people who could hear us when there weren't, "you see that?"

I examined the vicinity but didn't know what she was referring to. "What?"

Her head jerked towards the house. "That. There's someone watching us from that top window."

I followed her line of sight and saw that it was true, someone was watching us. "How long has *that* been there?"

"*That*? I think it's a *she* after all." Arwen was using her hand to shield the sun from her eyes, making it more than obvious we'd clocked whoever it was but, unperturbed, the person didn't even flinch. "Hey, doesn't it remind you of that film Psycho?" She waved to the distant figure. "Mother! Mother!"

I laughed and chucked a grape at her. "Maybe we can watch that when we get out of here." Was Psycho the right film to get a girl in the mood? Perhaps I could park the camper in an isolated wood because I was beginning to run out of ideas.

"I have a full battery and waiting," she turned away from the house, "anyway, I suppose the extra money won't do any harm, assuming we're being paid for this hard labour."

"And don't forget she's feeding us."

Which was true and the only reason Arwen had been pacified because we'd been promised a real Italian dinner and something better than what had been provided during the tour. I was sceptical, as was Arwen and with good reason. She wasn't Italian.

But the minute we returned to the house, it was obvious we'd underestimated her. We'd worked three hours, filled two cartloads with grapes and were beyond starving, especially considering lunch had been such a disappointment.

"Please," Dayna beamed and gestured to the table with its fantastic spread.

My belly was already rumbling and the smell was enough to prompt my saliva glands into awakening. It was all there, the cute red and white squared table cloth that for whatever reason screamed Italy, napkins of the same design, red and white roses poking out from used wine bottles in the centre, a beautiful vase filled with corks, a lit candle crammed down its neck and the wax from candles past that had dribbled down the sides and set, wine at the ready with the kind of fancy glasses reserved for posh guests, a large platter of bread and the most adorable olive oil container with a spout that resembled a miniature watering can and side dishes for dipping, fancy plates and the kind of weighty cutlery that just had to be silver. Soft Italian dinner music was playing and Arwen puckered her lips as we made eye contact from over our seats before pulling them out. Dayna had gone to much effort, maybe too much.

"How was your afternoon amongst the vines?" She made it sound so romantic and Arwen inhaled in preparation to speak and I was quick to cut her off.

"It was an experience," I emphasised with a nod to Arwen, thinking I sounded diplomatic and was rewarded with one of her cute little scowls.

Dayna smiled and carefully took her seat facing us. "Maybe sometime I'll show you how to operate the grape press." She said, tipping a dollop of oil onto her dish and reaching forwards for a cut of bread.

We both straightened at this and I felt Arwen's foot tapping mine beneath the table.

"We already saw that." She said with a flat tone and if I felt it necessary to intervene, nothing came to mind. Not that it mattered anyway because I didn't think Dayna had heard because the timer on the oven was loud and she was jumping up, in her state, and rushing to open the oven door and it all smelled so good.

"Be nice to her," I whispered to my friend and she responded by reaching for a piece of bread and tearing it apart with vigour.

"Bread's stale."

"That's because it's probably meant to be," I whispered whilst Dayna clattered about from not too far away, "and she was dipping it in olive oil." I took the liberty of pouring a small quantity onto Arwen's dish, rather a strange custom but when in Rome...

I used the opportunity to inspect the abode and yes, the whole thing was quite strange, for starters, that we were even here, and I had many questions even if Arwen didn't. For whatever reason, Dayna had taken a liking to us. Sure, we'd been pleasant to a certain extent and had happened to be around when Arwen brought on an attack of claustrophobia but we'd only been repaid that kindness by being emotionally blackmailed into toiling in the fields yet now, here we were, getting the royal treatment, but why? And why was this pretty pregnant lady here all alone but for some crazy woman locked in a room upstairs? Where were the men? Or other women, for that matter? Valid questions, the house was large and Dayna was the only apparent occupant.

I was about to inquire when an upstairs door slammed and Dayna, who was approaching the table with a large ceramic pot, stopped to glance upwards at the ceiling. There was the patter of feet and the rattling of pipes that could only come from bad water pressure and Dayna's eyes softened as she placed down the pot.

"It's Garganelli alla Bolognese, which means it's veal and pork mixed together with parmesan." She came back with another dish filled with those pasta tubes and I was about to go overboard with the ladle when she warned, "this is the first course."

Wow, we truly did have her all wrong, I think, although Arwen was giving me a knowing sidewards glance as she scooped a large dose of the meat sauce over her pasta.

I was so hungry but hadn't yet touched anything because I was polite and had been brought up correctly and, I assumed, we were about to be joined by the crazy but no, Dayna was already eating and there was no fourth table setting so I scooped up my first mouthful and hummed long and appreciatively. It was over the top amazing. "Oh, Dayna, I think this is the best thing I've tasted since arriving on the continent."

Arwen nodded grudgingly.

"You're too kind," Dayna dipped some bread into her sauce, "it's merely an every day Tuscan dinner. Well, I suppose I'm used to it."

"You live very well." I was absolutely inhaling the bounty.

Dayna reached for the wine then passed it to me because it required the use of a corkscrew. "You'd think I'd be used to it by now but..." she trailed off, slightly alarming me but then one glance at her set revealed she was drinking only water.

"Oh, I really shouldn't, we have to drive back to San Gim ... San something."

"San Gimignano, a beautiful place."

"Right, well somewhere there's a lay-by with our name on it."

"But one glass won't hurt, will it? Oh, go on, I insist, just one glass, it's one of *ours* ... our *premium* blend, to say thanks for everything you've done. You'll still get to your lay-bi. You must." She prodded the glass towards me and what could I do? Say no to the dear pregnant lady who'd gone to so much trouble? And there was more than a slight insinuation in her tone that great offence would be taken if I didn't imbibe in quantity, it was Vino di Giordano, after all. She waved a hand, "ignore me, it's up to you, of course. I'm just trying and failing at being an Italian host."

I reassured her by patting her on the forearm and croaked, "no, no, you're a wonderful host," which wasn't a complete lie, "well, I guess one glass won't hurt." I poured the fluid into my glass and Dayna was already looking on at Arwen in expectation.

"Go on, I'll have some too." Arwen gave me another sideward glance though I expected the wine would make her more agreeable.

There was a great difference between the wine I usually bought and the nectar we were drinking now. I'm no expert with the fancy descriptive words but this so-called premium blend was dry and easy on the palate, which had the effect of making me believe I wasn't really drinking anything and before I knew it my glass was half empty.

For several minutes the table slumped into silence save for the clatter of expensive cutlery and the creature causing another ruckus with the pipes. At one point, her feet bounded across the floor, which shook the boards and preceded a door slamming and at least two of us had to feign deafness and ignorance, all whilst Dayna set down her fork and began rubbing her arm. It was the elephant in the room, for sure, and I had to give Arwen credit for not mentioning it. Perhaps like me, she was beginning to believe this sweet, if rather odd, pregnant lady might be housing a character from every child's favourite nightmare about a monster hiding in the attic and the less said about that the better.

Dayna brought the second course out from the oven. "It's Tuscan porterhouse steak in red wine with parmesan roasted potatoes."

Arwen and I craned our necks as she brought it over and when she set it down the steak was hanging off the bone, the red wine still bubbled and the potatoes glowed and I was so happy I still had room in my belly because a decent home cooked meal was something I'd missed. She truly had gone to much effort and I wondered why we were so special and didn't the meat just melt in my mouth.

Noticing our wine had somehow been vanquished, Dayna took it upon herself to refill both glasses as she talked casually about how, six years before, she'd arrived at the vineyard for work experience and never left.

"And why would I? Giordano looks exactly like all those vineyards you see on the Tuscan postcards, the place is magical." She sipped her water and studied our expressions, neutral as I suppose they probably were. "I don't reckon the two of you would like a summer job or are travelling with anyone who'd like one, if only for a few weeks? Days even?"

It was another Dayna left field speciality and my head jerked without a prompt from my brain. Luckily I had a mouthful of steak, which gifted me valuable seconds to formulate a tactful refusal. Unfortunately, Arwen, who'd been less than subtle since our arrival, beat me to it.

"We don't." And that put a stop to Dayna's hopes at once.

I scratched my neck, hastily swallowed, and felt it necessary to add, "but thanks, Dayna, really. It's very kind of you but we have other places we need to get to and only so much time to see them."

Dayna leaned back and cleared her throat, just enough for us to notice.

"Rome beckons for us," I added with urgency, "we hear her distant call." What the fuck was that?

Arwen tapped my foot again and was struggling to contain herself after that one and then, at last, Dayna spoke.

"Of course, everyone should see Rome at least once in their lives. It's a bit overrated, extremely heavy traffic and the people aren't as friendly as you'd get in some of the other Italian regions ... say, Tuscany, for example. But yes, you should probably see it if you're travelling. Have some more wine." She emptied the remnants of the bottle into our glasses and I had literally no idea where the rest had gone.

How long had dinner lasted? Checking my phone was not the polite thing to do so I resisted the temptation. It was still light outside, so I reasoned we'd been eating around an hour or perhaps a bit longer. I thought again about finding a quiet spot on one of

Chianti's hills or valleys, snuggling in the sleeping bag with the girl I was in love with and watching Psycho but that hopefully we wouldn't be watching the film at all.

We finished and Dayna began to collect the plates.

"Would you let us do the washing?" I asked and Dayna shook her head.

"Don't be silly, you're my guests. Besides, we have a dishwasher." She engaged in that task and a minute later returned to the table. "But it's getting late and..." that was my cue to check the time on my phone, eight in the evening, "...the baby needs sleep as much as I do." She caressed her tummy with an expression of total love and warmth.

But I needed no more hints and pushed myself up, or rather, I tried but the effects of the alcohol unexpectedly surged to my head. Arwen had made it to her feet but was holding an arm out for the nearby wall.

A dainty hand found its way to Dayna's mouth. "Oh, what was I thinking feeding you both so much wine when you needed to drive back," Dayna slapped her wrist, "silly me. Oh, I really am sorry. What can we ever do?" She looked from me, to Arwen and back and I had a feeling I already knew where this was going. "Say..." and she touched a finger to her lip as though the idea had just come to her, "you should both stay over ... no, no, I insist. It's all my doing, oh, silly me, I truly apologise but you really shouldn't drive anywhere in this state."

"I..." but all I could do was exhale and wonder how I hadn't anticipated this from the offset.

Arwen risked unsteadying herself by standing arms akimbo. "We have to go, Dayna," she said sternly, "Rome ain't gonna come to us."

I was beginning to think we'd never see Rome nor anywhere else ever again, "right," I added, lamely and tried again to stand, failed and reached up for Arwen's hand but she was too far away to risk the trip.

Dayna shook her head, "no, no, you're over the legal limit, I can't let you leave like this, I'd never forgive myself if anything happened, but don't worry, we have spare bedrooms ... It's not a problem. No, don't be silly, I insist."

What could we bloody do? And we both recognised that attempting to resist this master manipulator would prove fruitless. I consoled myself with the thought that if we ever did manage to leave this vineyard, then it would be something we could both laugh about, probably.

"Follow me," Dayna commanded with a strange satisfied grin and we did, taking great care with the bannister for support, up two floors of creaky steps.

"You are such a bloody lightweight." Arwen swivelled her head to chastise me from in front and I had to avert my eyes from her rear end to reply.

"Says you, my dear."

The stairway possessed numerous portraits of families sat posing for the artist in traditional red and white Tuscan garb, which made everyone look like page boys from a fairytale and then I noticed the inscriptions which confirmed the images were actually the Giordanos from past generations. The further up the stairs we ascended so the portrait was of the generation after until the paintbrush changed to photography, first black and white and then colour. The final spot revealed no portrait of the present family, but an empty hook.

There were two opened doors on the right of the landing and we stopped at the first. I almost expected to find my name on a plate screwed into the wood but there wasn't.

Dayna gestured within, "Freya, this will be your room."

I stood awkwardly for a while, as did Arwen before she seized my hand, as well as an opportunity to get kicked out, and interlaced our fingers.

"You got a problem with this?" She was looking cold and deliberately at Dayna.

"Oh," Dayna sighed after a moment, she was tired, and smiled after the admission we were together because apparently, the two of us weren't giving off those kinds of vibes and that made me sad, "no, of course, I don't have a problem with this."

I realised that was the first time we'd ever told anyone we were in a relationship, for lack of a better word, and I wasn't sure what to think of how it went.

Dayna showed us both into the first room and gestured out with her arms. "It's the room I had when I first arrived. Better than a lay-bi, no?"

It was and Arwen nodded with a grunt as she plodded to the window and looked out over the vines in the twilight. Dayna wished us a goodnight and closed the door on us.

Arwen whipped around, "what the heck happened today?"

I shrugged and gazed hopelessly at the bed, a fourposter, which beat a sleeping bag. "I really don't know."

"I really don't know," she mimicked me, "we come here for a wine tour and end up picking grapes and staying the bloody night?"

I couldn't help but grin. "You said you wanted a wine tour, you got one."

"The nerve of the bloody woman," she continued, ignoring my humour, "how does she know we don't have opera tickets?"

"Yeah but we don't." I found myself being drawn towards her.

"Yeah but still, she doesn't know that." Her bottom lip was sticking out and I just wanted to bite it.

I moved to put my arms around her but she twisted away and stomped to the other side of the room. I exhaled and gestured to the surroundings, "it's a beautiful room."

And it was, like everything else in the house. There was an antique mirror on cast iron feet that looked incredibly heavy. It was one of those things that tilted in its frame and was presently reflecting Arwen's back, arse and everything else as she inspected the cabinet. This too was probably older than both of us combined and then some and had beautiful ornate floral carvings. Apart from the bathroom, which was en-suite, that was pretty much everything, minimalistic yet adequate.

I perched on the bed and felt myself sinking. "Arwen?" I waited for her to grunt before continuing. "Is there anything that strikes you as weird about this place?"

She turned around and leaned against the cabinet. "About Dayna? Sure."

"Did you notice the photo frames, how they're all facing away?" There were a few other things that had given me reasons to be concerned but it was the frames that would provide the easiest answers.

She folded her arms, considered her answer for a second and nodded. "My belief is that her husband knocked her up and ran. In a fit, she's unable to face the memories but doesn't want to lose all hope, so rather than destroy the images she turns them away, along with everyone else she meets and therefore has to resort to measures like this to get people to like her." She was jesting, of course, and I loved it when she was in this semi-belligerent mood, it totally brought out all her cute little expressions. "Can't say I blame him really and we've known her less than a day, imagine how it must be having to live with a woman like that."

My legs crossed the room without needing instruction and then I was pulling her in and inhaling the peaches that were infused oh so faintly and deliciously with the grape toiling sweat, all natural Arwen. "Say some more angry."

"I'm not angry."

"Yes, you are."

"No, I'm not." She squeezed me so hard that a burst of air was forced from my lungs.

"Scrunch your face up like you do."

"I will not."

"For me?"

"I won't"

And then my hand was finding its way beneath her skirt and working its way slowly up to graze her pussy.

She trembled, closed her eyes and all I could hear was her breathing muffled against my neck and, encouraged by finding her already moist, I began making slow circles with my middle finger but painfully soon, she pulled away so that the air against my finger, up to the distal interphalangeal joint, felt suddenly cold from her residue and the breeze left by her movement. My heart sank.

"Let's go down and see what she's hiding." She was filled with a sudden excitement that came from nowhere.

"Um, what?"

"The photo frames and anything else."

We decided to wait long enough to be sure Dayna would be asleep, whilst we used the interim to shower, separately.

And when the time came it was dark so we had to feel our way, slowly, down the stairs. My hand was on Arwen's shoulder as she led the way, step by step, every deafening creak causing a shudder. Even our breathing was like sirens as we passed the middle floor, the wooden steps cold beneath our bare feet and then we reached the landing and I could feel the warm woollen strands of a rug. The curtains were all closed and I regretted not thinking to bring my phone so that I could use the torch facility.

"Where's the light switch?" I hissed and Arwen stepped towards the wall from where we began sweeping our hands up and down the plaster in search of that familiar white box.

By now we were far beyond the landing and even the kitchen as we came to the living area and we had to navigate around a table that I remembered being positioned in front of the window.

And then I found a switch and applied pressure with my thumb.

The lights flicked on.

The girl on the couch was watching us and I fell into Arwen who had the presence of mind not to tumble to the floor with me atop of her.

"Holy fuck!" We both whimpered and staggered back.

She was brunette, an Italian, with hollowed cheeks, dark sunken eyes and nothing much behind them, eerily expressionless, and was sitting up straight with both hands resting on her knees.

Arwen and I had frozen, everywhere my skin pricking and then the woman simply stood and the loose white shift she wore flowed down to cover her legs and without a word, she stepped past the two of us to creak a slow journey upstairs.

Arwen's nails had been digging hard into my arm and I hadn't even noticed. "You were right," she hissed, "something's definitely weird."

DAYNA WAS ALREADY at the table when we came down for breakfast, another fancy spread. "Sleep well?" She looked surprisingly perky like she'd been up a while but then, I guessed, she had.

"Um, yeah, thanks." It was seven in the morning and the Tuscan brightness flooding in through the windows hurt my drowsy eyes, that now caught Arwen's, as we cautiously pulled out the chairs and sat and I knew what she was thinking. *How much does she know?*

But talk about being scared witless.

I was still feeling the anxiety from last night's encounter and I'll never know how we didn't end up smashing through the door and breaking for the hills.

Dayna considered us from over her small cup of coffee. "You met Alessia?" Ah, so she did know.

I shuffled as Arwen turned visibly away to glare at a bird that'd perched on a table outside. "Um, briefly. We came down for a glass of water. She was…"

"You were discussing the Fortezza Medicea di Poggio Imperiale?" There was an odd twinkle in her eye that unsettled me. "She said you were showing an interest."

Arwen's face, "the what?"

"My apologies. It's the Medici fortress in Poggibonsi."

Arwen gawked and turned back out the window, doubtless looking for signs of the moon.

Dayna shrugged, "her English is abysmal, so maybe she misinterpreted but I'll show you the place in a day or two. There's presently summer concerts, opera, stilt walkers, cake stalls, fireworks, that kind of thing. We can all go. Have some bread." She prodded the plate towards us and I realised Arwen's foot had been pressing down on mine for a while. "The first time I saw Poggibonsi, I actually preferred it to Lucca. Alessia calls me crazy." She laughed, which prompted the two of us to laugh nervously along with her. "Orange juice?" She raised the carafe and reached over to find an empty spot on the table, cramming the juice between plates of egg and freshly sliced tomato. "I made it this morning, fresh from the tree in the garden."

In which case, like the wine, I'd better not say no and I filled our glasses to the top. "Poggibonsi?"

"It'll be my pleasure. Ham? Coffee? And just so you're aware, in case you didn't notice the en-suite ... you know ... the one in *your* room," she made a strange downward inflection on the your, "it has fully functional taps and everything."

"What?" I asked, my head spinning from so many words too early in the morning.

"You said you came down for a glass of water." She was definitely one of those annoying morning people and it was hard to tell how much Dayna was enjoying this exchange but more to the point - *Our* room?

Arwen leaned towards my ear and if she was intending to whisper she failed because it came out more as a croak, "it looks like we now have our base, cos we ain't ever leaving this place," and I couldn't be sure whether Dayna heard or not.

She coughed and glanced at her watch. "Maybe we could do Poggibonsi after breakfast? Ah, damn it," she shook her head, "I have to drive to Siena to collect the labour," she made a fist and playfully struck the table, "oh, what a shame. I was a little worried, you know, in case I went into labour but there's no way out of it. Sorry." She was looking down into her fruit salad, bottom lip protruding and then her eye poked up from below.

But this wouldn't do at all, I'd told her only yesterday she shouldn't be rushing about in her condition. I readjusted myself on the cushion and was about to offer going in her stead when Arwen piped up.

"How about I go for you?" Her face was full of concern, which made me sceptical.

"What, really? You wouldn't mind?" Dayna stood and when her back was turned, Arwen stuck her tongue out at me and I knew it at once. She'd skilfully avoided having to harvest grapes, which I was sure Dayna was about to rope me into doing.

She approached the kitchen countertop, reached behind the spice rack and pulled out a sheet of paper. "Here's the address. There are usually three or four men waiting around, the usuals, and they'll recognise the minivan and jump straight in. When you drive them back, there's no need to show them how to pick the grapes, they already know how." How much of this was her sense of humour and how much her crazy? "Oh, and you wouldn't mind going to the supermarket? The items I need are listed below the address and if you can deliver the wine boxes that are already packed in the van to the address on the other side, that'd be a great help ... best get that one out of the way first, I'd prefer having the labour arrive sober."

Arwen stood to snatch the paper from Dayna's grasp and momentarily found herself unable to respond. Aye, the girl was literally speechless, which in my experience takes an awful lot of doing and on some levels, Dayna had to be congratulated. Arwen dumped herself back in her seat and began piling cheese, ham and bread onto her plate before finally managing her retort. "So Dayna, got any more tour victims lined up today?"

I cringed at that and this time it was I who pressed down on Arwen's foot because it had been a little uncalled for and Dayna definitely heard that one. I expected our host come jailer to reply on the defensive because her forehead furrowed and her mouth began to open when instead her tired face softened and her gaze shifted between the two of us and we couldn't help twisting around to follow her line of sight.

Because Alessia was traipsing towards the table, clutching her dressing gown tight about her body as though it was cold when it was anything but, her exceptionally long brown hair left free to roam down her back, brittle as it looked and in need of some serious care. Her eyes were indeed sunken, which tragic because they possessed a certain intensity, complimented by a jaw that gave her a hawkish appearance. She might have been beautiful, if not malnourished to the extreme, and I wasn't sure how happy I was to finally be getting a good look at the mysterious Alessia.

Arwen and I were invisible as Alessia seemingly floated towards Dayna and hunched over to carefully place her arms around the English girl in a warm embrace, no words spoken, and they kissed closed mouthed for a count of three or four.

Arwen's hand leapt around my wrist and I had to suppress a surprised yelp. I glared at Dayna's belly, surely only days from delivery, as the shock struck me.

Dayna was a lesbian?

Maybe that explained all the madness around here?

Alessia released her lips and their hands remained together as she trailed away and Alessia again grabbed the sides of her gown as she wandered out through the opened door.

Dayna was quick to call out, "mangia qualcosa stamattina, per favore, Alessia," her voice was heavy with worry, her face contorted with utter love and feeling. "Alessia?"

"No, non ho fame." She went farther outside and through the window I watched as she strayed aimlessly down the slope in her bare feet, to stop halfway before the first row of vines.

I pulled myself away in an effort to eat something but there were no tastes, the egg, ham and bread bland on my palate. Something had happened here at the Giordano Vineyard, my guess was it had happened recently and I was both intrigued and saddened.

Dayna had slid her seat to face the window and again, I glanced outside to see Alessia standing in the open, staring into nothing as the small breeze lifted her hair.

It was something that unfortunately I recognised. And the reason I recognised what I was seeing was because my very first childhood memories were so similar.

My mother had so often done the same.

———

AFTER MY MOTHER had crashed the car and injured my brother, she'd fallen into a depression that had lasted many months. At the time, I was a child of three, my cognition was only just forming and I was slowly beginning to realise I existed in this world. I do recall my mother, vaguely; her lying in bed throughout the day, refusing to speak, to look at me even, of seeing her shape standing in the garden as she stared out into the Highlands that surrounded us. She always wore that long grey gown that was so large for her petite frame that the ends would traipse over the soggy ground from where the mud patches became prominent. I remember seeing my dad cry once and that he'd hastily wiped his face when he noticed me watching.

Depression can strike any person for any reason and can cause symptoms of anxiety, sadness, helplessness, guilt, weight loss, fatigue and in the case of my mother, suicide. It can also offset sleeping patterns, as in the case of Alessia, and although I might not yet possess my piece of paper, I knew exactly what it was afflicting that poor girl.

It was approaching ten in the morning, the sun was already oppressive and I very nearly had my first full cartload of harvested grapes. Arwen had been gone a couple of hours and the silence of her absence had presented the opportunity for reflection. I finished stripping a vine of its fruit and whistled, hoping to attract the attention of Salvo who'd been in and out of the barn all morning. He looked down and I waved and a minute later he joined me by the cart.

"Ok, I handle."

"Let me help."

We both grunted as he pulled and I pushed. The dirt path had been so worn down by countless thousands of similar trips that the earth almost resembled asphalt and as long as we didn't veer off track and over the less travelled ground then the two of us made easy work hauling the load into the barn and parking it beside the ludicrous grape press.

"Here we remove grape and throw bad grape in there," he tossed a rotten one over his shoulder into an industrial-sized rubbish bin before expertly stripping an entire stalk into the press. "We make premium wine, which mean bad grape not go in machine. I say that well?"

"Well enough for me to understand."

He was a friendly looking man with a belly that slightly pushed out his workman's overalls, was overly generous with the smiles and again wore that red baseball cap that had a miniature flag of Italy on its peak. His face was heavy with stubble and I put him to be about forty years of age. "I thank you for helping Alessia," he said, gesturing with a hand that I should pitch in with the monotonous but essential task.

I tossed a bad grape towards the giant rubbish bin and missed. "I thought it was Dayna I was helping. It's her vineyard, isn't it?"

He laughed and shook his head. "No, not Dayna, Alessia. At least, it is now."

I stopped and considered that response. Why not, Alessia? Nobody had told me anything. But I decided against shattering Salvo's vision of the altruistic Freya by telling him we were only helping largely against our will, and still hadn't come to terms with how that had even happened. But since I was here, and working, apparently pro bono, I at least deserved an explanation as to why I was doing it, for the moment voluntarily, and all whilst my valuable travelling time was diminishing by the hour.

"I'd like to know what happened here. Could you please tell me?"

He hesitated but then after seeing we still had a full cart of grapes to strip for the press, decided there'd be no harm in talking. "A lot happened but mostly Alberto died and everything went to hell."

"Alberto was their," I struggled to even come up with a name for the term and found it even harder to say it, "he was their live-in lover?" I assumed that someone, somehow, probably had something to do with Dayna being pregnant but then I gave it a moment's thought and realised that explanation made no sense. Alessia was the one who'd taken the death of this Alberto far worse than Dayna.

Salvo's dark brows dipped and I didn't think he understood my words anyway. "He was Alessia's father."

"Ahhhh." I could occasionally be slow to catch on, was I supposed to be an expert on how lesbians lived suddenly? I only had my own experiences to draw on and they merely involved living nomadically with a woman who could barely bring herself to be touched.

After a second, I realised Alberto had to be the man in the photos and I recalled the small table in the house with the flowers and candles and how it was most probably a shrine. I'd since taken an opportunity to peak behind some of the other photos and found they were all images of either Alessia, Dayna, Alessia and Dayna, or another woman who looked strikingly like Alessia, who I put to be her mother.

Salvo continued to explain how Alberto had suffered a heart attack and died, which had happened only a few weeks before, at the worst possible time, as though there was ever a good time to die, and how those two poor girls had been left with the incredible task of running the family business by themselves, amidst a mass walkout of

workers, many of whom blamed Alessia's lesbianism for a long string
of bad luck, even as they were undergoing an expansion.

He needed a long time to explain and by the time he had, we'd
finished the task but I wasn't about to leave now.

"Who's the father of the baby then?"

He removed the cap and ran his fingers through thinning black
strands. "Beh, just one of Alessia's old friend ... used to love her, she
didn't love him and now he have baby with girlfriend of Alessia," he
laughed, "funny world, funny old world." With his fingers, he drew in
the air a crude rectangular outline and pumped his fist and I could
only imagine how it was intended. Of course, I knew all about
artificial insemination and assumed that was what Salvo meant. "But
he live in Switzerland and won't be part of family from what I know.
The girls do family on their own." He sighed and looked unhappy.
"They try anyway." He replaced his cap and leaned against the wheel
that would crush the grapes. "Do I say it right? My English
not good."

"Grammatical errors here and there but I understand everything
you're saying."

He grabbed ahold of the wheel but delayed turning it. "Alessia, I
know her many year but now she don't speak much ... has lots
all hope."

"*Lost* all hope," I corrected him.

He shrugged and peered into the trough. "I help best I can. I
been here many year and know nothing else, no other trade, only
wine. I do everything here now but I'm only one man and production
is down seventy percent. Without wine, contracts get cancelled and
Alessia lose her home and business. Alberto's daughter, my friend but
what can I do?" He turned the lever, the gushing commenced and he
had to raise his voice above the squelching of grapes and squeaking of
the wheel to say, "what they need is help, money and a miracle."

I returned with the cart to the vines feeling justifiably subdued.
Life so often had a way of kicking you when you were already down
and I had a terrible image of Dayna, Alessia and a baby losing this
place and finding themselves on the streets.

I reached for my phone and visited the reviews for the Giordano
Vineyard on TripAdvisor, bracing myself for the bad news.

'The worst tour in Tuscany! They should have their tour license
revoked, the brown haired girl wanted to be anywhere else but there,
a disgrace. The banging was non-stop, the food terrible, there was too

much walking in the dirt and I got sunburned. The wine was ok but ruined by everything else. Did I mention the wine shop was fully functional and operating - Funny that!'

There were several more similar mean-spirited reviews and I took a moment to write my own, praising the tour, the wine, the food, the staff, everything, though what good it would do now, I couldn't say. But I had to do something and such a small act, dispatched to cyberspace and left to its own destiny felt so futile against such overwhelming opposition.

I was training to be a doctor and knew nothing about business, especially running one and especially not running a vineyard but to be here and to experience this place, to view its scale and beauty, there was only potential, surely. I mean, the Giordano Vineyard had existed for four hundred years already. How much would be needed for the glory days to return?

Twenty minutes later I could see Dayna and Alessia, arm in arm, strolling around the grounds. Alessia was dressed now and wore a pair of grey jogging bottoms with a hoody. At first, they remained near the house, walking around its perimeter five or six times but later they ambled down the grassy section of the slope where no vines were planted. Instead, there were flowers and trees, some of which had oranges hanging from the branches. At the end of the slope trickled a stream and there together they spent a while standing as Alessia's head rested on Dayna's shoulder. Then Dayna left Alessia sitting on the bank and slowly made her way through the vines to where I worked.

"You're toiling very hard and I feel very bad." She looked larger than ever, to see her down here now, in a bright yellow maternity dress. Her face and arms perspired and she carried her trademark fan that she flapped a few inches from her face. "I spoke to Salvo."

I placed down my pruning scissors and gave her my full attention. "He told me what happened and I'm very sorry for your loss, as well as for all the rotten bloody luck you've been having around here. I'm sure it was the last thing you needed right now," she was about to interject but I was quick to cut her off, "and I'd just like you to know that if there's any way I can help then I'm here to offer you my service." Did I really just say that? I paused and then nodded, as much for myself as for Dayna. "That's right. So you don't need to worry or stress yourself out, at least not over plotting to have me stay because I'm staying, so please relax."

Her head tipped back and she took a deep relieving breath. "Thank you." Her cheeks flushed and began to glow like her arms and she had to blink rapidly to quell the onset of tears. "I feel so bad for taking advantage of your good nature, I don't know what I was thinking, or how I expected it to turn out." She fanned her face with more vigour and laughed. It was nice to finally speak to the real Dayna, no pretences. "I want you to know that I'm really not crazy but what choice did I have? Two kind-hearted girls turned up at my door and I took your arrival as a gift from God ... if he even exists. Alessia no longer seems to think so."

My head tilted, "how is Alessia, really?"

She gazed over the vines to settle on her broken lover still sitting on the bank of that small stream, her feet dipping into the water and I wondered what kind of a person she'd been only a few short weeks before.

"She took it particularly bad and it hardly helped that Alberto had been in such anguish when he died," her jaw clenched and I knew not to ask about that though usually, there was only one thing that caused men such pain. "Alessia adored her dad, Alberto was one of the best men you could ever hope to meet but for whatever reason, she's become convinced he didn't love her."

"Why?"

She shrugged and felt her belly, "because she never married and had children, or so she thinks, but it was never true, of that I'm certain. He used to bemoan not having a son but it always seemed in jest to me. Still, a man likes to leave a legacy, to pass down his knowledge, what he's worked for, his home, and instead, he had a lesbian daughter."

I recalled the many portraits adorning the stairs of the family's past generations, an ever-present reminder of Alberto's most important duty but I wasn't sure what I could say on the matter. Legacy was that one thing that rested heaviest on the minds of men but it seemed to me that as long as his children were good people then a father had done as well as he could. I thought about my own dad and how many of the same things occupied his thoughts.

Dayna stared blankly over my shoulder. "If only he'd told her more often that he loved her, all this could have been avoided."

I tried to recall a time my dad had ever said those words to me, or even praised me in any such way, and could not. That was something I'd always been aware of but had always thought it was an old aristocratic or Scottish phenomenon and that my dad was Scots aristocrat was a double whammy of stiff upper lipped, keep your loved ones at a distance bullshit that deserved to die out.

"And it came at such a bad time," she continued, "with everything else surging over us, that she's pretty much given up. These things, they can either make or break..." she stopped and blinked up at the sky before proceeding to aggressively fan her face, "I never get used to this bloody heat."

The minivan juddered up the dirt track, throwing out a large cloud of dust and I reached out to place my hand on Dayna's shoulder.

"I can't promise any miracles and I can't speak for that girl," I nodded towards the vehicle that had disturbed the peace, "but you got *me* for a maximum of five weeks. All I ask is for an arse kissing reference at the end, that wonderful bedroom and your company at breakfast. Anything you need of me then I'll do my very best to see it done."

This time she made no effort to hide the tears and I thought she was adorable. "Thank you, Freya."

"It will be my pleasure but I want you to lie down and take it easy." I retrieved the pruning scissors. "Now, if you'd excuse me, but I have work to do."

She did and a minute later Arwen was bounding down the hill with a train of men stumbling after her; five, six, seven, eight of them, a mixture of nationalities by the looks of it and they were all absolutely drooling. The girl had her strengths, I had to hand her that.

"Babe," she swiped an errant branch out from her path, "we have to talk." She was probably right about that.

"Arwen?"

She scowled at the cart as I threw in a large bunch of grapes. "You're actually still doing this, huh?"

"I actually still am, yes." I glanced beyond her shoulder to the eight men who were still standing behind her, mostly North Africans but also two sub-Saharans.

Arwen noticed and twisted around, "andate a prendere dell'uva," and after nobody moved, "will you go and pick some bloody grapes," she said louder and pinched the skin at the bridge of her nose. They scattered. "I thought they knew what they were doing. Anyway..."

"How was your errand? No trouble?"

"Oh, any idiot could do it but that's all by the by," she closed her eyes and shook her head, "anyway, why are you even doing this? Why are *we* doing this? We got the labour now, so put those stupid prunes down and let them do it."

"Prunes?"

"Those!" She cuffed at my pruning scissors and they fell into the soil. "Look, Frey, I brought the men, the crazy lady has her slave labour, now please," and she turned to jab a finger in the direction of our camper van, "can we just drive away, nice and easy, no fuss, and never look back. What can she do, really? She can't stop us. I want to see Rooooooome," she sounded whiny now, "and from there to Naples, Pompeii, the Amalfi Coast, Sicily and on to Greece."

I stooped down to retrieve the implement. "That's what I wanted to talk to you about..."

She nodded, "uh huh, and you're still standing here, why?"

"Look, Arwen, there's no easy way to tell you this, so I'm just going to say it. I'm staying to help out." I spoke as evenly as I could but to hear the words inside my head was to doubt them.

Her expression remained apathetic for a count of two. "You're serious? For how long?"

I shrugged, "I already promised Dayna ... five weeks."

"The fuck?" Her mouth fell open and she spun bodily away before returning to centre and raising her voice. "Are you insane? It's contagious around here, ain't it. That's the rest of your holiday. Are you for real? And were you not thinking to discuss this with me? The fuck, Freya?"

I nodded, conceding certain points. "I probably should have discussed it with you, of course, I just, kind of made a commitment to Dayna on the hoof and..."

"On the hoof?"

"Um, it means I wasn't thinking at the time but I made the promise and I'm not sorry I did because the thing with Dayna and Alessia is that..."

She kicked the cart then her eyes glazed over, "I know why you're doing this," and she held her finger up, "you're doing this just to prove to me that you're not that thing I called you." She made a friendly exhalation for my benefit. "Well, rest assured, Frey, you've already proven it, so consider yourself an unselfish person, I'm sold. I'm sorry, I apologise, now, can we please stroll over to our beautiful camper and quietly drive away without another word?"

I held out my palms, "Arwen, I'm sorry but I'm staying, I just feel like I need to be here because Dayna and Alessia really need..."

She held a hand up. "Fine! I'm going." She spun around and stamped away but turned back after three paces. "Ok, Freya, you're not selfish but now you're stubborn and stupid and being taken advantage of, so which do you think is better?"

I tried. I'd tried twice to tell her why I was staying but she wasn't listening and the horrendous thing was that I was almost certain that even if she could shut her mouth for long enough to allow me to explain the situation, I really didn't think it would make a difference. Who was the selfish one now? No, Arwen was more bothered about herself than anything else, and way more than I ever was, and that realisation appalled me.

But more than being selfish, I finally realised what Arwen's real problem was.

"You can't handle things when they're tough, can you?"

She stepped back, "what are you talking about? And what does this have to do with anything?"

I tilted forwards, "it's so true," I muttered to myself and then spoke up, "you're not stupid, Arwen, you can see what's happening around here but either you don't care, which I find hard to believe, or you literally can't handle life when it's even the least bit difficult." I examined her, the beautiful woman, but it was so true, "it is."

She folded her arms and stared fixedly at me. "Look, I just don't think it's right that either of us should waste any more of our time toiling in filthy fields, spinning big wheels or anything else. You said so yourself, this is literally the only chance in years you'll have to travel, yet you're wasting it all to be a slave here?"

I stepped forwards, "you really can't handle it when everything doesn't go your way."

It all made sense now. The tantrum she had with Dan when he drove her through the Alps, which might have been understandable but there were more obvious examples. The way she ran away when I rejected her, and how she was on the verge of doing it again when Dan refused to speak to her and I'd caught her sneaking away. She could quite happily turn down a wealthy nightclub owner but lost her mind back in that bathroom in Barcelona when I'd barely even rejected her and she'd proceeded to dance with every girl and guy who happened to be near. Now she was threatening to leave again and all because I wouldn't do what she wanted. Arwen lacked responsibility, she hated not getting her own way, and rejection made her lose her shit.

"You know what, Arwen, in this world, you can't always get what you want ... you just have to learn to deal with it. Occasionally, life can be hard." I glanced over to where Dayna was cuddling Alessia by the stream. "I'm sorry but I'm staying."

She kicked a lump of soil that flew into the vines. "Are you really fucking serious?"

It was strange but I wasn't angry, I wasn't hurt, I wasn't even upset, it was what it was because Arwen was the girl who she was. And now it looked like Arwen and I had reached the end of the road, and to prove it, I delved into my pocket and threw her the camper keys.

"It's yours, keep it. Consider it a parting gift." But still, I could hardly believe I was saying the words.

She stared at the keys and looked back to me as she sought the words. "Are you really saying goodbye?"

I shrugged and hoped it wasn't. "If it is then it's for the best. I'll remember you with fondness." I returned to the vine I'd left half-trimmed. "Now, if you'd excuse me, I must prune."

The last thing I heard was, "damn you."

And a few minutes later she was driving down the path and out of my life.

———

THE DAY AFTER ARWEN LEFT, I drove for the labour myself, arriving in Siena and selecting six men who were standing in a group of many dozens. It was the kind of thing I'd never imagined myself doing and really should have had an escort, or at least a can of mace, but until Dayna could find a new bunch of permanent staff, which seemed unlikely for the time being, I'd be doing this every day for many weeks, so I'd have to get used to it. The men were there to work, after all, which was why they were standing out in the rain at eight in the morning.

They were from Eritrea and a man named Tesfay, at least I think, spoke English for the group, not that much was said, but he shepherded his companions into the van from where he tried to negotiate a price for their labour.

"Hey, I'm just the driver, take it up with the office." By which I hoped that would mean some person other than Dayna.

Negotiating wages was a little beyond my authority but it forced me to ponder how Arwen had handled the very same thing only the day before, which then made me think more about the girl, her impossible curves and beauty, which I didn't need to be doing right now. I'd bought a burner phone in Nice and the only people who had my number were Arwen and Dayna, but I quickly dropped any thoughts of contact. I'd have them again and they needed to be fought. There was work to do.

With a large group of men working in the vines, I was able to spend the day doing other things, like crushing grapes in the press. It was a satisfying experience and an intense cardio workout but not something I could maintain for long periods. Later, one of the Eritreans, a man named Massawa offered to take over and Salvo showed me how to pump the extracted juice into the vats, an easy task which involved the turning of yet another wheel.

There were twelve vats in total, each almost as high as the ceiling and Salvo, in his broken English told me they were seventeen feet from top to bottom, each as wide as the camper van Arwen had taken off in. Most modern vats are made from stainless steel but of course, here they were constructed from oak and although they looked aged, I was told they were actually less than ten years old and had a limited lifespan, after which they'd need replacing.

This was the stage where the wine was fermented, remaining in the giant tanks on a rotational basis, the vat that had been full the longest was next to be drained and then the liquid was transferred via pipe into oak barrels and taken to the cellar to be stored for a period of one year.

This was by far the most time consuming part of the process and the real reason Giordano wine was considered premium and the day after I was tasked with filling the barrels and, by use of a pulley, lowering them down into the cellar from where Salvo would store them, again using a rotation system.

The barrels that had been stored for a year or more were brought up and due to the staff walkout, this was where the largest backlog existed, and so I was happy to be given the neat task of bottling and corking.

The bottling was completed using nothing more complex than a siphon, filling the bottles to the neck before the real fun part. They used a floor corker where the bottle was placed on a small spring loaded platform, the cork slotted into position and all I needed to do was pull down on a lever and the cork was compressed and thrust down the neck. The bottles were then labelled and placed in boxes of six before being stacked for delivery.

By the end of the third day, I'd experienced every part of the process and Dayna would frequently stop by to chat.

"I'm getting very bored." She complained and I told her to enjoy the boredom because all that was about to change, which quietened her on that front, though in truth, I knew she was still doing admin work but at least that was nothing physical.

I picked up bits of Italian from Salvo, the radio, TV and because I'd expressed an interest in languages, Dayna gave me a few basic lessons so that I was able to recognise the crazy verb system most other languages used and was the real reason English speakers found linguistics so difficult. Dayna herself had studied Italian at university, which was the reason she'd ended up living in Tuscany and so I had someone qualified to teach me which, she said, enabled her to finally use the skills she possessed and it was the least she could do. By the end of the third day, I was able to converse with Salvo using the basics.

I rarely saw Alessia because she scarcely left her room but Dayna often brought me news of how grateful she was that I was here and that she already considered me a friend.

"As do I," Dayna said, flapping her fan, and that was when her waters broke. "There goes my cup of tea and it was the last of the Earl Grey too. Feel free to finish the Kit Kats, I should probably stop eating them now. Oh well, I suppose I'd best get to the hospital then. Are you sure you'll be all right here on your own?"

My body was vibrating, "what? Just get out of here woman. Here, let me help you."

"You couldn't call Alessia, could you? She's sort of the love of my life. If she doesn't answer just tell her ... well you know what to tell her ... and she's sure to get a move on."

I hadn't been sure whether Alessia would be going to the hospital but I was relieved to find there were no problems with her rousing and it was the fastest I'd yet seen her move when she ran down the stairs and grabbed the keys to their Peugeot convertible.

When I waved them off it was early evening on a Friday and although the vineyard was operating at a much-reduced output, with a large section of the fruit remaining uncollected and going rotten, at least every process was being handled to some degree.

A large truck juddered its way up the path before using the carpark to turn around and manoeuvre itself so that the back was positioned at the entrance to the warehouse. A man jumped out, slammed the cabin door closed and as he walked towards the warehouse, swivelled his head and noticed me. He stopped mid-stride, paused for a beat and then continued.

At seven in the evening, I was in the office handing Tesfay an envelope for each of his companions. "Same time tomorrow?"

"We be there." He left and then another man entered.

"Ciao, sei la nuova manager?" He was leaning against the doorframe and cast a glance back at Tesfay until the house door closed.

I shut the desk drawer and gave the man my attention, "um, my Italian is very basic."

"Are you the new manager?"

I laughed, "only if I've been promoted without my knowledge. No, but I've been entrusted with certain responsibilities."

For a while, he continued to stare without speaking. "You should not be alone in the house with the immigrant workers, it's not safe. Next time ensure Salvo's here, or me if I'm around. I was watching today but next time I might not be here."

I readjusted myself, "I'm sorry, I assumed Salvo was busy filling up that big truck. Is that yours?"

He nodded, "I just returned from Milano. I make the deliveries now. I'll be away again in the morning." The man was of stocky build, had a dark complexion and wore a red bandana. He was probably in his mid-thirties but maybe older, had a handsome face and was not altogether unpleasant to look at, even if I wasn't sure what to make of his introduction.

"I'm sorry," I began, thinking back to his earlier words, "but Tesfay's ok, as are the rest of them."

He smiled, "of course, but you can never be too careful, a beautiful woman like you..." his gaze lingered and I had to look away. "Anyway, I just had to make sure nothing happened ... you hear stories about these people."

From somewhere not far away, the clattering of bottles found its way through several walls to reach my ears and when I looked up, the man was walking away.

He returned half an hour later and leaned against the doorframe, this time the manly smell of body odour was thick within the confines of the small office. "Two hundred cases packed, ready for Rome. I'll need my delivery list first thing in the morning."

"Oh, gosh, right." I subconsciously looked down at the desk, as though the list might be amongst the papers there. Finding that would be fun. Talk about being thrown in at the deep end.

"You look very beautiful when you're confused."

I glanced up at that and when I did, he was holding a bunch of flowers.

"In case you thought I was impolite before, I meant no offence."

My hand touched my chest. "Oh, thank you, but really, it's fine." I stood and walked over to take them and his eyes never left my own. There were several vases containing nothing but dead flowers and I chose one to make the exchange. "That will surely brighten the room."

"You're working all night?" His accent was different to most of the Italians I'd spoken to and I wondered if he was from a different region.

I blew out air, "I'll probably call it a night soon, I was just researching a few things." From what I'd gathered, working hours around here were far longer than in the UK and I didn't wish to be the one letting the side down, especially considering some of the new tasks I'd taken on were less physical than everyone else's.

"And what will you do for dinner?"

My eyes glazed over as I thought for the answer. "I think there's some lasagne left over from last night, or perhaps I'll attempt some Italian cooking myself."

He stepped further into the office. "I cannot allow that, it's Friday night and for only a short time, the opera is in Poggibonsi. Tonight, we'll eat good local food and listen to music in the fortress grounds."

I pinched my bottom lip, "oh, now then," I wasn't sure. He seemed ok and apparently I was completely unattached but now was far from the right time to start anything new with anyone, I'd only said goodbye to Arwen a few days before and I felt the need to do that some justice by leaving sufficient time. Indeed, the fact I was so busy had prevented her leaving from properly sinking in, which was why I wasn't, even now, balling my eyes out. Other than that, there was no reason why I shouldn't spend the evening with this exceptionally straight talking and forward man enjoying the opera, as long as that's all it would be. I was also a guest in someone else's house, though I hardly thought that would be an issue. On the other hand, it was Friday night and I had literally nothing else to do other than get drunk on yet more wine and take an early night. Opera for the first time in my life? Why not?

"Sorry," I began, "I wasn't hesitating, I was just thinking. Yes, that sounds nice and I'd like to see Poggibonsi." I held my hand out to the man. "Mi chiamo Freya, e tu?"

He raised both eyebrows, impressed by my minuscule Italian, and his rough, calloused hand took mine. "Sono Goro."

"Piacere."

THE GENTLE SLOPE that approached the Medici fortress was lined with stalls selling medieval wares, cheeses, wine, spirits, pastries and all kinds of edible delicacies made locally and the ham and cheese paninis looked so good that my feet stopped of their own accord. I was just about to pay for one when instead, Goro handed the cash over to the lady.

"Goro, you shouldn't. I have money."

He guided me away with a hand on my lower back and stuck out his chin, "you're out with me so I will pay."

He was one of those old-fashioned guys, for sure, brought up a certain way, which made me wonder if I had his age all wrong or if men were just really different down here. He'd been quick with the doors, which was a refreshing change from Gabe, but then he was also too eager to pay when it wasn't necessary, having already handed over fifty Euros for the two tickets at the box office. It wasn't that I minded overly he was spending money on me when we'd only just met, the issue was that doing so placed me in a position where it felt like I was supposed to reciprocate in some way. And since he was not allowing me to pay for anything, that could only mean one thing.

We had about fifteen minutes before the start of the show, a Vivaldi that promised to be memorable. The warmup act was playing now and we'd been able to hear the distant clashing of cymbals and the toots of brass instruments all the way from the carpark and people had been stopping in the street to join the queue for tickets.

We strolled past a stall selling bouquets of flowers and Goro must have observed me staring at them because he stopped to purchase a particularly large bunch. "They're red to match your hair."

I held out my hands to accept them, what else could I do? "Goro, you really shouldn't." The second bunch today. "What are you apologising for this time?"

He didn't get the reference and gestured up the slope for us to continue and I made a conscious effort not to show interest in anything else. We passed through the gates and down a long stone tunnel before Goro showed the attendant our tickets and then we emerged onto a large lawn with a stage and seats for several hundred spectators. There were also more stalls set around the periphery.

The clashes and honks of brass instruments echoed from the ancient stone walls as the venue filled with people, though if I'd thought opera would only attract a more mature demographic I was wrong because there were people of all ages taking seats. What I did notice was how well everybody was dressed, this was Italy after all, and I hoped I wouldn't be too conspicuous in jeans and blouse. Certainly, my date hadn't made any complaints.

Goro himself had changed, I think, in the cabin of his truck, so that he was no longer wearing overalls and bandana but a striking all blue suit over white shirt and tie. He even had a pocket square at his breast and I had to hand it to the guy, he'd made an effort and was striking to look at, if not for his natural looks then certainly for his style and I did notice the glances he was attracting from other ladies.

"You like wine?" He asked as we ambled around the periphery and I assumed this was likely a question about how I'd ended up sort of working in a vineyard. How to explain that?

I sniggered, "who doesn't like wine? And I'm having lots of fun working for Dayna and Alessia." I turned into him and looked up to meet his eyes, "and it's good of you to stay behind when others ditched them in their hour of need."

He avoided my gaze. "Have you ever tried Prosecco?"

"Um, Prosecco?" I squinted, "it's fairly popular back home but no, I can't say I've ever tried it."

"Then we'll get a bottle," he placed his hand on my lower back and guided me towards the stall, looks like I'd assumed wrong about the meaning of his question, and he signalled the vendor before pointing to a bottle on the top shelf. I had to look away because the item ticket indicated it cost one hundred Euros and then Goro was handing over the money.

I didn't even know what to think because the price was beyond extortionate, as delicious as I'm sure it was, but how was I supposed to enjoy it? All I could do was pretend I hadn't seen how much it had cost, I mean, the man drove a truck for a living and I didn't wish to be the one responsible for his not being able to pay the rent this month. To top it off, none of this was impressing me at all. On the contrary, it placed me under the pressure to somehow repay him and I wasn't about to do that.

Thankfully, the music was soon starting and after we found our seats, Goro popped the cork and filled our glasses.

"To an evening of music, culture and beauty."

"Right," I clinked and sipped, it tasted good, magical even but I should have been here with someone else.

Where was Arwen this night? It was now the third night without the strange girl and finally, I knew it, which I could only put down to being here, socialising, with someone else. But she'd gone and this time it really was for the best because in so doing, she'd proven we weren't the same.

The orchestra came out to an applause and I counted twenty-one musicians before they began with Four Seasons. It lasted for more than half an hour and Goro told me about each season as the music transitioned. Afterwards, there was a short intermission and he was keen to learn about my travels. Having come from the south, he'd explored most of Italy but had never left the country and my impression of the man was that he was intelligent and worldly, if constrained by his job, which stole so many of his hours. I asked how long he'd been driving trucks and he explained that the truck he drove for the vineyard was the only one he'd ever driven and he'd taken the job only after the recent walkouts.

"Before I picked grapes and now I drive a truck." His jaw tilted up. "When the opportunity came, I took it."

I nodded appreciatively, ambition was important. Then a large lady in a blue dress emerged onto the stage along with a big man in a tux and an exceptionally red face and Goro explained that the present piece was called Gloria. Twenty minutes into it, Goro took the handkerchief from his breast pocket and wiped the tears from his eyes.

His car pulled up at the vineyard gates. "Freya, I had a wonderful time."

I unbuckled my belt, "I had fun, Goro."

There was a moment of eye contact as he tilted slowly forwards but my hand was already on the handle, it clicked and he moved away. "Tomorrow I go to Rome but I will see you again soon, I'm very certain."

And since I'd be at the vineyard, there'd be no getting away from it. Had I been naive in assuming this evening would be nothing more than music and a chance to leave the vineyard? It wasn't that I didn't like Goro necessarily, he was straightforward to a fault, which could only be admired, was hardworking and presented himself very well. The problem was I'd felt nothing all night long and there could only be one reason for that - Where was she now? But I knew of all the people I'd ever met, Goro would appreciate it being given straight.

"Goro, I had fun but I don't think I'm interested in that way and even if I was, I'm only going to be here for another month, so there's not really any way anything can happen between us," I'd backtracked on the exit to face him, he was nodding and blinking slowly, disappointed but thankfully ok with the reality, "but we can certainly hang out and chat whenever you're knocking about the vineyard."

He took my hand and kissed me above the knuckles, very sweet. "Of course, and I thank you for that. Buona notte, signora."

"Anche a te, Goro."

Saturday was uneventful at the vineyard, which for this place was something to celebrate in itself, and I simply carried on with my tasks, collecting the workers in the morning and bottling and corking almost a thousand bottles of wine before dinner.

Alessia called late in the evening to inform me, in exceptionally broken English, that Dayna had given birth to their son and both were doing well. It was the happiest I'd yet heard Alessia and hoped the new addition might trigger a positive change in her emotional state, indeed, the vineyard was long overdue some good news.

It was Sunday evening when they returned and, not wanting to crowd them too much, I had to wait a full fifteen minutes from the time they ground into the carpark to them removing the baby from its seat and finally arriving at the front door, all whilst I stood vibrating by the window.

They entered the house without ceremony, Dayna red-cheeked and exhausted whilst holding a small lump wrapped in a blanket. Alessia had one arm around Dayna's midriff and her eyes darted about the lower floor as though an unannounced threat might be lurking somewhere. Both were beaming beyond happiness and the baby was wrapped so snugly that I could only make out its adorable tiny face as he slept.

"I made some stew, in case you were hungry," I whispered as they drifted wearily over to the table. Not knowing what state they'd be in, I'd wanted to have something prepared for their arrival just in case.

"Abbiamo fame," Alessia said, to my surprise, not only because she'd spoken to me before Dayna but because she was actually eating, "buono."

And so we ate stew, which comprised chunks of beef, potatoes, carrots and turnip, a Scottish thing, but nobody complained and the baby only occasionally made adorable squeaking sounds as Dayna was unable to put him down even for a second.

"Come si chiama?" I asked Alessia. She looked incredibly thin and her face was gaunt but where before there was a haunted aspect, now there was most certainly something else.

"Marco Alberto Giordano-Hayes," she slowly leaned down to kiss his cheek.

"Marco's Alessia's best friend, who's the biological father." Dayna yawned and ate another spoonful of stew that had to have gone cold.

It was all so sweet and perfect and over the next hour I fussed over the three of them as twilight arrived and Dayna recalled the experience of the last couple of days and Alessia inserted her bits, which Dayna had to translate, the baby's eyes never once opening and I hoped beyond hope that everything would be all right for them, and living was all about these very rare magical moments you remember the rest of your life and if I'd had any doubts about the decision I'd made to be here, I knew now I'd done the right thing and then the headlights from a vehicle flashed against the far wall and there was the crunch of gravel beneath wheels and then silence as the engine cut out.

And I knew at once that this perfect night was about to become heavenly.

———

"LET ME GUESS," I began as I strolled towards her at the camper, "you climbed mountains, descended into meadows, slept with pixies, met rockstars and made it all the way to Eldorado?"

Arwen dropped her bag and rushed to cover the distance,

astonishing me by slipping her hands into my hair and pulling me closer as our lips crushed together. My hand was trapped between our rib cages and I had to work to wriggle it free so that I could grab her by the waist and squeeze her as tightly as I could.

She released her lips, "no I didn't. Why do you do this to me?"

I was still trying to come to terms with her sudden arrival when our lips were again smushing together and our feet began shuffling towards the camper without instruction from either of us. "You really came back?"

"Apparently, I never left. Damn you."

"You're really here?"

"I couldn't go without you, it wouldn't be the same."

"Keep speaking."

She reached behind her back and the camper door flung open. "I can't be without you."

"That's good enough for now." My feet left the ground because she was lifting me up and then I was plonked inside. "Oh, the mess."

"Quiet." She slammed the door closed, enshrouding us in darkness and I could only see her outline as it moved towards me and then my breasts were filling her hands.

I was forced back against the stove and something, a liquid, spilled over the floor. I groaned into her mouth as she worked on my blouse buttons and I began to assist with that task as I found myself again being lifted bodily up and dumped on the countertop. What had to be a kingsized bag of crisps crunched beneath me as most of the contents fired across the camper and finally, I was able to discard my blouse as she unclasped my bra and my breasts fell free in her hands.

I was wearing jeans and flip flops, the latter already having been discarded as we both grappled for that tiny button, which wasn't easy in my present position so I hitched back to allow her access and as I did, banged my head against the cupboard.

She tugged off my jeans and underwear in one effort and feeling the warm air against my thighs, I wrapped them around her waist, clasping her into me tight. We were both already panting and I couldn't believe I was about to have Arwen inside of me again, only this time, she was the girl I loved.

She leaned into me as I tried to find a comfortable position with my head and back lodged where the edge of the cupboard met the shelf but she moved swiftly away and pulled her dress over her head, "here," before handing it to me for use as a cushion.

I only wished I could see her eyes as she slid her hand down my body but it only made her heavenly peachy scent all the stronger as her finger slipped so easily inside my passage.

"Arwen," I panted and let out an involuntary moan, my body seeming to go rigid and limp in one as I could feel her working inside of me, "I really fucking missed you."

"I missed you too." She croaked into my ear. "Oh God, there's so much dew down here." It was true, her finger was slipping and sliding around with such ease there was barely any friction, not that it was a problem for me but then her head was moving down my body and I knew she wanted to have her taste.

"We really need to fall out more often." I heaved and reached around in an effort to grab ahold of something and managed to find the driver side headrest and I slid forwards on the countertop so she'd have a better angle to access my most secret place.

"You really need to stop talking," her voice came out muffled by my thighs, "I want no distractions when I'm ravishing you." So hot!

I could feel her breath so cold against the warm arousal that was already discharging from my opening. "Now who's talking." Please don't keep me waiting.

She was in a crouched position, which her powerful thighs would have no problem maintaining, and then all I could see was the dark outline of her head as she inched forwards, centring herself between my thighs and I clenched hard to that soft cushion and braced. It was the one thing I'd wanted more than anything else, for so long, to feel her again, to be close to her, to be one with her. All the mistakes we'd made had led to this moment, all was forgiven, we were still together and this would be better than our first time because now there were no complications holding us back, this time I loved her more than anything.

Her tongue slid up the length of my folds and I almost evaporated, I was so wet for Arwen, and now my natural honey was inside of her. She angled up to envelop my pearl as her fingers commenced work, curling just enough to massage that place deep within that held so much power. She used her free hand to massage my thigh whilst mine was lost in her hair and all the time I could feel her mouth hot around my most intimate spot, her tongue flicking and nipping that bundle of nerves, her fingers pushing firmly in before sliding carefully out. My body jerked and then again and she increased the tempo. I grabbed tighter to her hair, pulled her into me, the sweet sounds her mouth made as it played and tasted and experienced my inside. I could see swirly patterns in the darkness and heaved as my hips tried to thrust up but she held me down hard so she wouldn't lose a single drop of my essence that was spilling from within me. My skin perspired, flushed hot and cold until finally, she returned to hold me tight and I couldn't help but crumple in her arms.

"OK, I have to know, did you honestly never leave?" I asked, still dizzy, caressing and touching her all over like she was the long lost love of my life. We'd since transferred to our bedroom from where we lay on the bed and the dimmers revealed five days had done nothing to diminish her perfection.

She grazed my belly with the backs of her fingers, sending small shivers delightfully down my spine. "I made it halfway to Rome on the first day," she spoke lazily, "that was when I was really angry at you. But a long stop for coffee made me realise ... Rome wouldn't mean anything without you, my travel buddy." Her words were like magic.

"I hope I'm a little more than your travel buddy by now." I rolled my head to kiss her on the shoulder and in return she squeezed me for a long time. There was no need to say it, I knew. "Continue."

She did but only after a long, soft kiss. "There's not much more to tell. How exciting is my story about turning around, driving back to San Gimmy and pigging out on garbage for five days straight?" She persisted in grazing my abdomen and her eyes suddenly focused on that area. "Only five days ... you're looking incredibly toned and it's sexy as hell."

"That'll be the manual labour," I flexed a bicep, "feel that bump."

She did and hummed appreciatively, "not bad, Frey," and then she slapped me on the arse. "And *you* were supposed to call."

I giggled into her armpit, the girl needed a shower, badly. "I'm not sure how much longer I could have lasted."

She shook her head. "Well, I'm glad you didn't because you were right and I needed to know that, I needed to work it out for myself." Her hand was now grazing that indentation just above my buttocks, the sacral or pilonidal dimple, and I was shivering from the sensation caused by so many nerve endings dancing to her fingertips. She gave me a look and it was one I didn't recognise. "I missed you so much and I'm so sorry for being a bitch, an awful, work-shy, lazy bitch. I really don't want to be that person."

I nuzzled into her neck and inhaled her natural scent infused with peach and God only knew what else but it was so delightful all the same. "Well, now we're even and can forget all the crap and just see where this goes."

She squeezed me even tighter. "I'd really like that."

It was the kind of beautiful moment I'd always remember, lying naked on a Tuscan four poster bed with the girl I loved as we decided we were now together.

"You know," she began as my body continued to shiver and react to her touches, "I think that deep down, it was all intentional, running off like that, because I wanted to test you and see what you'd do and the reason was that I wanted to forgive you." Her body was quivering from suppressed giggling, which only caused me to explode in laughter.

I slapped her on the shoulder, "you would take credit for that," and then our eyes locked and the laughter stopped, "but I'll let you have it." I'd let her have anything.

"When I said that to you, do you remember, the night after we took off from Lisbon?" She asked and I nodded, recalling that memory in a San Sebastián bar. "Well, I forgive you."

I closed my eyes and inhaled the moment. "Thank you, Arwen. And as for me, there's nothing to forgive."

She sniffed and when I looked up she was using her thumb to dab at her eyes.

"Buuuuut," I pushed up onto my elbows and the sight below was so heavenly that I almost didn't want to make the next suggestion, "you need to take a bloody shower."

"Do I really have to?" She hated not being clean, in fact, she hated it so much she was willing to bathe in streams and that she'd suffered through the last five days without washing showed how distraught she must have been.

I was happy to change that now and I stood and tugged at her arm, "don't you usually get all agitated when you can't shower? What happened to you out there all alone?"

She surrendered to my cajoling and came willingly. "I must have been too engrossed in Machiavelli to notice."

I rolled my eyes as we entered our en-suite wet room. "Always the multilingual smart-arse, some things never change."

She was taking tiny steps backwards, pulling me towards the shower even as our breasts squashed snugly together. "You know you love that about me and don't you dare deny it." Yes, love. "Don't think I haven't noticed the way your body stirs whenever I say anything you can't understand, it drives you mad with lust."

I reached over her head to turn on the tap and we both screamed when the cold water cascaded over us but then it turned warm and we fell into a fit of hysterics even as we seized each other tightly, my hands buried deep in her hair that began to quickly soak up water, her hands kneading my breasts as our tongues clashed and I tasted the warm liquid as it flowed down her face, thrust out my hips so that my pussy might find an angle to touch hers.

I pressed the soap dispenser, three, four times, "you need this," and began lathering her neck, shoulders, arms, back, hips, boobs and tummy as the starfish on the end of her belly button chain spouted a continuous stream of water. I went for more soap and as she stood over me, I crouched to begin work on those miraculous thighs, turning the soap to foam, thick and lemony whilst being unable to take my eyes from her jewel and the tiny strip of blonde just above as the froth from her body rinsed over it. She'd satisfied me twice, been loving and tender, ensured I was taken care of yet still, I'd not so much as touched her in that special place, indeed, I'd never so much as seen another woman's most intimate area this close, which might have gone some way to explain why my vision was glazing over as my fingertips stopped for a breather somewhere over her buns.

"I'd like you to ... if you want to." She spoke sweetly above the pattering of a thousand hot droplets striking tile and I was struck by a sudden apprehension, "you can't disappoint me, Frey. I just want to feel you inside of me." She got it, she understood, and I tilted up to find her reassuring eyes gazing back.

"I'd like to." There was nothing I wanted more than to taste her, to have her essence inside of me, to be one with her.

She settled back into the corner and I watched as her dainty feet with red painted toenails inched out across the tiles to fully expose her petite cleft to me for the first time.

I took an involuntary inhalation, I don't know what I was

expecting, it was no different to mine yet it still made my head fizz and swirl and I took one final look into her eyes as her hand came down to nestle in my hair.

Stealing myself for one heavenly moment of introspection, just to wonder at life and how much I'd changed in such a short space of time; this girl had done it all to me, I'd already given her my body and now she was about to give me hers. And then I gently ran my finger along her fold, which was all I needed to do to feel her tremble and, encouraged, I persisted, using my middle digit, massaging the slick flesh, working in tiny circles before increasing the area of contact, stimulating ever more nerve endings. I was only getting started and it was still sinking into my head that I was immersing myself in the natural juices of the most beautiful creature I'd ever seen when she astonished me by letting out a cry and her thighs convulsed and jerked and all I could do was stare open-mouthed at the girl, for she was one of the lucky ones.

"Are you serious?"

Her eyes were clamped shut, she was biting her bottom lip so hard it had turned white and I could feel her entire arm vibrating through the hand that was now clutching at my hair. "Frey ... don't ... don't stop."

If I aroused her that much, I wouldn't complain and I prepared myself for round two, saw how her beautiful bud had engorged without even so much as being touched, though I'd soon be fixing that, in fact very soon I'd be performing the most sensual act one person could do to another and that I would be experiencing it with a girl was still such a novelty, but one I couldn't stop no matter what, this was me now and I grabbed onto her hips for stability and tilted forwards to close my mouth around her berry.

She bucked immediately and as I began swathing my tongue over her pearl, tasting and savouring her most intimate part, I marvelled at how silky it felt to the tongue, completely intoxicating. I mean, I had one, of course, but it wasn't like I'd done this to myself, or anyone else, and I don't know what I was expecting but it felt beyond description and I had no doubt it was because I was devouring Arwen.

I increased the pressure as her breathing became deeper and hoarse and I sensed her arm reaching up against the wall to grab ahold of the window ledge, her back arching, as I continued sucking and nibbling her flesh. I brought two fingers to her opening and, not being able to see where they were heading, delicately searched the area being squidged beneath my chin, found what I was looking for and gently inserted the digits inside her passage, at first only enough depth to feel her pussy clamping around my fingertips before gently delving further inside to find that fleshy spot on her inner walls, already plump with fast-flowing blood. It was a lot to concentrate on, my mouth working one rhythm whilst finding a new and corresponding pulse with my fingers. At times I knew I was getting them fuddled, however, it was a skill I'd enjoy becoming proficient in.

The water continued to cascade over my shoulders and although I'd maintained a suitable vacuum around Arwen's engorged bundle of nerves, I could still taste the water running down her body and somehow finding its way inside my mouth. I felt the muscles in her thighs twitch as she made small thrusts into me, my mouth, tongue and lips combining with her clitoris to make the most delicious sounds. My fingers were curled and massaging her raw flesh with ever-increasing pressure as my thighs were only now beginning to ache from crouching so long but I would battle through the fatigue because I just couldn't tear myself away.

I had to swallow, a combination of water, soap and pure Arwen, a drug I'd never be able to get enough of and then a moan escaped her as I sank my hand into her buttock, her legs trembled and seized together, her pussy tightened around my fingers as her bud seemed to go both hot and cold in my mouth.

"Babe," she finally pulled herself away and sank down against the wall to sag into my arms from where we both collapsed to the tiles and remained as the water continued to rain down upon us.

I WAS in the barn when I received the long-awaited news. It came in the form of an email from the UK Foundation Programme and had been sitting in my inbox all morning without my knowing. Considering the contents were to dictate the next few years of my life, my reaction to it surprised me.

The gist was that I'd been accepted to three of my five residency choices; Royal Cornwall, The Priory Hospital in Chelmsford and Raigmore in Inverness, a choice I'd now have to make without Gabe.

I turned the phone off, thrust it back in my pocket and went back to stripping the long stems of their fruit, filling the press with grapes.

I found two smaller, shrivelled specimens and plucked them from the machine before tossing them over my shoulder, one after the other, and heard the satisfying smack of them striking the inside of the waste container before falling to their grave.

"A good shot," came the masculine voice and I looked up to see Goro leaning against the shutter, the sun blotted out by his head so that his long shadow cast deep inside the barn. He was holding something and now strode over to me at the press. "I've sweat for many hours on this laborious machine."

"I've been getting the practice in myself. Goro, it's good to see you again," I said more out of politeness than anything else.

It was two weeks after Arwen's return, a little more since my quasi-date with Goro, and this would be the third occasion in the interim I'd been visited by him and it looked like he had another gift for me, to add to the chocolates and perfume I'd already received. Don't date coworkers. I'd learned that lesson early, if a little too late.

I grabbed the handle, began turning and the wheel squelched the grapes most satisfyingly as the juice began to flow from the pipe into the tub. It was a physical task which demanded a concentrated effort, even if it was becoming easier, and besides, focusing on the press enabled me to disregard whatever Goro was holding, for a few more precious seconds at least.

"I arrived back from Torino and brought you this." His voice was gruff and close.

There was no escaping it and so I gave him my attention. "Oh, gosh, another gift? That's very sweet but really, there's no need. Please..." I let it trail off in the hope no more needed to be said.

He stepped forward and held out the bag, one of those glossy paper things with a rope handle, the type you might pick up from a jewellers. "No, it's for you, Freya Bella." That was what he'd started calling me the last time I saw him.

I sighed, hesitated, hoped he'd register my discomfort and stop buying gifts I'd done nothing to deserve and then finally, reached out to take the bag, which had the word Damiani in exquisite gold font stamped upon it. My scalp itched as I peered inside then carefully removed the black rectangular box from within, glancing up at him once, and lifting the lid to find a chain with my name, Freya Bella, staring back in gold. It was beautiful yet so over the top and unnecessary it left me momentarily stunned. Where was Arwen when I needed her? Ah yes, down at the wholesalers.

But I'd tried, I'd tried to be firm, honest and assertive yet nothing seemed to be working. The only thing left was to demand he stop spending his money on me because what was next, a car, a puppy, a trip for two to Rome?

"It's eighteen carats and look..." he pointed to the a in Freya, which trailed at its tail to connect to the B in Bella and I'd been so stunned I hadn't noticed the tiny diamonds, three, four, five in total that featured in the flourish and held the two words together, "I designed it myself and had it made by..."

"Goro, you really shouldn't have, it's too much ... far, far too much." My body felt limp but he wasn't discouraged by my discomfort.

The necklace was still in its box, from where I was almost too afraid to touch it, and he looped a section of chain around his fingers, "here," bodily turned me around and I felt the gold fall cold around my neck in the warm late summer heat.

I shivered, wasn't sure what to say, do, think as his hands were at the nape of my neck, my hair was swept aside, I felt the chain connect and his hands moved down to rest on my shoulders. Gravel scuffed from somewhere nearby and then Dayna appeared just as Goro's hands left my body.

"Oh, hi, Goro," she said in Italian as the relief flooded through my body, "how was the journey to Torino?"

He shifted and I wondered if his top lip curled upwards, though I probably imagined that. "Saint Christopher watches over my travels," he said, thrusting out his chest.

Dayna beamed, "I hope he watches over all of us."

Goro said nothing as Dayna demonstrated her ignorance of the patron saint of travellers.

She blinked then turned her attention to me. "Hold off on that batch, Scotty," another one of my nicknames, "dinner's ready. Goro, would you like some pappardelle?"

He grimaced, which coming from him somehow didn't seem rude, at least Dayna didn't seem to think so, "thank you but I must return to Poggibonsi."

"Are you sure? All those long trips deserve a reward and I've made my special sauce, my famous veal and pork combo, which Scotty will vouch for."

He shook his head and thanked her for the offer before leaving me alone with Dayna and it was testament to the stress she was still under that she didn't see, or perhaps she simply chose to pay no heed to, the very visible chain that had spontaneously appeared around my neck.

Later that evening, Arwen, however, had no such qualms. "Is this from your stalker again, Freya Bella?" She lifted the gold plate with a finger and smirked with mild amusement.

"It's not funny," my arms were hanging limply at my sides and it was all enough to distract me from her naked form, almost, "I'm not sure what to do about the man and if you ever met him you'd understand. He's, um, very particular ... oh, I don't know, it's such a mess."

She smushed her hips into mine. "So I have competition, do I?" She was enjoying my discomfort a little too much as she gave the plate a flick with her finger and her hands began drifting hungrily down my body. "Maybe we can send him on a delivery run to Sicily until after you're gone for good?"

"Maybe we can," I sighed, not wanting to think about Goro now, "it's all your fault."

"My fault?"

I grabbed an ample buttock. "You weren't here to stop it."

She snorted, "well then, you shouldn't be so quick to the rebound, should you."

I sniggered, "you're one to talk," and cupped a large, round breast with my other hand before letting out a silent whimper as I squeezed. "Can I take it off now?"

Her lips were on my neck and I shivered, "not yet, Freya Bella," she groaned close to my ear just as her fingers entered me.

Exhausted, we came downstairs for a snack a short time after midnight and were both surprised to find the office light on and Alessia leaning forward at the desk as she squinted into the computer screen, which could only mean she was working, irrespective of this quite bizarre hour.

Indeed, since Marco's arrival, Alessia had been spending ever less time in her room, carrying out basic household chores mostly, cooking as well as looking after the baby and to see Alessia around the sweet little thing was to think all was well with the world. I'd noticed she'd gradually been eating more, even if she often skipped breakfast, which was still the worst time of day for her moods, though nothing she ate made any difference to the way she looked, which was gaunt and pale in comparison to her photos from only a few months before. But to find her engaging in light admin work, even after midnight, was a new development and doubtless a welcome one because Arwen had been doing exceptionally good work acquiring new business, as well as badly needed recruits to fill a number of positions at the vineyard and all that meant an increase in paperwork.

I saw Dayna frequently but Alessia less so and when I did I could never be certain as to her state. Sometimes she'd smile and welcome me, even summoning the ability to attempt conversation in her exceptionally strong Tuscan dialect as I found myself gradually being able to converse with her. But other times she'd exit the room as I entered and once she even turned around and walked the other way when she saw me approaching the kitchen from the other direction. There was never any way of knowing how she'd fair from one day to the next though one thing I could be reasonably sure of was that she was beginning to have more good days than bad. Dayna, Marco, Arwen, myself, I'd like to think we all had something to do with it.

Of the two of us, it was Arwen who'd spent by far the most time with Alessia because the Australian had offered to restart the tours, which meant first having to take a crash course in winemaking, as well as learning about the history of the Giordano Vineyard and only Alessia could teach that. Arwen had visited all the local tour operators to let them know the Giordano wine tours were back on and they could start selling tickets again via their offices and websites and although there were a small number of initial sales, this wasn't good enough for my lover, who surprised everyone by driving to Poggibonsi and shortly after returning with a minivan full of tourists. I watched awestruck from the barn as they began filing out, one by one, a continuous stream of happy Americans, Brits, Germans and Chinese who crowded the carpark as they gazed with curiosity along the lines of vines that stretched down the slope and up again to disappear over the near vista.

"Arwen, how?" I'd asked later at lunch, scratching my head as the guests squeezed in at the tables and I tried not to panic.

She just leaned against the wall and propped a hand on hip. "Oh, darling, don't you know? I just used my charms." Of course, I should have expected such a response as I contemplated the damage this girl could do if she was working for commission.

The chef had been plucked straight from the local catering college, a nineteen-year-old called Lorenzo, and this being his first ever part-time job, he'd done exceptionally well not to freeze when the lunchtime rush struck as hard as it did, ultimately coping because he'd been well prepared in advance.

"If you had fun, don't forget to leave a review on TripAdvisor." Arwen was always mindful to say and so the reviews began to trickle in, which only created a snowball effect so that by the end of the second week, Arwen had given up touting for tourists in the local town because they were all finding their own way to the vineyard.

"If you ever decide to give up dancing, I'd say you've found your calling," I told her because she truly was sensational at being a tour guide. I had first-hand knowledge of this because I just couldn't stop myself from tagging onto the end of one of her tours and I watched in awe as she led the group of sixty from the vines to the barn, making them laugh, answering questions in French or Spanish and at the end, even posing for photos with besotted fans.

The gift shop was my responsibility, which thankfully was fairly low maintenance, apart from when one of Arwen's tours finished and then it was all hands on deck as the shelves were emptied and the cash register threatened to overload.

Now, two weeks and a day since Arwen's return, Dayna surprised us at breakfast by presenting us with the keys to her silver Peugeot 206 Coupe Cabriolet, the cute little convertible that hardly ever got used.

I raised a questioning eyebrow obscenely high, "they're the keys to your car."

She hummed as the baby's mouth attached to her nipple. "This is true and today you're taking the day off, and my car, to visit Saturnia."

I was about to protest because, as always, there was so much to be done but she cut me off before I had chance.

"Don't even think about it. You've both worked so hard and you deserve it."

And so, half an hour later, we were on a fast road south making the hundred mile journey to the village of Saturnia. It was a hot day, we drove with the roof down and the wind was loud as it played the devil with our hair and we sang along to Staying Out for the Summer at the top of our voices.

Then we arrived at our destination and the sight stunned us both. It was only ten in the morning but already the place buzzed with people and what's more, they were all completely naked.

"Come on, strip," Arwen commanded as she lifted the t-shirt over her head to reveal plump breasts straining within her red bikini top. "You knew this was coming so don't wussy out now."

I surveyed the scene, the many gentle cascades of a beautiful bright blue that curved around an ancient mill, the steam that drifted up from the hot water, the smell of sulphur in the air, the roaring sounds, and about a hundred people all topless as they lounged back and allowed the water to flow over them, curing all their troubles and ailments, supposedly. I wanted in and I wanted to do it properly, which meant there was no getting out of stripping, as hard as such a public display was for a girl like me.

"But you can keep your foof covered," she giggled, "because that really is for my eyes only and don't you ever forget it."

A surge of warmth to rival the hot spa flooded through me. "Not just your eyes." I had to clamp mine shut as the memories of last night, and this morning, came back so vividly to taunt me. I could do nothing to her with so many people around. And to make matters worse, when I opened my eyes and regained focus, she was unclasping her bra and I watched as I underwent the usual weakness of the knees and stirring in my belly as her breasts came free.

She was watching for my reaction, as she always did because she enjoyed nothing more than teasing me and she was sure to be getting off on this. "You look utterly deranged, you pervert, stop stalling and remove that bra at once." She stepped forward so that the peach overwhelmed the sulphur and then my bra was discarded to the pebbles, her eyes lowered and she displayed the same demented look I was surely guilty of myself.

"You damned, bloody hypocrite." I shook my head, even though it was absolutely thrilling, then we placed our arms around each other and waded into the water, which was lovely because it truly was warm, bordering on hot, like it wasn't what I'd been expecting all along. We had a few geothermal spas back in the UK, though I'd never been to any and now I knew I'd been missing out.

I tried not to be distracted by the inevitable prying eyes and just held my breath as we carefully waded over pebbles and stones towards a large step with fewer people in its vicinity and then we leaned back, submerged ourselves and breathed in the air. It was strange, peaceful, relaxing and wonderful, to be bathing outside in the open air, where the water should have been cold and dirty but it was hot and clean, where the steam was so thick you could see no further than a few feet in front of your face, where for thousands of years people would have come to this place for the same reason.

"Ain't this the life," Arwen remarked after several minutes. She was probably referring to this, now, being here, though in truth, for me at least, she could have meant the entirety of the last two weeks, which I could honestly say had been the happiest two weeks of my life.

"I wouldn't change anything." I shyly glanced at her before averting back to the nearby rim from where, every second, untold gallons flowed over to crash onto the step below and then she interlaced our fingers and I turned back to her.

The water cascaded over our shoulders as we leaned back against the ledge and it seemed like we were enveloped in a cloak of steam where nothing outside existed. She was gazing into my eyes as her teeth pinched her bottom lip in an almost vulnerable looking grin, which was a rare look for her but one I'd been noticing increasingly the last two weeks, her mouth moved and I expected her to say something but then her fingers tightened around mine and no words came and she released her fingers and splayed her hand out on her thigh. "Um, neither would I, I mean, I wouldn't change anything," she finally said.

I wanted so badly to ask what she meant, what she wanted to say, for her to elaborate and lift me up into the stars. I had a feeling, just a feeling, that I knew what it might be but I just couldn't bring myself to ask, to maybe make myself the happiest woman in the world.

Because what if I was wrong?

SHE CAME up from between my thighs and scrambled her way back towards my arms whilst licking her lips in a most beautiful act of perversion, but I was rolling away and off the bed, suddenly conscious I was still in orgasm as I wobbled towards the dresser.

"Hmmm ... ahhh ... ohh," I panted loud and raspy through my nose as I clasped the oak surface, held on for balance and rode it out as my vision fuzzed and the salt smacked heavy on my lips, my arms perspired and now, as my dilated pupils refocused, I could see in the mirror that the skin around my nose was dark red, which looked so odd yet appealing on my pale complexion. *Getting fucked by Arwen's good for you, Frey*, I sniggered too loud, as my legs trembled and my body bucked another two or three times from the hips, stars flickered yellow and the hairs on the back of my neck pricked. I was still making strange sounds when I managed to swivel my blurry gaze towards Arwen, who was lying back on the bed, head propped up with hands clasped behind as she looked on amused.

"Are you done?"

I shook my head, exhausted yet so alive, "Arwen..." and let it trail off. What was there to say?

"Because when you recover, it's my turn," she sprang from the bed and pottered over to where I was still grasping the dresser lest I let go and collapse, "did I tell you, you're getting real good with your tongue?" Her hips pressed against my buttocks, her boobs against my back as she reached around to cup my breasts.

"That's because I love nothing more than being inside of you." Which was true, but I hadn't meant to say *that* word, even in a context that shouldn't be construed as it usually was, and I felt a prickle on my scalp as my senses heightened to interpret any sign from her that she might feel different but then, after a second, her head pushed forward and her cheek came to press against mine and I turned to meet her lips from where we kissed passionately as my breasts heaved in her small hands and my heart danced and skipped and my head fizzed all over again.

For a long time now, I'd thought I loved Arwen, certainly from that awful month we were parted, but it all felt so very different now, different to the extent I could not be sure my feelings for her before had been a lesser form of love or something else entirely. All I knew was that my love had grown ever stronger by the day, which had brought us to this moment in time, and now I couldn't bear the thought of being parted from her.

She'd stayed, even when things had been tough, even when they were excruciatingly hard, she'd been true to her word and stayed and now I loved her more than anything else in this world.

And I did not want our time in this magical place to ever end.

I met her gaze in the mirror's reflection. "What did you ever see in me?" I sounded unsure of myself, which was hardly attractive, but I just had to know, she could have anybody, yet she chose me.

Her hands pulsed around my breasts, "Frey," and her eyes warmed as she studied my face gazing back at her, my large green eyes, thin lips, pale freckly skin and shiny red hair that framed my features, "just look at you, you're the most beautiful girl in the entire world."

My eyes clamped shut as my legs began to wobble all over again.

"But more than that," she continued, her voice soft in my ear, "you're determined, intelligent, kind of funny in your own way, and you're about the only person who never fell apart in my presence," even now, the girl was most inappropriately full of it, but that was what I loved about her, "you're a good person and you made me a better person."

I turned around in her arms as I took her hands in mine, "I'm in love with you."

There it was and whatever happened happened. I'd just given a drifter the power to destroy my heart, soul, life.

Her face crumpled and then I had to support her and I held her up and her tears were already starting, as were mine, and her cheeks flushed as her stomach warmed suddenly and then she made me the happiest girl in the world. "Frey, I'm in love with you too."

We held each other so tight for so long that I lost track of time and my arms began to ache as I repeated again and again that I loved her as she repeated again and again that she loved me and by the end we took ourselves to bed from where I devoured and lost myself within her and I'm not sure for how long I'd been down when she took me again and finally, when out of necessity, we both needed a rest, I floated over to the drawer and pulled out the Bordeaux.

"There will never be a better time."

It was a good wine, as it turned out, and although we often talked until late, tonight was different in the most magical way, as we enjoyed the wine that had been a gift from her to me on that night we'd first met. We regaled that strange night and I admitted to initially finding her a pain in the arse, an inconvenience, a freeloader, a gatecrasher and someone I'd wanted as far away from my man as possible. "And then you literally flipped me inside out."

She blew her knuckles and admitted to having a small crush on me from as early on as that night in Bordeaux but that her feelings had slowly grown the more time she spent around me, that she had an obsession with my breasts, which I'd kind of noticed, that our first kiss in Catalonia, under duress, as it was, had played havoc with her heart, and at that moment she'd wanted nothing more than for me to spend the night with her in that tent and when I didn't, she'd been so frustrated she'd fantasised about me for the first time, that putting the rich Spaniard's number in her purse had been a subconscious attempt at provoking a reaction from me, that Barcelona had been a dream come true but how bad she'd felt for my dilemma at the time and that soon after, the way I'd treated her and our subsequent time apart had ripped out her soul.

It was late and we were tired and on the way to being drunk but we were in love and my kisses began at her lips and soon found their way to that special spot nestled between her thighs and when I'd finished, she devoured me again and then, at some point, we both fell asleep.

Something buzzed and I stirred, fell back to sleep and then, sometime later, I gently roused.

Immediately, I knew something wasn't right because her feet weren't snuggled between mine and, panicking, I sprang up with a start.

"Hey," she was sitting beside me on the bed's edge and my nerves settled. How long had she been there? "Sorry, I didn't want to wake you."

"Arwen," I took her hand and she squeezed mine whilst continuing to watch me from her elevated position.

There was another odd look in her eyes, something else new, something else I'd never seen before. She was trying to smile but the eyes gave it away.

"What is it?" I asked, propping myself up on one elbow as a pulse beat noticeably in my throat.

Despite the obvious sadness, her voice was calm. "Frey, I have to leave."

"What?" I hissed the word. "You have to leave?"

She nodded and held out her palm. "I'd forgot all about it, but my ninety days are up, I have to leave today."

The buzzing that I heard, it was a reminder she'd set on her phone, and I knew instantly what it was as my elbow collapsed of its own accord and I fell back flat on the bed.

"Schengen."

"Schengen," she confirmed.

The Schengen law meant that once you were within its zone, an area that encompassed most of Europe, you could travel freely inside without having to stop at borders to show documentation. As a non-European citizen on a tourist visa, however, Arwen was only permitted to remain within the Schengen area for a maximum of ninety days out of every one hundred and eighty.

It was something that had never even occurred to me, that one day Arwen would be forced to leave and now that day had arrived, I could feel the weight of my own chest crushing me.

"Stupid fucking Schengen. You can't just ignore it?" I pleaded, knowing the futility of the situation.

She just shrugged, what else could she do? "If I don't leave today then I'll be fined, possibly deported and will get a nasty stamp in my passport, which will only make finding you again all the more difficult." She rubbed my thigh through the sheets. "Hey, I know, it's a real bloody farce, but it's the law and I know you wouldn't have me break it."

I was sobbing now, finding it hard to breathe and the palpitations were sure to follow. "I would if it meant I never had to lose you." But I knew that was being selfish and then an idea came to me, as forlorn as it might have been but it was enough to make me spring up nonetheless. "Don't you have Welsh ancestry? You're a dual citizen!" I demanded of her, praying the stupid straw would be worth something.

She smiled sadly and shook her head. "Sorry, I don't have that."

I threw her hand off my leg, instantly regretted it, and pulled her back. "You're not going." And I pulled her so tightly into me that if I chose, she'd never get away.

It was so unfair. Only a few hours before I'd had the most magical night of my entire life and now she was leaving, so abruptly, and there was nothing anybody could do about it. The last few weeks had been so unimaginably perfect, it was hard to imagine it should ever end, but reality had now crashed down upon me and life would never be so beautiful again.

The peach was so intoxicating that my lips soon found their way to crush against hers as the taste of salt from our tears mingled and for the next hour we made love for what I knew would be the final time in too long.

"Three months isn't the end of the world but," she sighed because a new realisation had just found her, "even if I was to return here, by that time you'd be back home training to be a doctor, learning to save lives, and that's more important." We were both curled up beneath the sheet, gazing into each other as we gently played with each others' fingers. "If I came back, it wouldn't be the same around here without you."

"Obviously." And my use of an Arwenism caused her to splutter tears over my face. But I wasn't laughing. In fact, I was completely serious. "What if I was to stay?"

Her fingers, that had been rubbing and caressing mine suddenly stopped. "Stay?"

I nodded and knew that even though I'd given it zero thought, it was exactly what I wanted, to remain at the Giordano Vineyard, with Dayna, with Alessia, with Marco, with Arwen, nothing else would make me happier. I nodded again, this time with even more certainty. "Yes. What if I was to stay?"

"Don't be silly, you can't."

"I'm not being silly and I most certainly can."

"No, you can't. You mustn't."

"I can and I'm more than willing to."

She saw in my eyes that I was serious and then she cast the sheet off from over us and suddenly we were both on our knees, grabbing ahold of each other by the forearms. "Are you really fucking serious?"

I laughed and wept. "Yes. Yes. I'm happy here, I don't want to leave, ever."

She laughed and backed away in disbelief but came right back to retake my hands. "But ... but you're supposed to be training to be a doctor."

I shrugged and barked out loud, "I no longer care about any of that, I want to be with you, I want to be happy and I've never been happier than in this place." I was getting carried away but apparently, as I was finding out, love did that to a girl and I didn't care and besides, the thing was that ever since waking, neither of us had spoken a word of English. In fact, we'd both adopted Italian and had spoken nothing else these last few days and it made no difference whether desperate, devastated or ecstatic, drunk or sober. I was meant to be here.

Her hands were tight around my arms and she never looked so happy and beautiful as now. "But Frey, I can't be responsible for you giving up your career and..."

I cut her off and shook her by the shoulders, "it's my decision and I'm making it so shut up and fuck me."

She did and when she'd finished and we'd calmed down, we were able to sit back and put some actual thought into this new plan.

It was simple. Arwen would leave the Schengen area, return after the expiration of ninety days and life would be perfect again.

"Where will you go?" I asked.

"I really don't care, anywhere, oh, but are you sure this is what you want to..."

I cut her off by mashing my lips against hers and by the time I pulled away, she'd got the message. "Not one more word about that, ok?"

She grinned but then her eyebrows drew closer, "we're forgetting one important detail. Because the day I step back on Italian soil, that annoying ninety-day ticker restarts and then I'll only have to leave again come the end of it. I want to be with you, Frey, but this isn't an arrangement we can continue indefinitely."

I nodded, recognising and cursing the stupid laws that prevented two people in love from being together.

We needn't have worried, however, because Dayna had the solution to everything.

"It's called a working visa. Over the years, we've helped several people obtain indefinite permission to stay in Italy." We were having a farewell breakfast picnic beneath one of the orange trees and Dayna, unpacking a batch of prosciutto from a cute straw basket, didn't even bother looking up as she handed us the lifeline. She'd literally just saved our lives and it was all nothing to the mad woman. "The trick," she continued as she sifted through the basket, "is not to quit or get fired because everything's dependant on the job." She brought out the cheese and delved back within, bringing out a long baguette. "Who was that guy who came over from New Zealand?"

"Jason." The name sounded strange being pronounced by Alessia. She was leaning back, fussing over and playing with Marco as he giggled and blew bubbles and kicked his legs most adoringly. "He lasted two weeks and couldn't take anymore, so he left."

"Which meant that stupidly, he had to leave the continent but he wouldn't listen." Dayna rolled her eyes. "Couldn't take physical labour, if I recall. People have romantic visions of working in a place like this, I know I did, and it is like that in its way, but it's hard work too. I'm sure he got his Instagram photos standing next to a row of vines though, so it all ended well for him." She shrugged and passed the platter of bread, ham and cheese. "Of course, you already know what to expect, you've been doing it without complaint for long enough." She perked unexpectedly, "so that's a *yes*, of course. Just lay low for a few months in Ukraine or wherever and we'll send you a formal offer of employment in writing and then you'll need to do the rest with your embassy." Dayna was good enough to speak slowly and

I understood most of what she said. It was always easier comprehending Dayna or Arwen's Italian than Alessia's but I hoped to fix that in time.

But we were beyond happy. It had been an emotional twenty-four hours with Arwen and I declaring our love for each other only to learn soon after we were once again to be parted, and then to be saved by our friends.

"Really, you two guys are the best." Arwen gave them each a hug in turn.

"It will be our absolute pleasure," Alessia said, pouring the dark coffee from a Moka pot into four small cups, "and we'll have a party when you return home. But since you're staying, you both need to start drinking your coffee black, like normal Italians."

And there it was. Starting in three months, we'd both be given paid positions at the vineyard and life would be perfect again and what better way of celebrating than a breakfast picnic with friends and loved ones whilst surrounded by such natural beauty as the sun began to establish its heat and Alessia opened an umbrella to shade the baby as we ate pastries and drank coffee.

Arwen repositioned herself to sit behind me and I felt weak as her knees came to settle either side of my hips. "I'm doing you another braid, my lover, and I'm warning you not to tantrum and pull this one out or you'll find yourself in the biggest trouble of your entire life. You remember what I'm like when I'm really mad?"

I recalled our very first encounter with fondness. "How could I forget?"

She blew on my neck and I shivered as I felt the gentle pulls and tugs of her hands going to work. "Just make sure you don't forget." She hummed, "it just so happens they last around three months, give or take, imagine that, you have literally no excuses so I want to see a weather-beaten, worn down, disgusting braid when I return and then I'll undo the thing myself, ok my love?" She had me.

Sensing we desired one final moment of privacy, Dayna and Alessia had begun discussing something in lowered voices as they propped themselves up on elbows and I was able to watch the two of them together. It was all in the way Dayna's pupils dilated, how Alessia twirled hair around a finger, the occasional touches and how neither seemed to blink as they spoke. They'd been together for years and even after their recent hardships were still besotted with each other. It was all so adorably cute and I could only bring myself to look away when they began kissing.

Arwen had been quiet and I wondered if, like me, she'd been eavesdropping, but then she finished my braid, moved around to my front and whispered, "I'm gonna try not to cry but I know I'll fail."

"Me too." I fell into her arms and within seconds, we too were sinking into a deep kiss and I knew the next three months would be the longest and most agonising of my life.

Something slammed, which caused me to break apart from Arwen, Dayna and Alessia had done the same, and I scanned the near distance atop the slope, the barn, house, warehouse and finally found Goro, beside the truck, standing and gawping in our direction. His vehicle had been parked there overnight, which wasn't unusual as he lived in Poggibonsi but now, I guessed, he'd either arrived for work on foot or had spent the night in his truck's cabin. Either way, he'd seen me with my tongue down my girlfriend's throat and now I wasn't sure what to think. At the least, it was enough to give me a hot flush and a weird sinking feeling in my belly because it was crap I had no desire to deal with now or ever.

"Is that the guy?" Arwen laughed and rubbed my back. "At least that ought to solve your little stalker problem. Think he'll get the message?"

I barked, what else could I do, and then the more I thought about it, I guessed that Arwen was right, "oh, I do hope so," because I'd told the man, I'd been honest with him and it hadn't made a difference. "Please say you're right."

Throughout this, Arwen's hand had been nestled snugly between my thighs and after what seemed like more than long enough to confirm my sexuality to the man, Goro finally jumped back inside his cabin, slammed the door shut and a minute later the truck was roaring down the path, throwing up clouds of dust, before disappearing through the gates.

"Yep, I'd say that'll do it, Frey." Arwen laughed again as I shook my head and slapped her on the knee.

"You are just terrible."

She nodded, "you've known this all along."

But it hadn't stopped me falling in love with her.

WE ARRIVED mid-afternoon at Pisa airport, Arwen only fifteen minutes before having purchased a ticket to Belgrade, and I still admired the way she could drift from one place to another with no real plan or idea of where she was heading. But then, life gets in the way and it doesn't matter what dreams you have or how much planning you put into them because everything can change in a second, just ask Alessia.

Of course, it was something I could also attest to and the sight of planes reminded me I should have been imminently boarding one myself because, in another world, I was only two weeks away from beginning my residency. Yet here I was having made new plans to live in Tuscany, with my lesbian girlfriend, no less. Life could be so fucking strange.

"You let me know the minute you arrive." Oh Christ, but my voice was all choked.

Her face screwed up and she pulled me in for an embrace so that I wouldn't see her crying but now I was crying too and sod it because I didn't care. "I'll miss you so much." When she brought me back to arms' length, her face was red and puffy. "And you'd better bloody stay away from all those Italian hunks, as well as the donnas, you hear me?"

My hands were tightly gripping her waist and it was hard to believe that in a few seconds she'd once again be leaving my life. "Then you'd better make sure it's not ninety-one days."

We embraced for the final time and then I felt woozy as I watched Arwen wheel her bag through the departure gates, round the corner and disappear and the only thing I could do was remain where I stood, numb and not knowing what to do with myself. Her leaving had all happened so fast, it might take some time to come to terms with.

A jet whooshed overhead and the nearby departure boards flashed with the names of a hundred destinations.

A quick call to Dayna was required.

Because I was due a few days off.

Chapter Twelve

GIBRALTAR

*I*t was funny because in order to arrive in Gibraltar, I first had to make a connecting flight in London, and that felt strange, to be surrounded by my own people after all this time. I mean, technically, Gibraltarians were British, English was their primary language but they spoke with a unique accent, which sounded somewhere halfway between Spanish and some long-forgotten English dialect. In truth, however, the accent of one man sounded different to the next. To look at them was likewise to notice a range of complexions. There were those who possessed the typical Spanish tan but also many you could place beside any English person and you'd not be able to tell them apart. Of course, there was a large military presence here, my sister had supposedly married one of them, and so there was no knowing who, as I sat drinking coffee on the main quaint street, was a Gibraltarian and who wasn't.

It was indeed a culture shock. Not two miles away the Spanish border gave way to a country that disputed Gibraltar's sovereignty and I'd learned that, even today, there were constant disputes and, hard as it was to believe, the occasional sea skirmish between the locals and Spanish.

From what little I'd seen, Gibraltar looked like someone had gone forty or fifty years back in time, picked up a pretty English town and dumped it on a sunny spot between a giant rock and the sea.

There were the red letterboxes of my country and even the old red phone boxes that today, you only ever saw in tourist towns. All

SALLY BRYAN

the shops were the usual British chains like Marks and Spencer, Debenhams and Costa Coffee. There were not the relaxed tapas bars of Spain but instead English pubs with names that would hardly be out of place in York, Bristol or London, establishments with names like Shakespeare's, Lord Nelson, Red Lion and The Angry Friar. There were even the old lantern shaped street lights that I loved so much because they reminded me of Edinburgh and all the buildings were in the typical British style, though many had their own unique twist.

But there were differences too. The weather was the most obvious distinction and the streets were lined with palm trees, oh, and for some reason, they drove on the right but by far the biggest and most pleasant shock for me was what I was seeing right now. Because on the pedestrian zone cobbles sat a monkey and he was grinning, scratching himself and causing an obstruction as people simply walked around and took little notice.

I took a photo and sent the image to Arwen, which was when I noticed she'd sent me one herself not five minutes before. She was standing between the two great bastions of a castle, making the peace sign with kissy lips and the message, 'missing you already.' I felt the stir down below and closed my eyes as the warmth flushed delightfully through me.

'WTF? Where are you? I don't think that's San Gimmy!' Came the fast response from her.

I laughed and fired back a reply, telling her I'd come to Gibraltar, on the hoof, in an attempt to find Lizzie, attaching another image of myself sitting at an outside table, drinking coffee surrounded by sunburned Brits.

'OMG! Just when I thought you couldn't surprise me anymore. I wish to God I could be with you but I can't, so I want photos and stories.'

It had only been a little over half a day and already, I missed her more than I knew how to describe and it was only sure to get worse. And then I kicked the table leg because I realised I'd fucked up.

Gibraltar was not in the Schengen area, which meant Arwen could have been with me now. I clenched a fist, watched as my knuckles turned white and decided to keep that annoying fact away from my woman, as well as hope she didn't find it out for herself - The perils of not planning ahead, à la Arwen.

It was time to move and so I drained the coffee and stood, not knowing what the bloody hell I was supposed to do next. What leads did I have? Not even a full name and I felt a stab of guilt because this was my sister and yet I had not even the most fundamental piece of information. I could phone Dad and tell him where I was but I'd asked for information before and he'd always withheld it and so I doubted my being in Gibraltar would change anything. Had this been a stupid idea?

I plodded down Main Street, forlornly scanning the passing faces, which just went to show how desperate I was. Gibraltar was small, it had a population of only thirty thousand and if I was to bump into Lizzie then we stood a greater chance of it happening in a place like this but still, could I even be sure I'd recognise her after eight years?

I passed a British expat store and, on a whim, decided to go inside. Lizzie always had an obsession with Scottish shortbread and I badly missed Highland tablet, clootie, blood sausage, stovies, bannock, bridie, skirlie and rumbledethumps, amongst others, though here, I was to be disappointed for the most part. Then I saw the Lea & Perrins Worcestershire sauce and didn't know how to react to that. Of course, it reminded me of Dan, which then made me think of Gabe and then I left the shop without making any purchases.

Of course, I hadn't taken time off work and flown all the way to Gibraltar with absolutely no idea of what to do when I got here, the plan was always to seek out some sort of authority, which was why I now arrived at 6 Convent Place, headquarters of Her Majesty's Government in Gibraltar. Finding it was easy, though I doubted the rest would be.

"Hello." The lady spoke with an accent that could have come from the English home counties.

I took a breath and hoped I could remember the winey speech I'd prepared, about how I wanted to know where my sister lived, except I didn't know her new name, and could you somehow provide me with her address please and honest, I'm not a crazy woman. Instead, I lost my backbone, or perhaps I was just playing it safe, and used her maiden name instead. "I'm looking for Lizzie Argyle."

The lady returned to her screen and began typing and for a brief moment, I thought she was actually searching some supposed database of every resident in The Rock and that she would actually hand my sister's details over but then I realised she was just checking names of the people who worked in the building. "I'm sorry, there's no Lizzie Argyle here."

Obviously! And damn you, Arwen.

Her colleague, another woman, who'd been sitting close behind at another desk overheard and after swiftly typing something into her keyboard, stood and made her way over to the front desk. "You're looking for Lizzie Argyle?"

My eyes widened, a miracle perhaps? It was all in her tone, something that most definitely suggested familiarity. "Yes!" My heart soared. "Do you have her address?"

Her head jerked back and she looked briefly shocked but why? My head probed forwards as I studied her face and I immediately knew I was being ridiculous because this woman was about twenty-five years too old to be Lizzie. But maybe she knew her? "If you would like to wait a couple of minutes..." she left it at that but remained standing, hands held in front of her belly, watching me whilst pretending not to be, and after a minute of not being able to read her face, I began to wonder what game she was playing.

Footsteps trod on nearby floorboards and then a security guard entered from a side door. "Good evening, would you like to come with me, please?"

I glanced at the two women who were now sneering back. "Is there a problem?"

"Miss, please." He held a hand out toward the exit and so I went, to be taken outside into a small annex of the main building, which had a heavy door, no windows and a grim aspect.

"Prison? Is that where you're taking me? For wanting to find my sister?" I screeched the last part and he scrunched his eyes closed and winced. "How dare you? I haven't done anything."

"Miss, it's not a prison," he held his hands up defensively and his voice had taken on a higher pitch from before, "but we need to run a few checks, if you wouldn't mind. You need to stay here for..."

"But why? I haven't even done anything."

"Yes, you said, please, don't scream." He cringed and managed to usher me into what had to be an interrogation room, which kind of looked like they did in the movies except they'd tried to make this place appear more comfortable, with magazines, a water dispenser and flatscreen TV that was running the BBC World Service with the volume muted. He asked for documentation and I angrily rustled through my bag for my passport before handing it over and dumping myself onto a seat. He closed the door on me and I was left alone in the small room.

After an hour had passed, I began to feel foolish and regretted this daft escapade. What did I think would happen, really? Why would the government hand over the address of one of its people to some crazy outsider?

After two hours the ceiling pattern was visible when I closed my eyes and I began to panic because it was late, I had no accommodation and could do nothing about finding any because they'd done something to block the phone signal in the room.

There was little else to do other than ponder the reasons for my detainment and I reasoned it probably had something to do with Lizzie's husband being in the army and they were paranoid about that kind of thing.

The door opened, which brought me from my semi-slumber, and a man wearing khaki stepped inside. I sat up and blinked. "Uncle Paul?"

He was holding my passport and grinned with those dispelling Celtic blue eyes of his, the type that always put you at ease, the sort you only found on Scottish men. "Trouble? So it really is you, I didn't believe it but here you are." He shot an angry glance through the opened door from where he came but before he could say anything to whoever was out there, I'd leapt up to throw my arms around him.

"I've never been so happy to see a friendly face." And my Uncle Paul was the friendliest.

Uncle Paul wasn't my real uncle, on account of neither my parents having any brothers, but he was the nearest thing I ever had. He was my dad's best friend, having grown up and been in the army together and even after we were born, they were always around each other, either on the moors stalking, playing golf, drinking or making investments. Though because he was a captain in the army, we'd often go long periods without seeing him. Now, I surveyed his uniform and stopped at a badge on his arm that said Royal Gibraltar Regiment. His other arm possessed a gorget patch with the insignia of a major.

"I see you're going up in the world." I was still grinning and knew without even having to ask that Uncle Paul would get me out of this place.

He shook his head and mirrored my grin. "Trubbs, it would seem you've been on a bit of a road trip." Either he'd been speaking to Dad or was privy to whatever checks security were making out there, not that I cared about such crap now.

"Yes, I've had a wonderful time, not long enough though. I feel I need another three of the same to even scratch the surface." I examined him from his now greying hair all the way to his boots that were so shiny they reflected the light from the ceiling. "I'm trying to think when it was I last saw you?"

Instead of answering, he guided me by the shoulder toward the door. I knew he'd get me out. "Obviously, we have things to catch up on but not here, anywhere's better than this depressing place."

He took me to a waiting army Land Rover, which was a thrill to be inside but unfortunately, it was now too dark to see Gibraltar or The Rock that dominated the territory like a freak that had no business being there.

"Wee place, huh?" This was in reference to the fact we were pulling into a gated residential after only five minutes of movement. "Wee and densely populated ... not much privacy."

"I bet you must really miss home?"

His lips turned down, "aye."

The iron gate closed after us and although the communal area was clean, green and pleasant, if I'd had the impression my uncle, who'd come from wealth, would be living in luxury, that impression was soon changed.

"Standard officer accommodation, I'm afraid, hence the security, but you're most very welcome." He slid a card through the reader, the door opened and as he led the way up a short flight of stairs, he began grinning like the monkey I'd seen on Main Street.

"Are you ok?"

He winked then pushed open the door and called into the flat, "just brought you a wee visitor."

I instinctively turned back to check if he was speaking to me but there were blurred shapes moving in my periphery and when I whipped back, there was a woman kneeling on the floor beside a child, both swamped in a large pile of building blocks scattered over the carpet.

I stopped mid-step and froze, my sister was doing the same, my hand rose to my mouth, she yelped, "I can't believe..." we said together and then she jumped up and we embraced as my skin tingled and neither of us could speak. She clasped me tight whilst, over her shoulder, my nephew hit bricks against the TV remote.

"I'll put the bairn to bed whilst you two catch up," Paul said from somewhere. Oh, I wanted nothing more than to know all about the wee bairn.

I was an aunt!

"It was Uncle Paul all along?" I asked, still ignoring the haggis, neeps and tatties on the plate. I missed this food but was far too excited to eat now.

Uncle Paul had been about to slice into his haggis but then landed back in his seat and folded his arms. "You mean, he never told you?"

I shook my head and Lizzie sighed.

"Oh, Dad."

There was silence after that, which gave me an opportunity to study my sister.

Where I was a redhead, she'd inherited the generic Scotch ginger gene and despite living in the sun, she still had a pale complexion as expected. We both had similar green eyes and our mouths were also very alike, though where my nose was slim and straight, hers was turned up slightly. She had many more freckles than I did and over the last eight years, it appeared I'd gained a height advantage of around two inches. She'd attained a slightly rounder look overall, of course, giving birth would have something to do with that, though she most definitely looked good.

Indeed, she was happy, and it wasn't merely because she'd been surprised by my arriving out of nowhere. She hadn't been the only one surprised and, not being quick to catch on, I'd wondered why Uncle Paul was taking the wee bairn to his room, having initially assumed he'd only driven me to Lizzie's flat because he obviously knew where she lived. Only then had I seen the picture frames. The small flat was crammed with them and I still found myself glancing over at various spots where they were concentrated. Yes, they were happy.

"That was four years ago." Lizzie followed my line of sight to a large frame on the wall, of what looked like a market on an endless sea of wooden rafts. "Vietnam. I was pregnant at the time."

"I can see." I indicated another because, having caught the travel bug, it looked like the kind of place I needed to be. "And that?"

"That was the Norwegian coastal road, through the fjords. We camped in the most stunning scenery imaginable."

I could have wilted and almost regretted the direction we'd taken this trip but then instantly abandoned that idea, knowing I wouldn't change anything for fear of never meeting Arwen.

Above the fireplace, my eyes rested on a large framed portrait of the wee bairn, impossibly happy and innocent with those same Celtic blue eyes. "Your son looks very much like you, Uncle Paul."

He squeezed his wife's hand, "thank God for that."

I snorted at my faux pas but knew he wouldn't mind, I was still getting used to this. "At least now, after all this time, I know why Dad was so upset."

"Upset?" Lizzie brought her hands in, "if that's what you want to call it."

I was starving so I ate the traditional Scottish meal Lizzie had hastily prepared. Haggis, neeps, which meant turnips and tatties, which were potatoes - Ah, Scottish cuisine but it was most suitable for tonight.

"Tomorrow we'll have to go on a hike up The Rock." She suggested, cocking a subconscious eyebrow at Uncle Paul.

He understood and jerked his chin toward the wee bairn's door. "I'll take him to the beach."

I wanted to spend time with my nephew but recognised that my sister and I most certainly had things to discuss. Oh God, but how would she take my news? I'd been so preoccupied with how Dad would react, I'd completely neglected Lizzie and had prepared nothing, no speeches or anything.

"When did we last see each other?" I asked my sister, "wasn't it the night before I returned to Fettes at the end of that summer?"

She nodded, "the four of us went for an Italian meal, that new place we all wanted to try."

"It's not there anymore."

She frowned at that but then her face filled with excitement. "Lachlan was being a pain that night, stealing my meatballs. I'll never forget it." Her hand moved atop my wrist. "How is he?"

My head tilted, "same, as expected, sometimes easy, sometimes not, always an experience."

Her eyes shimmered and Paul rubbed her shoulder. She didn't need to tell me how much she missed our brother and Paul looked down, mouth tightened, and I could only wonder how much he blamed himself for the entire predicament, for his wife being ostracised from her family, which was something I needed to know.

"How did this happen?" I opened out my arms to encompass the two of them and if I'd expected any discomfort from the question, they displayed none.

On the contrary, they gazed at each other and immediately, I could see it. They looked at each other the way I looked at Arwen. Were they such an unlikely pairing? Just because of the age gap? My sister was twenty-six, Uncle Paul in his late fifties and sure, it was unusual but not really.

"Growing up, I always felt close to Paul," Lizzie began, "as I know you did too but that doesn't mean anything inappropriate happened but try telling that to Dad."

"Ah, now I'm beginning to understand." I noticed Paul was sitting with his chin up, maintaining my eye contact.

Lizzie shrugged, "it wasn't planned or anything. You were at boarding school and I went down south to visit Heather at uni." She smiled at her husband. "Paul was on leave and it was an honest chance encounter in the street, he bought me lunch and after a year of not seeing him, things were different." She looked at me with deliberation. "Freya, I was *eighteen*." She was about to continue and Paul, seeing how difficult it was for her, took up where she left off.

"Gus accused me of grooming." He said as a matter of fact.

"Which is complete fucking bullshit." Lizzie snapped and then peered at the bedroom door as though fearing she'd disturbed her son.

I nodded, "of course, it's bullshit." And it was.

"But try telling that stubborn man," she put in. "If anything, it was *I* who seduced *him*," she jerked her head sidewards, "and only *after* I became an adult." Her forehead wrinkled. "Oh, Freya, he said some bloody hurtful things."

"He accused me of always being attracted to his daughters." He was trying to remain strong for Lizzie's benefit but the sadness in his voice was easy to detect.

Lizzie hooked a hand around his arm. "Paul is a good man. Would I still be with him, a beautiful child, married, if I'd been *groomed*? No, he just wanted me to marry someone my own age, which I can understand, but we can't help who we fall in love with."

"Right." I nodded vigorously, understanding that completely.

Everything now made sense. Dad had interfered in my own relationship to its detriment. When would he learn?

But what I saw here was love, real love. It was just so tragic they'd both had to lose so much for it.

Lizzie's head was buried in the crook of Paul's neck as he rubbed her back and he now spoke to me over her shoulder. "There's not much room in Gibraltar so I'll take the couch tonight, you can share the bed with your sister."

And so, after finally discovering the truth, I went to sleep in peace.

———

"It's the only place in Europe that has monkeys." Lizzie breathed heavily as she climbed the steps that ascended The Rock.

I'd already taken about a hundred photos. "They're everywhere."

She put her arm across the front of my body and we stopped because not far ahead, a tourist had just lost her camera to one particularly cheeky monkey, and it quickly ran and clambered up a tree from where it began banging it against a branch.

I laughed but Lizzie didn't find it funny, the dour Scot.

"Be careful with your phone and any other valuables because they'll have them."

"Lizzie, I don't think I could ever get bored of living here."

She released her arm and we set off again. "Well, you're welcome to visit anytime you like."

"Right, I will do my best but I have..." I almost said residency but then remembered I'd recently changed my life plans, "work," I said instead.

She didn't pick up on my discomfort or if she did she didn't mention it, which preceded a few minutes of silence, though that was mostly because Lizzie wasn't finding the climb as easy as I was. "You know," she panted, "there's twice the length of tunnels than roads in Gibraltar, and they're all under this rock."

"I remember reading there are war tunnels and a reservoir in it somewhere."

The steps phased into a dirt path, thick with bushes, which unfortunately obscured the view of Morocco across the Med, not to mention Spain over the other side. We'd already been walking for an hour and for the most part, the path was gradual and easy.

Lizzie took a sip of water and batted at a fly. "I see you decided to go straight to the office of the Chief Minister yesterday. It must have been a shock when Paul arrived."

I laughed and recalled the memory with fondness. "A lucky first port of call. I would have gone to the police after that and eventually resorted to asking strangers in the street. Luckily Paul spared me all of that and yes, it was a very pleasant shock."

"Not the only shock, right?" She remarked in an even tone and because I assumed she meant the shock of seeing her, there was no need to answer.

Instead, I asked my own obvious question. "Why was I detained? All I did was mention your name. Has Spain's proximity really made everyone around here so paranoid?"

She stared blankly at me. "You really don't know? Oh wow."

I slowed down and touched her arm. "That sounded a little ominous. Know what?"

She held out a palm, "we had a visit from your ex. Gable, was it?" Oh shit. "His friend too and a girl."

I stopped and wasn't completely sure I'd heard right. "You had a visit from Gabe? Wait ... if I couldn't find you, how the bloody hell did he?"

Her forehead creased as she took a breath. "A good question and the answer is they were arrested in the town centre for fighting."

"Jesus Christ!" I covered my face and groaned into my hands.

She gave me a mild disapproving frown, just subtle enough to notice because obviously, I made terrible choices in men. If only she knew. But I didn't want my sister thinking I'd turned out to be such a terrible judge of character. Oh Gabe, what happened to you? I was about to make an emotional outburst in my defence but she was too quick to continue with the story.

"Your ex-boyfriend, Gable Shoesmith, made a bit of a nuisance of himself, got drunk and fought in the street, was arrested, spent several nights in detention and all the while kept requesting to see a Lizzie Argyle, my maiden name."

"I remember it," I said dryly.

"And my guess is that your mentioning of that name prompted a response from the authorities because it was all still so fresh in their heads."

My ex must have left an impression but there was something potentially important I needed to know at once. "How fresh?"

She shrugged and her eyes snapped up, "five weeks? Or thereabouts." Which thankfully meant he'd be long gone by now.

I sighed, "my detainment was a precaution then. See ... I'm really not a criminal." Though I couldn't speak for some of my former acquaintances. "You met him?" I almost feared to ask because I couldn't imagine what state he must have been in.

She barked. "Are you crazy?" And there was another disapproving look from big sister. "Paul wouldn't allow that but he went instead, and my husband has ways of getting to the bottom of the matter." Whilst doubtless implying he should stop requesting to see his wife.

"I'm sure he has."

"He's protective over his family."

"As he should be."

Now she looked at me with something a little more friendly and smiled. "You tried to visit a few weeks earlier, didn't you?"

I nodded and blew out air, "yes, I'd wanted to come after Malaga," and then I realised that would mean nothing to her, "which was probably around two months ago ... you tend to lose track of what day it is when you're travelling."

"I bet. But you stole his car, or something," bloody hell, "and I'm guessing he thought Gibraltar would have been your logical first stop on the run."

I put my hand on her elbow and we came to another halt, "ok, I have to stop you there, because I did not *steal* the car, I..." my head was throbbing from the exertion and the walking and the accusations and the half-truths and I needed water, "first of all, it was a camper van and..."

Another disapproving glance, I should keep a tally, "looks like someone's gone completely off the rails."

My arms just fell limp and so I shut my eyes, counted to ten and decided to let the camper van issue go, to keep the peace, to keep moving, because she hadn't even heard the best part yet, or had she? Gabe, as it transpired, had a loose tongue and was likely trying to destroy me but I did count myself extremely lucky not to have been around when he was. He'd evidently travelled straight to Gibraltar from Lisbon, that camper would have been extremely conspicuous in such a small place, and it was hard to imagine what state of mind he must have been in. I didn't feel good about it, of course not, but neither was it easy to feel sympathy for Gabe after he'd been fighting yet again.

"Have you got any more of that water?" I asked.

She handed over the bottle. "I was very sorry to have missed you," she surprised me by changing tone, "I thought we might have missed the only chance we'd ever have and it made me cry, I must admit." She took the bottle back and stuffed it in her bag. "So, is this Arwen character your girlfriend?"

I stumbled on the flat surface. "Shit! You know?"

She shifted but then her face softened and she slid her arm inside mine. "Your ex was very keen to dirty your name to anyone who'd listen."

Did that mean Dad knew too? Or did Gabe fear him too much to risk it? Or perhaps he wanted to hold that one thing back to blackmail me with later? Or was I thinking too much into it?

"Bloody hell," I said under my breath.

"It's true then, Freya?" Her tone was absolutely disapproving.

"Yes it's true, I've met a wonderful woman and I'm in love with her." I tried to meet her eyes but it was she who couldn't bring herself to look at me. It was understandably something to get used to.

She shook her head, "Dad's really gonna love this news."

I laughed at that. "An understatement and I'm happy to take the pressure off you. In fact, you never know, after hearing about me, he'll probably come to you himself."

We'd reached the summit and the world opened out to reveal the Mediterranean reflecting the sun and beyond, the Atlas Mountains of Morocco that appeared almost close enough to touch.

She turned me suddenly around by the arm, forgetting the view. "Freya, is there anything you can do to facilitate a reunion? Please? Anything at all? I miss him, Lachlan, you, home. I just want the suffering to stop. Please."

―――――

"I DIDN'T BELIEVE it at first and why would I? It came amidst this car stealing thing, not to mention a tonne of other accusations, cheating, drugs, a gambling addiction?" She reeled that last one off whilst subconsciously leaning away from me, as though it was so much worse than stealing, cheating and drugs but I knew it was because she'd been around when our mother had succumbed to the casino slot machines and the thought that her little sister had been doing the same must have been particularly horrifying. Gabe had unknowingly touched a nerve with that one.

My head was spinning as I found it hard to enjoy the traditional English sausage and mash we were eating in a pub after the long hike. "Lizzie, you know bloody well I would never ever even think about gambling." I squeezed the knife obscenely hard because Gabe had been the one gambling that night I left him. Accuse the other side of that which you are guilty.

"The drugs are true then?" She asked in a high-pitched squeal.

I exhaled and kept a level tone, yet still had to raise my voice above the ringing of fruit machines and the blare of a football match playing on a large flatscreen attached to the far wall where a small crowd had gathered. "Of course." And when she physically jolted, I knew I couldn't continue with the joke, funny as it might have been, "I was taking ibuprofen for a stiff neck and headaches."

She wasn't sure how to take that, but after a short while nodded, evidently believing me. Stick one truth in with a bunch of lies and the whole package tends to get believed.

"Please tell me Uncle Paul didn't believe any of this slander?"

"Paul just rolled his eyes and dismissed the guy as some jealous ex who was taking a break up extremely bad, then told the police to release him when he'd calmed down and was no longer a danger to himself and others in the territory." She laughed nervously, "I mean, the guy had travelled all the way from Lisbon to find you." She cast me a disapproving eye as she used her fork to further smush up her mash. "How long were the two of you together?"

"Five years," I said flatly, knowing she'd be judging me again, "but he was never like..." I gave up, what was the use. Truthfully, it was a relief to have been having the time of my life in Southern France, as well as a bunch of other places, when Gabe had been shaming himself here. At the time it had never even occurred to me that he'd think to follow us to Gibraltar, that it was the logical place we'd go first. Thank God two girls on the run don't think logically, necessarily, and had fled in the opposite direction completely. "Did you hear from him again?"

She shook her head and shrugged. "Nope."

I breathed and relaxed, took a bite of sausage topped with caramelised onion and scooped in some mash and peas. It tasted better now.

Lizzie waited for a file of men holding pint glasses to pass our table. "Tell me about this Arwen person," she pushed the sausages around on her plate, "I can understand wanting to dump this Gable idiot, but run away with a woman? Are you bloody serious?"

I'd never really known my sister as an adult and now I wondered if she was trying to take the position of mum, though of course, she cared about me. "Yes, I'm bloody serious, Lizzie. I love that girl more than anything." I'd spoken the last three words slower as my eyes glazed over and my mind went into a small spasm for some totally unknown reason. I shook it away. "She's absolutely the best thing that ever happened to me."

"You don't sound very sure. Is she good enough to throw away your career?" She sliced through her sausage so aggressively that the knife made a cringy screech against the plate. "Christ, Freya? You always wanted to be a bloody doctor, it was the most important thing in the world to you. Does she really mean so much you'd give that up just to pick bloody grapes? *After* having wasted five years of your life studying, no less. She must be bloody good in bed." She was but I wouldn't say that. She continued, "I have to be honest because you're my little sissy and I love you but it seems to me like you've been travelling a little too long and have lost your mind ... you've literally run away with a bloody woman!"

If I'd thought our conversation on The Rock had settled it, I was wrong, in fact, now she knew it hadn't just been Gabe spreading bullshit, it appeared she'd used the entire descent to come up with a whole bunch of reasons to talk me out of it, to make me see sense.

In my paranoia, I briefly surveyed the near vicinity for eavesdroppers and spoke in a low voice in the hope she'd simmer down. "You know, Lizzie, that's exactly how it seemed to us when *you* ran away with *your* lover. For years, I thought you'd lost your mind and made a stupid irrational decision without putting any thought into it." When she had no response to that, and because I was too nice, I decided to save her from answering by referring to her earlier point, "and yes, I wanted to be a doctor but I really like working at the vineyard too and..."

"But Freya, you're not even a lesbian," she cut in, a little too loud, "don't think I don't remember that obsession you had with that actor ... who was he?" Her eyes shot up and I decided to help her out.

"Ewan McGregor, the guy out of Trainspotting. Lizzie, he's pretty famous." I shuffled and peeped again around the near area.

"Right, I remember the posters and how you spent hours

watching all his films, again and again, so don't you tell me you're one of those women who was born liking women because I know you're not."

"You're not wrong, in fact, you're correct, and I don't consider myself a *lesbian* necessarily, but I *am* in a lesbian relationship with a woman I'm besotted with," I'd again spoken the last few words slower, as I underwent another mind twitch. Had the hike slowed the blood flow to my head? I shook it away and tried to pick up where I left off but Lizzie was too quick to intervene.

"You don't even sound convinced about being besotted with her."

I slapped the table and because the knife was in my hand, the clang of metal on wood was unintentionally loud, "I really wish you could be supportive." I knew I wasn't doing a very good job fighting my corner but this was only a prelude of what was to come. How would I fare when confronted with Dad? Was I wrong to have expected that after all this time, Lizzie would be on my side from the start? The difference was we were both adults now but she'd always be my big sister looking out for me and I knew she was only asking the hard questions because she cared.

She made a wavering smile, "have you," she coughed, "can I see a picture?"

I smiled, "of course." I showed her a photo of Arwen standing beside Michelangelo's David in Florence and because we weren't supposed to be taking photos in the museum, she looked particularly cheeky.

Lizzie shuffled and looked away. "She's very pretty."

"She is and thank you," because I knew that must have been pretty hard for her to say.

She rubbed the back of her neck. "But she looks like a hippy. You can rely on that kind of a woman?"

I faced her straight on, "I can rely on Arwen and you're right, she is a hippy and there's not one thing I'd change about her." Other than her not being here now.

She began to eat and a few minutes later said, "tell me about her."

And so I did. I told Lizzie all about Arwen, her intellect, her life as a dancer, the languages she spoke, that she never stopped surprising and challenging me, her humour and warmth, her devilish mischievous streak, how we'd had the most magical time travelling through Europe and how we'd fallen in love in a Tuscan vineyard and by the end I hoped that if nothing else, Lizzie might understand, at least a little.

"And children?" She asked, almost managing to meet my eye.

I rubbed my chin and pretended to consider it. "You know, I'm not sure Arwen and I can have them, I learned that studying medicine."

She just barely cut a smile, the dour Scot. "Don't mess with me."

I shrugged and thought about Dayna and Alessia. "There are ways but I'm only twenty-three."

She rubbed her face, "well, I can tell you really *are* besotted with her. Maybe we'll get to meet sometime." Though she said it without much conviction.

Obviously, it was all quite difficult for Lizzie, in fact, I was sure she had no idea how to take any of it. She was only now learning her little sister wasn't just messing around but was actually in a lesbian relationship and it was the real thing.

"I'm sorry if I sounded upset." She said from across our empty plates.

My face softened, "it's big news, I kind of understand."

"And just so you know, it wasn't an irrational decision I made with Paul. I loved him."

I nodded, "I know now, and I love Arwen."

It wasn't that my sister had been impulsive and carefree growing up, it was more that it had appeared to everybody she'd made one impulsive, carefree and irrational decision and as a consequence had dismantled our entire family. But now I could see it was only as irrational as love itself. The truth was that like myself, Lizzie was a traditional girl in an untraditional relationship.

"You know," I told her, "you haven't really changed at all, you're still so much like Dad." Which made it all even more tragic. "And I promise to do my best to make him see sense." I nodded for emphasis and meant my words, despite not knowing what I could possibly do.

"Thank you, I knew you would," she stood and held out her arms for a hug and so I pulled out from my seat, stood and embraced my sister...

...as my eyes adjusted over her shoulder, three tables down, to the empty bottle of Lea & Perrins Worcestershire Sauce.

I pulled away, wide-eyed and cold skinned.

"Freya?" She examined the area around us, "what is it?"

I was frantically scanning the room but there was no sign of them, any of them, and finally, I breathed and was able to laugh it away. It was a pub, they served food and kept bottles of the stupid sauce for people with acidic penchants. What's more, it had been five fucking weeks, he wasn't on this stupid rock.

"Nothing," I rubbed her arm, "can we go see my nephew?"

That evening we did a few jigsaw puzzles and watched Peppa Pig whilst Paul worked his late shift. It was instant love with the little guy, who I was sure could recognise his mother in me and Lizzie said she'd always thought he resembled me more than anyone else, though in my opinion, apart from his red hair, he looked most like his father.

In the morning, after Paul had again left for work, I had to make a tearful goodbye for now, exchanging numbers with my sister, which seemed so strange, and crouching to embrace and kiss my nephew.

"From the town centre, there's a shuttle to the airport at a quarter past every hour." She wiped her eye and pulled her son off my leg.

I kissed them both again and tried to keep it together. "I can make the walk if I leave now. Oh God..."

"Stay in touch."

"Of course, we're sisters, and you're welcome to visit us in Tuscany any time you want." I hugged them both again and then I was out the door, walking down the steps, out the building, through the security gates and along a busy road that led into town.

Ten minutes later I was at the shuttle stop where an elderly couple and three solitary female travellers waited beside a stack of bags as the early morning sun cast their shadows far and dark across the pavement.

I closed my eyes and allowed my mind to conjure up images of my beautiful nephew and then, a minute later, Arwen pushed her way to the fore and I couldn't help but grin stupidly, caring not one bit how I came across to the strangers gathered around. I pulled out my phone and flicked through our many photos, rode out the familiar rush of heat she always caused because she was mine, and lamented it was a mere two days short of ninety before I could be with her again.

A new shadow moved over me and I didn't even need to look up to know who it was.

"Hello, Doctor."

IF I'D THOUGHT, after seeing the stupid Lea & Perrins bottle, that coming face to face with Gabe in the street would leave me panicked then I was to be surprised. It seemed the thought of seeing him, after five weeks, was worse than the act itself but then, so far, I'd only been gaping at him for a matter of seven or eight seconds. Gabe didn't scare me and he never would but I was still grateful not to be standing alone at the shuttle stop.

He was wearing the brown cargo shorts he'd donned through much of Western Europe, which were now severely frayed just above where they cut off at the knee, like he'd maybe scuffed them hard on the ground, or been dragged across it. His navy blue shirt was missing its top two buttons and his sleeves were rolled up, which was unlike him, and I wondered if that was to conceal any rips or torn fabric, indeed, his right elbow was badly grazed. He wore his flip flops, which had been a gift from me before the trip, and exposed a blackened nail on his big toe. The periorbital puffiness was prominent, like he wasn't sleeping, though it might also have had much to do with his alcohol intake, because he reeked of it. His right eye was bloodshot and he wore a pair of glasses I didn't recognise. He was also thinner than I'd ever seen him and his hair longer, though he'd managed to keep clean shaven, as though that was more important than showering, and his skin had flared again from mosquito bites.

"Surprised to see me, are you Doctor?" His eyes tracked over my face and ran down my body and only stopped when he unbalanced and had to reach out to steady himself against a rubbish bin.

There was no knowing how stunned I must have looked but considering everything, I was able to remain calm. "Gabe..." but what to say? How are you? What are you doing here? Nothing seemed apt for the moment.

He let go of the bin and came closer, flicking at my braid with a finger and sneering, "you look like someone but I can't quite think who."

"Gabe," I finally managed to find my senses, "are you ok?"

He laughed with exaggeration and it came out more as a cackle. "Am I ok, she asks." He rubbed his face as another two people arrived at the stop. "Do you really give a fuck whether I'm ok?"

"Gabe, I do, of course." My eyes flicked up to the digital display over his shoulder, the one that showed how far away the shuttle was. Three minutes. "Where's Dan?"

His eyes had narrowed in scepticism when I'd told him I cared and they were still squinting now, but then the sun was bright behind me, which contributed, and doubtless he was also hungover. "Dan? Oh, Dan. You just missed him. He took a boat to Morocco about an hour ago. He's banging Floor now."

"Right, well, good for him," please hurry up damn shuttle. "So, you're here in Gibraltar ... how are you finding it?"

"Fuck you!"

I jerked but remained placid. "I was only asking, Gabe. Did you get your passport?"

"My what?"

"Your passport. I mailed it to the hostel in Lisbon."

"I got it." He teetered briefly then brought himself back to equilibrium. "Are you going to tell me where you're going?"

I gestured at the shuttle shelter we were both presently standing in and tried not to sound condescending, "to the airport."

"I meant where fucking to," he snapped, "and don't play fucking dumb. You're going somewhere to meet that bitch you're fucking and don't fucking lie to me," he scratched again at one of the red splotches on his neck, "I already know she's not here."

From that, I gaged that he had been at the pub yesterday and decided not to ask if he'd followed me back to Lizzie's and waited all evening and all night for the moment I left her flat alone. "Gabe, Arwen and I are living in Italy." I decided to be as vague as possible with the location, naming only the country of sixty million souls in the hope that would be good enough. Thankfully, it was.

"Living?" He raised an eyebrow, which unsettled one of his spots.

The shuttle pulled in, early, and I breathed. "Gabe," I forced my hand to let go of the bag strap and held it out to him, "it was nice seeing you again. Stay safe, please."

He didn't take my hand but just scowled from close range.

"Ok, well, please take care." I turned, hefted my bag and knew after only two steps he was still there behind me and now, as I entered the bus and took my seat, he was still there. I dumped my bag on the seat beside me, which unsettled him for a moment, but then he landed on the pew directly to my rear and leaned forward, propping his elbows on the rail beside my head, as the stench of last night's beer pervaded my nostrils. "Gabe, you do know this is the shuttle to the airport?"

It pulled out, only to join the slow-moving traffic and I briefly considered stepping off and paying for a taxi.

He ignored my question and asked another, "what are you doing living in Italy?" His voice was suddenly deeper than before, which made it about as croaky as I'd ever heard it.

At the least, it was an opportunity to make him feel better about no longer being with me and I seized it. "I've taken a job working on a vineyard, so I won't be taking residency and..." I was about to elaborate that he could feel free to choose any of our options, safe in the knowledge I wouldn't be there but he cut me off by grunting, which turned into a mocking laugh.

"A vineyard? Doing what? Picking grapes?" It had been intended as a put-down, little did he know.

I nodded, "that's right, I enjoy it."

He barked and I heard him thump back against his seat. A second later his elbows were back near my head. "Oh, God, you know, I used to think you were rational, but you're just like all the rest."

"Rest? What rest?"

He flapped a hand and I saw the grazes on his knuckles, "all women. You've thrown your life away because of how you *feel*," and he screeched the word, trying to sound like some demented woman, "in the moment and when you come around, which you will, it'll be too late, cos I'm training to be a doctor and like your ogre of a dad says, I'll have the pick of the women, despite my *ridiculous hairline*," he said the last two words trying to sound like my dad, and I could almost visualise how that conversation must have gone.

I shook my head and sighed, sinking down into the seat and praying for this ride to be over. An old woman on the other aisle was staring directly forwards and we went over a bump.

"*Angus? Angus?*" Gabe began his monologue. "I always thought that was the stupidest name I ever heard. Not as stupid as your grandparents for naming him *Angus*. I Googled *Angus* ... turns out it's a breed of cattle ... also the title of a film about a fat boy who was bullied. Maybe that's why your dad, *Angus*, turned out to be such a pathetic weasel and a tyrant. *Angus!* And what's the short form? *Gus?* Oh, because that's so much better." He laughed and sat back. "I fucking hate your dad. He's responsible for all of this, for everything that happened to us."

Through it all, I'd been staring blankly out the window, as the small territory passed by, and the truth was I just didn't know what to make of it, any of it.

But he'd silenced, which was a temporary blessing, and now all I could hear from him were his fingers as they tapped against his phone screen.

The shuttle entered the airport, which was the smallest I'd ever seen, so small its runway crossed the main road that led into the territory and only one plane sat in an open space a short walk from the terminal, which was a single small glass-fronted building.

I hurried to file out amongst everyone else and strode in the direction of the terminal. "What the fuck, Gabe? What are you playing at?"

He was walking beside me, with a belligerent smirk, and I feared I already knew what he'd done. "Thought I'd keep you company on the flight."

I stopped on the tarmac, spun around, for whatever reason, and then continued toward the terminal. What was the use? I couldn't stop him from getting on a plane and since only four left every day, it wouldn't have been hard to guess I was flying to London Gatwick. "You really want to waste your money just to insult my dad and upset me? You don't even have your bag and what about your passport?"

He produced his passport from his back pocket, waved it in front of my face and gurned, which was when I noticed the chipped tooth.

I threw up my arms and checked in. The wait to board was around thirty minutes, the entirety of which Gabe spent sitting at the bar, watching me from a distance, beer in hand.

And what would you know, but I found myself sitting next to him on the plane and then we were in the air, beginning the three-hour flight to London.

I finally broke the silence after what must have been half an hour. "Have you honestly been squatting in Gibraltar for all of five weeks? All on the assumption I'd eventually turn up?"

He looked away, which said it all. "Let's see how you'd react if I stole your vehicle and drove away with some man I'd only just met."

I didn't know whether to laugh or cry. I did *not* steal the bloody camper and we'd already broken up by that point. "And where've you been staying?"

He scratched his neck and rubbed at the residue that stuck to his fingers. "Like you give a shit."

I turned suddenly to face him, "well actually, I do, but be like that. And I know you've been blabbing about my private life to anyone who'd listen but what I'd really like to know is if you spoke to my dad about it?"

"What, *Angus*?" He folded his arms and made a smug face. "Maybe I did, maybe I didn't." Five weeks, apparently that's all it took for Gabe to lose the ability to answer questions.

"Fine, and what are you going to do when you arrive in London? Because you ain't following me back to Italy, I can tell you that right now."

He fell silent and then after several minutes spoke again. "Are you honestly not taking your residency?"

I'd settled down since the last outburst and now sounded composed. "I'm honestly not, Gabe. I'm happy where I am."

His jaw trembled, "but ... but, you would really give up your career for her but wouldn't even marry me?" It was obvious that realisation cut him deeply, even though the two things were hardly the same. "Was I really so bad? I know I messed up at the end but ... but ... Freya, you're giving up your entire career." He bit his lip. "Is it because you don't want to risk being at the same placement as me?"

It was so tragic I was briefly lost for words. "Gabe, I'm not..."

"Because I've decided on Cornwall, so you should go somewhere else or," his hand seemed to float towards mine but changed its mind halfway, "or maybe you can come to Cornwall too?"

I tried to sound stern yet understanding. "This has nothing to do with being afraid to be in the same hospital as you, that would be ridiculous."

After a second, he stared down into his lap. "So, it's true then, you must really love her." He turned away, which saved me from having to respond, to hurt him even more.

On account of feeling sick, he left to use the bathroom on three separate occasions and because it was a small plane, and there were queues, I was left alone for much of the flight.

We landed and during that annoying period where everybody stands crowding the aisle waiting to disembark, Gabe watched me the whole time.

I occupied myself by sifting through my hand luggage and shortly after we were leaving the plane, walking through the bridge and converging in an atrium where there was a surge of passengers merging from other planes, many of whom were running to make connections. My flight to Pisa left in an hour, which meant I was in a rush and Gabe, well, I had no idea where he was going and doubted he'd tell me if I asked.

"Right," I turned to him and nodded, "this is it," I didn't want to remember him in this state but as the happy guy who got me through medical school. It was a damned bloody shame. "I have to make my connection so I must scoot. I wish you well in Cornwall but I would advise you to quit drinking before you start."

"Don't you dare patronise me," he said ungraciously.

"I wasn't," I shook my head and threw up my arms, "well, I tried, have a good life, Gabe." I was about to turn away but froze because he'd dropped to his knees and before I could move, or think, his arms were wrapped around my legs.

"Please don't leave me, Freya, please, I don't care what you did, I still love you and I forgive everything, I just want you back, I miss you so much, please don't leave me." He wailed and his arms were absolutely shaking as a huge crowd drew up to watch the spectacle.

I lost the feeling in my face as a chill rushed through my body. "Gabe, what ... please ... what are you doing? Get off me." I tried to stoop, to work his arms off me but couldn't and at least two people stopped mid-run to see what was happening, their urgent connections forgotten.

He felt me trying to squirm away and increased his hold around my knees. "Freya, please? I still love you, I don't know what to do without you."

"Gabe! You're scaring me."

The whole world shifted into slow motion as my heightened senses brought horrifying small details to greater clarity. People filming, laughing, covering their mouths, the digital clock striking seventeen past the hour. "I think he likes you, love," and, "get a room," were called and the laughter was unbearable.

His chin tilted up, his face white, tears soaking his cheeks, he looked so pathetic. "I can't take it anymore, if you leave me, I promise, I'm going to kill myself."

"Gabe? Please, you must let me go." I wasn't sure how long it had been, probably not more than thirty seconds, and from the direction I wanted to dash, passengers were fanning out to make room for three burly security guards in official uniforms who were running towards us.

The leading guard barged into Gabe so roughly that he was sent tumbling to the floor, knocking away his glasses, as yet more people began filming and laughing.

"Are you all right?" I was asked by the second guard and I nodded.

"Just my crazy ex ... need to catch my connection ... in a rush ... you don't need a statement I hope." I felt disorientated and my brain was blotting out much of the crowds and buzz.

Gabe was even more dazed, in fact, I could see now he must have hit his head and there was a small pool of red beneath his face which was being held down against the tiles as they pinned his arms painfully behind his back.

"It would be nice but you can email it if you're in a rush."

I nodded and he took the details from my passport. "What will happen to him?"

He shrugged, didn't seem too worried and I guessed stupid incidents in large international airports were hardly a rarity. "For now, he'll go to the immigration holding cell."

"He's British," I said, as though that might mean anything and then watched as they hauled the former love of my life to his feet, which were pointing limply inwards. "He should probably get some treatment. You've hurt him. All he ever wanted was to help hurt people."

The border guard laughed and looked at me funny and then Gabe was dragged past, his head sagging and blood dripping over the tiles. "I can fast track you through the gates if you're in a rush?"

"Huh?"

"Queues ... if you're late, I can get you straight through so you don't miss your flight."

I shook my head, "I think I've time but thanks."

He left and then several women, who'd been watching from somewhere close, came forward to offer comfort, or obtain gossip to satisfy their morbid curiosity, as I stood numb and a cleaner arrived to mop away Gabe's blood. He didn't see the glasses and accidentally kicked them across the floor. He made his way over to them and stooped, inspected the frames and seemed in two minds what to do with them. He was about to dump them in the rubbish but I acted quickly to intervene.

"Please, I'll take them."

He shrugged and handed them over. They were a cheap set of frames, probably temporary until he had chance to obtain a permanent pair.

The clock ticked twenty-six past the hour and I was still standing on the same spot, holding the frames at twenty-seven past.

The crowd had dispersed and there were no fresh surges of passengers coming from the seven bridges attached to the atrium.

Men. They place women at the centre of their lives, which gives us the highest power over them, whether or not we'd like to admit it, and women must learn to be careful with that power. He was once a fine man and look at him now.

A trail of blood revealed a path and a choice.

The clock struck twenty-eight.

THE BLOODY TRAIL did not lead to a holding cell, of which we were both becoming accustomed, but to a first aid room and when I entered, Gabe was sitting on an examination couch, pinching his nose to stem the flow of blood whilst staring into the floor tiles. A nurse was sitting beside him holding a bag of ice to his forehead.

"Freya," he croaked without looking up.

"You lost your glasses," I reached meekly towards the couch to place them on the edge and spoke to the nurse, "mind if I take over?"

She frowned at me, I must have had that look, and she seemed about to reject my request but then shrugged and handed me the bag of ice before walking to the other side of the room to begin typing into a laptop.

"They're a piece of junk but thanks." He groaned and because he was still pinching his nose, his voice came out nasally.

"You'll need them to get home, right?"

"If you're suggesting my travels are over, you'd be right."

I sat beside him and placed the bag against the bruise, "I'm not gonna lie, it looks pretty bad."

He flinched when I made contact with the ice, at least, I thought it was from the ice. "That bastard broke my nose."

"You could sue," I said softly, "plenty of witnesses."

"Freya, ugh, I'm so sorry. Sorry for Gibraltar and sorry for embarrassing you, as well as myself. What the fuck was I thinking?"

"Gabe, I hurt you really bad."

"Yeah but still … That is what you call hitting rock bottom and that is the lowest I've been in my entire life." He removed the cloth from his face, inspected the dark red contents, grimaced and braced for the inevitable continuation of blood which didn't come. "At least that's stopped." He winced from a sudden pain in his nose. "Sue them?" He hummed but after a moment shook his head. "No, I think I needed a clout on the head. Perhaps not quite so hard, but I needed something." He leaned back against the wall and I had to follow him with the ice, and then he began to laugh and only stopped because it hurt his head. "Don't they say you have to hit rock bottom before you can ... oh, I don't know ... and I can't think right now but you know what I mean."

"I do, it's just a shame things had to go this far, right? Here," I took the bloody cloth from his hand and wanted to inspect his nose, "look at me," he hesitated before shifting and could only meet my eye for a flicker. "It is broken, Gabe."

He closed his eyes and exhaled and I knew that the old Gabe would be thinking about the kind of impression he'd be making at his placement. "You'll miss your flight if you don't leave now."

"Sod the bloody flight, *you're* more important and *yes*, Gabe, I do bloody care." There was a short period of silence. "How long until your placement, two weeks?"

"Yep."

"Then let's hope you get lucky." This was in reference to the fact most broken noses required two to three weeks to heal, and Gabe was most definitely due some luck. "You worry me, Gabe. This talk about suicide?"

He stared blankly forwards. "Did I really say that? You know, I worry myself sometimes but you needn't. No, I'm fine, honestly, and it's weird, I have such a bad headache right now," he groaned deeply, "but the thing is, never before have I had such clarity of thought, even if I can't articulate the bloody words, I'm thinking clearly, for a change. I mean, Jesus Christ, Freya, fighting when I'm no good at it, drinking until I pass out. I've spent the last five weeks moping about Gibraltar, hoping to bump into you at some point, when I was in the worst shape of my life. How was *that* supposed to win you back?"

"That was trying to win me back?" I joked, even though it wasn't funny.

He stared blankly at the wall ahead. "I've not been me, not for a while ... I mean, I've been sharing a small room with a heroin addict." He was tapping his leg with a finger. "He kept asking for money and I had to spend several nights sleeping under a tree just to get away from the guy." He met my eye for the first time since my arrival in the room. "If that's not low then I don't know what is."

I took the hand that was tapping a nervous rhythm. "Please, Gabe, no more. You're so much better than that."

He nodded, "I'm glad you still think so, I was beginning to forget what self-respect felt like. This whole bloody trip, huh?"

I tried not to laugh, "it's been an experience for us both." An understatement. "What will you do now?"

"Can I just," he took the ice from my hand, "I'd prefer to see you when I speak to you." But all the same, it wasn't easy for him to look. "Now, I clean myself the fuck up. Get my head straight. Fix my bloody appearance. Try not make a fool of myself when I begin residency. Do my bloody best to make a success of it. And stay the fuck away from women. Well, for a while anyway."

"That's definitely a good idea," I remembered how shitty I felt that month without Arwen and could only assume that for Gabe, the feeling would be intensified many times over. He'd loved me a lot longer, I'd been his world and I left him in a way that prevented him from gaining closure. "I'm sorry I never said goodbye. You deserved that at least."

He opened out his palms, "that's just it, Frey, because had you done that you probably wouldn't have been able to get away ... I'd have pulled some shit to get you to stay, or followed you and sabotaged you in some way." He took a breath. "I needed to recognise when it was over. I've not been able to see it but now I absolutely do."

"We've both done some pretty shitty things these last few months, the fault is not all yours, I'm equally to blame," I admitted and he didn't argue.

He turned to face me so that his shoulder rested against the wall and maybe it was the head injury but his voice was so soothing that it sounded like he'd accepted everything. "I think that maybe we were coasting so easily through our relationship that it prevented either of us from growing up. People need adversity to grow, couples need challenges to grow together, and we've had five easy years in a study bubble that it only needed one trip to break us."

And it would have happened eventually whether or not I met Arwen. "You're making sense."

"You asked if I'd told your dad about being ... you know." He briefly looked away, unable to say the word and I realised that neither had he been able to say the name of the woman who'd taken me away from him.

I smiled, "yes, you seemed happy to keep that from me at the time."

"Oh, what an arsehole I am." He sniggered. "Well, I know I told him we'd broken up because I was sober when he contacted me, which was within my first few days in Gibraltar. I think he wanted to know how my proposal had gone and I told him not very well." He left it at that but his tone suggested there was more.

"And?"

"And apart from that, I'm not too sure. I might have been drunk and sent a bunch of angry messages, abusing him, taking the piss out of his name, which sounds like something I was capable of in that state but I just don't remember doing it, or not doing it."

My shoulders raised, "that's easy, you can just check your messages."

He shook his head, "I lost that phone and I've no idea where, which kind of proves everything. God knows how I've kept my passport through all this."

I paused for a while and then shrugged half-heartedly, "oh well, it is what it is. If he knows then I'll just have to deal with it." It was hard to imagine a scenario where my dad would know I was in a lesbian relationship and he wasn't on the first plane ready to drag me back to Scotland. It was probably about time we had that chat anyway. "I think, Gabe, you're going to be ok."

"Aye, I will but what about you? Aren't you the one giving up everything to..." he stopped because I'd slapped him on the knee and I was greatly relieved to see him making light of the situation, my life.

"Maybe we're both crazy."

"I will agree with you there."

I stayed behind for at least another hour as we caught up with each other because, at the very least, he'd missed me and had wondered what I'd been doing the past few weeks. I spoke about Dayna and Alessia, how I'd somehow found a new purpose, the work I was doing at the vineyard, whilst trying not to mention a certain person. He told me how he'd been so unhappy the last few weeks that even Dan had found his company hard to stand for more than a few days at a time, which was why his friend was now pretty much travelling alone with Floor.

"I need to get back to my former self," he admitted, "I miss the old happy guy."

If I'd been worried about his safety or sanity, I was now reassured. He knew what he needed to do and the nurse wasn't concerned either because she soon kicked us out of the room.

"No immigration holding cell?" I asked, wondering where the border guards had gone.

He scoped the vicinity with mock urgency, "shush, you'll wake them." Maybe his luck was about to change.

We were standing in an exceptionally long, narrow building that connected one part of the airport to another and there was a constant stream of people rushing to make connections. The roof was glass panelled and revealed the sight and sounds of the torrential downpour that pelted down upon it.

"I'm really back in England, aren't I. You should get off now before you destroy the illusion you're still travelling." He looked momentarily away. "Sorry I cost you your airfare."

"I'll buy another ... Gabe, promise me now."

He knew what I meant. "I'm sane, I promise and I will be ok." He placed his hands on my shoulders and I knew this was it. "I know what you're thinking and it's for the best."

I was beholding him for the final time. "You got me through med school."

"And now we go our separate ways."

Chapter Thirteen

CHIANTI 2

*T*here was no more delaying it, the procrastination had to stop now and I clamped my eyes closed as the phone rang, once, twice, thrice, if it gets to six I'll hang up, four, five, it clicked.

"Freya, what the bloody hell! You'd better be at the bloody airport. Shall I be coming down to collect you?"

My heart thudded, "hi, Dad."

"Where?"

"I said, hi."

"I know you bloody did. You're in Inverness? You'd better bloody be."

I was beginning to remember why I'd put this call off for so long. Unfortunately, it could not have been postponed any longer because today was the latest I was supposed to be back home, yet here I was, still in Tuscany. Not that calling last month would have made a difference after hearing my news.

"Dad ... listen ... um, I'm in Italy, near a town called Poggibonsi and..."

"I know where Italy is! What I want to know is why you're not in Inverness?"

There was no easy way of saying it and my dad always wanted things told straight, so here it was. "Dad, I'm not coming back. I've decided to drop out of medicine and I already have a job here ... a job here ... working in a vineyard." Kill me now.

...

...

...

"Hello, Dad? You there?"

"Get back here this minute before I come over there and drag you back myself." He boomed and I had to move the phone away from my ear.

"Dad, I've thought long and hard about this decision and I've made up my..."

"You've lost your bloody wits. That's what travelling does. You need to get yourself back here right now."

"Dad, I'm stay..."

"Where the fuck is this place?" He growled and I scrunched my eyes closed and pressed the phone against my forehead.

"Italy."

"I mean where ... the address ... give it me!"

And so, having no choice, I told him and now he was on his way and his voice, which I could still hear, would be in my head all day whilst I used the same to concoct my strategy, as futile as it would most probably prove to be.

"That didn't exactly go according to plan." I groaned to myself.

I'd thought long over my talking points and had even written them down because I knew that when the time came, my brain would turn to mush; Lizzie, Uncle Paul and if the convo went well, I might have mentioned I'd broken up with Gabe, that I was in a new relationship and left it at that. But I'd foolishly commenced with my plan to drop out of medicine to work in a vineyard, thinking it the least incendiary of topics to be covered, yet that was all it required for the man to blow his top.

I collapsed back onto the bed and moaned out loud. "I should have started with the lesbian thing."

Speaking of Arwen, and judging from the photos, she was waiting out her prison sentence dancing, meditating on beautiful mountain vistas and snorkelling off Croatian islands, whilst I was forced to chew over what my dad knew or didn't know and repeatedly question whether my news, what little I'd told him myself, would have been enough to prompt him dropping everything to visit, or did he know more?

The next evening, which happened to be eighteen days into Arwen's ninety, it appeared I would receive an answer, when Dad rumbled up the dirt track in a rented Land Rover.

I was in my filthy overalls and took my time trudging up the slope to greet him.

He heaved himself from the seat and slammed the door, "Trubbs," his arms were open, the smile wide and apparently real, "come for a hug."

I hesitated but then plodded forwards to accept his embrace. "It's good to see you but you didn't have to come out here just to..."

If I'd been confused as to why he seemed so genuinely happy, I soon discovered why when she stepped out from the vehicle...

In the form of a woman.

I pulled away from Dad as my eyes adjusted on her and for whatever reason, the first word that came to mind was *respectable*.

"Hello," she said in my own Highlands accent as she walked around the vehicle, I came to meet her at the front, and we shook hands, "I'm Eleanor, it's nice to finally meet you." The *finally* was a bit of a giveaway, that they were most likely dating and had been for a while and now she appeared to be scrutinising my features, the girl from the photos, and now here in the flesh. "Gus, she's very beautiful."

Dad slapped his palm against the bonnet. "Didn't I tell you?"

I was still recovering but managed to find enough wits to remember my name, as if she didn't already know it. "Sorry, I'm Freya," I cocked an eyebrow at Dad. I'd never known him with any woman besides my mother and I barely even remembered that. This might be weird for me.

"She wasn't about to let me come here without bringing her along." Dad was still grinning but finally pulled his eyes away from us to survey the vineyard and whistled. "It's wee wonder you don't want to leave the place."

"Aye," I had to quickly think whether to say more, "it's home and I love it." Was that too much? Probably. I was confused.

He nodded, it was all going a little too well, which was odd, and I could only put it down to the fact we hadn't seen each other since Christmas, maybe give it ten minutes. I glanced again at Eleanor, who was probably the other reason because she had to be having a mellowing effect on him.

She was tall and slim, though it was hard to tell what her figure was truly like beneath her long red winter coat, having doubtless been in the mid-September Inverness climate only hours before. Her brown hair rested upon her shoulders and she had intelligent eyes in a face that gave little away through expressions, another dour Scot, and despite my putting her at thirty-five years of age, she was remarkably free of wrinkles ... what never changing facial expression could do for you. Ok, Freya, stop being a bitch. I'd get used to it.

"Where are you staying?" I finally broke the long silence. "There's a spare room here and I'm sure it wouldn't be a problem for..."

He dismissed me by grimacing, "we're staying at the Villa San something, so don't worry about us ... won't be more than a few days." He clapped his hands together. "Have you eaten? It's been a while since I've devoured one of their famous Tuscan steaks."

"I've not, no." I checked the time on my phone, I was about due to turn in for the evening and so I gestured to my filth covered overalls, "I'll have to change first but I won't be long."

"Freya?" It was Eleanor who spoke just as I was stepping away. "Is there a bathroom I could use?"

I showed her to the facilities inside before rushing upstairs to change and then Dad drove the few miles into Poggibonsi from where we entered a restaurant called Leonardo's.

It was one of those family-owned places decked out to look old worldy, with vintage pans and other utensils hanging off hooks from the walls and because it was early by Italian dinner standards, the place was empty save for one couple who were speaking with American accents about seeing the Leaning Tower tomorrow.

The waiter took one look at my dad in his brown shoes, tie, tweed jacket and cap with his overall demeanour that somehow suggested you'd best not displease him and we were ushered to the only table with a window, which had a view over twisting roads and the many vineyards behind the castle in the foreground.

Dad and I sat as Eleanor removed her long coat and placed it over her chair, "excuse me one moment," she said as she headed towards the bathroom.

I watched her leave and centred on Dad. "She's nice. Very," I searched for the right word to use, "proper."

He was still watching after her then turned back to me, the warmth still in his eyes. "She's head of the Equine Business Management department over at the University of the Highlands." He said proudly, puffing out his chest.

"Ooh, very specialist ... a rider? ... a lecturer?"

"All of those, as well as a professor and a golfer, which is the main thing."

I was still trying to discern what, if anything, he knew of my situation and couldn't work out why, after thirty-seven minutes, he still hadn't raised the subject of the abandonment of my career. It was sure to follow, it was the reason he was here, after all.

Eleanor returned and my dad filled her glass with water and touched her hand. "Everything all right?"

She nodded and then the waiter returned to take our orders, we all going for the Bistecca alla Fiorentina, which arrived on its own trolley and then we watched as the waiter began to calve from the thick portion of meat that was still on the bone. It tasted beyond delicious, which made me wonder why, despite having been here so long, I'd only tried it that one time with Dayna and Arwen.

Dad finished first by a long way. "I was last in these parts with your mother, before you were born, before it became such a tourist trap. They're everywhere ... God's sake ... and we've barely even touched down." He grunted and gestured out the window as though there were tourists out on the veranda. "We counted twelve tour groups all waving those silly bloody flags, all swarming around the walls at San Gimignano, and they were just the ones we could see, we didn't go inside." He rubbed a piece of bread over whatever meat residue still remained on his plate. "At least the steak's still the same though. How are you finding it?"

This was to Eleanor and because she was chewing, politely raised her eyebrows in appreciation.

"Not too warm are you, my dear?" He asked and titled his face up towards the ceiling, as though doing so might somehow regulate the room temperature.

She hastily swallowed, "I'm fine, don't worry."

Who'd have thought my dad was such a considerate, um, boyfriend, which almost made me cringe to think. And he'd been considerate to us both by not raising the obvious subject in front of Eleanor because it had the potential to become heated, which would only have embarrassed her. That was also the reason I hadn't yet brought it up myself, it had nothing to do with being a coward, honest.

The restaurant began to fill with people and then Dad's next words proved I'd maybe thought too soon. "I'm happy you dumped that other one, by the way. I won't say his name because the less said about that man-child the better," he glanced at Eleanor who made little reaction, "what a fanny he was," his eyes were briefly distracted by the arrival of a trolley that went to the very next table and then a platter lid was lifted to reveal another steak, "I could certainly eat it all over again, anyway, Trubbs, you can find a much better man with ease," he said and I wondered if I'd heard a strange emphasis on the 'man' or maybe I was just going paranoid. "No, you were right, because you're moving up. There'll be other doctors where you're going and they'll be queueing up to date you, just wait and see." There it was. "Now..." he paused with a jabbing finger mid-air because Eleanor had touched his shoulder.

"Excuse me, one moment." She stood and her heels clipped against the flags on her way to the bathroom, which had to have been her third visit, not that I was keeping count.

"Yes, my dear," he stared after her then turned back to me, "where was I, ah yes, now ... you're coming home. No, don't interrupt ... you were meant to have been back today at the bloody latest and instead, I find you still here, prancing about in a Tuscan vineyard looking like a bloody farmer. Look here, you've had your fun, and I've kept quiet about it because you deserved it but now you must come home and go to whichever hospital you promised you were going to attend." His voice had risen in volume since Eleanor left and I sensed it was only the beginning.

"Dad, I made no such promises to any hospital because I made my mind up weeks ago that I didn't want to leave here." It was remarkable how quickly my accent had descended back to broad Highland.

"Aye, and kept it to yourself, which is why you're bloody lucky I play golf with the Chief Executive at Inverness, both of them, as well as the Chief Surgeon ... had him and his wife over just the other week. You could say I had a feeling you were about to piss away your future," Gabe had to have blabbed something there, "and you cost me a forty-one-year-old bottle of Glenglassaugh, and I can't tell you how much that was worth, but I was glad to do it, cos you're my absolute last fucking hope, even if your options are now down to one and even that'll fag out if you're not sharp, so don't make me drag you back by the bloody hair, because you know I will." His face had reddened to the shade of a tomato and my next words would take the kind of courage I'd never shown in front of my dad.

I gripped the table, "Dad, like I told you on the phone, I've decided to stay here."

There, I'd said it and now his eyes widened and the vessels in his face seemed to enlarge and he was just about to shout and cause a scene when Eleanor's return was perfectly timed, in fact, it had the surreal effect of snapping him into another person, almost like a Jekyll and Hyde type being. "Are you all right, my dear?"

She rested her hands on her coat. "I'm a little tired, Gus."

"Right! Il conto!" He surprised me by cutting the evening dead and waving at the waiter, who ran towards us and Dad settled the bill before driving me back to the vineyard.

"It was nice meeting you, Eleanor," I told her but Dad cut in before she could respond.

"I'll be back to deal with you in good time."

And I believed him.

Though I was lucky to have a one day respite, on account of being away for most of it, carrying out errands, visits to the wholesalers, some local deliveries and of course, collecting the labour from Siena. However, an evening conversation with Dayna revealed my dad had stopped by.

"Oh, my goodness, you spoke to him?" I shrieked, holding my chest as mental images of an eccentric Scottish would-be aristocrat stomping around in front of my friends flashed through my mind.

She spooned Bolognese sauce over her spaghetti, calm as I'd come to expect. "Of course, delightful man, a little hard to understand."

"Aye, his accent's very thick," I waved it away as the irrelevance that it was, "but what did he say?" I interrupted her as she was about to speak. "Wait, did you just call him delightful?"

"I did," she subconsciously glanced over at Marco, asleep in his buggy, "and he was asking questions, that's all. Would you like any more meatballs?"

"No, what was he asking?"

"Where's Alessia? She's late again. Oh, you know, just the usual ones, the banal, polite questions. What work is she doing, is she any good, is she having fun."

I wasn't sure I was hearing this. "Was there, by any chance, a woman with him?"

She nodded. "Indeed there was." Maybe that explained it then. Oh, there was more. "He was interested in knowing if you'd been on any dates."

"He was?"

She stared blankly through me. "Or maybe it was his female friend who asked that. Hmmm, I really can't remember. I was breastfeeding at the time and he was trying not to look. But of course, I spoke very highly of you, as did Alessia, but we wouldn't get involved in your personal business."

I rubbed at my temple. "And he didn't try coercing you into firing me?"

"Firing you?" She stopped with her fork halfway to her mouth. "No, he was nice, a gentleman."

I thanked her for this rather unbelievable account and sat down to eat spaghetti meatballs.

And so I began work the next day fully expecting him to come tearing up the path at any moment, but come seven in the evening he still hadn't turned up and neither did he come the day after that. In fact, I very nearly called to check if he was ok, half suspecting he might even have given me up as a bad job and flown back to Scotland but then he arrived just after ten in the morning, four days after I'd seen him last, and this time he came alone.

Though he didn't do me the courtesy of stomping immediately down the slope for round two but instead made me wait and I watched from the vines as he exited the Land Rover, walked around the house, poked his head inside the barn, stood speaking on his phone for twenty minutes and then finally hung up when Salvo happened past pushing his wheelbarrow. The two of them spoke for a while as I snipped at bunches of grapes and tried to keep an eye on them as they occasionally made gestures in my direction and I'd have killed to know what was being said.

But the morning's bizarre events were only just beginning as a bright red Porsche drove up the path, a conspicuous vehicle I'd never before seen here. The dust clouded thick around its wheels and it came to a skidding stop, the woman inside hastily shut the top, futilely batting at the air around her, and then continued towards the house at the summit.

My dad left Salvo to his work and managed to intercept the woman on her way to the house from where they began another long conversation.

After five minutes, I squinted up the slope and realised who the leggy woman, in flowing white summer dress might likely be, and wasn't sure how Alessia would take the arrival of her mother. I'd only seen the woman from photos but even from this distance, her profile, most notably her Mediterranean hips, were similar to Alessia's. My dad touched his cap, and the woman, who went by the name of

Maria, headed towards the front door, my dad strode in the opposite direction, making sure to turn around and check out her behind as he did. I cringed and then cringed again when he approached Goro, who was heaving boxes into his truck.

"Bastard," I called out.

"What, me?" It was Tesfay who spoke from two rows over.

I waved, "oh, sorry, I didn't mean you."

I knew what he was doing. My dad wasn't a fool. On the contrary, he was absolutely shrewd, worldly and wily. He'd want to be sure before making any irreversible decisions, decisions of the like my sister knew all too well, and right now he was speaking to as many people as possible, gathering information, before demanding again that I return home.

And if I didn't?

Alessia's mother left the house, only minutes after arriving, and Dayna stood watch at the door as she entered the Porsche and drove away, just like that, and I hoped her little visit wouldn't set Alessia back considering the remarkable progress she'd made recently.

He was still speaking to Goro, which made me incredibly uncomfortable but there was nothing I could do. Fortunately, my dad wasn't the type to take the word of an apparent unhinged, and spurned, former obsessive admirer on its own, but on top of what he'd learned from everyone else, including Gabe?

It was a little before twelve when he finally strolled down into the vines. I threw a bunch of grapes into the cart, propped an elbow on its handle and waited for him to arrive.

"Good morning, Trubbs," he spoke with an even tone and I immediately knew there was a problem, not because of his voice but because of his eyes.

"Dad? Are you ok?"

He stopped beside the cart and mirrored my stance, placing his elbow on the opposing handle. "I've been speaking to some of your colleagues," he began, ignoring my question, "it seems you have friends here."

"I would hope so, I love it here." I paused. "Dad?"

He surveyed the near vicinity, the vines, the orange trees, the stream that could just be heard trickling slowly over the small breeze. "I was thinking about the other day and I bet it must have been a bit of a shock to find I've been courting recently but I want you to know that nobody could ever replace your mother. Aileen will always be the love of my life."

I scrunched at the earth beneath my foot. "That's ok, you don't need to explain these things to me, I want you to be happy." Surely he was due some happiness because if anyone had suffered, it was my dad, even if much of it he'd brought on himself.

He looked like he'd not slept the last few days and I wondered if he might also have been weeping because the blood vessels in his eyes were red and dilated, though that on its own was not unusual for him, but the patches beneath were more prominent than when I'd seen him last. However, as so often with these things, it was what lay behind the eyes that so often gave it away.

"And I like Eleanor," I was quick to fill the silence, "how is she?" I immediately regretted asking because I realised the possibility they'd broken up during the interim might explain his present aspect but his reply quickly quashed that.

"She's been unwell these past days." He said, waving it away. So they were still together, at least, but if my dad didn't wish to talk about it then I'd press no further.

Warm weather colds were common when arriving in a warm climate from a place like Scotland and she had been fatigued at the restaurant. But wait, she'd also taken frequent bathroom breaks, which could rule out a cold. My dad had not stopped by at the vineyard in two days, and I knew it would take a lot for him to postpone speaking with me, considering it was his entire reason for being here. Again, I examined my dad's face, the irritation and something else, and feared what it might be, that maybe, just maybe, Eleanor had been in the early stages of pregnancy and miscarried? I was probably wrong, it was a wild stab based on very little, but was it really?

My elbow fell off the handle and I carefully propped it back, hoping it wasn't true yet not knowing what else it could be whilst knowing not to ask at the same time.

He coughed and straightened, "anyway, to business because we can't be having you wasting your time here when you're needed in other places."

"Dad, this again? Please..."

"No, I must say this and I must admit, I wasn't all that keen on the idea of studying for so many years when quite honestly, there are better things to be doing, but now I can perfectly see the logic behind it and I must say, it's quite brilliant in its way because where else would you find the best sorts of men? Aye, that fanny aside, of course. But because of him, you now have to start again and if you're to bag one of these doctor types then you need to be where the doctor types are, which is in a bloody hospital," he patted me on the arm, "didn't I tell you? Brilliant! And you have the best possible chance of succeeding whilst you're still young and pretty. You know, Trubbs, your looks will soon fade, so you have no time to piss about..." he opened out his arms, "...in a place like this, fun as it might be, for now at least, you're unlikely to find the kind of man you'll want to have children wi..." he abruptly stopped because his stare had settled on Tesfay, who'd dropped a grape and was even now stooping and turning it in his fingers as he blew away the soil. My dad shuddered and turned away, moving a little to the side, in the hope that doing so would block the Eritrean from my view, "no, no, Trubbs, a Scottish hospital, that's the place for you. Now..."

"Dad," I quickly cut in, "I can't say it any more plainly." I breathed and my knee was shaking, not so much for me but for him, because he only wanted what he thought to be best for me, and I was about to shatter his hopes. "I'm staying here at the vineyard, I really like it, I've made friends and I believe I can be truly happy here."

"Aye, with that woman by all accounts." The fact he knew did not come as a surprise and because I showed next to no reaction, it only confirmed the truth to him. "Yes, I thought so," he growled and the vessels in his face flared, "so let me say it again, Freya," which he only ever called me when he was serious, "you're coming home."

I stood firm, even though I was shaking on the outside and breaking on the in. "Dad, I'm staying here."

He laughed but it was out of frustration then raised his voice. "Are you seriously giving up everything, your career, a decent man, a family, all for a glorified farm and some ditzy blonde who'll leave the minute a man of money comes along?"

I knew it wasn't true, Arwen had already proven she wouldn't, but this was so very hard and I hated it. "I'm giving up one career for another, one plan for another."

He brought his two palms briefly together, as if in prayer, or to beg, but then parted them and one balled into a fist. "Freya, I'm asking you, no, I'm pleading with you to come home or...or..." he couldn't say it but I knew what he meant, that he'd do to me what he'd done to Lizzie.

I stood firm, swallowed, heard the ocean rolling in my head. "Dad, I love you but I'm staying here."

His fist pulsed, it unclenched and clenched again and then he brought it to his mouth and bit. "You're really fucking stubborn, just like your mother."

The gentle trickles of the stream were just barely audible above the lull in the breeze.

He nodded, seemed to want to say more, the appalling hurt, disappointment, loss even, clear upon his ageing face. He turned away, took a single step up the slope, then another, stopped and then did the unexpected, "I've never been so proud of you."

My mouth fell open and I stepped back, I must have heard wrong. "What did you say? Dad?" But he was stomping away, long, fast strides, heading towards his vehicle and I might never hear from him again, "Dad?" He was fast and the soft earth unsteadied my shaking legs. "What did you say?" I yelled as he neared the Land Rover and for whatever reason, Alessia flashed through my mind, the torture she'd suffered because of what her dad said, or didn't say, and this might be the final chance I'd ever have to say it, to shout it, "Dad, you have a grandson."

He stopped.

One foot was extended in front of the other, I don't know how long passed, and then his head turned part way to the side so that his ear faced me. "Is it true?"

The whole world was silent. "I found Lizzie, yes, it's true."

He didn't move, not one inch. "What's his name?"

"Angus."

His head sagged and I thought I heard something, a moan perhaps, but it could have been the breeze and then he continued towards his vehicle, fumbled with the keys, climbed in and drove away.

———

HARVEST SEASON ENDED in the middle of October, which meant the great bulk of the physical labour was finished until the new season. It also presaged having to say goodbye to our seasonal workers, and I had no idea what happened to them or if they found employment elsewhere.

Overall, it meant a shift in focus for me, from the production side of the business to the tourism. I was no Arwen when it came to dazzling the guests and even though I saw it as a chance for personal development, the very thought of taking my first tour group was still terrifying. Luckily, Alessia, who'd been running them intermittently since Arwen left, took me through a dress rehearsal and the next morning, at eleven o'clock precisely, a coach arrived from Genoa and sixty Germans trudged off.

I hastily sent a photo of the approaching flock to Arwen, who was in Odessa, a city in Ukraine, of which I'd never heard but what looked beyond incredible.

'Wish I could be there instead of here but I know you'll do great,' she replied and I closed my eyes, steadied myself and would try to do a good job for her.

Like I said, I was no Arwen, but after the first few minutes, I soon found my swing, my voice and nerves settled and although I decided not to read any of my online reviews, I was optimistic my group had fun and at the end, the shop made decent takings and I even posed for a selfie with a couple from Cologne.

Fifty-five days after Arwen left, Maria surprised me by again arriving out of nowhere, though luckily Alessia, Dayna and the baby were at lunch in San Gimignano. I sent Dayna a text to let them know who was presently sitting at their coffee table.

"You're using my best Amalfi pottery," she sat and sipped her drink, "not the best espresso though. You should never grind the beans and allow them to sit in a jar for weeks, you grind them when you use them and you should always heat the cups so you're not drinking it cold, a little hot water is all it takes." It was an awkward coffee.

I shrugged and spoke in English, "I'm really sorry but I don't understand."

"It was you father I spoke last month," she switched to English, oh shit, but then I perked at the mention of Dad, I'd not heard from him since that day on the vineyard, "he loves you very much. You break his heart."

My fingers began fidgeting with the espresso cup handle. "I love my dad but he's stubborn."

"Like my daughter, Alessia. She hate me because of what I did. I'm sorry, I try to make things best again but she won't speak to me." She was a striking woman, much like her daughter, with the same sharp features. From what I'd heard, everything had been perfect between Maria and her husband until the day she was caught out and from then it was like a switch had been flicked in her head and it was all out war, take, take, take whatever she could, because the law was on her side, and everybody else could go to hell.

I glanced from her Gucci bag resting on the table to the Porsche sitting on the gravel outside. "If you truly are sorry," I said, switching to Italian, "you could start by selling that car and giving the money to your daughter. Maybe then she won't lose her home."

Twenty seconds later she was out the door and I messaged Dayna to say the coast was clear.

"Alessia never wants to see her again," Dayna confided in me later that evening, "and I can't say I blame her, Scotty. Oh," she placed Marco in his cot, "it's a little over a month before your girl returns home. We should start thinking about that party."

The mere mention of *my girl* and *party* was all it took for the electricity to begin surging through my veins. I missed her so much and although I'd remained as busy as possible the entire time, I could barely get her out of my head and I wasn't sure if the photos she constantly sent were a help or death itself. Oh, she knew what she was doing, of course, and it wasn't hard to picture her laughing to herself even as she posed in the mirror, completely naked, before sending me the images. And then came the video of her lying on an empty beach, finger inserted as she panted my name.

No, it wasn't easy.

Thankfully, there were books on agriculture, no joke, to keep my mind off her, which meant I was now reading in Italian and that to me was as impressive as attaining a medical degree.

The next month involved fermenting, bottling and delivering, as well as being a tour guide, more than enough to stay busy whilst I planned Arwen's welcome home party. It would be a simple affair, good food, drink, music and friends, which would culminate in the hottest, most eagerly anticipated, steamy night of passion I'd ever know. Alessia told me that Marco, her best friend and biological father to their son would be coming down from Switzerland, which meant he'd get to meet baby Marco for the first time.

On day eighty-eight, everything was ready and I was so excited I could barely function, yet conversely I was operating on some zen level of awareness, rushing to finish tasks, which was futile because they were endless.

I dashed into Poggibonsi for my appointment at the beauty salon, not my usual thing, and had a Brazilian. The things you do for love. That night, Arwen sent me a photo of her flight confirmation, from Saint Petersburg to Pisa, and in return I sent her an image of my waxed pussy.

It was the morning of day eighty-nine when I received the call.

I was in the barn labelling bottles and placing them in boxes ready for a delivery to Arezzo when my phone began to ring and I plucked it from my pocket and saw the name on the screen.

"Oh," I hummed and tapped the screen to answer, "Lizzie, hi."

"Frey, are you sitting down?"

My heart, "what? No, hold up, ok. Lizzie, what's wrong?"

"I'm with Dad ... in the hospital." She was with Dad?

But there was no time to consider that revelation as the stabbing pain shot through my chest. "What? Is he all right?"

"Dad, erm, yes, he is ... it's Lachlan."

"Lachlan?"

"Freya, you need to come home right away."

EPILOGUE

*A*fter four days, we turned off his life support and we all watched as my big brother slowly slipped away.

"You're with your mother now, my son." Dad let go of his hand, took Lizzie's and walked toward the door, glancing back at me. "You coming?"

"A few more minutes." I waited for them to leave and took my brother's hand. "I want you to know that I'm back and I will fulfil the promise that I made to you."

If you don't have a purpose, you need to find it so you can bring meaning to your life. If you know your purpose then you have a duty to realise it. Circumstances, fate, life will distract us and throw all kinds of obstacles in the way. It's called living.

I BEGAN my belated residency at Raigmore Hospital in Inverness and was immediately given the responsibility of overseeing the ongoing care over a number of patients with diabetes, heart disease, cancer and even a few road traffic accident survivors who required routine checks. These fields would be rotated every few months, the intention being to give trainee doctors like myself experience over as large a base as possible.

Arwen understood, eventually. Judging from our many calls, she was beyond devastated, but she understood.

Her work visa required that she had to remain employed to avoid deportation and although she was entitled to the same breaks and holidays as any other worker within the European Union, what would you know, but the UK and Ireland were the only two countries within the EU not to allow her entry on a work visa. It was just another in a long line of setbacks we'd already had to deal with.

Regardless, I was busy, as was Arwen, and although we spoke regularly and made promises of "hooking up" at some point, as the months progressed our contact gradually diminished.

I'd arrived in Scotland on the eighty-ninth day, my braid unravelling under its own weight and on day ninety, I'd freed it and made my own. It wasn't anywhere near as good as the braid Arwen had done for me but the intent was there. I would keep a braid until the day arrived when Arwen could undo it herself, even if, under the workload, she began to occupy ever less of my thoughts, as unthinkable as that was, and I realised it was probably a defence mechanism of some kind, even if it took a whole year to reach that stage and then, because we were barely speaking anymore, I finally gave up on the idea of maintaining a braid. It was mostly because of my own circumstance, I was working exceptionally long hours and had heavy responsibilities and things with Arwen eventually fizzled out.

Besides, she'd probably moved on.

Though I will admit to feeling a small sensation of hope every time I was due a patient with a Welsh-sounding name, Miss Jones, Williams, Evans, only for the hope to be dashed when someone else entered. There was even an occasion when one female patient was speaking with an Australian accent from over the dividing curtain and I had to leave the ward in tears. They were futile dreams and such things shouldn't have been allowed to upset me but they did, it couldn't be helped, not that I wanted Arwen to be one of my terminal patients or anything.

The family had a long discussion over what to do about the pond that had claimed the lives of two of its members. Lizzie and I wanted to have more fish living in it and to possibly construct some kind of a permanent memorial, whereas Dad wanted the whole thing bulldozed, concreted over and steamrolled. He got his way.

The death of Lachlan had the effect of changing my dad's perspective on a few matters and although I was told his first meeting with Uncle Paul had resulted in the latter being punched on the jaw, they were playing golf soon afterwards. Besides, Dad had a grandson, which was the one thing he'd wanted more than anything else in the world and within six months, Lizzie, Uncle Paul and Wee Angus had relocated to the Highlands.

After two years, I finished my residency at Raigmore and progressed straight into my first of six years specialist training in emergency medicine, which meant rotating hospitals again and again and again. My responsibility involved being the first doctor to review incoming patients and from there, either treating the minor injuries, or else sending them onto the relevant specialist after making a diagnosis, which at first I did under very close supervision. Emergency medicine was exceptionally broad because there was no way of knowing who was about to walk, or be carried, through the door and there were times, Friday and Saturday nights particularly, when thanks to the fuel of alcohol, the once orderly department would turn to sudden chaos and then there'd be cut limbs, concussions, broken faces and stomachs to pump. The weekends were long and often went by in a haze and it was during one such usual Friday when I received the email informing me of yet another rotation and I was relocating from Yorkshire back to Scotland, Saint Andrews to be exact.

The home of golf it may have been, not that I had chance to play, or would be any good even if I did but I'd always thought of it as Scotland's most beautiful town. It had other things to boast, such as the third oldest university in the English speaking world, a castle and lovely beach, not that we ever had the sun to enjoy it.

"You had a call," Tracy, the department administrator and receptionist interrupted as I was charging towards Accident and Emergency.

I slid to a halt, "who was it?"

"I wrote it down on this." She held out a Post-it but I was in too much of a rush to consider it now.

"I'll grab it in a bit ... incident ... must go."

It was my first major cycling accident, which required my consent before sending the patient to theatre, as though the gaping hole in the guy's leg wasn't invitation enough. Two minutes later I was rushing back the other way, the downed rider on a trolley trailing blood, helmet still in situ and the strap clenched between the man's teeth. Just ahead, Doctor Swift was exiting his office and we only just caught up with his long strides.

His dark eyes passed over the patient as his large, brilliant, skilful hands were relegated to the task of fastening the buttons of his blue surgery coat that filled out so splendidly. He said nothing, just finished with the buttons before grabbing the handle, and it was like the trolley's weight disappeared completely.

It was ninety minutes later when I discarded the gloves, left the theatre and drifted towards the front desk, filled a cup from the water dispenser and enjoyed the short respite. "An experience." I quietly moaned, not immediately noticing Tracy because I was operating on some other level.

"She called again."

"Again?" I looked at her like she was crazy. "I've not spoken to anyone a first time." Then I remembered. "Oh, who?" To get a call at work was a first, I moved around all over the place to the extent that some of the time I didn't even know where I was or how I got there.

She shuffled through a mess of papers, "one moment," no rush, and then she found some scrawl made earlier on a Post-it, "someone by the name of..."

"Freya," it was Doctor Swift who was standing beside me and I jerked to attention, as did Tracy, as did the three female patients waiting nearby. He rubbed a dexterous hand over weary eyes that exhibited such intellect, "I wanted to say you did a great job in there. You kept a cool head."

"Oh, I didn't really do anything." I flapped a hand, forgetting it was still holding a paper cup half-filled with water and sent the lot splashing over his scrubs. "Oh, fu..." the heat.

It didn't even faze him, in fact, he was nice enough to find it amusing and stepped into my personal space. "Just for that, you owe me a round of golf," he said low enough nobody else could hear, our little secret.

"It would be my pleasure," I said too quick, "but my game will put all of Scotland to shame." Seriously, the last thing I needed was for Doctor Swift to witness me making a fool of myself on the world's most famous golf course.

He leaned even closer so that his scent was almost overwhelming, or perhaps I was augmenting it in my own mind, the first few strands of grey visible in his short brown hair. He'd make my dad happy, all right. "Then we can skip the silly game and go straight for dinner." He pulled away, leaving me questioning whether he meant it. "Again, great work. Was that really your first theatre?"

I nodded and swallowed, "I'm in my second year of emergency. The worst I've had so far was a sliced hand ... knife job ... no nerve damage so..." I had to force myself to stop lest I ramble and embarrass myself.

He nodded appreciatively, "I'm impressed. You're not afraid of a bit of blood ... a good start." He jerked his chin towards the corridor. "Anyway, I'll be seeing you about." He strode off as every pair of eyes followed after him and I had to hastily turn away when he checked back over his shoulder. "Oh, and Freya?"

"Huh?" I scratched my neck and looked up at the lights.

"Practice your drive, I'm holding you to that game."

"Um, yeah, I will," I watched him leave and muttered the rest under my breath, "practice my bloody drive." The room fell strangely silent and I turned back to Tracy. "Did someone walk into a glass door? Send him through."

It was eight in the evening when I could finally get away, donned my rather unimpressive, inconspicuous, but comfortable civvies, and ordered a club sandwich with a large glass of red in The Jigger. It was turning into a regular thing, which I didn't necessarily like, but who wants to spend precious time cooking a healthy meal after such a long day?

I took my drink to the corner, where I sat alone and brought out the stack of papers I had to read about the new technology relating to 3D wound visualisation, so exciting, more wine might be required. The tiny black text was blurry as I flipped through the pages and forced a yawn, just as the long blonde hair slinked into my dazed periphery.

"It's true what they say about doctors and alcohol," came the familiar Australian accent.

I looked up, "I'm not proud of myself," and smiled at her, "hi Charlotte, how are you?"

She set my club sandwich down on the table, "I gave you extra chicken because you're my favourite customer."

"Thank you, and you're my favourite employee of The Jigger."

She ran her finger subtly along the vein on my hand as it rested over the fork. "When do you want to have that drink together?" She was a lovely girl, my age, and could probably teach me how to golf. But it wasn't a good idea. She wasn't the real thing. So close yet so far.

"I told you, Charlie, you remind me of someone, it wouldn't feel right, but we most definitely can be friends, I know next to nobody in this town." I hoped she'd accept that.

She removed her finger and smiled. "Of course, but you can't blame me for persisting."

An hour later, I left, enjoyed a short walk around the town, its walls and stone harbour pier before returning to my small flat and meditating prior to collapsing bedwards.

The alarm woke me at six and I staggered into the bathroom and stared at my worn out reflection. I'd turned twenty-seven a couple of weeks before and the highlight had been coming home after a long day and lying on the couch. Life was turning into a blur, where everything seemed to coast by without incident or excitement, which was saying something considering I worked in the Accident and Emergency department. I looked into my eyes and for whatever reason thought of that one summer and chuckled. "Those were some wild times," and I was glad I did it.

I turned on the shower, removed my pyjamas and laughed louder as I stepped into the tub. "Did I really *steal* a bloody camper?" And not a stain on my reputation.

I arrived at the hospital before eight and changed into my uniform, green scrubs that identified me as a junior doctor, and went to see how many people in this small town had already managed to injure themselves this early on in the day.

Tracy prodded the form across the desk and turned away pouting. "She *says* she's got a sprained ankle, from dancing, yet she seemed perfectly fine walking."

I took the form and rolled my eyes, could someone please find her a man? I scanned the reception area, nobody there. "Where is she?"

She smiled mischievously and wiggled her shoulders. "CR6."

I narrowed my eyes for her benefit but said nothing, she'd sent a girl with a sprained ankle to the consulting room that was farthest away because, I'm guessing, she was young and pretty.

I decided not to get involved and paced down the corridor as I read the form, Miss A Llewellyn of no fixed abode, knocked once, "hello," looked up and gasped.

"Do you have any idea how hard it is to pin you down ... *Doctor?*" She spoke the last word in a voice filled with pride and struggled to restrain herself as she stood and for some crazy reason, the first thought that came to mind was, be careful, you're injured. She must have seen it in my eyes and because I was unable to utter anything, or even breathe, she spoke in my stead. "I'm fine, by the way, and that bitch out there knows it too."

"Arwen." For some unknown purpose, I goggled downwards to check the incident form but it was no longer in my hands. I could swear, the damned girl got off on doing this. We embraced and the intoxicating peach aroma smelled like coming home. "Three years, two months."

"And one week exactly since you made me leave you standing at that airport." She pulled away and slapped my arm. "And *you* were supposed to be there ninety days later." Her head tilted to the side, "you look bloody good though."

I slapped her back and my hand remained where it was. "Oh, stop it, I look totally knackered out and you better believe it was the hardest thing I ever had to do."

She smiled sadly for what could have been. "I know."

There was a short silence, evidently, my brain still wasn't convinced it was Arwen standing in front of me. How long would that take to kick in? I reached behind with my foot and prodded the door closed and we both opened out our arms for the second embrace.

"It's so very good to see you again," she croaked into my ear and sniffled as I felt her tears against my cheek, "I was beginning to fear you were avoiding me."

"Never, ever," I hissed and it was several minutes later when we again pulled away, even though our hands were unable to separate. "But how? How are you here?"

Her face was red, puffy and still the most beautiful thing I ever saw. "It must be for the golf courses."

I shook my head in alarm, "oh, please don't joke about that," and laughed.

"Why do you think I'm here, really?" She asked rhetorically, her hand stroking my shoulder and even after all this time, it felt so normal, yet if I had any awareness of self in this moment, I'd be sure I was shaking uncontrollably.

Arwen. She looked exactly the same but different, which was crazy. Still the same incredible figure, an impossibly narrow waist above hips that projected miraculously, perfect round breasts that pushed out her overcoat, something I'd never seen her wear before, and cute elfin features that always made her look like she was concocting mischief, probably because she usually was. The most notable change was her hair because the braids were gone and in their place was a straight, shiny mane of blonde.

There was so much to say, to ask, to feel, but I had to bloody work. "Meet at seven tonight?" It would be the longest day of my life.

She nodded, "looks like golf it is," and tilted forwards to peck me on the lips, which wasn't enough, not by a long way, but I understood her reasons. "I'll be standing outside the entrance."

She wasn't, instead she was there in the camper, which I guessed was another one of her surprises.

I jumped in the passenger side and slammed the door. "You still have this?"

She revved the engine and wiggled her eyebrows. "It doesn't get used much these days but what can I say? I love it, oh..." and she leaned sideways to kiss me properly and I capitulated in earnest, throwing my arms around her shoulders and pulling her so tightly into me that I feared for my lips longevity.

I hesitated to pull away, "Arwen, take us home."

She did and I knew she wouldn't care about the size of my place as I switched on the light and she dragged her trolley bag across the threshold. "Very cute, I see you've taken up yoga ... and astronomy?" This was in reference to the telescope that was set up by the window. For some reason, gazing at the stars brought me peace.

"They're both great de-stressors." I held on to the back of the sofa, still totally giddy and in a state of disbelief.

She pottered around the room as I stood and watched in silence, enjoying one of those rare moments in life. Her eyes passed over the medical books, the flowers and the collage on the wall that consisted of a few dozen photos of the two of us all over Europe. She glanced at the bathroom door then the one bedroom before her eyes settled back on me at the couch I'd probably be sleeping on tonight.

"Sorry," I patted the cushion, "please make yourself at home. Are you hungry? I have beef broth or we could order in a pizza?"

"Broth is fine."

"Or Chinese?"

"I'm happy with broth."

"Indian?"

She smiled warmly, "Freya, I'd love to try some of your broth."

"Ok," I found myself rushing for the fridge before dropping a spoon, then a knife, but I managed to convey the pot to the table without losing any. "We have bread as well."

She was rustling through her bag, such a mess, and pulled out a bottle of wine, "I have…"

"Oh, is that a Giordano?" I'd recognise the label anywhere and I dashed for the corkscrew and two glasses.

"It's a gift from Dayna and Alessia." She came to the table and opened the bottle whilst, with a shaky hand, I plunged the ladle into the pot and dribbled no small quantity over the tablecloth en route to the bowls.

She filled the glasses to the top and slid one into my hand, "drink," she encouraged.

So I did, maybe too much, it was needed and I stared into the golden liquid. "How are they?"

From across my own table, in my own flat, the only girl I ever loved told me the news. "They're well, very well. Happy. Business is good. I've been taking an average of two tours every day and teaching dance in town during the evenings. Oh," she brought out her phone and flicked through the images, "here's Marco."

"Awe." There was an uncomfortable gap between us and I had to lean over to see the image of Dayna, Alessia and Marco at the age of three. He was a beautiful, chubby little boy with dark hair and a big smile.

"I truly miss them … everything."

"You have your life here now." She regretted saying that the moment the words left her mouth because the insinuation was, as if I didn't already know it, that she'd soon be leaving again, and what then for me?

I exhaled deeply and the moderate gap between us suddenly seemed so much larger. "Arwen, why are you here?" It was finally hitting me as the emotions of having this girl arrive out of the blue were taking their inevitable effects and I jumped in, cutting her off before she could reply. "I can't … I'm sorry, but I can't go through this all over again with you."

She thumped the table, making me jump. "Frey, I'm *not* playing hard to get here and neither am I messing you about. I just drove that stupid camper all the way from Tuscany, just to find you."

"Yes," I sobbed, "but you'll leave again and I'll be left shattered and broken all over again and I just can't go through it any more…"

She'd been delving through the inside pocket of her coat and suddenly slammed a small brown packet down on the table, which cut me off. "There!"

I didn't move, just remained still because whatever it was could only disappoint me or worse.

"Open it!" She demanded, her smile long gone.

"What ... what is it?"

"Why don't you open it and find out."

I was almost too afraid but couldn't stop myself regardless and I reached forward, plucked up the packet, its weight and feel giving nothing away, and ripped it apart.

And felt the euphoria rush through me.

"It took a *long* time and if only you knew the hoops I had to jump through to obtain this." Her arm moved softly around my body. "So stop blubbering and let's celebrate."

I read the text aloud, lest I was unable to believe the words, "United Kingdom of Great Britain and Northern Ireland" and then beneath the coat of arms, "Passport," with its new blue design in all its glory. "You're British?"

"Hey, careful," her hand squeezed my arm but she kissed me apologetically on the cheek, "I'll always be Australian, just don't tell the authorities about my true allegiances."

I spluttered tears all over it and felt dizzy again. "But ... but you have work, you work in..."

"Not anymore."

I gaped at her, still not fully comprehending it all, the risks she'd taken in doing all this without any guarantees she'd find me, that I'd be single when she did or that I'd even be open to it.

"Frey, speak to me."

"I ... I..."

"Frey, you'd better not tell me I've wasted my time."

I shook my head, "no, you most definitely haven't." Was this truly happening?

She laughed with relief and wiped her forehead in an exaggerated way. "Well, that's a big bloody load off my shoulders." She moved her seat closer, enveloped me in her arms and held her forehead against mine. "I've missed you so much and I want you to know that I never stopped loving you."

My hands were still shaking as they gripped that little blue book and I put all of my being into feeling her body against mine. "I never stopped loving you either."

I don't know for how long we stayed like this but Arwen had come home and that was all that mattered.

"So tell me," she finally whispered, "am I sleeping on the couch tonight?"

I shook my head, "nuh uh."

I felt a small vibration from her body and then she took my hand and led me to our room.

ALSO BY SALLY BRYAN

Novels

Where Are You

A Petal And A Thorn

Novellas

Trapped

My Summer Romance